blue
rider
press

THE WAY *of* SORROWS

ALSO BY JON STEELE

FICTION

Angel City

The Watchers

NONFICTION

War Junkie

THE WAY *of* SORROWS

The Angelus Trilogy, Part 3

JON STEELE

BLUE RIDER PRESS
New York

blue
rider
press

An imprint of Penguin Random House LLC
375 Hudson Street
New York, New York 10014

Library of Congress Cataloging-in-Publication Data

Steele, Jon, date.
The way of sorrows : the Angelus trilogy, part 3 / Jon Steele.
p. cm.
ISBN 978-0-399-17149-9
I. Title.
PS3619.T4338W39 2015 2015016060
813'.6—dc23

Printed in the United States of America
1 3 5 7 9 10 8 6 4 2

BOOK DESIGN BY AMANDA DEWEY

This is a work of fiction. Names, characters, places, and incidents either are the product of the author's imagination or are used fictitiously, and any resemblance to actual persons, living or dead, businesses, companies, events, or locales is entirely coincidental.

for e.c.s.

The Essenes (so named in *The Jewish Wars* by the historian Josephus) were one of three sects of Judaism that included the Pharisees and Sadducees in the first century AD. Known for their settlement at Qumran, where the Dead Sea Scrolls were discovered in 1947, the sect also established communes across ancient Israel. They lived an ascetic life, abstained from animal sacrifice in religious practices, and performed good works on behalf of the afflicted. One community was encamped outside Jerusalem's walls near the "Essene Gate" (now sealed) at the time of the crucifixion of Jesus. After AD 73, the Essenes vanished from history.

The Church of the Holy Sepulchre marks the traditional site of Golgotha, the Place of the Skull, where Jesus was crucified and buried. Modern archaeologists and historians agree the church was erected over the ground where Romans crucified seditionists and criminals, and that most probably Jesus was crucified somewhere within the walls of the church in AD 36. However, there is no credible archaeological or historical evidence that Jesus was buried there.

The Dome of the Rock (built in AD 691) is the Islamic shrine that stands atop Temple Mount in Jerusalem. It is built over the site of the Second Temple of ancient Israel (destroyed by Rome in AD 70). Together with Al-Aqsa Mosque, also atop Temple Mount, the Dome of the Rock marks the third holiest site in Islam. It stands over what is known as the "Foundation

Stone." This stone is sacred to all three of the Abrahamic faiths. Jews believe it to be the place where Abraham nearly slaughtered his son Isaac in a test of faith as commanded by God. Christians revere the stone as a place where Jesus prayed in the time of the Second Temple. Muslims believe the stone to be the place from where Mohammed ascended to heaven.

The Third Temple (to be built in the time of the Messiah) was prophesied in the Book of Ezekiel and has yet to be built. Jews believe the Third Temple will provide a dwelling place for God to return and live among His people again. Messianic Christians believe the building of the Third Temple marks the "end of days," when Jesus will return to officiate the Final Judgment. Construction of the Third Temple would require the destruction of Al-Aqsa Mosque and the Dome of the Rock.

The exact year and circumstances of Yeshua ben Yosef's death are not clearly known. For the sake of this story, the author has drawn on archaeological and historical evidence as presented by Dr. Shimon Gibson in his work *The Final Days of Jesus*. Also, the author has chosen to denote historical dates as BC and AD instead of BCE and CE.

Thou hast made the earth to tremble; thou hast broken it: heal the breaches thereof; for it shaketh.

—*Psalms 60:2*

"We're lost! We're lost," cried the women, clasping their children in their arms.

—Nikos Kazantzakis, *Christ Recrucified*

PERFECTUM

אחת

In the name of the Pure G-d.

These words are written many years after the destruction of Jerusalem, which came on the ninth day of Av, 3830. Know that I am a son of the light who served the teacher of righteousness at Qumran near the Salt Sea. Our settlement stood three parsa'ot in distance from Jericho, which is also now destroyed. The destruction of Qumran came on the twenty-fifth day of Sivan, three years after the fall of Jerusalem. It came at the hands of the Tenth Legion Fretensis of Rome, who marched along the Salt Sea to conquer the Zealots at Masada and so end the Jewish revolt.

This is how it happened.

On the twenty-first day of Sivan, Roman outriders reached the summit of the mountain that separated us from Jericho's ruins. In doing this they discovered our commune on the plateau below them. The outriders observed us through the afternoon and left before sunset. In those hours they learned we had no fortifications or weapons of any kind. Four days had passed when a great cloud of dust rose from the desert and there was the clamor of boots and drums. Then appeared the vanguard of the Tenth Legion leading more than five thousand soldiers onto the Masada Road. Their helmets and lances caught the dawn and their shields bore the color of blood. By this sign we knew our sacrifice was at hand, as it had been prophesied to us by seven angels of the Pure G-d. And so it was that upon reaching the trail that climbed the plateau to our commune, the main body of the legion continued south while the fifth cohort of infantry and archers broke away to attack Qumran.

As this prophecy came to pass, and being the youngest of my order, I was instructed by the teacher of righteousness to take refuge in the cavern of solitude, which is set apart from the commune. It was a scriptorium for transcriptions of the holiest scrolls as judged by the teacher. Here, one of the chosen scribes would live alone for many days in proper meditation before writing the holy name of the Pure G-d.

I was young and had yet to be selected for this duty, though I longed to assume it. So it was with sadness that my ascension to the cavern was not as one of the chosen scribes but to bear witness to the annihilation of my order, and then live a life of isolation to the end of my days. Within the cavern were a bed, a table and stool, lamps, and sacred oil to burn for light. There were quills and ink-making tools and sheets of fine vellum. There were food stocks in jars and a cistern outside the cavern's entrance that gathered rain as it flowed from the mountains.

This duty was commanded of me by the teacher of righteousness so that one of our number might survive and continue to watch for the man of signs and wonders, who would come to reclaim the things entrusted to us by the seven angels of the Pure G-d. For the seven did know this man and guarded his tomb for a period of thirty-four years; from the time of the man's death until his tomb was abandoned when Jerusalem was destroyed. And upon abandoning the man's tomb the seven angels appeared to us to reveal the truth of the man's death, entreating us to aid them in their sacred purpose. Now knowing the cousin of this man, who was called the Baptist, and upon hearing the voices of the seven angels of the Pure G-d, the teacher of righteousness identified them as the forces of light named in the War Scroll of our order. We pledged our souls to them and agreed to watch over the way of the man's return. We pledged in full knowledge that the forces of darkness, who sought to wipe all memory of the man from the world, would one day destroy us as they had destroyed Jerusalem.

שתים

The cavern of solitude was located in the canyon above Qumran and hid from the world by an outcrop of rock at the entrance. There were narrow fissures in the stone allowing me to see down onto the commune and witness the slaughter of my order. All my brethren, including the teacher of righteousness, suffered greatly before giving up their souls to death; but all kept their vow to not reveal any knowledge of the man of signs and wonders, though this knowledge was cruelly demanded of them.

The cohort then raided our stores of food and wine. Becoming drunk they ransacked the scriptorium for plunder. Finding nothing to please them, they took up battering rams and demolished the commune to rubble. But this destruction did not sate them, and they were overcome with savagery. They pounded their chest armor with fists; their curses filled the canyon with wickedness. Some drew swords and hacked apart the bodies of the dead, others built great fires; then was my brethren's flesh roasted and eaten. This unholy feast lasted into the night until a stupor came over the soldiers and they lay on the ground to sleep. Black clouds concealed the moon and stars that night, and when the fires ended there was no light of any kind; as if all the world had gone into hiding from the evil befallen us. At dawn, and hearing no sound, I went to the entrance of the cavern. There was no sign of the fifth cohort but for the slaughter they had committed.

I had been commanded by the teacher of righteousness to not leave the cavern for forty days. In obeying his command I did not bury my brethren according to Jewish law. In so doing I watched the remains of my order devoured by the beasts of the desert. Many of my brethren's bones were carried away, though some remained that I might not be devoured by the beast of loneliness. But I did not touch the bones or bury them; I only watched them turn to dust. This had been commanded of me so I would not be detected by any forces of darkness who might pass; nor those foul spirits who feed on human souls; nor their progeny who were possessed of the same hunger and roamed the world in the forms of men.

In the month of Elul my forty days of hiding had ended. To replenish the cavern's food stocks I grew grains and vegetables on a nearby plot of irrigated land. This plot was long used by my order and not seen from the desert lowlands or the surrounding mountains. One parsa from this place were colonies of bees that did not abandon their hives, and I tended them for honey. Near Jericho's ruins, abandoned groves of date palm and pomegranate and olive trees, once belonging to Egypt's queen, continued to bear fruit, and I harvested them.

I was commanded also to lay aside the white robes of the order and take the appearance of a madman. For there are things to be seen in this desert that will deliver a man into madness if regarded too long and without enlightenment, and such woeful men are common along the Salt Sea. I sealed my robes and sandals in an empty jar to protect them from corruption. I ceased to perform the water purification rituals of my order. In summer I wore only a loincloth and walked the desert in bare feet; in winter I wore coarse animal skins for warmth. My hair and beard became long and matted; my flesh darkened and leathered. In doing all these things I would not be regarded as a son of the light.

I walked the hills and mountains above Qumran to watch over the caves in which were hid the holy scrolls of the Jewish people. Also hid were the scrolls of our order, including the Book of Community Rule and the War Scroll. And in a remote cave, five parsa'ot in distance from Qumran's ruins, were the things for the man of signs and wonders as entrusted to us by the seven angels of the Pure G-d. This place was named the cavern of secrets by the teacher of righteousness.

שלוש

Through innumerable seasons I watched people travel across the Jordan Valley, wondering if one of them would reveal himself to me as the man foretold to us. There were merchant caravans from the east, Syrians and Phoenicians from the north, tribes of nomads from the south. Some of these travelers camped within sight of Qumran. They grazed their animals at the mouth of the Jordan River where it flows into the Salt Sea. Some travelers, chasing after their wandering flocks, climbed the trail to the ruins of our commune. Finding Roman coins or arrow points or other things of use, and not knowing the history of the place, most were satisfied and left. Those more curious of the place dared to approach the caves.

I hurried through the cliffs by unseen trails and jumped out before all invaders. I threw stones and called to Baal and proclaimed this ground as my divinely given kingdom. I chanted in tongues, rolled my eyes, and spittle formed on my lips. I became a creature of such dread that the invaders feared the curse of desert madness would claim them, too, and they retreated.

I lost count of the days long ago.

I do not know the number of years I have lived since the destruction of Qumran. In this season of summer I became much weakened. It became difficult for me to walk the trails or gather food. Then did questions come to me. In the war between the forces of light and the darkness, as written in the War Scroll of our order, had the man of signs and wonders been vanquished? Was all hope of his return lost? If so, what had been the purpose of my terrible isolation? Why was I not sacrificed with the members of my order? But these questions were without answer and sorrow weighed heavily on my soul; the last soul belonging to a son of the light.

Then did a tempest come up from the land of the Edomites, and the sky became thick with dust and the sun yellowed as if diseased. I could not see the lowlands or the Salt Sea for the blowing sand. As night fell the winds increased tenfold; then came the wails of the world's unburied and forgotten dead. Included in their number were the members of my order who had sacrificed their souls to forever death. By these signs I knew forces of darkness were passing the ruins of Qumran in search of the cavern of secrets.

I grew fearful, with only the flame of an oil lamp for consolation. I cried out to the Pure G-d and begged Him to give me succor. But the tempest mocked me for my cries, and the ground shook and the outcrop of rock at the cavern's entrance fell away. A suffocating dust, foul with putrefaction, rushed in to extinguish the lamp and I was blinded. I heard the screams of the world's unburied and forgotten dead approach; I felt their tormented souls reach from the dust and claw at my flesh, wanting to drag me down to the woeful place where they were imprisoned by the forces of darkness. And they begged me to save them by revealing the way to the cavern of secrets. So torn between my oath and the pitiful souls about me that I was overcome with despair, I crawled to the entrance of the cavern to throw myself from the cliffs and so end my own torment. I reached the edge of the cliff, rose to my feet, and stepped toward the abyss. Then came the roar of a thousand wings, and the whirlwind so created held me in place, and I beheld a vision.

ארבע

The tempest vanished and I saw the Pure G-d asleep in an immense void above the earth and nothing moved. He stirred and awoke and saw that He was alone in his place. He breathed and a fire was born into the void. By this light He reached down to the earth and gathered the world's unburied and forgotten dead. He anointed them with tongues of fire and cast them into the void where they became the stars and spheres of the heavens. Then a great comet rose from the east and it hovered over Qumran's ruins. And the comet burst into ten thousand stars, and they did form the constellation Kesîl. From them appeared the seven angels of the

Pure G-d who had entreated us to aid them in their sacred purpose. They came down bearing a body bound in a linen shroud, and they laid it on the ground. Then the leader of the seven smiled upon me, as he had smiled upon us in the days after Jerusalem was destroyed, and he said:

"They will see the dwelling place of the Pure G-d,
They will see the time of angels,
They will see the coming of the light."

And the angel drew his sword and cut open the shroud to reveal the face of the man of signs and wonders, and he was of the light. And the angel said:

"By your words will he be raised from the dead,
So that the world will know the light."

The sun rose above Mount Nebo and I was returned to the world. I knew my years of isolation were not in vain. I knew the man foretold to us would return, but not in the time of men; he would return in the time of angels when the secrets of the heavens are so revealed. And thus, my own sacred purpose was made known to me. I must guide the way of the man's return from beyond the time of my death. I took a knife and cut my hair and beard. I took water from the cistern and performed the purification rituals of my order for the first time since Qumran was destroyed. I unsealed my robe and sandals and I dressed in them. With joy in my heart I prepared ink and quills and seven scrolls of velum, and after proper meditation and with joy in my heart, I became one of the chosen scribes of Qumran.

Now my work is finished. I await for my soul to be lifted to the heavens, where I may take my place with the world's unburied and forgotten dead.

Receive, then, these seven scrolls to know of Qumran and the sons of the light; to know of the seven angels of the Pure G-d who appeared to us in the days after Jerusalem was destroyed; to know of Yeshua ben Yosef and the crucifixion of the man of signs and wonders; to know how through him the world may be saved. In knowing these things you will find the path to the cavern of secrets, and there you will claim the things left to him. For you, beloved reader, are that man; and now is the time of your return.

Book I

THE CRUCIBLE

ONE

Did Marc Rochat have a soul?"

The girl's voice echoed through the dark of the nave.

. . . have a soul . . . a soul . . . a soul . . .

Harper didn't answer at first. He was too busy staring at the girl's face. He knew it was a genetic trait; all the half-breeds were the same. Same almond-shaped eyes, same emerald-colored irises. But just now, seeing those eyes watching him from under the brim of a black floppy hat, Harper flashed Marc Rochat as if he had risen from the grave . . . *Bloody hell.* Harper blinked, told himself it wasn't the lad resurrected; told himself it was the new one.

He checked back over his shoulder.

Krinkle, the rock-and-roll roadie in denim overalls and steel-toed boots, was on the altar square, leaning over Astruc's unconscious form and checking for a pulse. Sensing he was being watched, he looked up.

"What's wrong?"

Harper shrugged.

"I'm not sure."

"Yeah, well, I'm kind of busy with Brother Astruc at the moment. Stick with rules and regs. You'll be fine," Krinkle said, nudging Astruc into alignment with a heading of due east.

"Right."

Harper turned to the girl, his mind sorting rules and regs on revealing info about human souls . . . *Sod it.*

"Yes, mademoiselle, the lad had a soul. So do you, so do all the half—"

His voice was lost in the drone of the execution bell tumbling from the belfry and rolling through the nave. Clémence was the bell's name, and she was tolling in threes and sixes. *They're dying, the children are dying.* Harper watched the girl with the lantern hanging from her right hand, half hidden in the folds of her black cloak. Her eyes appearing to follow the waves of mournful bell sound now rounding the ambulatory, then looking at Harper.

"Where is it?" she said.

. . . *where is it, where is it, where is it* . . .

"Sorry?"

"Where is his soul?"

. . . *his soul, his soul, his soul* . . .

Harper ran through his timeline, trying to see the lad from the cathedral job again. The girl pronounced his name not ten seconds ago and the lad's face had flashed through his eyes. But the microchip embedded in Harper's brain kicked in one second later and presto: gone. No name, no face; just a silhouette on a timeline.

"I don't know where his soul is, mademoiselle. I wish I did, but I don't."

"Why not?"

"Just the way it is, I'm afraid."

The girl furrowed her brow. Harper scanned her eyes. The human half of her brain was releasing electrochemical signals in the form of memories at a speed of one five-hundredth of a second, but the part of her bred by Harper's kind was flashing a timeline even faster. The expression on her face read she was slipping from nowtimes.

"Mademoiselle, look at me."

She tried, but her eyes lost focus.

Harper clocked she'd gone back ten minutes in time, to where Harper shot his way into the cathedral. Then Harper and Krinkle hauling a battered Astruc up the center aisle and dropping him on the crossing square like a bag of lead, hearing their voices calling for Monsieur Gabriel the messenger, but Gabriel was gone. Then seeing their fierce and road-worn faces in the shaft of light pouring through the cathedral rose high in the south transept wall, knowing they were men of violence. But watching the one in the mackintosh, the one with bloodied bandages wrapped around the palms of his hands; watching him brush his brown hair from his face. *Is he the one?* Seeing his emerald-colored eyes, seeing he was younger than the other two men; but the lines around those eyes made him older somehow. Then listening to the sound of his voice coaxing her from the shadows:

"Be not afraid, I know who you are. I've seen you from my balcony, in the old city on Rue Vuillermet. I see you when you call the hour to the north."

"You haven't come to kill me?"

. . . to kill me, kill me, kill me . . .

"No, I'm here to protect you."

Harper watched the girl blink herself back to nowtimes, but it was too fast. Her human memories caught up with her timeline; the jolt shook her hard.

"It's all right, mademoiselle, stay with me," he said.

But she was suddenly unsure of the man who coaxed her from the shadows.

"Hann sagði að þú vildi vera einn. Það er það sem hann sagði."

She was speaking Icelandic. It took Harper half a second to upload the language. *He said you would be the one. That's what he said.*

"Monsieur Gabriel, you mean. He told you I'd come, yeah? It's all right, I know him. All of us know him."

She shook her head no. She edged back to the dark of the nave. Watching her reach the steps of the altar square, Harper realized the girl was damn good at hiding in shadows. Three steps down, tuck the lantern in her cloak, and she'd disappear for good. Something was off, Harper thought; this couldn't be the setup. The girl was far too fragile to be left like this. Like leaving a child with an acetylene torch. He raised the palm of his right hand, intersected her eyeline.

"Tecum sum semper."

The girl slowed, then stopped.

"Hvað viljið þér mér herra?" What do you want from me, monsieur?

Harper read her eyes again. Still here and not here at the same time. And the sound of her voice . . . familiar, waiting for him to find her.

"Tell me your name, mademoiselle," Harper said.

The girl waited a long moment, then her voice was whisper-like.

"Ella Mínervudóttir. I'm the new *guet de Lausanne*."

He worked her surname for lines of causality. *Mínervudóttir*: Nordic matronymic of Minerva, the Roman goddess of wisdom and crafts. A poet named Virgil called her the goddess of a thousand works. Nothing connected. He ran his timeline, landed on a briefing he received about her after the cathedral job. *Got it.*

"You're from Iceland. From Reykjavík, I think."

"From Selfoss, monsieur. It's in the south. It's very small and there are horses there. They're small, too."

"Horses. Small ones."

He could hold her for only three minutes before the free will of her human side would break the spell. He grabbed at something else he had heard: eighteen, vegetarian, shy . . . then he flashed one of Minerva's thousand works: goddess of music.

"I was told you play classical guitar in the belfry. You play near the oldest bell, the one that calls the hour. What's her name?"

"Marie-Madeleine. But she's not the oldest bell, monsieur. The oldest bell is Couvre-feu, the smallest one. Marie is the biggest bell. That's why she calls the hour."

Harper nodded.

"Marie-Madeleine, right. I've met her. She is big. And loud. They told me you play guitar to keep her company while she's resting. So she won't be sad, they said."

The girl smiled a little. She was pretty, Harper thought. Light brown hair hanging from under her hat, just touching her shoulders, framing the eyes of a half-breed.

"Marie likes the cello better, monsieur. She says the music is rounder, so I play cello now."

"Rounder?"

The girl made a circle with her left hand. *"Eins og svo." Like this.*

"Rounder, right. That's good. That it sounds rounder, I mean."

"Would you like to come to the belfry, monsieur? You can listen to me play for Marie-Madeleine."

A shuffling sound reminded Harper that he and the girl weren't alone on the altar square. He looked back, saw Krinkle pressing his big hands along Astruc's sides and stomach.

"Sure," he said, turning back to the girl.

"When?"

"Sometime."

"Soon?"

"Sure. But just now I want you to listen to the sound of my voice, all right?"

"Ég er að hlusta." I'm listening.

"The soul of the one you named, the lad who called the hour from the belfry before you. His soul was comforted at the time of his death and born into a new life. But I don't know where it is. That's just the way it works."

She accepted his words without question this time. Ella's eyes slid to Krinkle and Astruc. She watched the roadie press down hard on the priest's chest . . . A painful groan echoed through the nave.

"Why are you hurting him?" she said.

Krinkle realized the girl was talking to him. He stood, looked at her, no idea what it was she was talking about.

"What now?" the roadie said, looking at Harper.

Harper nodded to *le guet*.

"She wants to know why you're hurting him."

Krinkle adjusted the shoulder straps of his denim overalls.

"I'm not. I'm helping him."

The girl looked at Astruc's battered form on the floor, then to Krinkle. Her face was expressionless.

"The way Monsieur Gabriel is trying to help the dying ones at Mon Repos?"

Krinkle pulled at his beard.

"Um, what makes you ask that particular question, mademoiselle?"

The girl's face remained expressionless.

"Because you're doing it wrong. That's not the way to do it. He told me how to do it. He told me to show you how to do it."

Krinkle glanced at Harper.

"Now would be a good time to say something, brother."

"Like what?"

Krinkle shook his head, stepped directly in front of the girl, raised the palm of his hand to her eyes.

"Dulcis et alta quies placidæque simillima morti."

The girl became still, staring off into the big nowhere. Harper watched her breathing slow down, settling at one breath per minute and taking her heartbeat with it. He looked at Krinkle.

"Half-breeds can go into hibernation mode like us?"

Krinkle pulled a penlight from the pouch of his overalls and switched it on. He checked the girl's pupils with a lapis-colored beam.

"No, but they can be put in hibernation mode *by* us. Just need to change pitch accents on two syllables in the incantation. And have clearance from management, which I do and you don't."

"Rather cold, isn't it?" Harper said.

"How so?"

"A bit like training a pet. Sit, stay, roll over."

Krinkle switched off the light, turned to Harper.

"You needed her to stay put so you waved your hand and said the magic words. What's the difference?"

"I was talking to her soul. She could choose to accept my voice or not."

"And if she didn't?"

"I'd find another way to sort the manner of her thinking."

Krinkle shrugged. "Yeah, well, I suppose that sounds like a plan to a guy with issues."

"Issues?"

"You. In the head," Krinkle said, nodding to *le guet*, "with them. And your issues are getting in the way of our orders."

Harper gave it two seconds.

"Maybe you need to run our orders by me again."

Krinkle counted down with his fingers. "One: Break into a French jail, snatch one defrocked priest who's wanted for murder and thinks his only begotten son is the savior of paradise. Two: Put said priest on my excellent tour bus and get him juiced with potions. Three: Deliver him to Lausanne Cathedral by a certain time to be awakened by Monsieur Gabriel because, guess what, the defrocked priest is one of *our* kind."

Clémence, the execution bell, sounded from the belfry in threes and sixes again. Harper checked his watch, waited for Clémence to wail. Second hand still not moving. *A certain time?*

"We're locked in on the negative side of a bloody time warp. There's no way of knowing what time it is in the cathedral, or anywhere else, for that matter."

Krinkle shrugged. "Sure there is, considering we nearly crashed and burned because the enemy knew we were coming and tried to blow us to hell on approach. Not to mention the slaughter of innocents going down two miles from this cathedral and there's not a damn thing we can do about it. I'd say that makes it five minutes past fucked-up o'clock, here and every place else in the world. Hold that thought."

The roadie turned, walked to Astruc, got down on one knee. He checked the priest's pulse at the carotid artery.

"Bummer," Krinkle said.

He lit up Astruc's eyes with the penlight. Harper saw the ragged scar running down Astruc's cheek now illuminated by the lapis-colored beam.

"Double bummer," Krinkle said.

He anchored the penlight between his teeth, removed an injector jet from the pouch of his overalls. He unbuttoned Astruc's overcoat, tore open the priest's shirt, and felt along his chest. He set the injector jet between the third and fifth costal cartilages of the priest's rib cage, right of the sternum, right over the heart . . . *Click.* Astruc's body shook as the needle hit his heart and the potions rushed in. The priest snapped to consciousness, knocked the injector jet from Krinkle's hands, knocked away the penlight, and grabbed at Krinkle's throat.

"No! We must all die for our sins!"

Krinkle countered with a left cross and Astruc hit the floor stones with that same bag-of-lead sound.

"Not if I can help it, brother," Krinkle said.

He picked up the penlight, gave the priest's eyes a quick check. He switched off the light and dropped it in his overalls. He got up and walked toward Harper, scooping up the injector jet along the way.

"Now, where were we? Oh yeah. I'd be happy to keep juicing Brother Astruc while you and *le guet* discuss the nature of reincarnated human souls, but no way is a local, half-breed or not, supposed to hear that soul stuff from our kind. Not now, not ever. Besides, we got trouble. Brother Astruc is crashing in his form."

Harper looked at the priest.

"How bad?"

"Organs shutting down, heart rate at two-five-zero, you could call it dying."

"Sorry?"

"I got some flash traffic from management while you were breaking Brother Astruc from jail. He may have tweaked his homemade juice to trigger a suicide response if his blood came into contact with awakening potion."

Harper looked at the injector jet in the roadie's hand. There were traces of a purple and luminous liquid in the glass tube.

"And you gave it to him anyway?"

"Hey, if management tells me to hit him with the shiny stuff when he goes south, I do it. Point is, he's dying and *le guet* knew it was going to happen."

"I'm not following you."

"You don't need to follow me, you just need to park this in your cerebral cortex: Astruc is one of us. The moment his heart stops, he's supposed to have one hundred eighty seconds before lights-out. But as you say, we're stuck on the negative side of a time warp."

"He'll have zero seconds."

"Bingo."

Harper rubbed the back of his neck with a bandaged hand.

"Right. Seeing as you know what's going on and I don't, maybe you'd best talk to the girl. Find out what she knows."

"Nope. The cathedral is your patch. *Le guet* is off-limits to me."

"You just put her in hibernation mode."

"To keep you from spilling about human souls."

"This is bloody daft."

"No, this is friggin' paradise. Listen, brother, *le guet* knew Astruc was dying because Gabriel revealed himself to her and primed her. You know how it is with Gabriel, he comes and goes. Sometimes he goes for years and we don't see him."

"What's your point?"

"This girl wasn't hiding in the nave, she was waiting for you. She's been mission-activated by Gabriel."

Harper looked at the girl. *Mission-activated.*

"No, she's just a kid."

"Open your head, brother. She's been primed with intel we need to save Astruc, and you need to pry it from her before it's too late."

Harper tried to imagine it.

"I don't see it. It can't be."

"Bullshit."

"I tell you I don't see it!"

"And I'm telling you bullshit! You're choosing not to see it because of what happened during the cathedral job! And you need to get over it, pronto!"

Krinkle's voice echoed through the nave and flashes of time ripped through Harper's eyes. Three years back to the brain-injured lad who imagined Lausanne Cathedral was a hiding place for lost angels. Ended up with the lad falling through the sky, dying on the esplanade, never knowing he'd been mission-activated, never knowing he was a half-breed conceived by Harper's own kind. *Christ, what was his name?*

"All I see is a broken body on the ground, no face. There's never a face unless someone pronounces his name."

Krinkle paced in a slow circle, pulling at his beard, resetting his ponytail, mumbling to himself. He stopped, looked at Harper.

"Names. Okay, we're getting somewhere. Focus on this one: *Le guet*'s given name is Ella."

Like flipping a switch.

Ella: a name of unknown origin. Norman, Germanic, Greek meanings: *complete, other, stranger, fairy maiden*. Primary meaning in ancient Hebrew: *goddess*; secondary meaning: *torch, sacred light*. Harper lowered his eyes to the lantern in the girl's hand. He saw the delicate flame on the wick of a stunted candle. He raised his eyes to Krinkle.

"You knew all this before we got to Lausanne?"

"What I knew before we got here has nothing to do with where we are now."

"Meaning what?"

"Meaning we don't know what's happening outside Lausanne Cathedral, only that some seriously bad shit has gone down. You know rules and regs in this kind of situation: Proceed as if we're the only ones left."

Harper looked at *le guet*.

"You forgot her. Or doesn't being half our kind qualify her as a member of the club?"

Krinkle turned away, stepped to the girl, checked her eyes again.

"She's also half human. That means we're forbidden to interfere with the time of her death if that's what's coming down. With her or without her, we've got no choice but to survive."

Harper looked at the girl.

Just a kid.

"We are not them, they are not us."

"Amen," Krinkle said.

Harper felt a jab of pain in the palms of his hands. He saw fresh blood seeping through the bandages.

"Hey," Krinkle called.

Harper looked at him.

"If I could choose to interfere with the time of her death, I would. If I could've done the same damn thing for the Cathars at Montségur eight hundred years ago, I would've. It's nothing personal, it's the gig. Been that way for two and a half million years. But if it makes you feel any better, imagine my crew outside the cathedral right now. They're armed to the teeth and they'll protect *le guet* to the death, with or without us."

Harper saw them on his timeline. Five rock-and-rollers dressed in black leather; one young woman working as guitar tuner and sometimes chauffeur of Krinkle's magic bus.

"Your crew is a post-rock band from bloody Finland."

"And they do killer encores as required."

Harper rested his bandaged hands in the pockets of his mackintosh, listened to Clémence rumble through the nave once more. Flashes of the last seventy-two hours ripped through his eyes. Strange lights in the sky, stranger things on the ground. A sextant from a time before the locals knew the world was round. And there was a five-thousand-year-old mathematical proof of infinity engraved in the sextant's arc. That was just Paris. In Montségur, in the shadow of the Pyrenees, where the Cathars made their last stand—where it all went bad for Harper, Krinkle, and Astruc eight hundred years ago—there was a shed full of somber angels cast in scrap iron and a biscuit tin containing one-third of a clay drinking cup and one bloodied carpenter nail. Two thousand years old, from Jerusalem; so said the sculptor of the somber angels. Mad lines of causality, their courses plotted thousands of years ago, now intersecting and delivering the message that some of the legends and myths of men were being ground down to a point of singularity, ready to blow the lid of the truth about angels hiding in the forms of men in a place called paradise.

"Christ, I need a smoke," Harper said.

"Yeah, a hit of radiance would do a body good right now. But later. Let's finish this."

Harper looked at the girl.

"Remind me how 'this' works."

"Easy," Krinkle said. "I'll back *le guet*'s memory up to just before you spilled on the reincarnation of human souls. When she comes around, pronounce her given name, let her see the light in your eyes. The synaptic contacts of her entorhinal cortex will fire simultaneously and delete her declarative memory from that point on. She'll have no choice but to follow you back to nowtimes."

"Easy, you say."

"Yup."

The roadie walked to the girl, passed the palm of his right hand before her eyes. She blinked.

TWO

i

Consciousness returned.

She tried to comprehend the world in front of her. She was facing a steel door, buckled and ajar, seven inches thick. Like she was inside a bank vault. Her arm was raised, her hand held a gun; it was pointing at the steel door. Beyond the gun barrel was a wisp of smoke, and the room smelled of cordite.

She looked down, saw she was sitting on a narrow camp bed. Her left arm curved as if holding something no longer there. Before she could think what it might have been, a voice ripped through her brain: *Weapons check.* In quick moves she retracted the gun's breech, saw a hollow-point in the firing chamber: *Loaded.* She ejected the magazine, checked it: *Empty.* She shoved the magazine to the grip, aimed at the door again: *Fire ready, one round good to go.* Question: *Where the hell did I learn to do that? No idea* was the answer. She eased her finger from the trigger and rested the weapon on the bed. She saw a green plastic bracelet attached to her right wrist. She raised it to her eyes: no name, no markings, no clasp.

"Huh."

She looked up, saw a bank of fluorescent lights in the ceiling. She looked around, saw the pale green concrete walls of a large square room.

She looked right, saw the kitchenette built into a recessed section of the wall: sink, stove, microwave, huge fridge-freezer. Close by was a small wooden table and chairs next to the sink. Nearby shelves held glasses and plates, aluminum pots and pans stacked atop a big iron skillet. There were tall clear jars filled with tea bags and curious-looking smaller jars. She got up and walked to the shelves. She read the handwritten labels on the jars of tea: *Morning Light to welcome the day. Midday Buzz for harmony and balance.* There was a tea for afternoons, labeled *Violette's Garden,* that did something, and one called *Night Clouds* that did something else. And there were dozens of smaller jars stacked atop one another with labels written in the same script as the teas: *Molly's Tofu Stew, Molly's Veggie Mix, Molly's Yummy Homemade Alphabet Spaghetti.*

She pulled open the one drawer under the countertop: kitchen utensils, forks and knives, different-sized spoons. She closed the drawer, opened the fridge. It was loaded with bottles of UHT milk and *Molly's Finest Apple Juice.* The freezer was loaded, too: bags of frozen vegetables and complete meals in plastic tubs. Each tub was labeled with the contents and instructions on how to prepare them in the same handwritten script as the other stuff: *Ten minutes in the microwave and chow down!*

"Huh."

She looked at the table and chairs again. No; one adult chair, one child's high chair. She looked at the buckled steel door again. It wasn't a bank vault; it was a bomb shelter with enough food to keep one adult and one child alive for months.

"Where the hell am I?"

She closed the freezer, closed the fridge, saw a baby cot in the corner. She walked to it. The cot was made up with a clean sheet and blanket. There were folded pajamas lying on the blanket next to a stuffed bear. A repeating pattern of a sheep with a wide grin on his face was printed onto the pajamas; the stuffed bear was smiling, too.

She walked to the nearby wardrobe; floor-to-ceiling, three doors. She opened the first door: sweaters and blouses, shoes, socks, T-shirts, lingerie. She pulled one of the brassieres to her chest; it fit. So did all the clothes behind door number two, from the look of them.

"This is weird."

Behind the third door: children's toys on the lower shelf; three upper shelves with kids' clothes. Overalls, sweaters, shirts and trousers, socks and shoes. All the clothes were the same size as the pajamas; lots of blue, no pink.

"Blue means boy. So where's he?"

She looked under the dining table and chairs, the baby cot, the camp bed she'd been sitting on. No little boy anywhere, but half hidden under the bed was a black canvas bag. She walked over, reached under the bed, and pulled out the bag. It was open. It contained silver tubes, divided into six sections according to the colors of their plastic caps. Red, blue, yellow, green, white, purple. She removed a white-capped tube. Four inches long, half an inch in diameter. No label, but there was a button on the side. She pressed it . . . *Click.* A short needle poked through the cap and a jet of valerian-smelling liquid drained onto the concrete floor. She looked at the bag again. Inside was an information chart with a diagram of circles; some interconnecting, some connected by lines. Within each circle were lists of physical or emotional symptoms corresponding to a particular colored cap, or combinations of colors. Below the diagram were required dosages. She saw another silver tube on the bed with a small blue cap next to it; the needle had been released. She picked it up. It smelled of lavender. She checked the diagram, followed the colors and interconnecting circles and lines to the words:

> For severe shock or emotional trauma. Do not exceed one dose per 72-hour period. MAY BE FATAL.

"What the fuck?"

She checked under the bed again, saw an open book on the floor. She pulled it out, thumbed through it. It was a child's storybook about a giant caterpillar named Pompidou flying through a star-studded sky, circling the moon, and then over the Boiling Seas of Doom. On the caterpillar's back rode a band of silly-looking men. They wore paper pirate hats and waved wooden swords and shouted into voice balloons:

"Up, up, and away!"
"Me toos!"
"To the ice castle!"
"And don't forget to save the princess!"
"Oh yeah, oh yeah. Must save the princess!"

She closed the book and read the cover:

piratz
Une histoire drôle de—

"Wait a sec."

She reopened the book to the silly-looking pirates, read their dialogue again.

"It's French. I think in English but I can read French. I must be dreaming."

She tossed the book and silver tubes onto the bed—*clink, clink*. The sound bounced around the room, and she followed it till it stopped at a set of bifold doors on the wall opposite the kitchenette. She walked the twelve steps it took to get there, pulled open the doors. A small bathroom: toilet, shower, sink with mirrored cabinet above, a double-door closet to the right. Shelves next to the shower held soaps and creams, adult and baby shampoos, boxes of tampons, towels and washcloths. She stepped into the bathroom, opened the right side of the closet. There was a combo washer-dryer and cleaning products, a broom and a mop. The left side held stacks of clean cloth diapers wrapped in plastic. *Neat,* she thought. And she remembered the neatly written labels on the jars in the kitchenette; jars of Molly's this and that. She wondered if her own name was Molly because, thinking about it, she couldn't remember what her own name *was*.

She reached over, opened the mirrored cabinet above the sink. One electric toothbrush for an adult, one kid's toothbrush with blue bunnies on the handle. Toothpastes, disposable razors, dental floss, a child's thermometer, Band-Aids, and aspirin. She stepped closer, rose to her tiptoes, and checked the top shelf for a prescription bottle or anything with a name on it. Nothing. She closed the cabinet, saw a woman in the mirror staring back at her.

"Is your name Molly? Is that my name, too?"

No answer. But the more she stared at the woman in the mirror, the more *no way* seemed the answer. Molly was a neat freak; the woman in the mirror was a tramp. Messy blond hair, ashen face covered in dirt and sweat, looking out at the world with a vacant gaze. She touched the glass to make sure the image was a reflection and the woman in the mirror did the same thing. She saw the woman was wrapped in a black blanket. She stepped back from the mirror, held out her arms, and the woman in the mirror matched her moves again. It wasn't a blanket, it was a black wool cloak over a green sweater and blue jeans. All the clothes were filthy with dirt and twigs and pine needles. She focused on the sweater, saw a dark blotch of something damp. And there was similar spotting down the legs of the jeans. *Blood?*

"What happened to you? By the way, who the fuck are you?"

Not receiving answers from the reflection, she opened the sink's spigot. It gurgled and spat a few drops. There was an electric switch on the wall with a label: WATER PUMP. She flipped it and water began to stream from the spout. She leaned down, splashed a few handfuls on her face. She felt something trickle from the back of her neck and down her cheek, then drip into the sink. She watched a trickle of blood circle the basin before going down the drain. She wet a washcloth, pressed it to the back of her neck. A sharp pain raced up her neck and into her skull.

"Shit!"

She held the washcloth to the mirror, the woman on the other side of the looking glass doing the same damn thing. There was a nickel-sized spot of fresh blood on the cloth, like she'd been jabbed with . . .

". . . a needle."

She dropped the washcloth in the sink, hurried to the camp bed, and checked the black canvas bag. Twenty compartments up, twenty across made two hundred tubes; one ninety-eight still in the bag, plus two on the bed made them all accounted for. Had to be the stuff for severe shock she'd found when she came around. She reached behind her head, found the sore spot again. Wondered if she'd jabbed herself, or if someone else had. She looked back to the bathroom. The woman in the mirror was still watching her from the other side of the bifold doors.

"Anytime you want to pitch in with a hint, feel free."

The woman in the mirror didn't offer one.

"Big fucking help you are."

She quickly read through the symptoms on the lid of the canvas bag, searching for something reading, *Can't remember a thing? Try this.* Nothing. She sat on the bed, looked at the steel door. She stared at the gap in the buckled metal, saw a light beyond the door; then came a metallic, iron-like smell. She rose from the bed and walked to the door, more curious than afraid. Crimps in the metal were razor-sharp and the gap was narrow. Air flowed into the room and the metallic smell was stronger here. She turned sideways, leaned through, and saw a blood-spattered stairwell with a woman's body over the bottom steps. Face hammered to pulp, throat slashed, hair soaked in blood. The dead woman's right thigh was wrapped in a bloodied pressure bandage. It had come undone, and a thick shard of glass was buried deep in the woman's leg. Blood had ceased to flow, but it was fresh. Looking over the body again, she realized the clothes in the closet would fit the woman's body, too. She wondered if the dead woman was Molly, and if this was *her* place and the missing little boy was *her* child.

"So what am I doing in here and why are you out there? Where's your kid?"

Her eyes followed a trail of blood up the steps. At the top of the stairwell, two men lay slumped together, half invisible. It was the clothes they wore; uniforms of some kind, imprinted with a strange camouflage pattern that made them almost disappear. If not for the red blood seeping through the fabric, she would not have seen their bodies.

"Hello?"

Her voice echoed up the stairwell and the sound startled her. She eased back into the vault, wrapped her arms across her chest. An odd feeling washed over her; more the lack of any feeling at all. No fear, no panic inside a blood-splattered dream. Had to be a fucked-up dream. And the voice in her head reminded her how, in really fucked-up dreams, there's no choice but to ride it out till you reach the really scary stuff; then you wake up screaming. She turned to the bathroom, saw the woman in the mirror.

"That's your voice in my head, isn't it? I am dreaming all this, aren't I? Is that why I'm not afraid? Or is it because I haven't come to the really scary stuff yet? Or it was that stress-be-gone shit in the silver tube I got jabbed with? Because anything can happen in a fucked-up dream, can't it? Just have to ride it out."

Water overflowed the sink and poured onto the concrete floor. She rushed into the bathroom, pulled the washcloth from the sink, watched the water drain. She squeezed the cloth, watched blood drip from it. She slammed closed the spigot and faced the woman in the mirror, knowing she was looking at her own reflection, except for the eyes. The woman's gaze was more than vacant; it was soulless.

"It wasn't any stress-be-gone shit, was it? You got jabbed with some steal-your-soul shit, didn't you? That's why you're looking at me like that. You have no fear because you have no soul."

Silence.

"Who are you? What are you doing down here? What happened to those people out there?"

Nothing.

She turned and walked to the baby cot.

She picked up the perfectly folded pajamas. She lifted them to her face, smelled them. There was the mingled scent of soap and powdered skin, and smelling it, she remembered coming to minutes before. Right arm with a gun pointing toward the steel door, left arm curved as if holding something to her breast. She looked at the woman in the mirror.

"The little boy was in my arms, wasn't he? I was holding him, wasn't I? Did somebody take him? Did he wander off, or is everything about him part of this fucked-up dream, like you and the needles and all of it?"

Nothing.

"Say something, damn it!"

Silence.

"Fine. I'll figure it out myself."

She walked to the camp bed, laid the pajamas next to the children's book. Next to the book were the silver tubes with popped needles; next to the tubes was the gun. Her eyes moved slowly over the objects, trying to figure which of them made the most sense. Francophone pirates waving wooden swords while riding a giant flying caterpillar; the little boy's pajamas with the grinning sheep on them; the Glock 19 with one 9x19 parabellum round left in the firing chamber.

"The gun wins."

She picked it up, stuffed it in the belt of her blue jeans, and looked at the woman in the mirror.

"If I'm not back in an hour, send in the marines, bitch."

ii

"He told me you would come. He said I could trust you."

Harper scanned the girl's eyes. She was back with him, ready to spill whatever message she had from Monsieur Gabriel.

"That's good, mademoiselle. Did he tell you what else I would do?"

The girl lifted the lantern, turned a latch, and opened the small glass door.

"Inspirare."

She pronounced the word in slow cadence, evenly spaced, pitch accents all in a row. That meant it sounded like a command. *Funny that,* Harper thought.

"All right."

He stepped close to the lantern, leaned forward, and exhaled slowly. The fire in the lantern flickered, almost dying. Then the wick ignited and a brilliant light sparked and glowed. *Le guet* closed the glass door, latched the lantern shut. Krinkle stepped next to Harper, both their eyes locked on the flame.

"Whoa. Management said it might be here, but holy mother backbeat," Krinkle said.

"What would be here?"

"The first fire of creation."

"They seem to tell you a lot more than they tell me."

"They do."

"Swell. What else did they tell you about the fire being here?"

"Big bang, big show if it goes live."

Another switch tripped in Harper's brain and he raced back on his timeline to the cathedral job. Quick scenes flashed through his eyes: he and the lad finding the fire in a cavern under the cathedral, transferring it to the lad's lantern, carrying it to the nave. Fast forward: the nave flooded with devourers, the fire going out. Harper breathes into it to keep it alive. And they were not alone. There was a woman with them, a woman with blond hair, and he could almost see her face . . . Harper's timeline cut to hash for a second, then came back. Now he was holding the lantern and the cathedral was awash with radiant light . . . *Hash*. Harper blinked himself to nowtimes. The new one was standing before him with a lantern in her hand. A flame at the tip of the wick pulsing, now, like something ready to explode.

Harper reached for the lantern, but the girl pulled it back. She hid it in the folds of her cloak. The crossing square fell dark.

"*Ekki,*" she whispered.

"No?"

"I must hold the lantern and say the words. You cannot carry the weight alone anymore, monsieur. You have fallen two times. The third time will be the last. You must wait."

"Sorry?"

"That's what he said."

Harper stared at her.

"Are you quite sure that's what he told you, mademoiselle?"

"He said if you asked that question I was to tell you, 'I'm very sure.'"

. . . i'm very sure, i'm very sure, i'm very sure . . .

Harper listened to the words echo through the nave. The cadence, the tone, the determined delivery. He looked deeper into her eyes. Krinkle called to him.

"Hey, brother, snap out of it."

Harper turned to the roadie. "Something's not right, she's not making any sense."

"Would you cut it with the 'Something's not right' stuff? She's doing what Gabriel told her to do. And we need to get a move on. Brother Astruc is getting worse."

Harper glanced at the priest, saw the white froth at the corner of his mouth. Harper stepped closer to the girl, reached for the lantern again.

"*Ekki*. Get out of my way," she said.

"Sorry?"

She raised the lantern and the light drilled into Harper's eyes.

"He says he's very sure you need to get out of my way."

She passed between them, walked to Astruc, and circumambulated his form three times, clockwise, in ever-widening circles, always holding the lantern toward the priest. She stopped, faced him. The girl was a half a yard from Astruc's boots, standing on an imaginary line that ran through Astruc and toward the apse. Just then Astruc's body seized up and Krinkle rushed to him.

"Oh shit, here we go."

He knelt at Astruc's side, pulled the penlight, hit the priest with the lapis-colored beam. The priest's face was turning purple; he gasped for breath. Krinkle grabbed Astruc's head, arced it back to clear the airway.

"He's going down fast," Krinkle said.

Harper hurried to the girl, stood in front of her.

"Ella, listen to the sound of my voice. Give me the lantern."

"*Ekki*. You're too weak to do it."

"Ella—"

"I have to hold the lantern and say the words, not you. That's what he says."

Harper scanned her eyes again. No wonder she wasn't making sense. She'd been heavily juiced. With what, Harper didn't know, but it was kicking in and rushing through her blood.

"Mademoiselle, listen to me. *I* need to hold the lantern. That's how it works. Trust me and give me the lantern."

The girl spoke without looking at him.

"If you try to do it, the fire will die and so will everyone in the world. That's what he says."

Harper listened to her voice: *That's what he says.* The girl was speaking in the present tense.

"Ella, who is talking to you?"

"Him. He's out there, in the shadows. He's telling me what to do."

Harper scanned the nave.

"There's no one out there, Ella."

A death rattle gurgled through the nave. Harper checked over his shoulder, watched Astruc gasp and claw at his throat for breath. The roadie tilted the priest's head back, trying to clear his airway.

"Do not do this, brother. Do not do this," the roadie said.

Harper turned back to the girl. "For Christ's sake, Ella, no one is here. No one is talking to you but me."

The girl lowered her forehead to focus on the flame; her breath quickened.

"Not you talking . . . Marc Rochat."

Harper flashed the lad falling through the sky.

"What did you say?"

"He says you need to get your friend out of the way. He says, 'I'm very sure the fire will hurt him.'"

Same inflection, same tone; it was the lad's voice. *Bloody hell.* Clémence tolled through the nave, louder still. *They're dying, the children are all dying.* Harper spun around, saw the roadie gathering Astruc in his arms.

"Get away from him!"

"We cannot lose him!"

Harper flew across the altar square, slammed into Krinkle, and knocked him away from Astruc. They rolled over the floor stones, slamming into the wooden benches at the edge of the crossing square. The roadie broke free, reached for Astruc; Harper pulled him back.

"Leave him!"

"No!"

Then the lad's voice again:

"C'est le guet! Il a sonné l'heure! Il a sonné l'heure!"

Powerful, resonant, hitting a perfect third tone above Clémence; harmonizing, humming, rolling through the nave. A stream of radiant light shot from the lantern high into the lantern tower where it pulsed in time to the sound, then it broke into thousands of glittering shards, tumbling down and disappearing as they touched Astruc's form. Lausanne Cathedral shuddered a little, as if all the world had come to a gentle stop.

Harper looked at the lantern.

Only a delicate fire at the tip of the wick now, and a new bell sound rumbled through the nave; a deep-throated, comforting sound. It tolled seven times. *Marie-Madeleine,* Harper thought; *the biggest bell, not the oldest one.* Fading light passed through stained glass windows along the south aisle and caught bits of limestone falling from the lantern tower. The limestone bits sparkled in reds, blues, greens. Harper checked the angle of light passing through the face of God at the center of the cathedral rose set high in the south transept wall. The protected zone around the cathedral had rejoined real time. Evening it was, 19:00 hours. Harper sat up, leaned into the benches.

"Sicut erat in principio," he said.

"In principio erat Verbum," Krinkle answered, pulling himself from the floor to join Harper. He laughed a little.

"I have to say, brother, on a scale of one to ten on the exothermic reaction meter, I'd give that a billion. Was it like that the last time?"

"Sorry?"

"The first fire. Was it like that the last time it went live?"

Harper thought about it. "From what they allow me to see on my timeline, sort of."

Krinkle looked up into the lantern tower, watched as limestone bits fell.

"You know, I'm not too sure how much more of that this place can take," he said.

Harper brushed dust from the shoulders of his mac. "Not much, would be my guess."

They sat in meditative silence a few minutes, taking in the scene. It looked normal except for the young girl in the black floppy hat and long black cloak, holding a lantern over the form of a defrocked priest.

"Do I need to check on Brother Astruc?" Krinkle said. "I mean he's alive and all, isn't he?"

Harper looked at his wristwatch; the second hand was ticking now. He looked at the priest. Resting comfortably in hibernation mode; one breath, one heartbeat per minute.

"I'd say all's well for now," Harper said. "What are our orders from here?"

"Hold till relieved."

"Right."

Harper shifted his eyes to the girl. Her breathing had calmed and she relaxed except for her right arm. It was trembling from the weight of the lantern she still held toward Astruc. Harper got to his feet.

"Wait here a minute, would you? I need to talk to her in private."

"About what?"

"The nature of reincarnated souls, one soul in particular."

Krinkle got up from the floor stones, parked his butt on the bench. He reached into the pouch of his overalls, pulled a pack of gold-filtered smokes. He lit up and the radiance hit him fast.

"No problem. I'll just wait here and pretend to forget what you just said."

"You do that."

Harper walked to the girl. She didn't look at him.

"Could you take the lantern, monsieur? I'm very tired."

He scanned her eyes. The juice had dissipated and the girl was released from whatever spell it was that had had her. Harper took the lantern from her, stood it on the floor stones next to Astruc. He looked around the crossing square, pointed to the wooden benches opposite Krinkle.

"Why don't we sit down, mademoiselle?"

"Já, þakka þér." Yes, thank you.

"And maybe we could talk a bit."

"I'm very tired, monsieur."

"Sure. Come with me, we'll sit over there."

He led her to the benches and she sat. Harper sat at the far end of the same bench. She watched him with heavy, exhausted eyes, studying the distance between them. She got up, walked closer to him, sat down next to him.

"What did you want to talk about, monsieur?"

"It's about the lad. The one who called the hour before you. A little earlier, you said . . ."

Her heavy eyes closed and she fell toward him. Her head landed on his chest. Harper sat very still.

"Ella?"

The new one was sound asleep.

THREE

She squeezed through the gap and eased her way into the stairwell. She reached for the handrail, braced herself, and straddled the dead woman. There was a Glock 35 on the next step; the retracted slide said the gun was empty.

She stepped over the body and saw an iPhone in the woman's left hand. She leaned down, pulled away the phone, and pressed the power switch. The screen asked for a nine-digit code. Icons at the top of the screen read plenty of battery, but no signal. She slid the phone into the pocket of her cloak and looked at the body again. She saw a gold ring on the dead woman's left hand. The woman was married; had to be the missing boy's mother. She felt the woman's trousers and coat pockets: empty.

"Doesn't make sense. Why was I inside the vault with your kid?"

She counted her way up the steps, listening for signs of anyone ahead. At step seventeen she reached the two men in camouflage. Matching Brügger & Thomet submachine guns strapped around their shoulders; both breeches open, both weapons spent. The Glock 35s in their hands were spent, too. She patted down the men. No wallets or IDs, but they had phones hooked to their belts. She reached over and tested each one. Both asked for a nine-digit code; plenty of battery, no signal. She looked at the men's faces. Unlike the dead woman, they were still identifiable, but she did not know them.

She looked at the woman at the bottom of the stairs. The body down there was dressed in civilian clothes; the bodies up here wore matching camouflage. But all three had carried Glock 35s and cell phones locked with nine-digit codes. *All on the same side,* she thought. She pulled her own gun from her belt, set her index finger along the trigger guard. She remembered that's the way it was done; then she remembered her own gun was a Glock 35.

"We were all on the same side. But who the hell were 'we'?"

She leaned around the corner of the stairwell and saw a long hallway where the fluorescent lamps sputtered on and off like strobe lights. The passage was more tunnel than hall: one and a half feet wide, six feet high. There were brass casings and discarded ammo magazines scattered over the floor. She listened for a voice or a moan. There was nothing but the buzz of the fluorescent lamps.

"Nice and slow, whoever the fuck you are, girl."

She stepped up between the men's bodies and into the tunnel. She walked slowly over the brass casings, trying not to slip, trying not to make a sound. Her eyes adjusted to the erratic bursts of light and she began to see things. Walls pockmarked with bullet scars and slash marks and wild patterns of blood spatter. Closer: bone chips and brain matter embedded in the walls. The signs read there'd been a hellish firefight here resulting in multiple head shots. She didn't bother to question how she knew such a thing. She filed it away with knowing how to handle a gun and reading French.

"Got to go with it till we get to the really scary stuff and wake up screaming. That's the rule of fucked-up dreams, *n'est-ce pas*? Wait a sec."

She looked back through the flickering light, saw the two dead men at the top of the stairwell. They had been butchered like the woman outside the steel door, but none of the three had taken a bullet wound or head shot. *Meaning our side had the guns and the other guys had . . . knives?* And there was the blood. The bodies she had seen bled out red and their blood had a metallic smell. The blood on the walls was darker, more viscous, and it reeked. She looked at the blood on her sweater and jeans. Same color, same texture, same foul smell as the blood on the walls. She added it up:

She'd been in the middle of the firefight before ending up in the concrete room, one bullet in her Glock. That meant she'd unloaded fourteen rounds into . . . *men with knives*?

"Weirder and weirder."

As she thought about it, the idea of talking to herself was fairly weird, too; especially after thinking about it some more and not being able to remember her own name.

She crept to the end of the tunnel, her Glock pointing the way ahead. She looked around the corner. The passage continued ten yards, then cut left. Same scene: dark blood, bone, and brain matter on the walls; brass casings and ammo mags on the floor. She followed on to where the tunnel split into two. This way was clean, that way was a charnel house. She took the clean hall but hit a dead end thirty yards on. She doubled back to take the bloodied hall. She made the same mistake at another intersection and realized she was in a maze of tunnels and the only way out was to follow Charnel House Road. She backtracked, made three more turns, and came to another bloodied stairwell. She raised her Glock to eye level and aimed upstairs. Quiet. She climbed, counted thirty-nine steps to the doorway. She jumped around the corner, panned left to right with her one-bullet gun.

"Jesus."

She was taking aim at a large, windowless room of wrecked laptops on desks and banks of video monitors on a wall. The room had been sprayed with the same explosive pattern of black blood, bone, and white matter as the tunnels. The ceiling lights were not working here, but dull gray light filled the room through an opening where a steel door had been pried open. Not as thick as the door to the room at the bottom of the stairs, but just as solid.

"So there's outside. All we have to do is walk outside, see the really scary stuff, and wake up."

She stepped into the room, saw three clocks on the walls. No numbers on the faces; just black marks for the minutes and hours on white faces, black arms for hours and minutes, long red second hands. The clocks looked familiar, but she had no idea why. The left clock was labeled *PST* and marked the time at 1:29. On the clock in the middle, labeled *GMT*, it was 9:29; on the clock on the right, labeled *CET*, 10:29. *Time zones,* she thought. Pacific, Greenwich Mean Time, Central European. Question:

"Which fucking time zone am I dreaming in? Or is it all three?"

She noticed the clocks weren't running, and the second hands of all three were straight up. She looked at the bank of wall monitors. Only the big monitor in the center was still on, and it crackled and buzzed as a jumble of numbers, symbols, and letters flickered onscreen. She stepped into the middle of the room. Tucked in an alcove opposite the monitors was a desk. It took her a second to make out the body slumped across it. It was the body of a man, wearing the same camouflage as the dead men at the top of the stairwell. She kept her Glock aimed at the open door as she eased across the room. She rounded the desk, pulled away the body. It tumbled to the floor, landed on its back. He'd been sliced open, and his guts dripped onto the floor.

She knelt next to him, patted his pockets: nothing, and the cell phone clip on his belt was empty. She looked at his face again, saw the moist red slash across his throat. She touched the dead man's forehead. He wasn't warm, but he wasn't cold. Come to think of it, the rest of the dead were the same temperature. She thought about her dream so far. It consisted mainly of her seeing and touching dead people. She wondered if this might be a good time to scream her head off and get back to reality. But again, she realized she was unafraid.

"Nothing but a dream."

She looked around the floor for the man's cell phone, then atop the desk. No phone, but there were radios and speakers, rows of small monitors with distinct labels: *Sitting Room*, *Kitchen*, *Hallways*, *Bedroom One*, *Bedroom Two*, *Back Garden*, *Front Garden*. There were more, but the labels were splashed with red blood and a thickening pool had formed on the desktop. *Probably where the ones with the knives killed him,* she thought. There was a headset with an attached microphone hanging off the desk. It was connected to a panel labeled *Comms HQ*. She picked it up.

"Hello? Is anybody out there?"

The line was dead.

She dropped the headset. It landed next to a wireless computer keyboard. She stared at it. It was clean but for eight keys; letters and numbers plus the shift key. Each of those keys bore the same bloodied fingerprint.

```
  1  2  3
                    U
                G
            C       N
```

She looked at the main monitor on the wall. The screen sputtered with one line of data: 1 @ 3 U c G n. Seven characters: three keys using the shift key, four without it. She looked at the dead man on the floor, remembered she found him slumped over the desk. She leaned down to check his hands. His hands and fingers were bloodied but for the index fingers. Both were smudged as having touched something. *It's him,* she thought; *he typed the characters before he died.* She looked down at the dead man, trying to remember if in any of her really fucked-up dreams the dead could speak.

"Can you tell me what it means? Is it a password?" she asked him.

The man stayed dead.

"Guess not."

She stood up, looked back through the tunnel, then ahead. So far there'd been four bodies; four bodies from her side from the look of it. And though there were clear signs that dozens of attackers took head shots at point-blank range, not one of their bodies was anywhere to be found. Perhaps all of the attackers were gone. She turned to the open steel door leading outside.

"Only one way to find out."

She took a slow breath, raised the Glock, stepped ahead. Halfway across the control room she smelled fire smoke, and the fumes grew heavier with each step. She stopped short of the exit, saw a screened porch beyond the steel door. The screen door was swinging slightly in waves of heat. Beyond the porch was a long yard; at the end of the yard a two-story house was in flames.

"Keep moving, it's only a dream."

Stepping through the doorway and onto the porch, the burning house was revealed in wide shot. Its roof had collapsed, and broken pipes spewed water over blackened timbers and licks of flame. All the windows had burst, and she saw the fire inside the house. Her eyes were transfixed, as if gazing into a churning furnace of white-hot flame. If anyone was in there, they were dead. Next to the house was a driveway where two vehicles had caught fire in the radiating heat. Burning tires cast off oily smoke that blocked any hint of safe passage; not that there was anywhere to go. As best she could see, wherever this place was, it was surrounded by a forest of tall evergreen trees. Nearby branches were singed by hungry flames, but the trees did not catch fire. She watched the smoke. It rose in a black spiral and formed a mushroom cloud above the forest, but the cloud did not drift away. And like the fire in the house, the cloud seemed to churn. No, it wasn't churning; it was pulsing, as if breathing. She looked at the swinging screen door.

"Jesus, this is . . ."

Something caught her eye. On the underside of the mushroom cloud hovering above the trees. Shreds of black mist broke away from the cloud and sank into the forest.

". . . so fucked-up."

She eased through the screen door, keeping her Glock ahead of her. She stopped at the top of the porch steps, saw slaughtered bodies scattered over a smoke-filled yard. She counted twenty-six all wearing the same strange camouflage as the men outside the bunker. Some of them had Brügger & Thomet machine guns slung over their shoulders or Glocks in their hands; others lay empty-handed next to discarded weapons. She stepped down into the yard. Her eyes locked on the tree line, watching for anyone watching her. She could see only a few feet into the forest, where the trees and underbrush became a darkening web.

The smoke was thick and she coughed and covered her face with the collar of her cloak. She counted ten steps to the first body. It lay on its back, and she eased it over with her foot. She didn't know him. She tucked her Glock into her belt, dropped to one knee, touched the man's forehead.

Same as the man in the control room—not warm, not cold. She didn't bother searching his pockets or checking his cell phone, but she went through his ammo magazine pouches looking for bullets. Not one bullet left. She zigzagged her way up the long yard, stopping at each of the bodies to conduct the same examination. In the center of the yard, three men were squeezed together back-to-back as if they had been surrounded, firing outward till they ran out of ammo, then they were sliced to death.

"Who did this to you?"

She reached fourteen bodies near the tree line and peered into the forest as far as she could see, but there were no more bodies. She looked back at the burning house, then to the building from where she'd come into the yard. Wood planks had been ripped from the exterior to expose concrete walls underneath. The few planks still attached to the building bore slashes and gouges from ground level to the roof. She imagined a swarm of hungry beasts clawing their way into the building. First through the wood planks, then solid concrete.

"And why not? No weirder than anything else in this place."

She lowered her gaze to the bodies on the ground. Some of their faces were identifiable, most were disfigured. She sensed the men were European, then wondered why she did. She remembered reading and understanding French in the child's book she'd found in the concrete room, and the three broken clocks in the control room marking three different time zones. The one on the right marked *CET*. *Perhaps I'm in Europe; perhaps this is France.* She did a slow three-sixty of the scene. Wherever the dream was taking her, it was leading her through a wasteland. *Confusing,* she thought, adding that it might help if she could remember who she was besides some subconscious representation of herself wandering an imaginary wasteland without a trace of fear. And she remembered the woman in the mirror down in the concrete room; the bitch with no soul who wouldn't offer a clue as to where this place was or what had happened.

"So it goes."

She remembered the cell phone she'd collected back outside the vault.

"Or not."

She found it in her cloak, touched the control button. It lit up, asking for the nine-digit code; plenty of battery, no signal still. She held it up, turned in a circle. Not a blip for a signal. She returned the phone to her cloak.

"Just have to figure it out yourself, whoever the fuck you are."

She retraced her zigzag steps, looking at the way the fourteen men had fallen near the tree line.

"Huh."

The bodies were evenly spaced in two close-set lines, like the point of an arrow. There was a trail of dark blood coming from the forest, cutting through the men. The trail led to two more men, then six in a row, then the three in the middle of the yard with their backs to one another. Then, finally, to the man who lay a few steps from the porch.

She turned back to the men at the point closest to the tree line. Her imagination kicked in again. They were first to take on the swarm as it charged from the forest. They were overrun and the swarm rushed ahead, killing every defender in its path. The swarm clawed at the outbuilding until it broke in. They killed the man in the control room who died typing a sequence of letters, numbers, and symbols. The swarm then rushed into the tunnels, where two men and one woman in civilian clothes made a last stand at the stairwell outside the concrete room where she was alone with one bullet in a gun. *Down to me?*

No, she remembered the signs of a little boy in the room; a little boy who was missing. She looked at the dead scattered through the smoke-filled yard. Why would there be all these dead and not the little boy? She looked at the burning house, wondered if maybe he'd been trapped inside. *Or perhaps he never was,* she thought. Perhaps he was missing from the scene because he was a dream within a dream, guiding her through the wasteland of wherever the hell she was.

"So where are you guiding me now, little boy?" she mumbled.

Her eyes searched the forest.

"Are you out there, or are you only in my head?"

There was a growl behind her, and she turned quickly around as a stairwell within the house collapsed into the flames. Heat rushed through the yard and washed over her.

"Shit."

She backed up into the trees, crouched down, and covered her face with her cloak. She waited for the heat to pass. She stood and looked around the forest. There really was no way out of here, not that she could see. She turned back and walked toward the yard. Her boots caught a fallen branch—*crack*.

A cry sounded from the forest. She looked back.

"Is somebody there?"

She stepped forward, pushing low-hanging branches from her face. The cry came from the left now, then from the right.

"Is it you, little boy? Where are you?"

She followed it deeper into the wood.

"Come on, help me out here. I'm doing the best I can. Where are you hiding?"

She saw shreds of black mist slither over the ground as if leaking from the underbrush. She retreated a few steps, then turned and hurried into the middle of the yard. She stopped, looked back. The mist emerged from the tree line and spread over the yard. Over the scattered bodies, over her boots. It rose to midcalf before stopping. She moved one foot, then the other; the mist rippled.

"Fuck me."

She began to walk slowly, like moving through a shallow pool of dark, thickening goo. She stepped up to the porch and the goo dripped from her shoes. She turned, faced the yard. Pulsing smoke, churning fire, a pool of whatever the fuck it was.

"No little boy out there, that's for damn sure."

A radiating pulse of heat circled the yard and whipped up the smoke and soot. She gagged, backed into the control room, choked and coughed. She wiped her mouth and nose on the back of her hands. She looked at them, saw streaks of mucus on the skin. She wanted to vomit.

"Dream or no dream, I need to wash this shit off, right now."

She headed to the stairwell and back to the concrete room. The one working monitor on the wall flickered and sparked with the same data as before.

`1 @ 3 U c G n`

Seven characters typed by a dying man as life drained from his body. The last deliberate act of his life. Perhaps it wasn't a password; perhaps it was a message, she thought. A warning that they were being overrun and needed help . . . *But nobody came.*

She wiped her hands on her cloak, walked to the desk, and stared at the keyboard. Seven character keys plus the shift key were bloodied; the rest of the keys were clean, including the return key. She looked at the dead man on the floor.

"You didn't live long enough to press the return key to send the message, did you?"

She looked outside, saw the shreds of black mist over the dead. Then came the oddest sensation so far in the dream. *Whoever you are, girl, you have* so *seen this shit before.* She looked at the dead man again.

"This is what I'm supposed to do, isn't it? This is how I get out of the dream, isn't it? I press the key, then I wake up in a bed with fluffy pillows, isn't it?"

She turned back and leaned over the keyboard.

"Here goes nothing."

She pressed the return key and a high-pitched tone screamed through the control room.

"Shit!"

She tumbled back, tripped over the dead man, fell into the wall and down to the floor. The tone rose in pitch and sliced through the room. She locked her eyes on the broken clocks, trying to steady herself. Just then, the clocks advanced by one minute, and the second hands of all three clocks moved ahead in perfect marching order. The screaming tone climbed higher. She covered her ears with her hands.

"God, it hurts!"

The data on the screen began to shift left to right, right to left, the characters passing through one another and rearranging itself, holding a moment as if searching for meaning and shifting again till it locked in place.

`@ n G 3 1 U c`

One by one the characters flipped into uppercase letters: @ to *A*, *n* to *N*, and as each letter appeared, the screaming tone rose another painful pitch until it pierced her hands and ears and seeped into her brain.

"Fuck!"

The last character flipped from *c* to *S*, and a word flashed in her eyes.

A N G E L U S

A N G E L U S

A N G E L U S

"For fuck sake, make it stop!"

FOUR

i

The north transept doors flew open and real time rushed in. Silhouettes lingered against the fading evening light, unable to enter the cathedral till time equalized throughout the cathedral. Harper checked his watch, figuring the volume of the nave meant equalization would take ninety seconds. But nine ticks later the silhouettes crossed the threshold, and touching the stone floor of Lausanne Cathedral, they took human form.

Krinkle glanced at Harper. "Some entrance," the roadie said.

More like an apparition, Harper thought.

"It is at that," he said.

On point were five men in black leather and boots. They wore comms headsets and night vision gear. They carried a mix of machine pistols and submachine guns, and Gurkha knives were sheathed at their belts. Two of them held positions just inside the doors as the others marched ahead. Harper made them for Krinkle's post-rockers on the Older Than Dreams Tour, having traded their Stratocasters for kill kits. Then came a young woman with her blond hair half covered by the hood of her sheepskin jacket. A set of japa mala beads dangled from her right hand, and she swung them like some sacred censor. Harper tagged that one as Karoliina, the crew's guitar tech and muse. The two rockers at the door fell in step behind her. On the magic bus from Toulouse, Krinkle let slip that Karoliina was a dream catcher. First one in three hundred years, the roadie told him. Seeing her surrounded by her own rock-and-roll army suggested it was true. Krinkle called to her.

"How on earth did you do that, sister?"

"Wasn't me. It was the cop."

"What cop?"

Karoliina kicked back her head—*Behind me*—to where two huge lugs in ill-fitting suits walked on either side of a well-tailored gent in a cashmere coat. Krinkle looked at Harper.

"Someone you know?"

Harper nodded.

"Management. Inspector Jacques Gobet of the Swiss Federal Police. Runs the Special Unit Task Force out of Bern. That's his cover, at any rate. The other two are his muscle, Mutt and Jeff."

"Mutt and Jeff?"

"Rhyming slang for *death*."

Krinkle eyed Gobet. "Trippy."

The north doors slammed closed, and a rollicking *boom* echoed through the nave. Harper looked down at the girl next to him. The noise had not disturbed her, and she continued to lean against his chest, fast asleep.

"Ahem."

Inspector Gobet was standing at the foot of the crossing square now, considering the scene before him. Krinkle in denim overalls, slumped on the wooden bench to the left, puffing on a gold-filtered cigarette. On the bench to the right was Harper with one arm around *le guet*; both his hands were wrapped in blood-stained bandages, and the girl's hands clutched Harper's mackintosh. In the middle of the crossing square lay one Christophe Astruc, OP, renegade priest, father of a half-breed son. Near him was *le guet*'s lantern, the first fire of creation waxing and waning on the tip of a dripping candle. For a moment it seemed the inspector did not know where to begin. He settled on Krinkle.

"The laws of Switzerland forbid smoking within public spaces—that would include gothic cathedrals."

Krinkle searched the cop's eyes for recognition. Maybe he wasn't convinced Gobet was the real deal; or maybe the cut of the cop's clothes irritated the rock-and-roll remnants of Krinkle's 1960s-edition form. The roadie pulled another hit of radiance.

"Says who?"

Mutt and Jeff made a move to explain who with their fists. The inspector beat them to the punch by raising the palm of his right hand into the roadie's eyeline.

"Omnia mutantur nos, et mutamur illis."

Krinkle froze, and Gobet held him a long moment before releasing him. The roadie pulled his cigarette case from his overalls and ground out his smoke on the lid. He dropped the roach in the front pouch of his overalls.

"Just checking it's really you in that form, Boz. You have to admit, it's so not you."

"You will address me as 'Inspector.' And as far as the form before you, get used to it."

"Because?"

"As I have explained to your crew, after a rather unpleasant standoff at gunpoint with a company of Swiss Guard tacticals, all of you are to be placed under my command effective immediately."

"Doing what?"

"Security around the cathedral until we reestablish the protected zone over the old city, for starters. From then on, whatever I tell you to do."

"But we're in the middle of a world tour. We've got confirmed dates in Tallinn next week."

"Canceled in lieu of an extended run at a small club around the corner from the cathedral. It will serve as your base of operations until further notice. Your associates will have a place to perform and you will have secluded parking at the back of the club where you will continue your radio broadcasts."

Krinkle looked at his band.

"I don't have a choice about this, but you guys do."

Karoliina pulled the hood of her coat from her head.

"We've made our choice, Krinkle. We're staying in Lausanne. We're needed."

Krinkle listened to the sound of her voice. She was telling the truth; her free will was intact. And knowing her, she was speaking for the rest of the band.

"Cool. How many of his Swiss guns did you hold off?"

"Lost count at fifty. Luckily, the cop showed up with his two pals before someone pulled a trigger."

Krinkle smiled. "Even more cool."

Harper watched the roadie and the dream catcher stare at each other. He read unspoken words passing between them. He checked Inspector Gobet to see if he'd picked up the vibe on his copper radar. *No* was the answer. The inspector was looking at Astruc. Harper read solemnity, as if the cop recognized a battle buddy from long ago, once strong and righteous, now fallen low because he could not bear the weight of his sins.

"Joy be the consequence," the inspector said quietly to himself.

The words popped hot in Harper's brain. Shakespeare, *Merchant of Venice*: act three, scene two. A line about the folly of choices costing a pound of flesh further down the road. The inspector recovered, signaled his muscle to take Astruc.

"Tell the medics I want him conscious and ready for interrogation by tomorrow morning. Tell them I don't care how they do it."

Mutt and Jeff moved quickly onto the square and looped their elbows under Astruc's shoulders. They peeled the priest off the floor and dragged him down the center aisle. The heavy curtains at the narthex billowed as two of the inspector's tacticals pushed open the great west doors. There was an ambulance pulling up onto the esplanade; its spinning blue lights splashed against the doors and highlighted the hole where the iron latch used to be, the hole Harper had drilled with his SIG to break into the place. The ambulance backed up to the main doors, and its rear hatch opened to receive Astruc. Inside, two white-smocked medics were standing by in a mobile operating theater. Mutt and Jeff lifted the priest, tossed him on the gurney, and jumped in behind him. The hatch slammed shut, the ambulance sped off, and the tacticals pulled closed the doors—*boom*. Harper looked at Gobet.

"Sorry about the front door. It was locked."

"Oh, don't trouble yourself with the door, Mr. Harper. Easily repairable," the inspector said, brushing limestone dust from the sleeves of his cashmere coat. He stepped onto the square and walked to the lantern. He picked it up and held it high to cast as much light as possible on Harper and the sleeping girl. "But perhaps you would care to explain what on earth you are doing with Mademoiselle Mínervudóttir?"

"Sorry?"

"Le guet de Lausanne."

"I got the name, Inspector, it's the question I'm struggling with."

"You appear to be holding her in your arms."

The cop's thinking came through loud and clear. Harper's kind were forbidden to touch the locals without clearance from management. It's what started this bloody war to end all wars. The first of Harper's kind, two hundred of them, were sent to paradise to watch over the creation. After a few thousand years of watching, the Two Hundred decided the local females of the species were the business and that ruling this cosmic outpost could be profitable. The Two Hundred took the forms of men, propagated their own race, and infected the creation with greed and fear. *Book of Enoch: chapter six, verse two,* Harper thought. *Read all about it. Wasn't supposed to be this way.*

"Appearances can be deceiving, Inspector."

"Do tell."

"I'm not touching her, she's touching me."

The inspector raised an eyebrow. "I beg your pardon?"

"She passed out at the end of the operation and fell into me."

"Passed out?"

"That's right. Shouldn't be a surprise to you, seeing as she'd been—"

"Mission-activated," Krinkle interrupted.

Inspector Gobet looked at him. So did Harper.

"That is, Boz—uh, Inspector, we got here looking for Monsieur Gabriel, found the girl instead. Took us a while to understand she'd been mission-activated and that she's extremely sensitive, more than most of the children. Maybe it was stress, maybe nervousness, but I can verify she passed out and fell into Brother Harper. No unauthorized physical contact. Simple as that."

The inspector gave it three seconds, then turned to Harper. *"Estne verum?"*

Harper flashed back on his timeline, saw the girl's glassy eyes, juiced into a trance, thinking she was delivering messages from the dead lad, raising the lantern and releasing the first fire of creation on her own. He glanced at Krinkle, caught unspoken words: *It's true enough for now, brother.* Harper looked at Gobet.

"Verum est."

The inspector could wrench the details from the prefrontal cortex of Harper's brain in half a second. It would be painful, and Harper was sure it was coming. Instead, Gobet turned to Karoliina and offered her the lantern.

"Mademoiselle, would you and the members of your orchestra escort *le guet* to her quarters in the belfry now? You will find a box of chamomile tea for her in the loge. Brew a cup for her and keep her company through the evening. See to it that she remains calm after the stress of today." The inspector nodded toward Krinkle. "Your equivocating ringleader is correct. Mademoiselle Mínervudóttir is sensitive. She requires a certain level of care."

"Yes, sir," Karoliina said.

She pulled a Smith & Wesson from her sheepskin coat and handed it to the tallest of the rockers. "Secure the belfry, but stay out of her eyeline. I'll check in after the three o'clock bells when I put her to sleep. Signals?"

"The call is 'side one, track three.'"

"Answer?"

"'Black Metallic,'" the rocker said.

Karoliina smiled. "Nice tune. *Nähdään.*" *Later.*

"Nähdään."

The rockers checked their weapons and slipped away. Karoliina stepped up to the crossing square and took the lantern from Gobet.

"Do take care with that, mademoiselle. We have never used the first fire to call the hour."

"But it's a dark and stormy night."

"Quite."

Karoliina walked to Harper, lantern in hand. She stopped in front of him, looked at *le guet*.

"How is she?"

"Exhausted," Harper said.

"I can see that. Anything else I need to know?"

"Like what?"

Karoliina smiled. "Something she may have forgotten under the stress of being mission-activated, of course. Something I can replant in her dreams when I put her to sleep. Something kind."

Harper thought about it, wondering when the last time "something kind" was part of his job description. He flashed his timeline, saw Karoliina on the magic bus to Lausanne. She called children like the girl and the lad, like all the children from Mon Repos, "half-kinds." A better word for children born on the right side of the light, she said. And she said it was time for the likes of Krinkle and Harper to get with the twenty-first century and stop calling them "half-breeds." Harper looked down at *le guet*, noticed how graceful the young girl's hands were, how long the fingers, how they held on to him.

"She asked if I'd come to the belfry to listen to her play the cello for one of the bells. Marie-Madeleine, the big one."

"And you said?"

Harper looked at Karoliina. "I said I would. One night."

"Wow."

"Wow what?"

"Wow you." Karoliina rested the lantern on the floor and knelt before *le guet*. She lifted the japa mala beads, rubbed them together in her hands, and filled the air with the scent of tulasi wood. *"Vakna, litla."*

Le guet opened her eyes to the voice calling in her mother tongue.

"Hver ert þú?"

"My name is Karoliina. I'm from Finland."

Le guet rubbed her eyes and yawned. "As the bird flies, Finland is one thousand three hundred and sixty-eight miles from Iceland."

"Yes, it is. But how do you know this?"

"I like to look at maps in school."

"I like looking at maps, too. They tell where you are in the world."

"That's what my teachers at Mon Repos say. They are all dead now. They were killed with the children."

Karoliina touched the girl's knee. "Yes, but you're not alone. I'm going to be your teacher now, *litla*. We can look at maps and read stories and go for walks in the day."

Le guet smiled and tilted her head. "How did you know my nickname is *litla*? No one calls me that in Lausanne. Only my mother did. In Selfoss, before she died."

Karoliina stood, held out her hand to the girl. "Why don't you take your lantern and show me the way to the belfry? I'll make you a cup of tea and we'll talk."

The girl looked at Harper.

"All's well, mademoiselle. You go with her."

Le guet let go of Harper's coat and took Karoliina's hand. She stood, picked up her lantern, and allowed herself to be led away. Then she stopped and turned back to Harper.

"It was very nice to meet you, monsieur."

Harper heard the lad's voice again. He scanned the girl's eyes. They carried no remnants of what had happened in the cathedral just minutes ago. He thought maybe it was better there wasn't a chance to ask her about the nature of reincarnated souls—one soul in particular.

"And you, mademoiselle."

Darkness had seeped into the nave, and Harper watched the two women walk away in a pool of lantern light, disappearing behind stone pillars, then reappearing between the arches of the north aisle. He heard their voices:

. . . i like your beads. they smell nice . . .

. . . i can teach you to use them if you like . . .

. . . to do what . . .

. . . nice things . . .

. . . okay. we go this way now . . .

The women stopped at a narrow wooden door in the south wall. There was a chiming sound as *le guet* pulled a ring of keys from her cloak and unlocked it. The women crossed through with the lantern and the door closed behind them—*boom*. A notion in Harper's brain: With all the comings and goings and banging of doors, Lausanne Cathedral was like the grand concourse of a train station for angels and shadows and wandering souls. Someone said that once. The lad from the cathedral job maybe, before he was killed. Sounded like something he'd say.

ii

Harper looked at Inspector Gobet.

"Was she right about Mon Repos? They're all dead?"

The inspector nodded. "Three hundred children, one hundred partisans caring for them. Monsieur Gabriel is on-site searching for remains. As you can imagine, it is a ghastly business."

"And the other orphanages?" Krinkle said.

"Same scenes. We are facing the hard fact that many innocent souls will be lost before the comforters find them."

Harper looked at the both of them. "What other orphanages?"

The inspector climbed to the altar and took hold of the sanctuary lamp. A cumbersome thing it was. Solid brass, a meter and a half tall, a votive candle burning in a vase of bloodred glass atop it. The inspector lifted it with the greatest of ease. He stood it under the lantern tower and it brightened the crossing square a little.

"There were four more orphanages for the children of our kind, Mr. Harper. Three more in Europe, one in Hong Kong, all of them twice the size of Mon Repos."

"Twice the size?"

The inspector did not respond.

Harper leaned forward, rested his arms on his knees, and cupped his bandaged hands together.

"Correct me if I'm wrong, but after the cathedral job you said it was a one-off. You also said, if I'm not bloody mistaken, that you shut it down years ago."

"I don't care for your tone of voice, Mr. Harper."

"Turns out we've used the locals to create our own master race on a grand scale, same as the enemy, and you're worried about my bloody tone?"

"I remind you the children of our kind were not bred to wreak havoc in the world so that we might rule over it. It was an experiment of desperation following the decimation of our kind. And I did shut it down, the moment it became obvious our children all shared the same genetic trait."

Emerald green, almond-shaped.

"They have our eyes."

"Yes, Mr. Harper, they have our eyes. Combined with their unforeseen talents and sensitivities, the children made for easy prey. I established the orphanages to protect them. Or so I had hoped."

Harper looked at Krinkle. "How long have you known all this?"

"Long enough," the roadie said.

"And given the score, you didn't think it worth a mention?"

"Given the score, there wasn't time to mention it. Besides, I wasn't cleared to pass along the info to anyone, including you."

Harper sat back in his bench. The nave echoed with the sound of creaking wood. "That's funny."

"What's funny?"

"You found time to pass along the info on the kid in Portland. The one your dream catcher knew about before our own kind did."

Krinkle seemed confused.

"Let me help you with your timeline," Harper said. "I haul Astruc onto your bus, you and I talk about the prophecy. Get the picture yet?"

Krinkle's expression read that he did not. Harper continued.

"First I heard of the prophecy was in Montségur, from a man who made angels out of scrap iron. Turns out he's the only living descendant of the Cathars. The prophecy was a family secret handed down from the eighth century. But you already knew about it. A child conceived of light, born to guide the locals through the next stage of evolution, you said. Your dream catcher spotted him in downtown Portland, knew the child was the one she'd seen in her dreams. You reported the intel to HQ. A boy, eighteen months old maybe."

Krinkle pulled at his beard. "I told you that?"

"You did. Of course you were drinking one of management's teas at the time. Babbling like a speed freak, you called it."

Krinkle looked at Gobet. *Oops.*

The inspector shrugged. "It happens, especially with that particular blend. But seeing as you believe yourself to be in the know, Mr. Harper, why don't you let your imagination run with it?"

Harper watched lines of causality intersect in his eyes.

"You didn't mention an orphanage in the States, so I'd say the child was held in a secure location, protected by a time warp and one of your Swiss Guard tactical units, most probably. The fact Krinkle's dream catcher saw the kid in Portland, out in the open, says two things: the secure location is somewhere within driving distance of Portland, somewhere that doesn't exist on a map. It also suggests the mother is with the child and oblivious to the fact she's living in limbo, a few minutes behind real time. Your tacticals on-site take them out now and again to give them a feeling of normalcy. As a complete wild guess, I'd say you're the only member of management who knows the location, or that the kid even exists. At least you thought you were. Doesn't matter given the big question, does it?"

"That being?"

"Thousands of innocent children, hundreds of partisans were slaughtered at five different sites around the world to get at one little boy you had stashed in the States. At least that's the score I'm reading at the moment. Tell me, was it worth it?"

The inspector bristled. "Do not dare to cheapen the loss of their souls with sarcasm, Mr. Harper."

"I'm not. I'm asking the question in their name, before their souls and names are forgotten forever. That's what happens, isn't it?"

The inspector didn't answer.

Harper scanned the massive interior of the cathedral: the vault, the upper balconies, the nave bound on two sides by seven great arches. *A bloody big, dark place it is when the sun goes down,* he thought. He looked at Gobet.

"You put the first fire in the belfry tonight, Inspector. You did that for a reason. You're hoping it will guide the children's souls to the cathedral. I realize it's hard to tell without Monsieur Gabriel at his post, but who knows? Maybe a few souls are already here, hiding in the shadows and waiting for comfort, or an explanation."

The inspector studied the flame of the sanctuary lamp. He held his hands above it, moved them slowly to cast shadows into the lantern tower above.

"The enemy embedded a virus in the SX grid," he said. "Once activated, it was unstoppable. We lost operational control of the grid just as the attacks began in a wave from Hong Kong to Lausanne. Same attack profile in each instance. The time warp above a site was disrupted for sixty seconds, giving the enemy time to get inside, reset the access codes, and lock us out. When Mon Repos was hit, the protected zone around the cathedral became highly unstable. Every line of causality I could see indicated the cathedral would be next. At this point our mechanics regained partial control of the grid and I ordered them to reinforce the cathedral's defenses. In doing so, I played into the enemy's hands."

The inspector stopped talking and lowered his hands to his sides.

Harper filled in the silence. "The moment you reinforced the cathedral, the enemy went for the real target. Ground zero was in the States. The slaughter of the innocents around the world was a feint."

The inspector nodded. "I warned the tactical unit on-site, only to learn they were already coming under the heaviest attack so far. Communications became difficult before ceasing altogether."

Krinkle got up from his bench and joined Gobet at the sanctuary lamp. The roadie looked up into the lantern tower, read the shadows still hanging against the milk-colored windows of the lantern tower.

"Want me to take over awhile?" he said.

"Thank you," the inspector said.

Krinkle began to move his hands over the lamp in the same pattern as the cop. Harper, still on his bench at the edge of the crossing square, leaned down and looked up into the lantern tower. He couldn't get the angle to see what the roadie was up to; he sat back. The bench creaked and echoed through the nave again.

"What's the latest recon from ground zero?" Harper said.

The inspector shook his head. "Unlike the orphanages, we have not been able to reenter the American site to assess the situation."

"Why not?"

"As you already imagined, Mr. Harper, the location doesn't exist on a map, it exists in a temporal limbo, not a few minutes, but a few hours behind real time. When the enemy retreated, they reversed polarity in the time warp mechanisms to create a gravitational singularity over the site. We're stabilizing the situation as best we can, but the pressure of real time is bearing down."

Singularity . . . There's that word again, Harper thought. A place in space-time where mass is ground down to a point of infinite density and zero volume. Anything, everything, is suspended in a moment of time with no way of escape. Then he flashed why the word had planted itself in his consciousness. He had already received a "no way out, singularity ahead" notice from Inspector Gobet one starry night in the vineyards above Lac Léman, just after the Paris job. Seems his own eternal being was trapped in the physical form of Captain Jay Michael Harper, the inspector explained over tea. And sooner rather than later the weight of the dead man's form would crash down. *Wham*—lights-out. An "undefined metaphysical condition," the cop called it in the vineyards of Grandvaux. "Royally buggered" was the diagnosis Harper found more appropriate just now. He rubbed the back of his neck.

"The location will collapse in on itself. It'll be no better than a dead zone."

The inspector corrected him. "In point of fact, it will be more like the ninth circle in Monsieur Alighieri's *Inferno* for any human soul left alive."

Harper flashed up an episode of the History Channel he watched once: *Visions of Heaven and Hell*. The program featured some mad-as-a-hatter drawings by a Renaissance painter, Sandro Botticelli. Sandro visualized the descending levels of eternal torment in Dante Alighieri's tale. Last stop: the ninth circle, where Satan is trapped waist-deep in ice. The six-eyed demon spends his eternity trying to break free of the ice by flapping his six massive wings to melt it, but the resulting windstorm refreezes the ice and keeps him well stuck.

Hang on . . .

Harper looked at the inspector. "Are you telling me someone is still alive in there?"

The inspector adjusted the silk scarf under his cashmere coat. "The mother and child both wore life status bracelets. They were constantly monitored by my team at Bern HQ. As transmissions from the site began to fail, we could not get an exact location on their whereabouts within the perimeter. There is an underground bunker at the house, a safe room, if you will. We don't know if they got to it in time. To complicate matters, the enemy duplicated the signals, putting mother and child at several locations at once so that we would lose track of them, then all communications were lost. All we know is, up to that point, mother and child were alive."

"How alive is that?" Harper said.

"Good question, and I'm sending you in on a recon mission to answer the question yourself, after you attend to a small errand in Lausanne."

"What sort of errand?"

"One to help you understand what is happening in paradise so that you may better execute your mission. And frankly, it gives the chief mechanic one more day to plot an infil solution through the shifting sands of time, so to speak."

Harper let the inspector's last sentence sink in.

"You want me to infiltrate a place that doesn't exist on a map? And you want me to do it by tunneling through the bloody shifting sands of time?"

"Indeed."

"And how am I supposed to do that?"

The inspector pointed to the north doors where he had entered the cathedral. "You just witnessed a field test of the technology. We've been developing it over many generations while you were in stasis. Works surprisingly well, I think, though engaging it in unstable temporal conditions may prove otherwise."

"Terrific. Why me?"

"You have specific qualifications for the job, of course."

Harper felt a touch of vertigo—or maybe it was a measure of gravitational singularity.

"No great loss if I end up trapped inside, you mean, seeing as I'm half dead already."

The inspector nodded. "That would be one reason."

Swell, Harper thought. *Out of the cosmic frying pan, into an infinitesimal point of space-time with no escape. And Satan thinks he's got it tough.*

"Right then."

Harper stood and walked across the crossing square to make it a threesome around the sanctuary lamp. He leaned back, looked up into the lantern tower, and read what the cop and the roadie had been signaling to the outside world: *Mortem tuam annuntiamus et tuam resurrectionem confitemur. mortem tuam annuntiamus et tuam resurrectionem confitemur.*

"'We proclaim your death and confess your resurrection,'" Harper said.

"Yup," the roadie confirmed.

"What's it mean?"

"Depends on whether you're a local or one of our kind."

Harper lowered his eyes to Krinkle. "What kind of an answer is that?"

"The only one on offer at the moment, brother."

Harper thought about it.

"You know, mate, since we met in Toulouse, you've always been two steps ahead of me. Why is that?"

"It's my job," Krinkle said.

"How long has it been your job?"

"From the beginning."

"Fair enough."

Harper reached in the pockets of his mackintosh, found his own gold-filtered fags, and lit up. He took a deep hit of radiance and held it. He felt the weight of his physical form lift from his eternal being.

That's better, boyo.

He released the smoke straight into Inspector Gobet's face.

"I give up. What's the other reason you want me to take the mission? Unless you want to arrest me for smoking in a gothic cathedral and call the whole bloody thing off."

Inspector Gobet waved away the smoke.

"The woman in the States, the child's mother, her name is Katherine Taylor."

FIVE

i

The screaming tone stopped but reverberations ricocheted off the walls like stabbing things, and she remained paralyzed. The reverberations decayed, and she gasped for air.

"What . . . what was that?"

Her voice sounded strange. She lowered her hands from her ears.

"Hello?"

The words resonated in her chest, but were barely audible passing her lips. She sat up, braced her back against the wall. She clapped her hands twice; the sound was muffled and dull. She looked at the dead man on the floor. His unmoving eyes were locked on hers.

"What is this place?"

The dead man did not answer, still.

"Why is everyone dead but me?"

Nothing.

Smoke blew into the room on another wave of heat. She caught a whiff of something foul. Her stomach convulsed, and vomit rushed up her gullet into her mouth. She gagged, leaned over, coughed and spit for half a minute. She wiped her mouth on the sleeve of her cloak.

"Jesus, I'm deaf and eating my own puke. When does this fucking dream end?"

She looked at the dead man again, hating him for being near her.

"Stop looking at me!"

She kicked the body over on its side, got to her feet, looked out to the yard.

"What the fuck?"

The black mist lowered as if draining away, and the dead bodies in the yard emerged like islands. She thought goo was dripping from the bodies in streams, then she saw it was moving like knowing threads, wrapping themselves around each of the dead. A thought hit her: *It's alive. It's feeding.* Then the sensation she felt before touching the return key doubled down: *You have* so *seen this shit before.* She shook her head.

"I need to wake up. I really need to wake up."

She saw the monitor on the wall, the word *ANGELUS* still flashing at her.

"Fuck you!"

She rushed at the monitor, tried to yank it down. It was bolted in place.

"Fuck you, I said!"

She grabbed a laptop from a nearby desk, threw it at the monitor.

"Enough of this fucking shit!"

The monitor sparked and sizzled and spit glass. It was dead and the flashing word was gone. She heard a dull buzz in her ears and it made her dizzy. She leaned back against a desk to balance herself, but the room began to spin. She closed her eyes.

"God in heaven, what now?"

She sensed consciousness leave her body for a moment, then the dizziness passed. She opened her eyes, looked at the world beyond the porch. Mushroom cloud above the forest still pulsing, fire in the house still churning, but the black mist was gone. And where the twenty-six dead men had lain, there were now twenty-six tightly woven cocoons. Black, oily, hardening in the flaring heat.

"Bad shadows," she whispered.

She did not know what the words meant or why she pronounced them, but she knew the words to be truth. And for the first time since finding herself in this fucked-up dream, she was afraid.

"Fuck!"

She ran from the room and down the stairs to the tunnels. She ran faster, following the black-bloodied walls through the concrete maze. The flickering fluorescent lights in the ceiling made the tunnels appear longer than they were before, as if stretching ahead as fast as she ran. Panic seized her. *You'll never make it back, you'll never make it back, they'll find you!*

"Enough! Please, enough!"

With her heart racing and pounding in her chest, she reached the two men slumped at the top of the stairwell leading down to the vault. She jumped over the bodies, got halfway down the stairs, and lost her footing. She grabbed at the handrail, missed it, and fell.

"No!"

She crashed down on her knees, landing next to the slaughtered woman who lay outside the steel door.

"Get away from me, damn it!"

She tried to get to her feet, but slipped in the woman's blood. She kicked against the woman's legs and shifted the body.

"Get the fuck away! I don't want to end up like you!"

She backed up against the steel door, getting as far away from the slaughtered woman as she could. She drew her throbbing knees to her chest, saw bloody scratches and cuts through the rips in her jeans. She wrapped her arms around her legs, felt herself shudder.

"Why won't I . . ."

She saw something in the woman's right hand. Something green, barely poking through the woman's fingers. Something the woman was desperately trying to hold on to even in death.

". . . wake up?"

She reached over and pulled the thing from the woman's death grip. It was a small green band made of rubber, or it was before it had been cut open. She held it to the light, saw a thin metallic layer in the rubber. She looked at the bracelet on her own wrist. Except for the size, it was identical. She tried to pull hers off to get a better look at it, but the hoop was too small to slide over her wrist. The only way it would come off was by cutting it. She held the smaller bracelet before her eyes, connected the severed ends to form a ring. It wasn't just small, it was very small; designed for . . .

"A little boy."

She looked at the dead woman. Remembered first seeing her through the gap in the steel door, wondering if the woman was named Molly and if the missing child was hers. She got to her knees, checked the woman's right wrist; no bracelet, and she didn't remember seeing one on any of the dead. *Me and the little boy,* she thought, *we were wearing bracelets; only us.* She touched the inner side where it would have rested against the little boy's skin. It was like touching . . . *my son?*

"Oh, my God."

She grabbed the handrail, pulled herself from the floor. She squeezed through the gap in the steel door and marched straight to the bathroom, where the woman in the mirror was waiting for her. She held the small bracelet to the glass for the woman to see. The woman in the mirror did the same thing.

"I don't care how fucked-up this dream is supposed to be, you need to give me some answers, bitch, right fucking now. The little boy, he's not an illusion, is he? He was here and he was wearing this, wasn't he?"

Silence.

She held up her right wrist; so did the woman in the mirror.

"Look, I've got one, too. No one else in this dream does. Not the woman outside, not any of the men. Just me and the little boy that was in here with me. I know he was in here, so do you, because you're wearing one, too. I was sitting on the bed out there, pointing a gun at the door because the bad shadows were coming in and I was holding the boy, like this. Yeah, that's it, just like you're doing. I was trying to protect him, wasn't I? The bad shadows killed everyone outside and were coming in this vault because they wanted the little boy, because he isn't an illusion in my head, because you wouldn't put a bracelet on an illusion, would you? Because I've got one and I'm real."

The woman in the mirror did not answer.

"Look, I know you want to stay down here, but you have to know what's out there. The bad shadows are feeding on the dead and wrapping them in cocoons. That's what they do to the dead. I know, I've seen it before. I don't know where, but I fucking promise you I am not making this up. We have to find the little boy before they do the same thing to him. He's hiding somewhere out there, I heard his voice. I did, in the forest . . . Yeah, that's where. I know it was him, but the bad shadows chased me back. I need to wake up so I can find him because I'm trapped in this fucked-up dream and he's out there. He needs me."

Silence.

"I know they did something to you, I can see it in your eyes. It was in the needle, I know. They pumped you with something that stole your soul. That means they did the same thing to me. But you have to help me wake up so we can find the little boy before it's too late."

Silence.

"Please, don't you get it? If he's my child, then he's yours, too. But you're just a reflection, so I'm the only one who can find him. I need you to help me. I *need* you to show me how to wake the fuck up."

Silence.

Rage.

She pulled the Glock from her belt, pointed it at the woman in the mirror.

"You need to tell me how to wake up! Talk to me!"

The woman in the mirror had pulled her own gun and was pointing it from the other side of the looking glass.

"Please, help me."

Desperation.

Hopelessness.

"Fuck it!"

She put the gun barrel to the side of her head; so did the woman in the mirror.

"This is what you want, isn't it? You want me to pull the trigger, don't you? Because those fucking bad shadows turned you into a soulless fucking bitch who can't even remember her own son, so what's the point of living, yeah? This is what you want and you want it right now, don't you?"

A smile formed at the corners of the reflection's mouth.

Yes, do it. You're not a mother; you're nothing but a whore.

She stared at the soulless woman's eyes for long seconds, her finger squeezing the trigger.

Do it! Do it, you fucking useless whore!

"Go to hell."

She pulled the Glock from her head, stuffed it in her belt, and went back to the kitchenette shelves. She grabbed the handle of the iron skillet, yanked it free. Everything on the shelves tumbled to the concrete floor. Jars of teas, jars of kids' food, glasses, pots and pans hit the floor in muffled clangs and crashes. She turned, charged at the woman in the mirror. She saw the woman charging toward her, raising the skillet, swinging it down.

"Ahhhh!"

The mirror cracked and shards crashed into the sink and onto the floor. She hammered at the mirror till there was no more glass in the frame, no more woman staring at her with a vacant gaze. She stared at the wreckage on the floor.

"This dream wasn't big enough for the both of us, you soulless bitch."

She dropped the skillet. It rang with a muffled *gong; like a bell,* she thought. She staggered from the bathroom, crossed the concrete room, sat on the camp bed. The storybook and little boy's pajamas were next to her. She picked them up, rested them on her lap. She traced her fingers over the handwritten script on the book's cover.

piratz

Une histoire drôle de Marc Rochat

pour Mademoiselle Katherine Taylor

She flipped through the pages, following the adventures of a band of silly-looking men in paper hats, waving wooden swords, riding a flying caterpillar through the stars on their way to rescue a beautiful princess from an evil wizard's ice castle. She waited for words or pictures to connect the dots in her memory. When they didn't, she picked up the little boy's pajamas and laid them over the book. The repeating pattern of the grinning sheep seemed a happy thing; something that would make a little boy smile. She lifted the pajamas to her face and smelled them. There was the mingled scent of soap and powdered skin again. The scent sank deep into the hollowness of her womb, and there it rested.

ii

The Gulfstream G650, registration N3287, made a steep descent from thirty thousand feet before banking to starboard. It leveled off and lined up for its final approach on a heading of 071 magnetic, 090 true. When the jet's airspeed slowed to 120 knots, its landing gear lowered. As the jet overflew the threshold markers of runway 7R, its two Rolls-Royce engines throttled back to idle speed and its nose flared seven degrees. The Gulfstream touched down at 00:17 hours. Reverse thrust engaged and the jet rolled twenty-seven hundred feet before decelerating to fifty knots. It exited the runway onto taxiway E, away from the main passenger terminal. The landing lights and anti-collision strobes of the jet then switched off. For a moment the plane was invisible except for the red and green navigation lights at its wingtips.

High-intensity lamps mounted in the nose gear came on and illuminated the yellow centerline painted on the concrete. N3287 followed the line at a speed of fifteen knots for one hundred yards before turning onto taxiway H. It rolled by a series of aprons dotted with private aircraft, but there was no activity on the flight line. The jet continued another eight hundred yards to an isolated apron at the end of the taxiway. Power was increased to the right engine and the jet turned one hundred eighty degrees. The nose gear lamps panned over the façade of a blue aircraft hangar, highlighting a sign above the hangar doors.

ARCTIC X AIR SERVICES

ANCHORAGE, ALASKA

ELEVATION: 44 METERS

CURRENT TEMPERATURE: −9 F/−22 C

Engines shut down, all lights switched off.

N3287 sat shadowlike until the hangar doors opened and the building's interior lamps washed over the apron. Agent Kerr of Homeland Security exited the hangar and walked toward the jet. It was parked as far as possible from the hangar, and a bitter wind was blowing off Cook Inlet. He pulled the hood of his parka over his head.

"Don't worry about me. You go ahead and park on the other side of the damn runway if you like."

As he neared the jet, the forward passenger door opened and a set of stairs lowered to the ground. Agent Kerr waited for someone to appear in the open hatch. No one did.

"Fucking shit."

He mounted the stairs and stood on the platform outside the jet. There was a small galley inside; the doors to the flight deck and passenger compartments were closed. A quick look at the fittings, not to mention the automatic door and stairs, said the owner of this aircraft was loaded well beyond its $65 million price tag. The fucking interior was painted in twenty-two-carat gold leaf. Then again, Arctic X Air Services was the hub for Texas oil barons, Russian oligarchs, and Asian taipans who wished to remain unnoticed on the hop across the north Pacific. He knew better than to just walk onto a VIP flight and open a door. Walk in on some oil baron fracking his secretary and it could cost him his job; so he stood outside the hatch and let the cold seep into his boots.

"Anytime, folks."

"VIP" didn't begin to describe the way these people were coddled. No need to deal with the trials and tribulations of the little people, not them. No pat-downs or removing of shoes to board a flight. Lots of "Yes, sir" and "I'll get right on that, sir." And their flight plans were like state secrets to protect them from terrorists or kidnappings—or so it was said by the politicians in DC who made the rules the rich paid them to make. Which was why Agent Kerr had been hauled out of bed in the middle of the night to clear two unscheduled VIP flights. Still, standing in the cold wind waiting to be allowed to do his job was beyond the call of coddling.

He kicked any offending dirt from his boots and boarded the aircraft.

He felt a sudden blast of heat in the galley. Whoever owned this jet liked it kept warm. He pulled back the hood of his parka and unzipped the coat to reveal the uniform and badge underneath. He faced the cockpit door, stood where the pilots could see him through the spyhole. He banged on the door with his gloved hand.

"Homeland Security. Anyone flying this thing?"

The door unlocked from the inside; Agent Kerr pulled it open. He leaned into the flight deck. The pilot and copilot removed their headsets and turned to him. Their shirts and ties were black, like the jet. They regarded the uniformed man with indifference. Agent Kerr was used to it; servants to the rich often put on airs.

"How long were you two planning to let me freeze my ass off out there?"

"We assumed you would come to us when you were ready," the pilot said.

"Well, I've been ready and you're late. I expected you three hours ago."

"Our sincere apologies," the copilot said. "We were delayed at our last stop."

Agent Kerr removed his gloves, stuffed them in his parka.

"Identification and flight documentation, please."

"Certainly."

The copilot extended his empty hands as if handing something over. Agent Kerr saw the TSA IDs of two American nationals, papers listing the aircraft's registration and flight plans, passenger and cargo manifests. He took them, read through them. He could feel the texture of the paper on his fingertips.

"From JFK New York via PDX Oregon. PDX is where you were delayed?"

"Yes."

"What was the nature of the delay?"

"A faulty warning light in the fuel system. It needed to be replaced before takeoff."

Agent Kerr looked again at the imaginary papers in his hands.

"Says here you have five passengers, all Russian nationals. Connecting with a turnaround charter from VVO Vladivostok."

"Yes."

"You two are staying in the States?"

"We have accommodations at the Hilton and will return to New York tomorrow evening."

The copilot looked at his watch. "Pardon me, sir, is there any word on the turnaround charter's arrival? Our employer is anxious for information regarding its progress."

Agent Kerr looked at the copilot's watch, too. A man would have to be blind to miss it. A matte black Zenith with SuperLuminova-enhanced hands. Sapphire crystal back, four hundred thirty-nine parts. The world's twenty-four time zones marked in the bezel for those who had to know the hour anywhere, anytime.

"Last I heard it was inbound. I'll be notified when it's on final approach. Says here your onboard cargo is listed as artwork, a wood carving valued at sixty million dollars en route to VVO with your passengers?"

"Yes."

"May I have the export documents, please?"

The copilot made the same motion with his empty hands. "Certainly."

Kerr received the imaginary paperwork. He saw descriptions of the artifact, export and duty fees paid, photos of the artifact in a metal shipping container.

"What is this thing? Because it looks like a casket."

"It is a *tulo*."

"A what?"

"A religious idol of the indigenous people of Siberia, from the Heremchin tribe of the Lake Baikal region, to be exact."

"What was it doing in the United States? Why is it leaving?"

"It was part of a private collection of indigenous artwork. Our employer has purchased it from the collector in New York."

"Your employer is one of the passengers?"

"Yes, our employer wished to accompany the artifact personally."

Agent Kerr studied the imaginary photographs some more.

"If he's shelling out that kind of money for it, I'm not surprised. This thing is in the cargo hold?"

"Yes."

"I'll need to give it a visual inspection before it's loaded onto the VVO flight."

Agent Kerr looked at the two pilots. Waited for them to respond, or blink even. They continued to regard him with an indifferent gaze.

"Passports of passengers departing the United States?" Kerr said.

It was the pilot who made the motion with empty hands this time.

"Certainly. They are here."

Agent Kerr received five Russian passports. He flipped through the imaginary pages, studying them as he had the photos of the artifact. He nodded to the passenger cabin door.

"Would you let the passengers know I'm here so I can confirm their identities?"

"Our employer gave us instructions he was not to be disturbed until the Vladivostok flight is ready to board for takeoff. He is resting at the moment."

Agent Kerr was not amused at the piss-off.

"I thought he was anxiously awaiting a progress report on the inbound. I can deliver the info directly and verify his identity at the same time."

The pilot coughed slightly. "I hope you understand, but we must follow orders. You know how that is, I guess."

"Yes," the copilot said, "in lots of ways we're just like you."

Flying a private jet with a gold leaf interior while wearing a $28,000 watch?

"You bet."

A radio crackled.

"Five Oscar Tango, Five Oscar Tango, this is tower."

Agent Kerr reached inside his parka, pressed the button on his radio handset.

"Five Oscar Tango. Go ahead."

"Be advised VVO is on final approach and will proceed to Arctic X upon landing."

"Roger that. Will finish with N3287, clear VVO, and advise. Five Oscar Tango out."

"Tower out."

Agent Kerr backed out of the cockpit.

"All right, here's what happens, gentlemen. My truck is in the hangar keeping warm, it's a mobile immigration and customs station. I'll run the passports and paperwork and be back for the visual IDs. Then, and only then, will the ongoing passengers and goods be escorted, by me, to the VVO flight. In the meantime no one gets on or off this aircraft. Same thing goes for the inbound. Do it my way and your boss will be on his way soon enough. Are we clear?"

Indifference again. Agent Kerr wondered if there was something other than jet fuel keeping these two in the air.

"Sit tight, boys, I'll be back."

Agent Kerr disembarked with his imaginary documents in hand. He tucked them inside his parka to protect them from blowing away. He hurried across the apron and disappeared into the hangar.

Fifteen minutes later: A second Gulfstream G650, registration RA 9991, approached on taxiway H. Nearing the hangar, it made a one-eighty turn, then shut down its lights and engines. The two black aircraft were parked side by side; their long wings fluttered in the bitter wind.

Twenty minutes more: The rear cargo doors of both jets opened simultaneously and red lights in the cargo bays bled onto the tarmac.

Ten minutes later: Agent Kerr walked from the hangar and stopped in his tracks. There were four men in black leather coats at the tail of N3287. They were off-loading the metal shipping container he'd seen in the export documents. They lifted the heavy thing to their shoulders, two men to a side; they carried it toward the VVO flight. They walked slowly, carefully.

"Well, how do you like that?" he said.

Agent Kerr pulled out his flashlight, switched it on, and marched straight for the parade.

"Hey! Put that thing on the ground, right now!"

The four men stopped. Agent Kerr circled them with his flashlight, his mind matching their faces to four of the imaginary passports. They had that same air of indifference about them, and like the pilots they weren't big on blinking, either, not even when facing into the wind.

"What in the hell do you think you're doing? I said put that thing on the ground."

Then a paregoric voice wrapped in a Russian accent: *"Memento, homo, quia pulvis es, et in pulverem reverteris."*

Agent Kerr spun around, saw a tall man with long silver hair. He wore a black sable overcoat and a black scarf around his neck. There were dark glasses over his eyes.

"Where did you . . . What did you just say?"

The tall man stared for a long moment from behind his dark glasses. Agent Kerr matched the shape of the man's face and the color of his hair to the fifth passport. Had to be the one the pilots called "our employer." Just standing there the man oozed wealth and power.

"Tell me your name," the man said.

"What?"

"Tell me your name."

"Uh, Kerr, sir. Agent Richard Kerr. I'm with Homeland Security."

"Thank you, Agent Richard Kerr. I will remember you."

Agent Kerr knew a rich man's threat when he heard it. They had to be batted away with mink gloves.

"Sir, I told the pilots no one was to get off the aircraft until I got back."

"I was concerned with the time you were taking in processing our departure. I asked my associates to transfer the artifact to hurry things along. The fault, therefore, is mine."

Agent Kerr glanced at the four men standing with the container on their shoulders. They had not budged; they were still staring into the bitter wind.

"I'm sorry about that, sir, but processing a sixty-million-dollar antique for export requires a little extra paperwork. Now that it's done, I'll be happy to escort you and your associates to the Vladivostok flight, check the pilots' passports and flight registration, and you're free to leave."

"I would be most grateful," the tall man said, turning away.

"As soon as I make a visual inspection of the container's contents, sir."

The tall man turned back and smiled. "Do you simply wish to cause me the loss of more time, Agent Kerr, or do you suspect me of criminal activity?"

Kerr suspected every rich man coming through Arctic X Air Services of criminality, though proving it was like trying to pin a tail on a runaway donkey. *Just once would I like to nail one of them.*

"Not at all, sir. It's procedure, that's all it is. And it's for your own protection, too, to assure your indigenous religious idol is intact before it leaves the United States. I'd hate to think of the insurance nightmare you'd have if you got all the way to Russia only to find it was in pieces. Sir."

"Of course. You have your duty."

He signaled his associates to lower the container onto the tarmac, and it was done. One of the men leaned down to unlock the latches and lift the lid. There was the hiss of releasing air pressure. Agent Kerr leaned over with his flashlight. He saw a glass lid, and under the lid was a meter-long wooden pole carved with depictions of stars and moons, bears and eagles. It was topped with an oval-shaped head bearing an Asian-looking face; it matched the description and photos in the export documents. Agent Kerr laughed quietly to himself. *Sixty million bucks for that piece of junk?*

"Are you satisfied with your inspection of the artifact?" the tall man said.

Agent Kerr did not see what was truly under the glass. He did not see the circuits and wires, the breathing tubes and air tanks, the blinking monitors labeled HEART RATE, BLOOD PRESSURE, BODY CORE TEMPERATURE. He did not see the little boy with black hair strapped to a small hospital bed or the oxygen mask over the boy's face, his eyes closed as if he were sleeping. He did not see the small blue rubber hammer in the boy's right hand.

"It's all good. They can load it now."

The command was given. The container was sealed and carried to the jet bound for Vladivostok. For a moment, Agent Kerr was mesmerized by the sight of them, like they were carrying a coffin to a funeral. He snapped out if it.

"Oh, one last thing, sir," he said, sorting through the imaginary passports. He found the one with the photo of a man with silver hair.

"I have a visual on your associates, but would you remove your sunglasses for identification Mr. . . . Excuse me, how do you pronounce your name, sir?"

The tall man took off his dark glasses and revealed his silver-colored eyes.

"Komarovsky. My name is Komarovsky."

Book II

THE ARK

SIX

i

Coming down the hill Harper saw Lac Léman through the taxi's windshield. A passenger ferry was pulling away from the Ouchy docks for Évian. The French town seemed no more than arm's length across the lake, but it was an optical illusion. In the real world it was a thirty-five-mile trip. Turning right onto Avenue de Rhodanie and cruising along the shore, another illusion played in Harper's eyes: Évian sank under a watery horizon as if swallowed by a great flood.

"I know the feeling," Harper mumbled.

At the roundabout the taxi got off the main road to avoid morning traffic coming into Lausanne. Amusingly, the detour took Harper by the International Olympic Committee HQ on Route de Vidy. He saw the windows of his old office above the entrance to the parking garage. He hadn't been there in two years, but no one seemed to notice. His salary as a security consultant found its way into his mailbox on the twenty-fifth of each month like clockwork. After the cathedral job Harper thought someone should tell the IOC there was no reason to keep sending him a check. He ran the idea by Inspector Gobet; the cop was appalled.

"The laws of Switzerland require all foreign residents holding a Permis B to show proof of meaningful employment."

"You could pull a few strings, surely," Harper had said.

"Mr. Harper, the Swiss are most adamant regarding their immigration laws."

The copper's sentiment was backed up by the cabbie Harper hailed at Place Saint-François earlier, the one driving him by the IOC just now. Last week a referendum was passed in Switzerland calling on the government to renegotiate the Schengen Agreement with Brussels. The object was to stop an alleged invasion by foreigners, especially those from Eastern Europe and Africa. The driver couldn't stop banging on about it.

"*Oui*, we are in Europe, but it does not mean we wish to be 'European,' monsieur. We are Swiss. We do not want foreigners coming to Switzerland to steal our jobs."

Harper considered asking the cabbie's opinion on creatures born of light who came to Switzerland from an unknown somewhere and hid in the forms of dead men while collecting a monthly check for doing fuck-all. That was when the cabbie went off on "those filthy Romanians." Harper kicked the back of the man's seat. The cabbie glanced into the rearview mirror, saw the palm of Harper's right hand reflecting into his eyes.

"Zip it," Harper said.

Harper dropped his hand and the driver went back to driving without a memory of the previous conversation.

"Nice weather this morning, isn't it, monsieur?"

"That it is."

He looked out the window, watched the evenly spaced and perfectly shaped chestnut trees at the side of the road. As the taxi gathered speed the trees began to bend in the corners of Harper's eyes . . . *Whoosh, whoosh, whoosh.* The sound carried him back to the wee hours of the morning. In his flat, polishing off a bottle of Swiss red, watching *Units of Time, Measures of Wonder, and the Scientific Method* on the History Channel. It was a program on Max Karl Ernst Ludwig Planck. Born in Germany in 1858, he mastered the piano while learning to walk. He wrote complex pieces of music and several operas before finishing eighth grade. His parents hoped their wunderkind would be the next Mozart. Alas, young Planck was led astray by the muse of theoretical physics. In university he composed elaborate mathematical equations articulating his perception of the universe. At the turn of the century he wrote a paper on dimensional analysis in mathematical physics. The paper was Planck's magnum opus and became the hymn of quantum theory. When he was awarded the Nobel Prize for Physics in 1918, every physicist on the planet already knew the score for Planck time.

It looks like this:

$$t_p \equiv \sqrt{\frac{\hbar G}{c^5}}$$

It works like this:

$$\approx 5.39106(32) \times 10^{-44}\ \mathrm{s}$$

Planck time equals the time it takes for one quantum of electromagnetic energy, traveling through a vacuum at the speed of light, to cross one "Planck unit" of distance. Theoretically, at 10^{-44} of a second, a Planck unit is the smallest measure of time possible. Empirically, it is impossible for a human being to perceive any measure of change from one Planck unit to the next. But as Harper was a creature of light hiding in the body of a dead man, his ability to perceive the measure of change was keener. Enough to flash Katherine Taylor's face, one Planck unit's worth, the moment Inspector Gobet pronounced her name on the crossing square of Lausanne Cathedral last night. Just as fast, Harper's eternal being crashed through the microchip embedded in his brain and unscrambled redacted sequences on his timeline. He lifted one thousand frames before—*wham*—lockout. The surviving frames uploaded in Harper's eyes and presto, he had 41.6 seconds of his timeline back.

Hash.

The cathedral job; two and a half years ago.

Katherine Taylor on the crossing square of Lausanne Cathedral, telling Harper about her dream. A strange man wearing ragged clothes carries her into the streams of color flooding through the stained glass of the cathedral rose.

"To purify the light before it touches the life within you," the bum tells her.

Her eyes afire with emerald-colored light.

Hash.

The images faded. But somehow, Harper knew he'd recognize her if he saw her again. A strange sensation it was. He wondered if that's what a human memory felt like. He reconnected with real time . . . *Whoosh, whoosh, whoosh* went the trees by open farmland now. He dropped back into last night's timeline; staring at Inspector Gobet on the altar square, knowing the cop in the cashmere coat had broken every rule in the book to give him a glimpse of Katherine Taylor. Question was: *Why?*

"Interesting," Harper said to the cop.

"Considering the trouble involved, Mr. Harper, I was hoping for something more insightful."

Harper took another hit of radiance; his eyes tracked the lines of causality crisscrossing in his eyes till they slammed to a stop at the intersection of Luke Chapter 1 and Verse 28.

"And the angel came in unto her, and said, 'Hail, thou that art highly favored, the Lord is with thee: blessed art thou among women,'" he said.

The inspector nodded. "Full marks, Mr. Harper."

Click.

Harper blinked himself back to nowtimes again. The taxi meter had ticked up to 18.90 CHF. It was carrying him through an underpass now, and there was a face staring back at him from beyond the darkened windshield.

"Hello there, boyo."

Captain Jay Michael Harper, formerly of Her Majesty's Special Reconnaissance Regiment. Born in London, 1972; died thirty-seven years later in the tribal regions of Afghanistan. His body was still alive and kicking courtesy of the medics in Vevey. The face had a broad forehead and a prominent jaw, light brown hair, dark eyebrows, and darker lashes over piercing, emerald-colored eyes.

"Not bad for a corpse."

He heard the dead soldier's voice in his head.

Cheers, and remind me, why the hell are we in this taxi?

Harper thought it only polite to explain.

After letting Harper see Katherine Taylor for 41.6 seconds, Inspector Gobet ordered him to stand down and return to his flat in the old city. The inspector and Krinkle would maintain their candlelight vigil on the crossing square until dawn.

"I am advised that you need to tend to your wounds," Inspector Gobet told Harper. "And by the way, *bon appétit*."

Harper had smoked his fag down to the filter by then. It didn't make the cop's valediction any clearer. Not till Harper came through the door of his flat and found a club sandwich, a side of chips, and a bottle of Swiss pinot noir laid out on the kitchen table. A takeaway job from LP's Bar at the Palace judging from the logos on the plate and serviette. It looked swell; it also looked like a last meal being offered to a condemned man.

"Veni, vidi, edi."

He took off his mackintosh and sports coat. He unharnessed his kill kit and laid it next to the pinot noir. As he tucked in, an envelope was slid under his door—*swish*.

Harper took a sip of wine and stared at the envelope. He set his glass on the table, walked over, and picked it up. The envelope bore the seal of the Lausanne Palace Hotel and was addressed to *Notre Cher Client*. He carried it back to the table, sat down, and opened it. Inside was a handwritten letter from the hotel's concierge. The cursive script was perfect.

Harper emptied his glass, refilled it, and read the letter.

Le concierge hoped *notre cher client* was enjoying the food and drink and asked him to *please remove all personal belongings from your clothing* and to place all clothes, with shoes, into the laundry bag provided in the lavatory *and to deposit said bag into the hallway, posthaste*. He would find a robe and slippers in the lavatory for his convenience and *your clothes will be cleaned and returned by dawn*. He would also find ointments for the cuts and bruises on his face, as well as potions for his hands *for your use only*.

"Thoughtful."

Harper slipped the letter into his back pocket, pulled his Glock from the kill kit, and loaded a round in the firing chamber. He took a sip of wine, popped a chip into his mouth, and headed to the loo. He kicked open the door. Clear, and all items listed in the letter were as advertised.

He noticed a pale blue box, wrapped in silver ribbon, sitting on the edge of the bathtub. The wax seal on the ribbon said the box was from the hotel gift shop.

"Interesting."

He made the Glock safe, rested it on the toilet seat. He pulled the letter and continued to read. *Le concierge* described how the ointments would heal most cuts and bruises overnight. *The seeping wounds on the palms of your hands* were a different matter. *Accordingly, please find in the box provided* one pair of fingerless gloves to be worn 24/7. Harper opened the box. The gloves were beige in color, cut from fine Italian leather. The letter instructed him to apply the potions to his hands after showering, and before the potions dried *insert hands into gloves, one each*. When he did, he got a closer look at the gloves. They weren't cut from fine Italian leather; they were sheets of artificial skin grown into polymer sheaths perfectly formed to the shape of his hands. He touched the gloves with his fingertips. Lightly padded at the palms, hardened over each knuckle, like some high-tech special ops kit.

"You must be bloody joking."

Click.

Blink.

Harper focused on the fare meter on the dashboard: 57.60 CHF. He had lost thirty-five Swiss francs' worth of real time explaining things to the dead soldier in his head, who had vanished from the windshield to be replaced by a long concourse lined with identical modernist boxes for buildings.

"Where am I?" Harper said.

"EPFL," the cabbie said.

Harper thought about it. *EPFL: École Polytechnique Fédérale de Lausanne.* "Right."

He handed over sixty Swiss francs and told the cabbie to keep the change.

"Oh, merci. Très gentil, monsieur."

Harper alighted from the taxi, closed the door, and headed for the big map posted on the bigger sign at the top of the concourse.

"Excusez-moi?" the cabbie called.

Harper turned, saw the man lowering his side window.

"Where did you say you were from, monsieur?"

"Romania," Harper said.

The cabbie smiled. *"Oui, je me souviens.* Welcome to Switzerland, monsieur. Nice to have you in our country."

The cabbie raised his window and drove off. Harper looked at the palms of his gloved hands.

"Wow, me."

He looked at the big map. EPFL was a big place. Here was the Center of MicroNanoTechnology, there was the Institute of Condensed Matter Physics, and over there was the Rolex Learning Center. Down here was the Large Hadron Collider research center, down there was the Mathematics Institute of Computational Science and Engineering.

Harper reached into the inner pocket of his mackintosh and found the letter from the concierge. After the instructions on getting his clothes cleaned and wounds sorted there was a final paragraph.

Please report to the lobby of Building J of EPFL's Quartier de l'Innovation by 10:45 hours. Re: briefing. Door code: #6969821003.

The concierge did not state the subject on which Harper was to be briefed, but he signed off with *Bonne journée*. Harper returned the letter to his pocket and found Building J on the big map.

"Got it."

He walked along the concourse, where the buildings had glassed-in lobbies with secured entrances. There were students rushing across the concourse, loaded down with books and laptops. Harper thought about revealing himself to one of them just to double-check his directions, but all the faces read: *Not now, I'm terribly busy.*

There were a small kiosk to the left and a few students sitting at nearby tables. They drank coffee and ate pastries while reading books or tablet computers. A gang of pigeons waddled at foot level, pecking at the fallen remnants of croissants. Harper stopped at the kiosk, waited for the South Asian man behind the counter to see him.

"Oh, hello. Have you been standing there long, monsieur?"

English. *Odd,* Harper thought. He wondered if he had walked into a trap. He looked back at the crowd on the concourse. Students of all colors from all around the world. Maybe not; maybe English was the lingua franca of EPFL.

"I'm looking for the Quartier de l'Innovation," Harper said.

The man pointed to the left.

"Go that way and make a right at the Association Euratom, then make a left at the Cyberbotics Center."

"Cyberbotics? What goes on there?"

"I don't know what goes on there, monsieur. I sell coffee here."

"Of course you do. Have a nice day."

Harper waved the palm of his right hand before the man's eyes to delete any memory of their encounter from his consciousness. He walked on, passing two students at a table. A lad and a lass flipping busily through tablets. The lad was wearing headphones, listening to music with a heavy *thump, thump, thump*. The lass had short hair and a spiderweb tattoo at the back of her neck.

Harper moved closer.

The lad was searching through pictures labeled "X-ray free-electron laser images of single-layer bacteriorhodopsin proteins." The lass was reading an article titled "A New Model for Isolating the Effects of Nutrients on Gene Expression and Physiology." *Smart,* Harper thought; they probably used Planck's equations as e-mail passwords. He moved away before the students sensed his presence; he continued down the concourse. Four minutes later he was standing at a map for the Quartier de l'Innovation listing buildings A through K. He located Building J. He saw the list of the building's occupants. It was a list of one.

BLUE BRAIN PROJECT

Harper's timeline ripped back, locked, and replayed the greatest hits from the Paris job in three quick flashes:

Hash.

Trapped in the tunnels deep beneath the streets of Paris. He thought he'd been down there three hours, but he'd been down there three days talking to a rotting corpse. He cuts open the palms of his own hands to shed his blood and rub it into the dead man's eyes. Rescuers reach Harper, pull him from the corpse. Harper has no idea what he's doing. "From the looks of it, I'd say you were trying your hand at raising the dead," a rescuer tells him. With his clothes and flesh reeking of death, he's dragged to the roof of a town house in the 6th arrondissement. It's a starry night. Inspector Gobet and his computer geeks are kitted out with Crypto Field Terminals and AEHF satellite stations. Everyone's waiting for the big show. Before Harper can ask what it is, a blazing comet appears in the constellation Draco and hovers above the City of Light at a magnitude of –7.5. No one in paradise knew it would happen; no one but Christophe Astruc, OP, and a young man named Goose. Astruc is one of Harper's kind, but he went off the rails with his homemade potions and ended up barking mad. He believes Goose is the fulfillment of a prophecy: that a child born of light had been born to guide the creation through the next stage of evolution. He believes it because he can't handle the truth: Goose, a sickly creature suffering from paedomorphosis, is his own begotten son.

Fast forward. Lock. Roll.

Astruc and Goose were on a mission. Stage one: Snatch a five-thousand-year-old sextant from the tunnels beneath Paris and leave Harper for dead. Stage two: Escape to the ruins of the Cathar fortress at Montségur. Astruc tracks the comet with the sextant; Goose switches on a laptop he'd built from spare parts, hooks it up to a satlink, and hacks into a supercomputer named Blue Brain four hundred fifty-seven miles away in Lausanne. Goose begins a series of impossibly accurate triangulations between the comet's trajectory, the ruins of Montségur, and a billion different stars. He's building a 3-D model of the Earth's exact position in the universe. He loads the coordinates into Blue Brain and lets the supercomputer run with it. At the same time Harper watches a mirror image of the hack with Inspector Gobet's computer geeks. Best guess: The kid is building a cosmic clock that would—

Hash.

Harper blinked himself to nowtimes.

"That would what?"

He checked his watch. Ten forty-five on the nose.

ii

Harper punched in the door code for Building J.

The glass door slid open and he walked into a sun-drenched atrium. There was a palm tree in the middle of the place reaching five floors up to a roof of steel-framed glass. He circled the tree, saw glassed-in offices on the higher floors. People hustled about up there, but down here nobody was waiting for him.

In the north corner of the lobby was an entrance to something called Puur Innovation Café. He walked over and looked through the glass doors. It was a decent joint with a rather nice wine bar. This being Switzerland, the bar was already open for business. The dead soldier in Harper's head suggested they go in for a glass.

"Later."

He strolled around the lobby and saw a small sign at the base of the palm tree: VEITCHIA MERRILLII OR ADONIDIA OR CHRISTMAS PALM. On the other side of the tree he saw another sign: VISITORS PLEASE REPORT TO ADMINISTRATIVE OFFICE, FLOOR THREE.

He walked to the lift, pressed the call button, and the doors slid open. He stepped in and saw floors one through five; no floors below ground level. He pressed the button for the third floor. The doors closed and up he went. Two signs were posted in the lift. One with a picture of happy people, drinks in hands, pissed to the gills. Accompanying words read, HAPPY HOUR AT PUUR INNOVATION CAFÉ, 5–7 P.M. The sign next to it was an evacuation map for Building J, with the words IN CASE OF CHEMICAL, BIOLOGICAL, OR RADIOACTIVE FIRE, DIAL 115 AND USE ONLY AUTHORIZED EVACUATION PROCEDURES. The emergency number to dial was printed within an exploding ball of fire. Harper's eyes went back and forth between the two signs till the lift went *ding* and the doors opened.

"My kind of place."

He stepped out. Still no one to meet him. He looked down over the railing to check the atrium. Still no one down there, either. He followed the walkway toward the office entrance. There was a doorbell, and he'd almost pressed it when he heard a door creak open behind him.

"*Pssst*, over here, if you please."

He saw a round face under a head of thinning gray hair. The face wore bottle-thick eyeglasses and was peeking from behind the stairwell door.

"You talking to me?" Harper said.

"Yes, this way, sir. Quickly, please."

The man turned away, and the door closed. Harper slipped his hand inside his mackintosh, grabbing hold of his killing knife.

"Sure."

He walked over and pushed through the door. He saw a small man in a white lab coat scurrying down a set of metal stairs; two returns per floor, and the man was already two floors down, chatting as fast as he scurried.

"Terribly sorry I was late, sir. I was monitoring a reboot of one of Blue Brain's vector machines. A tricky thing when dealing with four thousand quad-cores of supercomputer. But it went very well, very well indeed. I say, I'm so glad I found you before you pressed the doorbell."

The small man unlocked a door that was marked JANITOR'S CLOSET: NO UNAUTHORIZED ACCESS. He walked in.

"I thought I was expected," Harper said, following him.

"Oh, yes, sir. By me. One moment, please."

The small man waited for Harper to get into the closet to close the door. With the brooms, buckets, and mops, it was a tight fit. The man pushed aside the mops and repeatedly rapped his knuckles on the wall opposite the door.

Beep, thunk.

The wall slid open. There was another stairwell going down.

"This way, sir."

"You first."

The small man passed through and waited for Harper to exit before pressing a button to close the wall.

Beep, thunk.

"This way, please."

Heading down, Harper considered how nothing in paradise surprised him anymore, not even a set of stairs hidden in a janitor's closet. But the dead soldier in his head had other ideas. *Oy, what's this shit?* Harper tuned him out till reaching the seventh set of stairs; then he heard the dead soldier scream, *No, not again!* Harper pulled his killing knife, jumped ahead of the small man, and forced him to the wall.

"Ten seconds. Who are you?"

"Sir, I don't understand."

"Me neither. Seven seconds."

"Wait, sir."

"Six seconds. I knew a lad with a lantern once. I can't see his face or say his name, but I do recall he taught me the importance of counting steps."

"Please, sir, wait—"

"Three seconds. We're already seven floors under a building with no basement and still heading south. I don't like being underground. It gives me the creeps. Two seconds. Who are you?"

"But you know me."

"One second. Wrong."

Harper set the blade to the small man's throat.

"Wait! After the incident at Lausanne Cathedral, we had dinner together at Café du Grütli in Lausanne. I'm the light mechanic from Bern. I installed the Arc 9 filters in the streetlamps around the cathedral."

Harper raced through his timeline; found him. Same round face, same eyeglasses, full of breathless excitement explaining how the Arc 9 filters improved the ability of Harper's kind to detect increased levels of black body radiation. The better to see bad guys in the dark, the small man tells him.

Harper blinked himself to nowtimes. "You're the guy who keeps pictures of cats in his wallet."

"Yes, yes. Pictures of cats. My cats. That's me."

Harper pulled away the knife. "Right. Sorry."

The man gasped and coughed. "Oh, my word."

"You'll be okay. Just breathe," Harper said.

"No, no, I'm fine. I assumed you would recognize me."

"I should have, sorry. Just keep breathing. And you might want to loosen your tie."

"Yes, yes. Thank you."

Harper took a slow breath himself. "Look, I thought I was here for a briefing on Blue Brain."

"You are. With me."

"You're a light mechanic."

"I was promoted. I'm now head of AI."

"Artificial Intelligence?"

"Yes."

Harper returned his killing knife to its sheath. "Congratulations."

"Thank you, sir. Shall we continue? It's only one more floor, and we are on a schedule."

"Sure."

The man led Harper down the stairs to a narrow corridor hemmed in by a wall of gray cinder block. At the end of the corridor was a steel door; no locks, no doorknob. The man rapped his knuckles on the second cinder block right of the door, five up from the concrete floor. *Taptap, taptap, taptap; tap, taptap, taptap, tap* . . . the exact pattern of raps he'd used in the janitor's closet. This time the dead soldier in Harper's head identified it as Morse code: O-P-E-N S-E-S—

No bloody way.

—A-M-E.

Beep, thunk.

"This way if you please, sir."

Maybe there were still a few surprises left in paradise after all, Harper thought.

"Cheers."

It was a large square room with a low ceiling. Harper had to walk between the hanging lamps to avoid hitting his head, but it was a comfy arrangement for the small man in the white lab coat. The walls were made of the same cinder block as the corridor, but painted white. Like the concrete ceiling and floor; like the desk and chair in the middle of the room. On the table was a white box-shaped computer terminal. Next to it were a white keyboard and mouse, both attached to the computer by white cables. The computer's nine-inch screen was greenish-blue, and there was a word scrolling across it, then dissolving and scrolling again.

hello

"What the hell is that?" Harper said.

"That? Why, that's Blue Brain."

"That's four thousand quad-cores of supercomputer?"

"Oh, no. I'm afraid I didn't get the opportunity to explain on the way down. This is an Apple computer, circa 1984. When it was originally manufactured it held only 128K of memory with a CPU of eight megahertz. Compared to a present-day cell phone, this computer is from the Stone Age."

The small man pressed a button on an interior cinder block to close the steel door.

Beep, thunk.

Harper looked around the room, tried not to think about being underground.

"So where's Blue Brain?"

"We're not allowed to go near Blue Brain or interfere with its operations in any way. We're only observing certain operations within its processors."

"Certain operations."

"Yes."

Harper thought about the people he'd seen upstairs. "The locals working upstairs don't know you're down here, do they?"

"I'm sure they would find it most distressing."

Harper looked at the thing from the digital Stone Age.

"And you're observing their supercomputer with 128K of memory?"

"Not quite. You see, this particular Apple machine was modified by George Muret."

The name popped hot.

"Astruc's son, Goose. That's his real name, yeah?"

"Indeed, sir."

"He made this?"

"Yes, sir."

"So this is no ordinary piece of Stone Age junk."

"No, sir. Inside, it's a technological marvel. It surpasses anything our own technicians could fit in such a limited space."

Harper imagined the misshapen kid, his small head at the end of a long neck leaning over a workbench as he wired bits together. Then he flashed meeting Astruc in Paris as Goose hid in the shadows.

"Don't underestimate him," Astruc tells him. "His IQ is above two hundred, along with having a photographic memory."

Harper blinked, saw George Muret's technological marvel staring at him.

hello

As the word dissolved, Harper felt a wave of vertigo. He rubbed the back of his neck.

"Are you unwell, Mr. Harper?"

"No, I'm . . . Remind me, what's the purpose of Blue Brain?"

"To map a single synapse of the human brain, sir. Like mapping the human genome, only a billion times more complicated."

"And it is one of Inspector Gobet's toys, yeah?"

"In a manner of speaking, as is all of EPFL. Inspector Gobet provides operational funding through third parties. But we don't interfere with any of the operations, including Blue Brain. We are only observing the workings of the machine's processors in response to triangulations introduced by Goose on the night of the comet."

Harper stepped closer to the computer. "To find Earth's exact position in the universe."

"Yes."

Harper leaned down, faced the screen.

hello

"So did Blue Brain figure out where we are yet?"

"Actually, it's more of a matter of understanding where we are going."

Harper stood and looked at the small man. "Sorry?"

The man removed his glasses. He blew on the lenses, then wiped them on the sleeve of his lab coat.

"Earth orbits the sun at sixty-seven thousand miles per hour. Our solar system orbits the center of the Milky Way galaxy at nearly five hundred thousand miles per hour. At the same time, our galaxy and our neighboring galaxies are racing through the universe at more than three hundred fifty miles per second. All this while the total mass of the universe is expanding away from us at forty-six miles per hour per megaparsec."

"Per megaparsec."

"Three million light-years in distance, sir, a little less than eighteen trillion miles. At two megaparsecs the universe expands from us at four hundred sixty miles per second. Given that the diameter of the observable universe is seven-point-two megaparsecs, the edge of the universe is expanding away from us at a speed of—"

"Pretty damn quick," Harper said.

"Yes, sir."

"So there's a chance of what? We might be left behind?" Harper said with a smile.

The small man in the white coat did not respond to the joke.

Something buzzed under the desk. Harper stepped back, bent down, and saw a rack packed with flash drives. Green lights blinked happily.

"What's that?"

"That is how we receive data from Blue Brain, sir. The data is downloaded onto the disc drives and brought here for processing."

"You're not physically connected to Blue Brain?"

"No, sir. That would be a violation of our operational protocols."

Harper walked around the table. Two white coaxial cables were attached to the back of the Apple. One was coming from under the desk and labeled INPUT. The second cable, labeled OUTPUT, split into five, then ten, then fifteen, then fifty. The cables ran to connectors mounted in the opposite wall. He took seven steps and touched the wall; it vibrated. He leaned closer and heard an oscillating hum from the other side; two hundred forty hertz from the sound of it.

"What's the kid's computer connected to?"

"A DBXL-3 Data Compressor and an ATU-1 Extraordinary Optical Transmission Unit."

"I have no idea what those things are."

"Neither does anyone else without proper security clearance, sir. Suffice it to say the data harvest from Blue Brain is being relayed in real time to the antennae array at the Madrid Deep Space Communications Complex."

Harper looked over the setup. "Inspector Gobet does like his toys, doesn't he?"

"In fact, the antennae array belongs to the National Aeronautics and Space Administration of the United States."

"The Americans?"

"Yes, sir. Inspector Gobet has made arrangements to borrow it."

"Borrow it?"

"Yes, sir."

"In the same way he's borrowing Blue Brain?"

The small man remained quiet. Harper studied the man's eyes.

"What's your security clearance?"

"Level eight."

Harper was impressed. "That's rather high. Tell me something . . ."

Vertigo nailed him again, then a crushing weight pressed down on his eternal being. He stumbled.

"Oh, bollocks."

"Sir?"

Harper steadied himself, tried to laugh it off. "Must be all that racing through the universe at all those megaparsecs per second whilst standing still."

The small man pulled the chair from the desk; he opened a drawer and removed an ashtray.

"Sir, would you care to sit down and have a puff of radiance? I was advised you have not been feeling yourself of late."

"Bad news travels fast at level eight, does it?"

"We are doing everything we can, sir. To turn things around, I mean."

Harper looked at the man's eyes. They registered compassion; they also registered that the man knew the odds of turning things around were slipping fast.

"Cheers. I appreciate it."

Harper rummaged through his coat for his smokes and matches. He lit up, sat down. He looked around the room again and waited for the pressure to ease.

"None of this makes sense. Well, some of it does, some of it doesn't."

"How can I assist you, sir?"

"This room, the cables and toys behind the wall. I get how Inspector Gobet's boys could drop a time warp over this place and build all this with the locals being none the wiser. But what about that?" Harper said, nodding to the computer on the desk. "How did we get our hands on it?"

"It was found in a hidden workshop at Astruc's base of operations on Rue Visconti. In Paris, sir."

"The house in the sixth, from where I saw the comet."

"Yes, sir."

Harper looked at the computer.

"That doesn't make sense, either. Astruc and Goose were barking mad killers, but they weren't sloppy."

"Sir?"

"They wouldn't leave something like this lying about. The enemy was after them, we were after them."

"In fact, sir, it was left on the workbench in plain sight."

"You said it was in a hidden workshop."

"Hidden in the sense that George Muret was hiding this particular computer from Father Astruc. With the computer, also, was a spiral notebook containing technical schematics and protocols necessary to receive data from Blue Brain plus all security codes required to transmit the data to the Madrid Deep Space Communications Complex."

Harper took a deep hit of radiance. He exhaled slowly.

"Are you telling me Goose was working with us, behind Astruc's back?"

The small man did not answer.

"The kid left me in a hole with a rotting corpse for three days," Harper said.

The man cleared his throat. "Regarding George Muret, I regret I am not authorized to comment further. From this point I am restricted to the purpose of his computer."

As if hearing itself mentioned, the kid's computer screen activated.

hello

"Why do I get the feeling it's talking to me?" Harper said.

"To you, no."

"Sorry?"

The small man opened the desk drawer again, this time removing a black-and-white photograph and setting it on the table. Harper looked at it. A laboratory; men in white coats gathered around what looked like a small satellite dish with mechanical arms. There was a time stamp in the lower right corner of the photograph: APRIL 17, 1977. Harper scanned the men in the photo. One of them had a round face and wore thick glasses; he was holding a gold disc in his hands.

"This is you," Harper said.

"I was much younger then. Still in university, in fact, when selected to work on this project."

"Selected. By Inspector Gobet."

"It was when I chose to enter service to your kind, yes."

Harper held up the photograph. "So what is this thing with the arms?"

"The space probe Voyager 1 as it was completed in the Jet Propulsion Laboratory."

Harper added it up. "The kid's homemade computer is allowing Blue Brain to talk to a space probe?"

The man fell quiet again. Harper smoked, waited. The man wasn't holding back this time. He was overcome with fervor in the presence of Harper's kind. It happened sometimes, especially to the compassionate ones. It was called the "Angelic Effect" in the book of rules and regs. There were nine pages of strict must-do's to deal with it. *Sod it.*

"What's your name, mate?"

"Peabody, sir."

"Doctor? Professor?"

"Professor."

"Right. Professor Peabody, for starters, you don't have to call me 'sir.'"

"I could not presume to not—"

"Fine, call me 'sir' if you have to, but I need you to help me out."

"Help?"

"Until the cathedral job I'd been in stasis since Easter Monday, 1917. Now, since I was reset in a new form, I've seen all sorts of things on my History Channel feed, from the physics of bell hum to Planck time. I've even seen human beings walking on the moon. But for some reason, a space probe named Voyager 1 never made the screen."

The small man named Peabody was coming around but confused. "Sir?"

Harper held up the photograph. "I have no idea what this thing is."

The small man realized what had happened and blushed.

"Oh, yes. Please, excuse me. Voyager 1 was launched from Cape Canaveral, Florida, on September 5, 1977, at precisely 12:56 Universal Time. It weighed seven hundred twenty-two kilograms and was powered by three radioisotope thermoelectric generators, or RTGs. Each RTG contained twenty-four plutonian-238 oxide spheres that generated slightly more than four hundred watts of power. Voyager 1's mission was to gather rudimentary data as it passed through the Jovian and Saturnian systems. This mission was completed three years later, in 1980, but Voyager 1 continued to travel outward. To date it has traveled a distance of more than eleven billion miles. And as you and I sit in this room, the space probe is crossing the heliosphere."

"And that would mean?"

"Voyager 1 broke free of our solar system a few years ago and is now sailing into interstellar space."

Harper focused on the younger Professor Peabody in the photograph, saw him holding the gold disc as if it were something precious.

"Let me guess: It's carrying a message that you and Inspector Gobet planted onboard, yeah?"

"Yes."

Harper looked at the Apple computer made by the hand of a misshapen half-kind.

"A message that's being updated by the data now spilling from Blue Brain."

"That is correct, sir."

Harper drew a heavy hit of radiance. "What's the message?"

Peabody leaned forward, careful not to touch Harper. "If you would allow me."

He tapped the space bar of the Apple keyboard. The screen flicked to life and a series of impossibly accurate triangulations between the comet's trajectory, the ruins of Montségur, and a billion different stars cascaded down the screen. Harper flashed the night of the comet, on the roof in Paris. Him with Inspector Gobet's computer geeks, watching a real-time mirror image of Goose's hack into Blue Brain. The kid was building a cosmic clock, the geeks said. A clock that would . . . *That would what?*

"It is, sir, an SOS from your kind in the name of life on Earth."

"To whom?"

"To whatever life-form there is waiting to receive it."

SEVEN

i

It was nearly eleven-thirty at night when Oleg Kabulov finished his tea and rose from the small wooden table. He put on his greatcoat and trooper hat. He picked one more tea cake from the tin and ate it slowly. It was delicious, coated with the perfect amount of powdered sugar. His dear Svetlana baked the tea cakes each workday, as she had for the last thirty-five years. She would arrange them in the same old tin and hand them to her husband as he left for Vladivostok train station in the late afternoon. Svetlana saw him off with the same joke each time.

"Smotri, chtob tebia transsibirskii ne pere'ehal." Try not to get run over by the Trans-Siberian.

"Horosho." Okay.

The clock on the wall chimed for eleven. He stepped outside the wooden shed that was the tapper's hut and he locked the door. He put on his work gloves and picked up the long-handled steel hammer resting against the wall.

"Come, Kukushka, let's go to work."

He rested the hammer on his shoulder and crossed three lines of track to the service path running through the switching yard. The path was covered with ice, so he shuffled as much as he walked. He followed a long train of freight cars to the break in the line. An eight-axle freight locomotive sat thirty feet up the track but wasn't backing up. Kabulov crossed carefully. Slip and bang your head on the rails, you could end up getting rolled over. It was one thing to die under the Trans-Siberian, but a freighter? Svetlana would wail for weeks in shame. He cleared the tracks.

"We have luck, Kukushka."

Crossing through a set of switches, he met the main line. From here he could see the station terminus and boarding platforms. He stopped, scratched the top of his hat as if it were his head.

"Bozhe moi."

He wondered if his clock in the tapper's hut was wrong, or perhaps he had the wrong day. The high-speed Sapsan train to Moscow wasn't at Platform One as it should be. In its place was a black P36 steam locomotive with a red snowplow and the red star of the Soviet Union mounted over the smokebox door.

"Holy Mother of God."

Not that Kabulov minded not seeing the Sapsan. He hated that train. It was a train that did not need him. Its steel wheels were monitored by young men with handheld computers instead of hammers. He would have lost his job long ago, except so many foreign tourists had read guidebooks that mentioned "the quaint man who walked the length of the Trans-Siberian Express and back, tapping the wheels to check for cracks." Foreign tourists paid a lot of money to make the seven-day trip across Siberia, and they expected a tapper to see them off, so the railway kept Kabulov on.

"Kukushka, do my eyes deceive me?"

Coming closer, Kabulov saw the locomotive was highly polished. The red star was blinding in the spotlights set around it. And though the streamlined side panels were black, they reflected the lights of the terminus like stars. The rails and pipes were red like the star; the main rods, side rods, and brake shoes were silver-colored; the steel wheels gleamed.

"Why, it looks like a museum piece."

He stepped back, saw the tender box. It was black like the locomotive and reflected as many stars. There were five cars hooked behind the tender; all of them were the same color as the locomotive. Oddly, all the windows were tinted black. He stepped back, shielded his eyes from the blinding red star, and looked at the locomotive's windows. They were darkly tinted, too.

"I've never seen anything like it."

Stepping around the front of the locomotive, he saw Platform One was empty. No passengers with baggage waiting to board, no ticket ladies, no service crews. Then he noticed the rest of the station platforms were empty, too. No people, no other trains.

"What is this? Where is everybody?"

He climbed the steps of the platform and walked to the doors of the station. Inside were the grand staircases and great clock and murals of Russian village life; all the lights were blazing, but there were no people at all, not even the police. He walked the length of the terminus, checking all the windows.

"Mogu vam pomoch?" May we help you?

Kabulov turned around.

Two men stood on either side of the steps to the forward passenger car. They were dressed in black leather jackets; they had earpieces in their right ears. They had the look of FSB, successors to the dreaded KGB. And as Kabulov walked toward them, he was sure that's who they were.

"What is going on? Where is the Trans-Siberian Express?" Kabulov said.

"It has been rescheduled for tomorrow for technical reasons."

Kabulov nodded to the black train. "But what's this?"

"This is a private train."

Kabulov looked back into the station, then to the men. "I don't understand. Where is everyone?"

"The station has been secured until this train departs."

That's when Kabulov remembered the empty platforms and tracks. And all the way from the tapper's hut to the terminus, no shunting of trains in the switching yard; no activity at all. He looked at the black train again, saw there were no registration markings. *Only someone of great importance could reschedule the Trans-Siberian and close down Vladivostok station,* he thought. The last Russian of such importance was Stalin. Another thought came to Kabulov: If the man on the train *was* as important as Stalin, and the two men staring at him now *were* FSB, then he should stop asking questions and leave immediately.

"Uh, well, I'm sorry to disturb you. No one told me about the rescheduling. I'll go back to my hut."

He turned to leave, praying they would let him go.

"Stop," a voice called.

Oh, no.

He turned around and faced the men. "Yes?"

"I believe you have a duty to perform," said one man.

"A duty?"

"You must tap the wheels of this train."

"You want me to tap *these* wheels? They look brand-new."

"The passenger, as we are sure you have imagined, is someone of great importance. He also has romantic regard for tradition. He would expect you to perform your duty."

Kabulov brightened. "Oh, I'd love to. The P36 was always my favorite train, and this one is a thing of beauty. They built these trains in Kolomna, you know, the last one in 1956. But they were green and the wheels were . . . Say, you're not taking this all the way to Moscow, are you?"

"Why do you ask?"

Kabulov was sure they were joking, and he laughed. "Oh, come now. There hasn't been a steamer on the line since Brezhnev. The coal stations required to refuel are long gone. And it's almost ten thousand kilometers to Moscow."

"We will leave the line at kilometer 1776."

Kabulov scratched the top of his hat again. "That's in the Ural Mountains. Where Asia becomes Europe."

"You know the place, do you?"

"Of course I do. I know every section of track from here to Moscow. There's nothing there but an obelisk marking the top of the Urals. It says 'Europe' on one side and 'Asia' on the other. There's not even a station, not even a loading platform. Well, there is a madwoman, and another fellow who lives on wild berries he collects in the summer. Sometimes the local stops there, but never the Trans-Siberian."

The men smiled at him. "Thank you, *dyadya*. We appreciate your interest in our affairs," one said.

"Yes, dear *dyadya*," the other said.

Kabulov should have felt better hearing them call him uncle; it was a term of affection and respect from the old days. Except just now, being thanked for his interest in where the train was going, Kabulov saw something vicious flare in their eyes. The men were toying with him like cats with a mouse. He froze stiff, waiting for something terrible to happen. Instead, the men responded to a signal in their earpieces.

"The passenger is arriving with his entourage," one man said.

"Perhaps you should begin your duty so that we may leave on schedule," the other said.

"Yes. I'll do that. Thank you."

Kabulov took the steps down to the tracks, walked to the far side of the locomotive. A feeling of relief washed over him.

"Let's do this quickly, Kukushka, and be done with it."

He lowered the hammer from his shoulder and walked along the driving wheels and trailing wheels, tapping each one.

Cling, cling, cling.

Kabulov listened. He had been a tapper all his life. He knew the sound of every train wheel in Russia. But this . . . the rings weren't just true, they were hitting harmonics like church bells, and the sound sustained and swirled through the deserted train yard. He continued along the tender and passenger cars, adding tones to the sound from the locomotive. The train's running gear began to hum with a low frequency drone as if vibrating on the rails. He swung his hammer to test the last wheel of the rear car.

Cling.

"Something tells me this train isn't running on coal, Kukushka."

He came around the back of the train, climbed onto the platform, and reached down with the hammer to tap the wheels.

Cling, cling.

He sensed movement. He looked up and saw a tall man with silver hair exit the terminus. He wore dark glasses over his eyes and seemed to float across the platform in his black sable coat. The FSB men bowed as the man boarded the forward passenger car. Then from the terminus came four more men, walking two by two. They didn't look like state security, they looked odd; from Western Europe perhaps. And they carried a metal container between them. They loaded the container into the third car with solemn care. Kabulov was telling himself it looked like a coffin when he realized the FSB men were watching him.

"Oh, dear."

He quickly lowered his eyes, continued forward. As he passed the two men, he felt their terrible eyes watching him, still.

Cling, cling, cling.

By the time Kabulov reached the locomotive, his hands were trembling. He considered jumping off the platform and slipping away to the tapper's hut. But maybe the FSB men would feel insulted and cause him trouble, he thought. Agents of state security may have changed their initials from KGB to FSB, but their claws were just as sharp, especially these days. No one dared to question them. There were rumors of secret gulags in the Tomsk Oblast, and talk of people disappearing for no reason. Kabulov gathered his courage and turned to say good night . . . but the two men were gone.

"Hello?"

Just then the great clock inside the terminus rang for midnight and the Tannoy above Platform One exploded with music as it did with every departure of the Trans-Siberian Express. Always at midnight; always the anthem of the Soviet Union. Then the train's whistle cried and there were slow chugs of steam from the chimney. The beautifully gleaming thing began to pull away. The chugs came faster and the train disappeared into the night.

Oleg Kabulov stood very still, listening for the sound of steel wheels. He did not hear them; he only heard that same drone from the running gear. Pulsing, fading. *Like the chanting of priests in Blessed Nicholas Cathedral,* he thought. Yes, that was it . . . like vespers. When the sound vanished, Kabulov shuddered. He signed himself three times.

"O angel Bozhiy, khranitel moih svyatih, okhranyu svoyu zhizn v strakhe Bozhyem."

He raised his hammer to his shoulder and shuffled back to his hut.

"Kukushka, that was a very strange business. Best not mention it to Svetlana. She's very superstitious and would worry so. She would think evil has returned to Russia. This will be our secret, *da*?"

ii

She did not know how long she had been sitting there. It felt like a long time, or the next second; she couldn't tell. She was still holding the pajamas to her face, holding the scent of soap and powdered skin deep within her body. She wanted to stay in the moment; it was safe here. There were no dead outside her door, or bad shadows lurking in the forest. Here, she could keep the fearful dream away. But a primal urge overcame her and she lowered the pajamas from her face to breathe. She folded them neatly and rested them on the camp bed.

"I need to . . . I need . . ."

She looked about the concrete room.

It looked like a bomb had hit it.

Glasses, plates, and jars scattered over the floor. Most of them broken, some still intact. There were spilled foods and teas and shards of the bathroom mirror that had flown wildly when she attacked the bitch with the vacant gaze in her eyes. *What a fucked-up place,* she thought. But it was better than ending up in a fucking cocoon woven by bad shadows. If she stayed down here, stayed quiet, the bad shadows would not find her. They'd gone back into the forest; she saw it happen in the dream, and they were telling her to stay underground until she woke up. She closed her eyes and wished the fearful dream away.

They won't find me, they won't.

She took a breath and opened her eyes. She stared at the storybook on her lap. She opened it and turned slowly through the pages, wondering if she had ever read the story to the little boy.

"You must have. Somewhere, sometime."

She slowed her breath and tried to imagine it . . . then she could almost see it happening. The little boy wearing his pajamas after a bath and sitting on her lap. He snuggled against her body, looking at the pictures and listening to the sound of her voice as she read the story about a band of silly-looking pirates who rescued a beautiful princess. She imagined the boy pointing to the characters he liked. The giant flying caterpillar named Pompidou would've been a big hit, and the silly-looking pirates with the paper hats, too. Even the evil wizard named Screechy was pretty silly-looking in his long robe embedded with stars and his matching conical hat with a rooster on top. And there was a fat gray cat named the Miserable Beast who was actually very nice in the story. It was the Miserable Beast who found the beautiful princess locked in the tower of the evil wizard's ice castle. And in seeing her, sitting alone while combing her hand through her long blond hair, the Miserable Beast fell in love with the princess and told her so with a heartfelt *Mew*.

She stared at the drawing of the princess and cat nose-to-nose. They sat across a small wooden table in a narrow room of wooden walls and a crooked roof. There was a bed in the background and an old radio on a shelf. A sensation came over her: *I know that place.* She sat back on the camp bed, rested her back on the concrete wall. She turned through the pages, picking up the story.

The funny-looking pirates fly above the Boiling Seas of Doom on Pompidou and arrive at the evil wizard's ice castle. The Miserable Beast leads them to the captured princess, and the pirates rescue her. But before escaping from the tower, the princess reminds the pirates about the future-teller diamond and all the pirates say, "Oh, yeah, the future-teller diamond." As long as the evil wizard had it he could control the princess and command her to return to him. So the Miserable Beast takes the pirates and the princess through the secret passages of the ice castle to where the evil wizard hides the future-teller diamond. It's locked behind bars, and only the cat can fit through. But he's a little too fat, and the pirates must get behind the beast's butt and push him through with a mighty, *"Vers l'avant!" Forward!* The Miserable Beast slips through and he takes the future-teller in his mouth and the pirates pull him back through the bars with a mighty, *"Vers l'arrière!" Retreat!* The cat slips through the bars again and they all run away to find Pompidou. But before they take off, the princess says they must take the Miserable Beast of a cat, too, because he helped them. All the pirates say, "Oh yeah, we have to take the cat because he helped us." So they all jump onto Pompidou the giant caterpillar and fly back over the Boiling Seas of Doom and around the moon and past the stars. They hide the future-teller in a secret cave under a cathedral in the land of Lausanne. They all drink tea in a vineyard overlooking a crescent-shaped lake. It's a spring day. The swallows are coming back to Lausanne. Everyone's happy.

Fin.

Her eyes moved over the drawings: vineyards, a crescent-shaped lake, a cathedral in the land of Lausanne . . . *I know that place.* She turned back to the page with the princess and the cat sitting nose-to-nose in the small room. She imagined the little boy on her lap reading the story with her, imagined it was one of his favorite pages. Imagined him pointing his finger at the cat, imagined the little boy's voice.

"Boo."

She had no idea what the word meant, only that it sounded like something the little boy would say. She imagined the little boy's finger sliding from the cat to the princess. She heard his voice again.

"Maman."

That was a word she knew; it was French for *mother*. She looked at the woman in the drawing, leaning with one elbow on the table, facing the fat gray cat and combing her hand through her hair. She pulled at her own hair, held it before her eyes. Her hair was filthy, but it was the same color as the storybook princess.

She lifted the book closer for a better look. A folded piece of paper slipped from the back and landed on her lap. She laid the storybook on the camp bed and unfolded the paper. It was finely woven cotton and bigger than the book's pages. On it was a series of drawings—an artist's study of a woman asleep. A damn good artist at that. There were close-ups of the woman's hands, her hair, her face.

"Hold it."

She leaned over the princess in the storybook, stared at her. She looked at the sleeping woman in the artist's study.

"This is the same woman."

She closed the book, glanced through the title.

"Une histoire drôle de Marc . . ."

She looked at the portrait. There was a scrawl in the corner of the page. It was the same name.

"Marc Rochat."

She set the name on the paper close to the dialogue balloons in the book. The script had been written by the same hand. Same woman, same artist.

"Marc Rochat knows who this woman is."

She looked at the drawing of the sleeping woman.

"Not only does he know her, he loves her."

She closed the book, stared at the title once more.

piratz

Une histoire drôle de Marc Rochat

pour Mademoiselle Katherine Taylor

She got up and walked quickly around the room, looking for the biggest chunk of mirror there was on the floor. She found one shard the size of a carton of cigarettes. She kicked the surrounding debris aside and cleared a space on the concrete floor. She knelt down, laying the storybook and portrait above the chunk of mirror. She looked into the glass. All she could see were a pair of vacant eyes; the eyes of the woman in the mirror she'd tried to murder with the skillet, but it seemed the bitch refused to die.

"Get lost, I'm busy."

She looked at the princess in the storybook. The eyes were the same shape as those of the woman in the mirror.

Wait. Something was different.

Slowly, Katherine turned her head from side to side, watching her reflection. She could not detect a difference, then she realized the eyes in the mirror were shaded. She looked up at the ceiling, saw she was directly under the light. She used the sleeve of her cloak to push away the debris to her left. She scooted over and shifted the chunk of mirror around until the light hit it and reflected into her eyes. She moved her head from side to side again.

There. Stop.

The vacant gaze in the woman's eyes was fading. Eyes the color of emeralds were emerging now, or trying to. Something else. There was a tiny flaw in the left iris; a silver squiggle. She reached for the storybook and pulled it closer. She looked at the princess, the close-up of her face nose-to-nose with the cat. She saw the same squiggle in the left iris of the princess.

"Well, well, what do you know?"

She got to her feet and walked in slow, clockwise circles. Bits of glass crunched under her shoes as she reached the perfect orbit between the storybook, the artist's sketch of the sleeping woman, and the mirror, her eyes focusing over each thing. Seeing her eyes in the mirror this way, they were in shade; that way they reflected the light from the ceiling. She kept walking and coming into the light. *Fuck me.*

"My name is Katherine Taylor."

She heard the muffled sound of her voice; she continued her orbit into the shade and spoke louder.

"My name is Katherine Taylor . . ."

Then seeing the princess, then the sleeping woman, then the light returning to her eyes.

Clink, clink.

Her foot knocked a glass jar. It skidded over the concrete floor, hit the legs of the camp bed. She stared at it, tipped her head the better to read the handwritten label: *Violette's Garden*. She walked over, pulled the Glock from her belt, and tossed it on the bed. She reached down, picked up the jar. It was one of the teas from the shelf.

Violette's Garden: for remembrance of pleasant memories.

". . . and this is not a dream."

EIGHT

i

Harper finished with Professor Peabody in the basement of Blue Brain HQ and came up for air. Standing under the palm tree in the atrium again, he didn't know what to do next. He dug out the letter from the concierge to double-check he'd done all that was required of him.

"Sorted. Now what?"

He stuffed the letter back into the pocket of his mackintosh. He leaned to the side of the palm tree and saw Puur Innovation Café across the atrium. He checked his watch: 17:05.

"Happy hour it is."

The joint was well packed. Harper cruised the buffet, grabbed a Gruyère and lettuce in a baguette. He cruised the wine bar, spotted a *cinq* of Swiss white among the bottles. A *cinq* held five glasses; a little more than a French half bottle, a little less than a full one. The Swiss were very sensible people, Harper thought. They always managed to provide him with solutions to complicated problems, like what to do next. When in doubt, grab a *cinq*. He found an empty table in the corner and sat down. Five seconds later the locals in the place forgot he was there.

Sipping through glass number one, he wondered if he should call Inspector Gobet and report in. Seemed the thing to be done; if nothing else, to prove he had completed his to-do list and was awaiting further orders.

A thought fell into Harper's head: In the years since he was awakened for the cathedral job . . . *I've never called the cop; he calls me.* He pulled his cell phone from his coat. *I don't even know his bloody number. Or mine.*

He dropped the phone into his pocket and scanned the locals in the café. Professors, researchers, grad students working on PhDs. He wondered if one of them was working for Inspector Gobet. Someone planted in the crowd to point him in the general direction of what to do next. Had to be. There always was someone or something to guide him on. Two days ago, chasing Astruc and Goose across the south of France, Harper landed in Montségur. He arrived in the middle of the night with the same question: *Now what?* Then appeared a Great Pyrenees dog named Shiva. The huge slobbering animal took Harper for a walk through a forest, ending up at the Field of the Burned, where the last of the Cathars were slaughtered in 1244. The dog at the lead, sniffing along the path, pointing to clues that brought Harper to this very moment in space and time—sitting in a café with a *cinq* of Swiss white after having his brain stretched from here to the edge of the observable universe. An amusing moment it was. Harper raised his glass and offered a toast to the noble mutt.

"Good dog."

As he sipped, another thought fell into his head. *How the hell did we superior creatures of light survive two and a half million years in paradise while spending great swathes of time not knowing what to do next?* Answer: *If we're being led around by the hands of locals, or the paws of dogs, maybe we're not all that superior.*

He finished his glass, poured number two, and took a healthy swig. He was thinking the wine had a pleasant grassy taste with a touch of effervescence when bursts of blue light raced through his eyes. Harper looked at his glass. The wine had been juiced, as if someone knew he would grab that particular bottle, someone who wished to help Harper focus his mind. He glanced at the wine bar. Bottles, bottles everywhere. Full bottles and half bottles . . . *and you picked the only* cinq *on offer, boyo.*

"Of course I did."

He sipped the wine again, watched the bursts of blue light in his eyes. Each burst uploaded a point of information to augment his briefing on

Blue Brain. Item: Lines of causality were constantly intersecting in paradise, like woof threads crossing warp threads at right angles once and again, once and again, weaving together the stuff of life on Earth. Item: Somewhere in the weave, one thread was deliberately introduced by Harper's kind. They had been sent from somewhere two and a half million years ago, bearing the first fire of creation. No idea of who had sent them or why. Orders were orders. They waited tens of thousands of years atop the volcanic pluton at Montségur. One day, they saw a tribe of *Homo ergaster* humanoids emerge from the forest and settle on the plain far below. That's when it happened: Some of Harper's kind came down from the pluton and revealed the first fire of creation to the humanoids. Item: Soon after, those same humanoids mastered fire, made tools, observed the stars. Then the humanoids began to imagine questions: *Who made this place? What is this place? Why does this place exist?*

The bursts of blue light faded, leaving ghostly contrails in Harper's eyes. As his vision returned the contrails floated through the room, touching this local and that one, then every local in the café. Item: These were the descendants of those *Homo ergaster* humanoids, burning off steam after a hard day's work. *Rather amusing that, too,* Harper thought. *Homo ergaster* was Latin for *working man*. More amusing was the objective of their day's work. And not just this crowd; people like them all around the world—scientists, artists, philosophers. They all thought they were seeking answers to *who?*, *what?*, and *why?* What they were also doing was seeking the source of a spark of light the locals called a soul. They didn't realize that's what they were doing, but it was the truth nonetheless. Item: The soul had been implanted into the forms of their extinct ancestors by Harper's kind. Item: A couple million years later, their descendants in nowtimes were at the point of "knowing all things." Or so said Professor Peabody in the basement of Blue Brain HQ. Harper flashed the small man in the white coat, chattering away with more info.

"Simply put, sir, the photograph you are looking at now represents the ability of the descendants of *Homo ergaster* humanoids to imagine—"

Hang on, Professor.

Harper's sense of time and space was out of sync. He stopped his timeline, drained glass number two, and poured number three. Between the bursts of blue light in his eyes and the trips between nowtimes and beforetimes, all while speeding through the universe at whatever megaparsecs it was per second, Harper felt the need for more of the whatever-it-was in the wine. He drank deep and settled . . . *That's better, boyo.* He backed up his timeline and let the beforetimes roll.

Wham.

Back in the basement of Blue Brain HQ, the Stone Age computer on the desk still spilling triangulations of the Earth's exact position in the universe. Professor Peabody lays a second photograph before Harper. Harper pulls his eyes from the triangulations, sees two funnels of luminous clouds rising in darkening sky and four brilliant stars hanging between the clouds.

"What's this?"

"The gas pillars of the Eagle nebula in the constellation Serpens. This particular formation is known as the Pillars of Creation."

Harper looked closer at the photo. Clouds of cosmic dust, hydrogen, helium, plasma.

"Taken by Voyager 1?"

"No, sir. It was from the Hubble Space Telescope launched in 1990 and still in service. The photograph was taken five years later."

"Another one of Inspector Gobet's toys, is it?"

"In fact, the Hubble telescope is a wholly human endeavor, and that is the point."

"Because?"

"Simply put, sir, the photograph you are looking at now represents the ability of the descendants of *Homo ergaster* humanoids to imagine the mechanics of the universe and to make the necessary tools to *see* those imaginations, thereby pointing the entirety of the human race toward a new spatial-temporal reality."

"Pointing. Like a Pyrenees mountain mutt?"

The small man lost his train of thought.

"I . . . I believe, sir, the Great Pyrenees is an agricultural breed used to guard flocks of sheep, whereas the pointer is a gun dog used for the flushing out of game birds and retrieving them."

Harper realized the ability of his particular line of life-form to imagine the mechanics of a joke, and then tell it, were not up to human standards.

"My mistake."

He looked again at the photograph of the Pillars of Creation. There were hundreds, thousands of smaller sparks of light hidden in the clouds of cosmic dust. *Like wombs giving birth to stars.*

"How old is this place?"

"A million and a half years old, sir."

"And how far away from paradise?"

"Seven thousand light-years."

The mechanics of distance were mind-boggling. Harper lost track at seven thousand light-years times 5.878625 trillion miles. Then it hit him: This photograph wasn't about mechanics. It was about *seeing* the birth of stars as it happened long ago, and just now, all at the same time.

"Beforetimes. The locals are watching beforetimes."

"Not in the same manner as your kind, sir, but in their own way, yes, that is exactly what they are doing."

"How far back can the locals see?"

"To date Hubble has allowed humanity to see thirteen and a half billion years back in time. Another billion years back and they will see the Big Bang itself."

Another episode from the History Channel flashed through Harper's eyes. *In the Beginning* it was. Black screen; nothingness; a mighty explosion. Suddenly, all the universe is, and all it will be, exists.

"Assuming humanity knows where to look, of course," Harper said.

"Sir?"

"My kind have been here for two and a half million years watching the same stars, and we sure as hell don't know where to look."

"Yes, well, human scientists imagined that problem and developed the mechanics to resolve it, too."

"You must be joking."

"No, sir."

"How?"

"A radio telescope at the South Pole called BICEP2 is searching for PGWs emanating from the most dense quadrant of the universe."

"That's a lot of letters, professor."

"In the first instance the letters stand for Background Imaging of Cosmic Extragalactic Polarization. PGWs are primordial gravitational waves."

"Primordial gravitational waves," Harper said.

"Yes, sir."

"Professor, I'm afraid PGWs are like Voyager 1—they never made my History Channel feed."

"Well, the universe is flat in shape, like a disc. If you imagine it to have an aqueous surface onto which a pebble is tossed, concentric circles would emanate outward from the point of impact."

"Ripples. Echoes."

"Precisely, sir. PGWs are the ripples and echoes of the Big Bang somewhere in the range of 10^{-36} to 10^{-32} of a second after it happened."

The numbers popped hot. If the locals found PGWs, the locals would be within an infinitesimal fraction of a Planck unit in seeing the moment of creation.

"Rather big news then," Harper said.

"Well, actually, sir . . ."

The *really* big news was a deep-space telescope nicknamed JWST that would be launched in 2018. It would travel through the solar system and park itself one and a half million miles away from paradise. It was fitted with eighteen hexagonal mirror segments forming a reflective surface nearly twenty feet in diameter. Each segment would be turned in such a way as to search the cosmic dust and target those primordial gravitational waves; the telescope would then focus its mirrors into the densest part of the observable universe. Meaning the descendants of a tribe of *Homo ergaster* humanoids who once gathered under the volcanic pluton at Montségur would witness the creation of the universe as it happened fourteen and a half billion bloody years ago, and in the here and now at the same time. It was quite the trick, and Harper let it sink in. In searching for secrets of the universe, the locals had found a way to travel through beforetimes. They were on a cosmic trip to the Big Bang.

"And in finding it mankind would reach the point of knowing," the professor said.

"Knowing what?"

"All things, sir."

Harper thought about it. Sounded swell. Too bad about the second thread woven into the stuff of life on Earth by Harper's kind, the one where two hundred traitors of the creation took the forms of men and bred fear and greed into paradise. He looked at the triangulations of Earth's position in the universe dripping down the screen of the Stone Age computer in front of him, info now heading into interstellar space on the back of Voyager 1. An SOS, Professor Peabody explained. *No shit,* Harper thought, now seeing the message buried in the triangulations. SOS: paradise heading for a mass extinction event.

"Non est ad astra mollis e terris via," Harper said.

"Sir?"

"There is no easy way from the earth to the stars."

ii

He blinked himself back to Puur Innovation Café.

He was staring into the bottom of an empty glass, feeling dizzy as hell. He looked up, saw the happy hour crowd still at it. He also saw he wasn't alone at his table in the shadows. Krinkle was sitting opposite him, spinning his own empty glass by the stem.

"Hi there. Mind if I join you?"

"Do I have a choice?"

"Nope."

Harper shoved the *cinq* the roadie's way. "Be forewarned, it's juiced."

"Yeah, they told me. I was ordered to have a glass."

Krinkle poured out the last of the Swiss white into both glasses. He patted the bottom of the carafe to get out the final drop.

"I could get another one," Harper said. "A real one, just to wash down the *cinq*."

Krinkle sipped. "No, that's all right," he said. "We're on a schedule."

"What kind of a schedule?"

"A tight one."

"So maybe we should drink up and get going."

Krinkle leaned across the table. "Relax, brother. Just because the schedule is tight doesn't mean there isn't room to move. Oh, great track. I need to get it on tonight's broadcast."

"Track?"

"'Room to Move.' John Mayall. Recorded live at Fillmore East, July 12, 1969. I did gigs there with the Dead in February of the same year."

"Which dead?"

"The Grateful Dead. I told you before, my form was one of their roadies. He overdosed on bad smack. Anyways, Mayall left the Bluesbreakers and gave up on electric instruments for a while. He teamed up with Jon Mark and Johnny Almond. 'Room to Move' is an acoustic rock classic, and Mayall blows a mean harp, almost as good as Boz—I mean, Inspector Gobet. Anyway, Mark and Almond formed their own band and went into a whole jazz-rock riff. They recorded this thing called 'The City.' Eleven minutes, forty-nine seconds of headphone bliss, especially the last two minutes and twenty-six seconds. See, this guy is sleeping out in the woods under a redwood tree and—"

"What the bloody hell are you talking about?"

"I'm talking about a song. See, this guy is sleeping in the woods. And he doesn't want to go back to the city because it's nothing but a long taxi ride."

"The drive back, you mean."

"No, the city, the perception of it. It's steel and concrete and nothing but a long taxi ride going nowhere."

"So we're talking philosophy."

Krinkle gulped at his glass. He wiped a dribble of wine from his long gray beard. "Dude, I know you've just had your head stretched—"

"You know?"

"Yeah, I had the same briefing last week."

"I have questions."

"Dude! I know you have questions, but right now we're talking about a friggin' song."

"Got it."

They sipped again. Krinkle continued.

"Okay. This guy doesn't want to go back, but he hears the taxi coming and he keeps singing *I hear the taxi coming, I hear the taxi coming,* and the music gets quiet and drifts, then out of the left speaker, from far away, comes this twelve-string acoustic guitar. It grows and it swells and pumps up the volume. Then from left of center comes a bongo laying down this Latin thing, then from the right speaker comes someone tapping a wood block in counter time, then way out there, from somewhere, come these rattles and zills. Then dead center of the headphones this Fender fretless bass explodes like the voice of God and it melts into your consciousness and you are held in awe. Then you're carried away in the taxi, heading back to the city because you have no choice. Fade out."

Krinkle sipped, Harper scanned his eyes.

"Are you on some new tea?"

"No, but I got a booster shot for something or other in Vevey this morning, so things are a little racy at the moment. That's why they ordered me to have a glass of this shit. Fizzy, isn't it?"

"Wait for the bursts of light in your eyes."

"Yeah, what color?"

"Blue."

"Cool."

Harper looked over the tables, studied the faces of the locals. "Do they realize how close they are to the point of knowing?"

Krinkle shrugged. "A few of them, the sensitive ones, sure. But ninety-nine point ninety-nine percent of the locals don't. Life is hard in paradise, brother. Most people are just trying to get through it one day at a time. No time to consider the big picture. What's in the baguette?"

"Gruyère, lettuce, butter."

"No ham?"

"No."

"Good on you."

A disembodied voice entered the conversation.

"You have a message."

Krinkle fumbled in the front pouch of his overalls for his cell phone.

"You have a message."

"Yeah, yeah. I heard you the first time." He pulled out the phone, tapped the screen, and read through the message. He tapped at the screen, traced a few circles, typed numbers and letters. He hit send and returned the phone to the pouch.

"Where were we?" he said.

Harper sipped at his glass while talking. "It's the same for you then? One-way phone calls, handwritten notes telling you what to do? Watching the History Channel or drinking a *cinq* to gather intel? Waiting in joints like this for someone to tell you what to do next?"

"Yes and no," Krinkle said.

"Meaning?"

"Meaning yes, it's the same. And no, not exactly."

"What?"

"I'm in communications and public relations, you're a killer of bad guys."

"A minor point, surely, given you practically beat Astruc to a pulp in the cathedral last night."

"Yeah, but he's one of us and I had orders to keep him in line. But no, I don't get handwritten notes and my phone goes both ways. I don't watch the History Channel, either. If management wants to slip me intel, they turn me on to a bootleg."

"A what?"

"The Dead jammed for thirty years, through the sixties and seventies. From the Fillmore in San Francisco to the pyramids of Egypt. Their shows were epic, they'd run for hours. And everywhere the Dead jammed, people recorded the shows with little recorders, ergo, bootlegs. When management wants me to know something, they slip the info into one of the recordings, put it on YouTube, and I give it a listen. And yeah, sometimes I end up in joints like this waiting to be told where to go next. That's why joints like this are here."

"This café, you mean."

"Yup."

"So you're here to tell me what to do next."

"Not quite. I'm taking you to where you can do what you're supposed to do next."

"Sorry?"

"I hear the taxi coming, brother."

Something moved in the corner of Harper's eye. He looked outside the café windows, saw Krinkle's tour bus with the tinted windows and blue running lights ease into the parking lot and stop. Harper looked at the roadie.

"Let me guess: Inspector Gobet's clever lads have plotted an infil solution through the shifting sands of time."

"Yup."

"Who's driving?"

"Me, if I have to."

Harper glanced at the bus. The side door opened and chrome-plated steps lowered to the ground.

"Who's driving the bus now?"

"Nobody."

"The bus drove itself?"

"More like it called me and relayed a message that coordinates have been synced with the particular time-warp madness at the destination. Then I programmed the bus to pick us up."

"You drove your bus by cell phone?"

"Twenty years from now every local on the planet with a car will be doing the same thing, *if* they make it that far."

Harper scanned the room, watched the locals talk and laugh. "Not looking good for them, is it?" he said.

"Or us."

Harper laughed a little and raised his glass in a toast. Krinkle matched him.

"Cheers."

"Amen."

They drank in communion, rested their empty glasses on the table.

"So it's just you and me making the infil then?" Harper said.

"Yes and . . . Shit."

Krinkle rubbed his eyes a few seconds, then looked at Harper.

"No. I drop you off, you infil and recon the site. I stay on the bus and hang at the perimeter for fifteen minutes."

"Then what?"

"If you come out with Katherine Taylor, I bring you both to Lausanne and get her to the clinic in Vevey."

"And if we don't come out within fifteen minutes?"

"I assume the site has collapsed with the two of you inside."

"Fifteen minutes is all I've got?" Harper said.

Krinkle shook his head and rubbed his eyes harder this time. "Shit!"

"What is it?" Harper said.

"Those friggin' blue lights. Fuck, they're bright. What was I saying?"

"Fifteen minutes."

"Oh yeah. Here's the deal: The site is crashing, so time is looping within the perimeter. A minute will seem longer than it is, which is why you need this."

Krinkle reached in the front pouch of his denim overalls again. This time he pulled out something small enough to be hidden in his big hands. He set the thing on the table and pushed it toward Harper. It was a small plastic chicken, sitting on a round base with ruler markings around the diameter.

"What the hell is that?"

"An egg timer. Actually, this one goes up to fifteen so you can time other stuff with it, too. You know, pasta and stuff. But it's an egg timer, basically."

"What am I supposed to do with it?"

Krinkle picked it up, gave the chicken a twist till its red beak lined up on the number fifteen. The chicken started to tick.

"You get inside the time warp, you set the timer to the max at fifteen, and you put it in your coat pocket. It counts down and rings, you reset it and do it again. You'll have four goes at it. If you don't get out before the fourth ring, you don't get out."

Harper added it up. "So in reality, I've got sixty minutes."

"Yeah, *inside* the perimeter, but *outside* it's only fifteen minutes. You're talking about two different temporal realities. Don't get confused."

"I'm already confused."

"Look, the real-world watch on your wrist won't work inside the warp. The warp you're going into is collapsing. Bottom line is you can get seriously fucked in there and never see it coming. That's why you need this."

Krinkle twisted the chicken again, lined its beak to zero.

Riiiinnnng.

The sound caught the attention of the locals in the café. Krinkle and Harper lowered their eyes. The locals looked at the table in the shadows, but they did not see Harper or Krinkle; then they all started checking their own cell phones.

Krinkle laid the plastic chicken on the table, looked at Harper. "The time mechanics said it's the best they could come up with on short notice."

"An egg timer that looks like a chicken."

"No, the chicken was me. The mechanics said any fifteen-minute egg timer that could be manually rewound would work, as long as it contained no electrical circuitry. Something about erratic electromagnetic pulses or some shit. I got messaged to pick up an egg timer on the way here. I made a stop at a hardware store in Renens. This was all they had in stock."

Harper leaned across the table and stared at Krinkle. "The locals have taken photographs of dust clouds giving birth to stars seven thousand light-years away. They put a telescope in low Earth orbit that can see thirteen and a half billion bloody years back in time. At the South Pole they've got a radio telescope that's looking for echoes of the Big Bang as we speak. In a few years they'll park a new telescope so far away it will see the creation of the bloody universe as it happened and live at the same time. Not to mention just now, seven floors under our feet, there's a Stone Age computer built by Astruc's half-kind son that's plugged into a supercomputer named Blue Brain. Together those computers are updating an SOS about a mass extinction event to a bloody space probe presently breaking into interstellar space."

Krinkle nodded. "Yeah, and what's your point?"

Harper held up the plastic chicken.

"I'm being sent on a recon mission through the shifting sands of time with this."

Krinkle stood up. "I know. Trippy, isn't it? Let's go. Bring the sandwich."

NINE

Guitars clanged through the bus like a wall of sound, loud as the seven bells of Lausanne Cathedral ringing out over the town. Harper sat in one of the bolted-to-the-floor chairs of the passenger cabin. He watched Krinkle lean over a Neve 8028 audio console. The roadie's eyes were closed, a set of Audio-Technica ATH W5000 headphones were over his ears, and his big frame swayed from side to side in his swivel chair. His fingers danced over the faders, sliding them up and down, or pressing a button to isolate a specific audio source. A kick drum or a snare, the ticking of a clock, a bass guitar or a screaming lead. Then he'd tweak EQ knobs to get the exact sound he wanted, release the button, and the wall of sound would clang through the bus again. Above him a huge bank of reel-to-reel tape machines rolled in sequence at fifteen inches per second. When a tape ran out, Krinkle jumped up to thread a new reel. Every once in a while he'd check his cell phone, then glance ahead through the windshield to check the bus was driving itself as programmed. Checking, this time, the roadie didn't like what he saw on the cell phone. He turned to one of the three laptops next to the console and typed furiously. A satellite shot looking down at the A9 north of Lausanne appeared onscreen. The shot was live, with Krinkle's black bus in the frame, cruising at speed. He hit a few more keys and the screen zoomed in ahead of the bus and highlighted a section of the motorway running south before banking left to run in a straight line due east. The computer marked that section in green before the road disappeared into a hillside.

Just then Harper felt the floor of the bus vibrate with the same cycles per second as the wall of sound. He'd felt it once before, on the bus ride from Montségur while bringing Astruc to Lausanne. Feeling it this time, a thought dropped. The wall of sound wasn't just as loud as the seven bells of Lausanne Cathedral, it was creating the same massive subharmonic hum: *ommm*. He looked through the open door to the driver's compartment, saw the empty driver's seat, saw the steering wheel turn this way and that way on its own. He had the urge to grab the wheel before realizing he had no idea how to drive. He felt Krinkle's hand tapping his shoulder.

Harper looked at him.

The roadie had spun around in his swivel chair and was pointing ahead through the windshield. His lips moved, but Harper couldn't hear a word for the music. Harper pointed to his own ears and shook his head. Krinkle spun in his chair again, brought down a fader, and lowered the volume to a dull roar. He pulled his headphones from his head and faced Harper. The vibrations coming up through the floor of the bus calmed.

"We've got a problem," the roadie said.

"Hearing loss?"

"Funny, but no. The road."

Harper looked ahead through the windshield. It looked like any Swiss highway of an evening. Dual carriageway, BMWs and Mercs and Audis with drivers ignoring the speed limit and driving as fast as they damn well pleased. He looked at Krinkle.

"What's wrong with it?"

"We hit acoustic levitation in less than two minutes, but the only stretch of road long and dead-east enough runs through the Belmont-sur-Lausanne tunnel. At the speed we need it'll take sixty-three-point-four seconds to clear the tunnel, and we hit levitation at sixty-five. If the bus's onboard computers don't get it right and we don't clear the tunnel in time, it won't be good."

"Define 'won't be good.'"

"Imagine a gasoline truck slamming into a truck loaded with nitroglycerin. In a friggin' tunnel."

"How about waiting for another stretch of road?"

"Any hope of getting you in and out of the location before it collapses means we need to go not just now, but *now* now."

Krinkle glanced at the table near Harper, saw the Gruyère and lettuce in a baguette Harper had brought from the café at Blue Brain HQ.

"You going to eat that, brother? I need some food to settle this blue shit in my eyes so I can see straight."

"Bon appétit," Harper said.

Krinkle grabbed the baguette, peeled away the paper wrapper, and took a healthy bite. He tapped at the laptop, watched numbers crunch on the screen. With another bite he looked at Harper.

"More drone," he said with a full mouth.

"Or maybe you could just take the bloody wheel and drive the bus yourself."

"Too busy with the music. I'll take the wheel on approach."

"You can't be serious."

"Hey, the music is how I get the drone. The drone is how I get the giddy-up into the go, got it?"

Not really, Harper thought. "Whatever you say, mate."

Krinkle reset his headphones over his ears, spun around, and kicked a drawer under the console; it slid open. Inside were kill kits, jars of potions, boxes of injector jets, and one tall green bottle with a black label.

"Pour us some whiskey. There's some coffee mugs behind you. I'll be back after the break."

Krinkle hit a button; the wall of sound came roaring back till the guitars slammed to a stop and a whirl of harmonics was suspended in the air. Krinkle leaned into the console's microphone, pushed up a fader on the board.

"Epic post-rock visions from Sweden's pg.lost. 'Crystalline' is the name of the track. *In Never Out* is the LP. Welcome to the evening. You're tuned to the last radio station on planet Earth. Next up, a special mix of 'When You Sing' from School of Seven Bells out of Brooklyn, New York. Listen close, brothers and sisters, these are good vibrations for a world in need. Close your eyes and open your hearts, for you are not alone. Come, fly with me to a place in the stars where you may witness the ascension of the watchers."

He closed the microphone and raised another fader, and ethereal sounds sailed through the bus. Then came a rhythm guitar climbing through a progression of major chords, then a perfect silence for half a breath . . . then a massive drone rushed forth. Harper felt it before he heard it. It was like being caressed in something warm, light maybe. Then came voices from the far beyond.

When you sing
You sing loud.
Rewind
And build the fires
Around my heart.

Round and round went the drone. The floor vibrated again, then came the hum of Lausanne's seven bells—*ommm*—and the bus raced into the Belmont-sur-Lausanne tunnel.

Weirdness commenced. The tunnel's tubular walls pulsed to a four-four beat. Headlamps and taillights of speeding cars melted into streaks that stretched and broke apart into threads of red, violet, and blue. Sixty-three-point-four seconds ahead, at the far end of the tunnel where vanishing point met horizon, Harper saw a brilliant white light.

"Will wonders never cease?" He laughed to himself.

He grabbed two coffee mugs, slammed them on the small side table. He reached for the tall bottle in the drawer. He looked at the black label: single malt, 1999, from the Ardbeg distillery on the Isle of Islay. Straightforward label for a pedigree single malt . . . except instead of a picture of a grouse or stag or a family crest, there was a silver spaceship rising from the Earth and heading to the stars. Then there was the whiskey's name: *Galileo*.

"Or the wonders could just keep coming."

He opened the bottle and poured two fingers' worth into both mugs. He stood, set one mug next to the audio console. Krinkle snapped it up, raised it to his nose, breathed deep, then drank. Harper did the same. The roadie went back to his broadcast. Harper stepped to the driver's compartment and stared ahead through the windshield. The white light at the end of the tunnel was coming fast; then everything slowed, then the threads of colored light seemed to hold in place. Harper felt a sense of being lifted up, floating; maybe it was the whiskey.

Ziiiiing.

Rushing ahead now, separating from the ground, crashing through the light at the end of the tunnel and coming out in a place somewhere between heaven and earth with a lone star, dead east, to guide them. Harper could only stare, almost forgetting to breathe. Then he heard Krinkle's voice behind him.

"And more I admire thy distant fire, than that colder, lowly light."

Hearing the words, Harper realized the wall of sound had quieted. He turned around and saw the roadie with his headphones around his neck and his legs propped up on the console.

"Sorry?"

"Edgar Allan Poe. 'Evening Star.'"

"Right. What happened to the music?"

"Once I get it off the ground the bus goes by itself till we get to the location."

Harper looked at the lone star again, then to the reel-to-reels rolling fast above the console, then to the roadie sitting comfortably below.

"What did you call it? Getting off the ground?" Harper said.

"Acoustic levitation."

"And it works how?"

"Standing waves, transverse waves, the angle of incidence equalizing the angle of reflection. Or you could just call it letting the earth spin under our wheels."

"It's the up-and-down part that's hard."

"What?"

"You said those words the last time coming from Montségur. Sideways, west to east, is easy, you said. It's the up-and-down part that's hard."

Krinkle nodded. "Not a problem this time. The location is only one degree north. We'll get to where we're going in three hours instead of six."

Krinkle reached for the bottle, poured himself another two fingers' worth. He offered the bottle to Harper.

"In the meantime, we got work, brother," the roadie said.

"Such as?"

"You need to know what to do when we get to where it is we're going."

"In the States."

"Yup."

"Where in the States exactly?"

"Sit down, would you? My arm is getting tired holding the bottle."

"Sure."

He walked back to his chair and sat down. Krinkle poured a healthy measure into Harper's mug.

"Like you said in the cathedral, where we're going doesn't exist on a map. It exists in a time warp wedged in at 45°47′29.41″ north by 121°57′43.42″ west. Your mission is to get in and sweep the site from the town to the house ending up at the bunker. You're looking to confirm or deny life status of Katherine Taylor and her son."

Hearing her name, Harper saw her at another point on his timeline—two and a half seconds' worth. Just after the cathedral job, standing on the esplanade below the belfry with the lad's cat in her arms. She was heavily juiced, so much so she didn't know she was pregnant. She was getting ready to leave Switzerland with . . .

"Officer Jannsen."

"Say again?"

"Miss Taylor's bodyguard. One of Inspector Gobet's Swiss Guard gang. A Swiss German girl with a solid left hook, yeah? The last time I saw Miss Taylor she said they had become friends."

Krinkle sipped his whiskey and smiled. "Weird the way it starts coming back in nonlinear drips and drabs, isn't it?"

Harper nodded. "Somewhat."

"It's going to happen a lot more now. Don't rush it. Too much too fast can cause some bad shit. And it hurts. And as she's had a child, it's Madame Taylor to the likes of us."

"Right."

"And they were more than friends."

"Who?"

"Madame Taylor and Officer Jannsen. Jannsen recently requested to be decommissioned so they could get married. They were going to be a family, they were going to raise Madame Taylor's child. We know they were together in Grover's Mill when the shit hit the fan. That's when comms went haywire. The one coded message we needed to hear, *Angelus*, telling us mother and child were secure in the vault, was never received."

"You don't sound all that hopeful on anyone's life status."

"Would you be?"

Harper thought about it. "If I had a choice in the matter, probably not."

"I hear you, brother."

Harper took a long sip of whiskey. "I've got an image of Miss Taylor on my timeline, two now, actually," he said. "But what about the child?"

"What about him?"

"I don't know what he looks like. Do you have a photograph?"

"There's never been a photo taken."

"HQ had to be monitoring the site's CCTV cameras. There must be a screen grab of him."

Krinkle shook his head. "Gobet ordered the child's face be put in silhouette at the point of transmission. No one outside the time warp knows what the child looks like."

Harper sipped again. "But you saw him with your dream catcher, Karoliina. In Portland, wasn't it? You could describe him."

"I could, but I won't."

"Because?"

Krinkle leaned toward Harper. "Because it doesn't matter. Because if the bad guys got him, there'll be nothing left but remains. Because it'll be easy determining if they got him or not, as he was the only child in the place. Katherine Taylor was one of hundreds of adults, so identifying her could be more difficult."

"Right. What do I do if I find their remains?"

"If they're hers, leave them. If they're his, bag them and bring them."

"And if I don't find any?" Harper said.

The roadie sat back, took a swallow of whiskey. "Then maybe mother and child are still alive. Maybe the bad guys are saving the two of them, or one of them, for purposes unknown."

Harper sipped. "And maybe that gives us a shot at turning things around," he said.

"It is the longest of shots, brother, but it's the only one up for grabs. Which is why Gobet is sending you in. And despite his riff about your undefined metaphysical condition making you expendable, it would be best if you got out before the site collapses. We need to know who's dead, who's alive."

Harper searched the pockets of his mackintosh for his smokes. He found them and set one between his lips. Krinkle had a match at the ready.

"Cheers," Harper said.

He leaned over, touching the tip of his fag to the fire. *Inhale, hold, exhale. Clearer.*

"You know the truth about the prophecy, don't you?"

The roadie stared back. "I'm not sure I follow the manner of your thinking."

"It hit me crashing through the light at the end of the tunnel. In a few years the locals will witness the very moment of creation. Voyager 1 is entering interstellar space with a mass extinction SOS our kind smuggled onboard. Then there's Astruc's son, Goose, who may or may not have been working with our kind, even though he tried to kill me, and after he thought he killed me, he started updating the SOS with Earth's exact position in the entire bloody universe. Then there's Madame Taylor and her son mixed up in a prophecy about a child conceived of light and born to guide the creation through the next stage of evolution. Lines of causality they are."

"Still not reading you, brother."

"Then focus on the SOS line. 'In the name of life on Earth,' Professor Peabody said. That was the beginning of the SOS. From our kind to whatever life-form there is waiting to receive it. I mean, how much of a long shot is that one? Even so, that causality line is running ahead of all the others, and it's racing to intersect a human imagination called salvation."

Krinkle gave it a few beats.

"Salvation is a heavy word, brother."

"It should be," Harper said. "It's carrying ten thousand years' worth of myths, legends, and religion on its back. Want to follow the rest of my thinking?"

"Go ahead."

"It isn't just the salvation of paradise and the locals we're dealing with, it's about the salvation of our kind, too. Raises the question: Who are we really trying to save, the locals or ourselves?"

Krinkle shrugged. "And what makes you think I'm the guy with the answer?"

"Because while Astruc may have been the priest, you're the preacher man. That mixing board is your altar, the microphone is your pulpit, and this magic bus is your flying church. You're spreading good vibrations to a world in need. And despite all the rules and regs on we-are-not-them and they-are-not-us, you're telling the locals they're not alone."

Krinkle took a long sip from his glass. "Are you suggesting that I'm promoting an unauthorized symbiotic relationship between our kind and the locals?"

"I'm suggesting you know we're finished without them."

It was the roadie's turn to light up. He took his time. Harper watched him, listened to the *ommm* of the magic bus. A few puffs later the roadie sat up.

"Okay, don't ask me how I know, but it breaks down like this: The only ones on this side of the light who knew about the prophecy were Astruc and Goose. Neither of them are spilling intel yet. Astruc might, soon as they pry open his brain, but Goose may never regain consciousness. Too bad—most of the intel on the prophecy is from him."

"How so?"

"Peabody, the EPFL wizard, he told you about the spiral notebook at the hideout?"

"The one they found with the kid's Stone Age computer? With the specs on connecting to Blue Brain?"

"And more. Including where you could be found in the tunnels under Paris."

"So he was working with our kind."

"Goose was half human and half our kind. Call him conflicted. Which half told him your ass was worth saving, I don't know. I imagine he let Gobet know where you were as a sign of good faith so he would trust him."

Harper inhaled a deep hit of radiance. He released it slowly. The roadie's good faith line made sense. "Trust the kid enough to hook up his homemade computer to Blue Brain and sync it with Voyager 1."

"Check. The kid is friggin' brilliant. We're not sure how he found out about the SOS. Couldn't have been Astruc, because he didn't know. Only ones who knew were Gobet, Professor Peabody, and me. But how the kid found out isn't even the interesting part. He had these incredibly vivid imaginations as a result of it. He imagined the same lines of causality you were talking about two minutes ago, except he imagined them fourteen years ago when he was twelve friggin' years old. He wrote them out in a thesis. Thirteen hundred pages of handwritten script in the classic Latin of the Roman Republic, no less. And get this: He wrote it with quill and ink. *De motu orbium et vita in terris*, he called it."

Harper smiled. "*On the Motion of the Spheres and Life on Earth.* Quite the title."

"And quite the read. It's an analysis of human history and how their history was shaped less by free will than the manipulations of the bad guys. The wildest part is he *imagined* their endgame when we didn't know what it friggin' was. The bad guys weren't just out to hijack free will in paradise, they needed to hijack the prophecy to hold on to it. Also, the thesis states the bad guys knew exactly when and where it would drop in space and time. That's why the world is the mess it is."

"Because?"

Krinkle took a slow sip of whiskey, then started up again.

"Dig it. The prophecy was supposed to drop in a world that *is* paradise, not the cesspit that currently passes for human civilization."

"A little harsh, isn't it? I mean there was the Axial Age, Renaissance, Beethoven. Not to mention the scientific method."

"True, but according to the thesis those achievements and all the others like it, including $E = mc^2$, mark diminishing returns more than progress. All through human history, especially after the scientific method dropped, the bad guys found ways of twisting the locals around and dragging them a hundred miles back for every small step they took away from superstition. I mean, look at the state of the world spinning beneath us right now, brother. The locals don't need the bad guys to lead them astray with fear and greed anymore. For all their friggin' enlightenment, the locals have become addicted to killing. Killing each other, killing the planet. They were supposed to have not only figured out that it's all one living organism, but living accordingly by now, that whatever they do unto the planet they do unto themselves. They still slaughter sentient creatures for meat, for friggin' sake. As far as Goose saw it, paradise was hitting the tipping point over which there was no chance of survival. The only hope was in the hands of the dreamers with brains enough to reach out to the universe, trying to get back to the beginning, to let everyone on the planet witness the Big friggin' Bang with their own eyes and understand the truth about life on Earth. Goose was doing everything he could to help mankind get that far."

Harper flashed through his briefing in the basement of EPFL.

"Professor Peabody called it 'the point of knowing.'"

"Peabody was quoting Astruc's son. And I'm telling you, I would, too. You read the kid's thesis and you understand why Astruc believed his son was the child of the prophecy. That and the fact Astruc had pretty much fried his own brain on homemade potions and couldn't handle the fact he had fathered a half-kind son."

"And Goose? Did he think he was the child of the prophecy?"

"Like I said, the kid was conflicted, so who knows what he thought? Besides, Astruc was pumping him with homemade potions, too, just to keep the kid alive. And double besides, what Goose thought of himself doesn't concern you and me or your mission, it's what he wrote about the prophecy's child in his thesis."

"Conclusion or prediction?"

"More like reading the handwriting on the wall. The locals reaching the point of knowing and the arrival of the child of the prophecy aren't just happening at the same time, they're codependent. The bad guys knew that one from the beginning. They've been waiting for the child to be born through ten thousand years of myths, legends, and religion. And now, as all those lines of causality would have it, they found him."

"Madame Taylor's child."

Krinkle nodded. "Killing the child is how the bad guys hijack the prophecy," he said.

Harper thought about it and sipped the last swig from his mug. "Prophecy null and void. No salvation for the locals or us."

Krinkle nodded again. "Only question is whether the child is dead already. That's why you need to get in and out of the time warp to tell us if we're as friggin' doomed as the locals."

"And if we are, what then?"

"Fuck if I know." He held out the bottle in pour position. "You want some more?"

"Sure. Nice to drink something that isn't juiced," Harper said.

"Who says it isn't?"

Harper sniffed his mug. "What was in it?"

"No idea, but where do you think that rush of babble came from? Which, according to the microchip in the hippocampus region of my brain, is now over. I'm being directed to brief you on the infil."

"You have one, too?" Harper said.

"Have a what?"

"A microchip in your head that switches things on and off."

Krinkle smiled. "You keep mistaking me for management. Told you before, I'm a grunt, the same as you. I just know a lot of things you don't."

The roadie refilled both mugs. Harper almost sipped.

"One thing before your microchip engages," Harper said.

"Make it fast."

"Madame Taylor's child, does he have a name?"

"His name is . . ." The roadie stopped talking and stared without blinking for two solid minutes.

"Am I supposed to guess?" Harper said.

The roadie snapped out of it and took a sip of whiskey.

"No, brother, you're supposed to give me time to hack through the friggin' microchip that engaged as I was about to tell you. Wait . . . got it. His name is Max."

TEN

i

It took Harper time to get his bearings. He was standing in the middle of a two-lane road that ran through an evergreen forest. He looked up at the watch on his wrist. The second hand had stopped. The watch was stuck somewhere back in real time.

He looked up, saw dull gray clouds churn above the trees. A fine mist fell and grazed his face. It had an oily texture and it reeked. He wiped the wet from his eyes, looked at the gloved palms of his hands. He saw streaks of filth.

"Whatever it is, it isn't rain."

He walked ahead and saw a sign posted at the side of the road:

GROVER'S MILL
EST.: 1932
POPULATION: 970

A hundred yards beyond the sign was the town, or what used to be a town. Buildings on either side of Main Street had been wrecked. Doors ripped off, windows smashed, façades pockmarked with blast damage. The street was strewn with rubble and debris. He took a step forward, stopped.

"Hang on."

He patted the pockets of his mackintosh, found the egg timer. He twisted its beak to the fifteen-minute mark and the thing began to tick. Not that it mattered. While rejoining the spinning earth and driving his bus toward the infil location, Krinkle had received flash traffic from Bern HQ: *Site increasingly unstable. Singularity imminent. Hold and standby. Orders to follow.* Instead, Krinkle crashed through the time warp's perimeter and opened the door of the bus.

"Here's where you get off, brother."

"They told us to hold and standby for orders."

"Too late. We were committed on the infil and there was no stopping without saying good-bye to half the Pacific Northwest. I think all bets are off inside this place, but stick with the timer anyway. Clear the town, get to the house as fast as you can. I'll circle around and crash through at the exfil point. Be there, or else."

Watching the bus back up through the perimeter and disappear into real time, Harper figured the odds on getting out of this bloody time warp before "or else" kicked in; a billion to one seemed a reasonable bet, especially considering the definition of the term. *Or else*: When a time warp is no longer able to resist the pressure of real time and collapses in on itself in less than a second, thereby reducing contained mass to an infinitesimal point of matter no bigger than a grain of sand. Just now, watching the plastic chicken count down the minutes to crunch time, Harper thought his billion-to-one bet was a sure thing.

"*Tempus rerum imperator,*" he said.

Harper dropped the timer into the pocket of his coat and walked toward Grover's Mill. There was a breeze blowing down the street. It smelled as foul as the filth falling from the sky. At the edge of the town Harper got a whiff of death. Coming onto Main Street he saw mangled corpses amid rubble and debris. Tens, hundreds of bodies. Partisans, the lot of them; pretending to be townsfolk, the roadie said on the bus. The corpses bore all the signs of slaughter at the hands of goons juiced to the gills on dead black. Throats slashed, disemboweled midsections, patches of skin carefully sliced from backs and legs.

Harper stood quietly and listened.

No murmurs, no cries, no souls begging to be comforted at the time of their death. The goons would have torn the partisans' souls from their bodies and cast them adrift. Like frightened things the souls would hover close to their dying forms, and then the devourers would sweep in to feast.

Harper walked slowly through the slaughter, scanned what was left of the faces. He counted two hundred seventy-three partisans, all of them adults, none resembling the image of Katherine Taylor on his timeline. Halfway down the street the wreckage was thicker. Chairs, seat cushions, tables; smashed plates and flatware, rotting food; a car door, a fender, shards of metal and nails. Farther up the street, cars and pickup trucks sat with melted tires or on their sides, windows blown out, side panels and roofs scarred by fire and flak from two separate directions. Twenty feet farther a blackened crater marked ground zero for a car bomb. He looked down to the rubble at his feet. He kicked over a table top, saw an arm that had been blown from its body. Scanning the street he saw more body parts and patches of dried blood. Again, all body parts belonged to adults; nothing suggested a child had been killed in the blast.

Riiiinng.

He grabbed at his coat and dug out the timer. He reset it, dropped it back in his coat pocket.

"One chance to get out alive down, three to go."

He looked at the building closest to the debris field. A one-floor, burned-out shell. Had to be Molly's Diner, he thought. According to Krinkle's brief the diner was one of four places Harper was to check for signs of Katherine Taylor and her son. Two in town, two at the house. The town and the house were separated by nine and a half miles, Krinkle said on the bus.

"I'll never make it from one place to the next with the time I've got," Harper told the roadie.

"There's a jump point."

"A what?"

"A quick way from one place to the next. It's a top-secret prototype built by Gobet's time mechanics. It was being tested on-site when the attack hit. Data received in Bern said it worked but only one-way, which is why you're going from town to the house. It's called Angel's Gate."

"You're joking."

Standing amid the slaughter just now, staring at the nothing that was left of Molly's Diner and the body parts scattered like rubbish, Harper considered what a bad joke it was. The kind that left a foul taste in the mouth, foul as the whatever it was falling from the sky. He scanned the street one more time, added it up. There had been two bombs here. Primary blast was from inside the diner, killing everyone inside and some in the street. Partisans locked within the perimeter rushed to the scene to render assistance. Then comes the secondary blast from a car bomb, killing many more. Survivors turned to run away. They were the unlucky ones; they ran straight into the killing knives of the goons.

He turned around, saw the wrecked storefronts across from the diner. One of them would be the small shop where Katherine Taylor worked; it was the second place to clear in town. Krinkle called the shop the Candle Lodge. A sign with that name was half hanging above the gaping hole where the door and windows used to be. He walked over, looked through the doorway. Twenty-nine partisans had come in here to hide. The goons found them and cut them to shreds. All adults, none matching the image of Katherine Taylor.

He walked into the shop, stepped over the dead, and checked the back rooms. A blond-haired woman lay on her stomach, her face turned to the wall. She'd been stabbed so many times, her limbs were barely connected to her torso. The blond hair popped hot on Harper's timeline. He moved closer, knelt on one knee. He almost touched the body, then stopped. Even dead a human form was not to be touched by Harper's kind without authorization from HQ. There was a smashed chair nearby. He picked up a chair leg and used it to pry the dead woman from the wall and roll her body onto its back. What was left of the woman's face didn't belong to Katherine Taylor. He dropped the chair leg and stood to leave. The woman's dead eyes were watching him. He gave it ten seconds to make sure her soul was gone.

"Aeternum vale."

He left the back room, walked out of the shop and onto the street.

The oily mist was heavier now and settling over everything. He checked the clouds again, then it hit him: The climate control system within the time warp was failing, causing humidity to spike. Harper looked at the filth on the palm of his right hand. He touched it with his fingertips, smelled it.

"Jesus wept."

The corruption of human flesh and blood was mixing with the humidity, then evaporating and rising as steam to the dome of the time warp. Up there, in the churning clouds, the steam coagulated and fell back to the ground as fetid mist. In Lausanne, forty-eight hours ago on the altar square, Inspector Gobet said this place would be like the ninth circle of Dante Alighieri's *Inferno* for any living soul trapped inside. Harper looked over the killing ground, watched the mist settle on the corpses and body parts. So far everyone in this place was dead. Maybe that was a good thing, Harper thought. Then, question: If the enemy's surprise attack went down just over forty-eight hours ago, why did the dead of Grover's Mill look like they'd been lying in the street for weeks? *Maybe the humidity is speeding decomposition,* the dead soldier in Harper's head offered.

"Yeah. Maybe."

The intersection ahead marked Elm Street. Krinkle told him there'd be a small park down Elm on the left side of the street. In the park, hidden behind a dogwood tree, was a path leading into the forest; thirty yards in was Angel's Gate. Pass through and you're one hundred fifty yards from Katherine Taylor's house.

Riiiinng.

Harper dug the timer from his coat pocket. Reset it to fifteen.

Tick, tick, tick, tick, tick . . .

"Two down, two to go."

He dropped the thing back in his coat.

He walked quickly, rounded the corner at Elm, saw the park ahead. He scanned the asphalt for any remains; none, but there was a coagulated blood smear coming from Main Street. It read someone had dragged a body around the corner. Didn't make sense, he thought. Goons didn't kill solo; they got off watching one another inflict suffering and death on the innocent. He followed the blood smear until it stopped. He saw a faint set of bloody boot prints on the asphalt. The prints continued down Elm Street and into the park. Harper crouched down for a closer look. The prints were made by a heavy-duty work boot with a neoprene sole. Then he saw the bloody imprint of a small wheel winding around and lining up with the boot prints. They looked recent.

"Like someone was pushing . . ."

He looked at the shop on the corner. BILL'S GARDEN AND HOME SUPPLIES, read the sign on the pockmarked wall. Like the other shops on Main Street the place was wrecked, but Harper could make out the merchandise that had been on offer. DIY home supplies, garden tools . . .

"Wheelbarrows."

He looked back and saw the drag marks of the body coming from around the corner. The marks stopped where the wheel imprint began.

"Someone was taking a body for a ride in a wheelbarrow."

He followed the boot prints into the park. They seemed to circle the brick walk a few times before finding the path into the forest. He walked to the edge of the brick walk, leaned around the dogwood, and saw the start of a dirt path leading into the forest. The boot prints and tire track went that way.

He thought about it.

After the attack, someone had carried a corpse from Grover's Mill to Angel's Gate. Questions: Who? Why? He reached inside his mackintosh, pulled his SIG Sauer from his kill kit, and loaded a round into the firing chamber. He raised the weapon, walked ahead. The path zigzagged now and again, but always moved deeper into the forest. He counted eighty-seven steps before he came to a clearing surrounded by tall evergreen trees. The path crossed the open ground, then returned to the forest, but not before passing through the lancet arch standing in the middle of the clearing. He didn't know which was stranger, seeing something that looked like it belonged in an English garden instead of a forest in the Pacific Northwest, or the boot prints and tire track heading straight for it.

Harper scanned the clearing with his SIG: no one. He walked toward the arch. It was made of very old limestone; the rise and span appeared big enough for someone pushing a wheelbarrow to pass through without ducking. Stepping closer Harper saw the path continue through the other side, but the boot prints and wheel track ended at the arch. He picked up a stone, tossed it through. The stone vanished midflight and the air between the stones wiggled. He walked up to the arch, reached out, and watched his gun disappear through the opening.

"What will they bloody think of next?"

He took a breath and passed through.

He saw the boot prints and tire track in the dirt again. He looked over his shoulder and saw the arch, but the limestone thing was standing in a completely different part of the forest. He reached back to the opening, this time touching an invisible wall. He tapped the barrel of his gun against it. It was solid and rang like steel.

"Definitely a one-way trip."

Then he felt it.

The temperature this side had fallen twenty or more degrees and it was hard to breathe. He looked up. The dull gray clouds were still churning, but instead of mist falling down there was a powderlike ash. He grabbed the collar of his mackintosh and pulled it across his nose and mouth. He continued along the path to where it met a one-lane asphalt road with a heavy log across it. He panned the road with his SIG: no one, and not a sound except for the ash falling through the trees. Off the road, down in a ravine, the shattered hulk of a GMC truck lay on its side. Harper saw skid marks on the road swerving away from the log, then wide tire tracks in the dirt down to the ravine. He looked back down the road, from where the GMC would have been coming. Ten yards that way was a traffic sign:

GROVER'S MILL 9.5 MILES AHEAD

DROP IN AND SAY HOWDY!

Harper holstered his SIG and climbed down into the ravine. He got to the truck's undercarriage, saw the slash marks of killing knives, saw them rise over the frame where goons swarmed over it. He circled around, saw the open hatch into the trunk: no one, but the interior roof was splashed with blackish blood and brain tissue. Signs read a goon had taken a head shot inside the truck. Coming around to the roof he saw the truck's exterior had sustained blast damage. Nothing like the bombs in town, more like a series of light explosives; hand grenades all gone off at once, most probably. Harper looked back to the road, imagined the scene. Whoever was in the truck had come from the town and been forced off the road. The passengers were surrounded, no hope. Somebody waited for the goons to attack and set off the grenades to take them down. Question: diversion, suicide . . .

"Or both?"

Harper leaned over the roof, looked inside the truck. The dashboard was loaded with technical kit and empty weapons mounts, the kind that read Swiss Guard tactical squad. Front seats were smeared with human blood; the smears read one or both passengers up front had been severely wounded before the blast. He looked in the backseat. No one and no blood. He saw something on the floor between the front and rear seats. Harper hauled himself up. He leaned into the truck, got hold of a piece of hard plastic, and pulled it out. He felt a cold shudder seeing the thing in his hand. It was a child's car seat.

"Mother and child were here. They survived the attack in town."

He scanned the ground around the truck, saw a trail of human blood and two sets of ash-covered footprints heading into the forest. He dropped the car seat, jumped from the truck, and hurried to the footprints. He knelt down, blew away the ash. The prints were weeks old, older than the boot prints he'd followed from town, and there were two sets here: one set of trainers, one set of boots. But these boots bore a different tread and size than the prints coming through Angel's Gate. Depth and angle of impact read both sets of prints were made by people on the run; sizes read two women. Katherine Taylor and Officer Jannsen, one of them carrying Max, Harper thought. *Had to be.* One of the women was bleeding badly. He flashed the blood in the front seat of the GMC. The Swiss Guard would ride up there, meaning Officer Jannsen was the wounded one.

She'd taken a bad hit; she was bleeding out. He looked ahead, his eyes following the prints.

"And she was trying to get mother and child to the bunker."

He walked quickly, his heart pounding in his chest. Forty yards on he rounded a bend and stopped cold at the sight before him. Just off the path, under a tall evergreen tree, two wooden crosses stood atop two fresh graves.

ii

The wind swelled and stirred the ash. She straightened up, listened for the cracking sound. It did not come this time.

"No fear, Kat."

She planted the shovel in the dirt. She pulled the PVC-coated gardening gloves from her hands and dropped them to the ground. She pulled the black scarf from her face and wiped ash from her eyes. She reached in her black wool cloak, found a small jar of Vicks VapoRub. She opened it, dipped her finger in the ointment. She smeared the menthol-scented stuff above her upper lip, just under her nostrils. She closed the jar, put it back in her cloak. She retied the scarf around her hair and face, leaving only her eyes exposed to the world. She reached down for the gloves and slipped them on. She grabbed the shovel and continued to fill the hole in the ground. She'd lost sight of the body a while ago, but six feet deep by one foot wide was a lot of hole to fill. Scoop and dump, scoop and dump, until a small mound of dirt equal to the mass of the buried body rose above ground level. She pounded the mound with the back of her shovel one hundred times, shaping it, forming it into something dignified. She coiled the rope she had used to lower the body into the grave and tossed it over her shoulder. She picked up the shovel, walked to the wheelbarrow. She laid the shovel across the pickax and draped the rope over the handles of the wheelbarrow. Next to the pickax was a wooden cross. She stared at it, thinking she had become much better in making them. They weren't much; just one piece of two-by-four nailed to another. But at three feet high and two feet across, the proportions were reverently crosslike. She dug through the rest of the tools and found the club hammer.

"Let's get it done."

She grabbed the cross with her right hand, the hammer with her left, and she walked back to the grave and laid the things on the ground. Nearby was a jug of Violette's Garden tea and four square-shaped stones. She picked up the jug and opened it. She pulled the scarf from her mouth and drank. It was the same routine each time. Dig down into the earth, hollow out a grave, lower a mutilated body into the ground, and bury it while drinking a jug of tea. One more swallow and she knelt down. She rested the jug on the ground, then arranged the hammer and the cross and the four stones as she always did. This act, too, was part of the routine. It wasn't an act of madness; it was an act she performed each time to prove she *wasn't* mad. Nothing random these days; everything organized. When all things were as they should be she pulled the permanent marker from the back pocket of her blue jeans and uncapped it. She wrote slowly along the arms of the cross.

Unknown Swiss Guard #30

She capped the pen and returned it to her pocket. She balanced the foot of the cross on the mound, grabbed the hammer, then, with four solid strikes, she anchored the cross into the grave. She lifted the stones one by one and set them around the cross. She pounded them into the dirt to brace the cross so it wouldn't blow over in the night's howling winds. When the stones were set, she laid the hammer on the ground. It was a good grave, she thought. She picked up the jug, got up, and faced the cross. She pulled the scarf from her face. She drank some tea to clear her throat.

"Here's where I make a speech. I try to say something different each time, but it always comes out the same, more or less. I don't know your name. I'm not even sure which one you are because there wasn't much left of your face. You're the thirty-third body I've buried and number twenty-nine of the unknowns. I'm sorry you're lying sideways instead of on your back. See, Anne was the first one I buried. I got the depth and length right, but the width was too narrow. When I lowered her down I couldn't get her on her back. Then I remembered Anne liked to sleep on her side. At least she was always on her side when I peeked in her room to watch her sleep. And as she was Swiss Guard and you guys were Swiss Guard, and the people in town were all working for you, I put you all on your sides, thinking you all might sleep better.

"After Anne, I buried the two guards I found at the top of the stairs leaving the bunker. There was one more in the control room and twenty-six in the yard. That's a whole other story. See, they were covered by bad shadows and cocoons for a while. When I saw it happen I ran the fuck away because I'd seen it before at Lausanne Cathedral. That's where Marc Rochat and . . . Sorry, you probably know all that stuff, don't you? Just because you're dead doesn't mean I have to bore you to tears.

"Please don't think me flippant. But I'm trying to hold on, see. And talking through what happened with each of you, each time . . . well, it helps. Each time I remember something else."

She took a long swig from the jug.

"I've been drinking my teas again, and they help, too. Though it's weird to be drinking this particular tea at the moment. It's called Violette's Garden. It's for the remembrance of pleasant memories. I haven't had any yet, but that's what it says on the jar back in the bunker. It's what I'm supposed to drink in the afternoons, so I do. Even as I dig graves. I suppose the fact I haven't jumped in with one of you and pulled the dirt down on top of me means the teas are working. But I have been tempted, you know? Jump in, pull the dirt down onto both me and the dead one just to end it. But I can't. There are still so many to bury. That's why I keep up with the teas.

"I always figure each of you wants to know what happened. Whether you died for something worthwhile or if it was in vain. You deserve to be told. It just takes me some time to get there so, please, bear with me."

She looked up to the tops of the trees. They were beginning that weird swirling motion. The winds were beginning, and the shade of gray in the clouds said she had another hour of daylight.

"As far as I can tell, after the bad shit happened, I stayed down in the bunker for a couple days. I think it was a couple days. There are no clocks or calendars here, none that work, anyway. I keep track the best I can and all I know for sure is it's been a while since I lost my son and Anne, and Molly and Lieutenant Worf, and the rest of you. But after however long it was, I decided I needed to bury Anne. See, drinking the teas helped me remember who she was. And I remembered I loved her. Did you know that? Did you know she loved me? No, I suppose not.

"Anyways, I dragged her up the stairs into the backyard to bury her. That's when I saw the other guys weren't wrapped up by bad shadows and cocoons anymore. They were just bodies on the ground. But that's a whole other story, too. I mean, before the house was burning nonstop, but it never burned down, and Jesus, it was so fucking weird. But getting up top with Anne's body, the house was just a massive pile of steaming ash. Then these howling winds came and blew the ash into the sky. At first the winds only came at night, now they come earlier in the day. And sometimes there's this cracking sound. First time I heard it I thought it was thunder. Now I can't tell. It just sounds like the world is breaking apart. Anne told me the truth about this place on the last day, when we were trying to get back to the house after the bombs in town. I remember her telling me we were locked inside . . . a time warp, she said.

"Jesus, I sound like a lunatic again. Stay with me, I'll get to what I want to say. Each time I bury one of you, I start free-forming it. Each time I find myself saying something more than planned. It's like talking to you guys is helping me. Like you're still protecting me. Burying you is the least I can do to repay you."

There was a swell of wind, and she lifted her arm to protect her face from the ash. Sometimes it felt like it wasn't just blowing by her, but nipping and biting at her. When the wind calmed she lowered her arm.

"Anyway, I needed tools to bury all of you. I couldn't find anything at the house so I walked back to town. I made the same walk with Anne lots of times. First time was right after I realized I was pregnant. That was the day I first met Molly at the diner. I was thinking of getting an abortion. Anne said I could if I chose to. But sitting with Anne that day in the diner, she told me I was carrying a boy and something happened. I wanted him to be born, and I wanted to protect him from harm. With Anne, with you guys, I thought I could be tough enough. You guys taught me how to shoot, and all that Krav Maga stuff. But I wasn't tough enough to protect him."

A glob of ash gathered at the back of her throat. She coughed, leaned over, and spit. She wiped her mouth with the back of her sleeve.

"Anyways, I was still a little dopey then, going to town after the bad shit happened, I mean. Otherwise I never would have gone, not if I had half a notion what I'd find there. I knew the killers were . . . well, I know they weren't human. Anne told me the truth about the killers the day the bombs went off in town. She called the killers goons. And when she told me, I remembered I'd seen them before at Lausanne Cathedral a long time ago, and there was someone there who called them goons, too. Did I tell you about the cathedral already? I can't remember if I did . . . Hold on a sec. This fucking ash hurts my throat."

She took a long drink of tea.

"In town there's a hardware store on a corner—you know the one I'm sure—and I went in and helped myself. Tools, tarps, gloves, rope, Wellington boots because my trainers were soaked with blood. The boots were a size and a half too big, but with the three pairs of work socks I stole, they fit all right. I stole a bunch of cleaning stuff, too. A couple pieces of lumber, some saws and hammers and nails. And I went back in the street and started walking through the dead to go home. Then I remembered that last day again, when bombs killed everyone. I remembered seeing Molly's body lying in the street, her head was somewhere else. I couldn't leave her that way. I thought she deserved to be buried, too. And as I had just stolen all the tools I needed, I thought—I know it's awful—*Dead people all over the street and I'm choosing to take care of just her,* but that's what I did. I picked up her body and put it in the wheelbarrow, then I found her head and did the same thing. It was weird, you know? The wheelbarrow never seemed to fill up, no matter how much I put in it. Like a dream . . . but it was real. I remembered there was this little park at the edge of town. I thought she'd like to be buried there. Then I thought perhaps she'd like to be farther away from the town so she wouldn't have to look at it. No, that's not it. I felt like I could hear her telling me she didn't want to be buried in town. I know it sounds strange, but that's the way it felt. *Take me to the park, honey,* she said in my mind. And when I got to the park she said, *Take me into the forest.* So I did. I was having a conversation with a dead person. I kept asking her, 'How about here, Molly?' And she said, *Just a little farther, honey.* I found this place with a stone arch and was really surprised, because I had never seen it before. But I guess Molly knew about it because she took me there. She said, *Over there, other side of the arch, honey.*

"I'm not sure what happened next. It was strange. I must have just kept walking and walking. Thing is, the strangeness of it didn't bother me. Like I said, I was still dopey as hell, so strange was the new normal. Somehow I got to a road, and I knew I was only a short way from the house. I knew because I saw the truck where Lieutenant Worf died, and I had passed it on the way to town to find the tools a few hours earlier. There wasn't a lot of Worf left. I collected everything I could find to be buried.

"Worf isn't his real name, I know. He told me his name once, but I can't remember it. See, we had this game. We both liked *Star Trek*, and he called my son Captain Picard and I called him Lieutenant Worf. My son . . . you remember him, don't you? I'm sure you do. I can't say his name. I know it, but I can't say it. If I do . . . I'll sink. And I need to hold on till I bury all of you. Anyway, my son tried to say 'Lieutenant Worf' but it always came out 'Woof.' That made us laugh, then my son laugh. Anne laughed, too. I remember that."

She took a breath, bit her lip.

"I was tired by then, and night was falling. So I left Molly with Woof—I mean Worf. I covered them with a tarp, secured it with rocks, and I went home with the wheelbarrow. Back there I secured tarps over the bodies in the yard, too. The next day I got up, went upstairs, and went to work. Took me a day and a half to bury Anne. When I finished I stood at the foot of her grave, like I am with you, and I wanted to cry but I couldn't. Believe me, I have wanted to cry at all your graves, but I can't."

She calmed herself, drew a long breath, and stared at the cross.

"I know how much you suffered trying to protect my son. You fought to the last bullet, then you fought with your bare hands. I wish I could tell you what happened to him, but I don't know. All I can tell you is there's a hollowness in me that says my son is gone forever. Probably not what you wanted to hear, but that's the truth of it. You didn't deserve to die so horribly, none of you deserved what happened to you. I am so sorry for everything. That's all I wanted to say."

She tucked the jug under her arm and retied the scarf around her face, leaving just enough of an opening for her eyes to see. She picked up the hammer from the ground and walked away. She loaded her things into the wheelbarrow, grabbed the handles, and lifted it. She looked back at the grave.

"If I don't come this way again, it's not because I forgot about you. And if the winds ease I'll go back to town and bury the rest of them, I promise. But the winds are coming earlier each day now. At first they only came at night. Sometimes there's this cracking sound. First time I heard it I thought it was thunder. Did I tell you that? Did you ever hear it, lying out here in the night? No, I suppose not. Rest in peace, number twenty-nine."

She pushed the wheelbarrow up to the road and headed home.

ELEVEN

i

Riiiinng.

Harper pulled the egg timer from his coat, reset it to fifteen.

Tick, tick, tick, tick . . .

"Three down, one to go."

He dropped it in his pocket and picked up his pace down the one-lane road. He'd lost precious seconds staring at the crosses in the forest where conflicting sensations held him in place. The locals would call the first one relief in seeing the names on the crosses didn't belong to Katherine Taylor or Max; the second would be guilt in feeling relieved. *Emotions,* Harper thought, *are not the things of our kind.* He shook them off.

"Focus."

He flashed the scene at the graves as he walked to make sure he got it right. The crosses, the scripts reading *Molly* and *Lt Worf.* Someone, the same someone he'd been tracking from town, had taken great care in burying the bodies. Someone capable of expressing benevolence and sorrow in equal measure. *But who?*

A raw wind shook the forest, and he blinked himself to nowtimes. He looked up, saw the tumbling ash-choked sky and the tops of trees bending wildly; then came the sound of thunder.

"Bloody hell."

He broke into a run till the road cut right and ended at the torched hulks of two GMC trucks in a tree-lined driveway. The trucks looked set in a defensive position to block access to the house but had been quickly overrun. Beyond the trucks, across a yard, was a great slag heap of ash, sodden from the humidity, but the cold wind kept the top of the heap dry and a funnel of ash wound its way up into clouds so thick that the fading light of day could not pass through them. Had to be the house, Harper thought, and there was nothing left of it to clear.

He squeezed by the trucks, hurried up the driveway. Krinkle said there was an outbuilding thirty yards up the drive; it was the last site to be cleared. Coming clear of the trees, Harper saw the battered structure with its broken screen door flapping in the wind. Three more steps and he saw the whole of the backyard. There were rows of graves in the middle of it. Perfectly set, identical to the forest graves.

"Bloody hell."

His mind tried to sort it.

Inspector Gobet's mechanics thought time within the warp had stretched to a ratio of four to one since the attack. That would yield a max of eight days within the perimeter while real time outside clocked only two days. Two graves in the forest, plausible; more than two dozen more in the yard?

"No bloody way."

He flashed his timeline: Krinkle's bus crashing through the time warp, seeing the roadie behind the wheel. He opens the door for Harper to get off, telling him all bets were off with time in the perimeter . . . use the egg timer anyway. Harper blinked himself to nowtimes, pulled the timer from his mackintosh. Silence. For a moment he thought the plastic bird was done for. He gave it a shake . . . *tick*; another shake . . . *tick*. Seemed crunch time had already begun and seconds were being squashed like swatted flies. The sound of thunder cracked again.

"Swell."

He dropped the egg timer in his pocket and quick-marched along the graves to check the names. In the last row of three: *Unknown Swiss Guard #28, Unknown Swiss Guard #27, Unknown Swiss Guard #26.* The next row counted down twenty-five to twenty, then nineteen through fifteen. All the graves exactly the same, all the names on the crosses written by the same caring hand. He got to the first row. Unknown Swiss Guards numbers four through one and one more. He faced the name on the cross.

Anne Jannsen

He staggered under the weight of a new sensation. Back in the forest, seeing that the two graves did not belong to mother and child, he'd told himself they were still alive. He realized it wasn't a deduction based on fact; it was nothing more than a desire with expectation of attainment, aka hope. He'd seen it a billion times on a billion faces and never understood it. But standing before the graves, Harper *felt* it.

"This cannot be real."

The dead soldier in his head chimed in again: *It's real enough, boyo; keep moving.*

He turned, jumped up the porch steps. He looked inside the control room while brushing ash from his hair and coat. The place was wrecked with all the signs of a hellish last stand. He saw the door across the room leading to the bunker and marched straight for it. Three steps on he realized he was walking on a path that had been cleared through the wreckage. There were boot prints on the floor, coming and going dozens of times. The prints matched the ones from town; the treads were marked with blood, mud, and ash.

"It's got to be her. If she's alive, then maybe Max . . ."

He flew down the stairs to the first tunnel. Krinkle said there were nine false turns and dead ends, that it might take a bit of hit-and-miss to find the way. In fact, the slash marks, bullet scars, and black blood on the walls made it easy. All signs read the goons chased after their prey like famished beasts. And that the last of the Swiss Guards put up one hell of a fight to get mother and child into the bunker. He ran faster, slammed into walls at sharp turns.

"Sod it!"

Around one more corner. *Stop.* Staring at two dark tunnels: one to the left, one to the right. He dug his cell phone from his coat, tapped the screen, pointed the dim blue light toward the tunnels. Going left was clean. The right tunnel bore slash marks and bullet scars, but no black blood. He moved into the right tunnel and picked up the scent of detergent and bleach. He traced his fingers along the wall; the surface was damp.

"She's been scrubbing the place clean."

And as he uttered those words, the tunnel ended.

He was standing at the top of a steep stairwell. A heavy wool blanket had been strung across the bottom of the stairs. Light and fresh air bled over the top of the blanket. Between his phone and the light from the bunker, Harper saw the stairwell had been well scrubbed, too.

He dropped the phone in his coat and walked silently down the steps. He listened for proof of life from within the bunker; nothing. He got to the wool blanket, almost called out her name. *Negative. Get in, raise your hand to her eyes and put her under, get the hell out of there.*

Harper eased aside the blanket. The primary smash job on the steel door was pure goon. But three heavy lengths of timber had been used since to pry open the door even more and anchor it in place.

He crossed the threshold, stood still.

A camp bed and crib over here; against the wall was a kitchenette with a small table, one adult chair and one child's high chair; an open door to a bathroom over there. The bathroom would be the only place anyone could hide down here, and he listened for a breath or a heartbeat; nothing. The place was empty.

He looked at the camp bed again. He saw small scratches in the concrete wall, eye level with the pillow. He walked closer and leaned down for a better look. The scratches weren't random. They were like the graves in the backyard—all perfectly set. Eight groups of five, side by side in two rows of four. Each group was made up of four vertical scratches with a fifth scratch cutting horizontally through them. He saw a string tied to the side of the camp bed. He pulled it and found the six-inch nail tied to the end of it. He stood, touched the sharp steel point, then stared at the scratches on the wall. She'd been marking her time. Two rows of four, eight groups of five.

"Forty bloody days?"

He pulled the egg timer from his coat. It was still. He held it to his ear, shook it. The gears rattled and hummed . . . *tick.*

"This cannot be good."

He dropped the timer in his coat pocket and walked slowly around the room, thinking the place had been smashed up but made neat. No slash marks or bullet scars on the walls. The battle ended at the stairwell, he thought. The smashup inside the vault was a result of anger or madness; the cleanup was submission to a brutal fate.

Something gnawed at his guts.

He turned around, scanned the place again. His eyes locked on the table and chairs, the way they faced each other. *Look down, boyo.* There were skid marks on the floor where the adult's chair had been moved in and out at the table. The floor under the high chair was spotless. He walked to the shelves, saw the jars of baby food. All evenly stacked as if never touched. He looked at the dish tray next to the sink. There was one dinner plate, a fork and spoon, one glass; all washed and left to dry.

He walked to the bathroom, turned on the light. He saw the empty frame above the sink where a mirror used to be. He saw an adult's electric toothbrush and a half-used bar of soap on the sink; he saw one towel hanging from the rack. He stepped in, touched it. The cloth was damp. He opened the medicine cabinet behind the ex-mirror. The child's toothbrush inside had never been used. He walked back into the living space and stood at the crib. He saw the neat bedding and the pajamas with grinning sheep printed on them. The pajamas were folded crisply on the blanket, never worn from the look of them.

Sensation: hope slipping away, aka despair.

Click.

He felt a gun barrel touch the back of his skull.

ii

"Do I have your complete attention?"

It was a woman's voice, worn but familiar.

"Quite," Harper said.

He heard boots shuffle back over the concrete floor. He counted seven steps.

"Turn around, slowly."

"I'm not a threat. I'll raise my hands to prove it."

Silence.

"If your hands so much as twitch, I'll paint the wall with your brains."

The tone registered don't-fuck-with-me serious.

"Slow it is, then," Harper said

He paced his turn to a five count. The woman he expected to see wasn't there. In her place was a ghostly, ash-laden form with emerald-green eyes. The ghost was pointing a Glock 35 at his head.

"Madame Taylor?"

Without taking her eyes off him or lowering her gun, she used her free hand to loosen the scarf wrapped around her head. Ash fell from her as if shaking off snow. The scarf was black; so was the cloak she wore. And when the scarf dropped to the woman's shoulders, Harper saw a shock of raggedly cut blond hair.

It was her and not her at the same time.

The facial features matched the image on his timeline. But the once smooth skin was marred with scratches and scrapes. More than anything it was a face barren of expression.

"Well, well. What do we have here?" she said.

"Do you recognize me, Madame Taylor?"

She eased her free hand under her gun hand to support her targeting.

"You're Jay Harper. You're a security consultant at the IOC. At least that's what you said you were when last we met. Lausanne Cathedral, wasn't it? I was stoned to the gills, shot up with potions given to me by little men in white coats. You pretended to care. And you called me 'Miss' in those days. Gone all formal on me, have you?"

This time the tone registered bitterness.

Harper focused on the Glock. She held it like a pro. Her grip was firm and her finger was inside the trigger guard. He figured the odds of making a move, came up with 1,000 to 1 chance of getting to her and knocking the gun away before she could fire.

"Go ahead. Make my day," Katherine said.

"Sorry?"

"The move you're thinking about. Go for it. I know you guys can move fast. Question is, are you faster than a speeding bullet?"

Harper stared at her, wondering how the hell she got inside his head.

"That's right, Harper, I know what you are. Anne told me the day before your friends came to town."

"My friends?"

"Killers, bad shadows, devourers of souls . . . your fucking friends. After all, you're all the same, aren't you?"

"No. We're not the same."

She tilted her head slowly to the left as if to get a better look at Harper's face.

"Ah, let's see, you and Inspector Gobet, you're the good guys? And the ones who raped me in Lausanne, slaughtered Anne and the others, they're the bad guys?"

"Yes, that's how it is."

She tilted her head to the right, studied Harper's face from that angle.

"Oh, how the lies drip from your lips. You're really good at it. Like your 'I'm no threat' line. Soon as you said it I remembered you in Lausanne Cathedral. Waving the palm of your hand before my eyes and sending me to dreamland so you could do with me as you wanted. Is that what you guys did to Anne and all the others to make them trust you? You waved the palms of your hands before their eyes, fed them fairy tales in their sleep about good guys and bad guys? Is that what you did to Marc Rochat?"

Harper flashed the lad falling through the sky, saw his body on the ground.

"The lad chose to protect the cathedral, to protect you, of his own free will."

She edged to the bed with Harper in her gun sights. She reached down and pulled something from under her pillow. She threw it to Harper and he caught it. He saw the halting script on the cover.

piratz

Une histoire drôle de Marc Rochat

pour Mademoiselle Katherine Taylor

"He was a brain-injured child in a man's body. He could barely write his own name. He lived in a world of angels and bells. So let me tell you how it is, Harper, how it really is with the poor kid who wrote that book, with Anne, with everyone. Once upon a time, the cop, you, and all your fucking friends crawled out of the same stinking gutter, and you've been fucking us over and calling it 'free will' ever since. Everywhere you go people die. Everyone I love dies."

She'd talked long enough for Harper to get a read on the manner of her thinking. Katherine Taylor's mind was broken by an unspoken grief. Just then a faint rumble echoed in the tunnels. No matter how much time was getting squashed, this bloody world within a world could only be a few ticks from destruction.

"Where is Max?" Harper said.

Her jaw clenched tight and she did not speak.

Push her.

"Is Max dead?"

Rage flashed in her eyes. She rushed at Harper, set the barrel of her gun to the side of his head.

"Shut up! You do not get to say his name. No one gets to say his name. Just shut up about my son. He was never my son, he was always one of them. He belongs to them. I was only the hooker who delivered him."

He could grab her gun and put her under now . . . *No, keep her awake till she spills the intel on Max.* He waited for her to blink. When she did, she lost focus long enough for Harper to scan her eyes. He found phantom images in the axons of her optic nerves, images she was hiding from her consciousness. As he uploaded them into his own eyes, he sensed her body relax, as if a great burden had been lifted from her. He had her now. He let the images roll in his own eyes and he forced Katherine Taylor's broken mind to see them.

"This is how it happened. Officer Jannsen was rushing you down the stairs. Two guards at the top of the stairwell were holding off the killers, but they ran out of ammunition. Then you heard them scream as the killers went at them with knives. Officer Jannsen got you into the bunker and started to close the door. You begged her to get in with you and Max, but she didn't. You heard the killers charging down the stairs. Jannsen told you she loved you, forced the door closed on you. The hydraulic bolts slammed into their sockets. It was quiet. Max was in shock. You hit him with an injector jet from the med kit. You were holding him, comforting him. For a moment, you hoped he was safe. Then the killers started to break in."

Harper felt the barrel of the gun shake against his head.

"You put the gun to the side of your son's head, same as you're doing to me just now. You were going to kill him, but you hesitated. That's when the killers cracked open the steel door and seeped in. You panicked, pointed the gun at them as they took human form, and fired. The shot passed through them and into the stairwell. They got to you, tore your son from your arms. You reached for him. You saw his face as they carried him away. He was looking at you, he was afraid. Then one of the killers jabbed you with a needle and you were paralyzed. The last thing you remember is your son screaming *'Maman.'* It all happened so fast, you were left with your arm as it was when you last held him. You hate yourself for panicking, for not killing him. You can't bear to imagine what's happened to him. You can't even say his name. If you do, you'll sink."

He scanned her unfocused eyes. He was deep within her consciousness.

"Madame Taylor, listen to the sound of my voice. Max is still alive. Do you hear me? Max is still alive."

As if being hit with a live wire, she bolted a meter from him, then adjusted her targeting at the kill spot between Harper's eyes.

"You're right, you're not the same as the bad guys. The bad guys only raped my body, you just raped what was left, you filthy piece of shit."

The concrete room shook and the sound of cracking thunder rumbled through the outer tunnels. She quickly glanced to the stairwell; looking back she saw the palm of Harper's right hand in her eyeline. She froze and held her breath, waited for her soul to be guided. He almost spoke the words of the spell to put her under, but her desperate voice replayed in his head: *He belongs to them. I was only the hooker who delivered him.* Then he flashed the vestibule of Lausanne Cathedral. His first trip to the place on Inspector Gobet's orders years ago, before he was awakened, even. When the heavy wooden doors closed behind him it was quiet, but he had the feeling he wasn't alone. He looked up. Above the high arch that opened to the nave there was a statue of the Virgin Mary. She was enthroned under a sky of faded stars painted on the stone ceiling. Her head and hands had been sawed off. Long ago, from the look of it. The stub of her neck suggested she was looking at him anyway, and the articulation of the arms suggested she'd been holding a child at her breast. He blinked back to nowtimes, saw Katherine Taylor standing statuelike and still.

And the stone was made flesh, he thought.

He closed his palm into a fist, slid both his hands into the pockets of his coat.

"Max isn't one of them," he said.

She'd been primed for guidance and she would remain still until her soul realized it had to find its own way and reconnect to her consciousness. If the plastic egg timer in his pocket was working, it'd clock the wait at 3.2 seconds. Coming to, she snapped the gun at him.

"What did you say?"

"Max isn't one of them. He doesn't belong to them."

"What does that mean?"

"The ones who raped you in Lausanne didn't make you pregnant."

"They drugged me and raped me for days. I woke up in a semen-soaked bed."

"I know what they did to you, but that's not how you fell pregnant."

She shook her head, afraid to believe him. "How then? Who did it?" she said.

"No one. Max is your son and your son alone."

"What?"

"When I waved my hand in front of your eyes years ago at the cathedral, the way you were talking about. The three of us were there, you, me, the lad with the lantern. Do you remember why I did it?"

He could see her mind working.

"Yeah, I had a dream."

"That's right. You said you dreamed about a man on the altar. You said he walked you around the altar, stood you in the light passing through the cathedral rose in the south transept wall. He turned your palms to the light and told you he was—"

"Protecting the life within me."

"That's right."

She became anxious. "It was a dream, Harper. And the man of my dreams was a fucking bum."

"The bum's name is Monsieur Gabriel. He's one of us."

"Stop it."

"Listen, there's a prophecy about a child conceived of light, born into the world to guide the creation through the next stage of evolution."

"Stop it, I said."

"Max is that child."

"Fuck off!" She put the gun to her own head. Harper saw the wet of tears forming in her eyes. "No more fairy tales, no more lies, Harper. Find yourself another whore to play with."

She took a breath, closed her eyes. Harper reached for her.

"Don't!"

Then a booming voice down the stairwell. "Hey, anyone down there lose a cat?"

Katherine wobbled and Harper charged. He ripped the gun from her hand. He made the move before she could open her eyes—not quite as fast as a speeding bullet, but fast enough. And it left Katherine Taylor disoriented. She stumbled, fell back onto the camp bed, and opened her eyes. Now heavy steps down the stairs.

"What is happening?" Katherine said.

"Not sure, actually."

As he said it, the ash-covered roadie appeared at the bunker's entrance with a fat, ash-covered cat dangling from his hand. The animal was disoriented and submissive. Its legs dangled in the air like limp spaghetti. Harper thought the beast looked familiar.

Mew.

"Monsieur Booty?" Katherine said with a disbelieving voice.

And as she pronounced the cat's name, Harper saw the beast on his timeline. In the belfry during the cathedral job. It was the lad's cat. *More of those wonders never ceasing,* Harper thought.

Mew.

Tears formed in Katherine's eyes. "Oh my God."

Krinkle lowered the cat to the floor. It ran to Katherine and jumped on her lap. At first, she was afraid to touch it.

"It can't be . . . How?"

The cat snuggled close to her.

"Jesus, Boo, it is you. You're alive."

Mew.

She cradled her arms around the beast. "They took Max, Monsieur Booty. They took him away."

Mew.

The cat purred, and Katherine lowered her head. She took a sharp breath, then trembled and wept as if holding the only living thing left to her. Harper looked at Krinkle. The roadie had his index finger to his lips: *Quiet, brother.* Harper knew what was coming. *No.* But Krinkle had already shifted space and was standing behind Katherine Taylor; he had an injector jet at the back of her neck.

Click.

She did not react for a moment, then slowly, she raised her face. Harper saw a heavy dose of comfort flood through her eyes. She blinked, saw Harper. He scanned her, got a read. It was as if a sword had been embedded in her heart and there wasn't enough comfort potion in the world to ease her suffering. He walked to her, knelt before her on one knee.

"Max is alive, Madame Taylor. Do you hear me? Max is alive."

She looked at him as if trying to comprehend his presence. "Harper?"

Down the stairs came a squad of Swiss Guard in tactical gear; they stopped at the entrance of the bunker. Krinkle waved them in with a whisper. "Get her to the bus. We're out of here, pronto."

The guards surrounded Katherine Taylor and wrapped her in a shock blanket.

"You're safe now, Madame Taylor. Come with us."

"But what about Monsieur Booty?" she said.

"Bring the cat with you, madame."

She rose from the bed without resistance with the cat in her arms, and the Swiss Guards led her slowly to the stairs. When she disappeared from view, Harper looked at Krinkle.

"I suppose it was bloody necessary to juice her up. Not like she hasn't had enough."

"I do what I'm told to do."

Harper nodded to the stairwell. "How long have you been out there?"

"Long enough, brother. I was just waiting for the proper moment to announce myself, apparitions being what they are."

"Apparitions."

Harper walked around the room with the Glock in his hand. A camp bed and crib over here; against the wall was a kitchenette with a small table, one adult chair and one child's high chair; an open door to a bathroom over there. He looked back at Krinkle.

"And the lad's cat? Where did you find it?"

"We crashed through the time warp, opened the door, and there it was. It mewed, turned around, and led us here. Smart friggin' cat."

"That it is. Why hasn't the bloody time warp collapsed yet?"

"Couldn't say, just yet."

"Meaning not until I ask the right question."

"That's generally how a mission debrief works."

Harper made the tour around the room again, stopping at the kitchenette to look at the lad's book on the table. He read aloud the words on the cover.

"Piratz, a funny story by Marc Rochat for Mademoiselle Katherine Taylor."

There was a flash of light in his eyes and he saw himself with the lad. On the roof of the belfry as evening fell on the last day of the lad's life. He pulled the book from his black coat and showed it to Harper. It was full of drawings about a caterpillar and little men in paper hats and an evil wizard and a beautiful princess and a fat gray cat.

"I made this story for her when I thought she was an angel," the lad said.

"It's swell," Harper said to him.

"Merci."

Looking at the lad's face, Harper could tell something bothered him. "What is it, mate?"

"I know the truth about her now and don't know what I should do with the story, monsieur."

Harper smiled at him. "I think you should give it to her. I think she'd like it."

"C'est vrai?"

"Yes."

The lad pulled a pen from his long black coat and held it to Harper. "I'm not very good at spelling, monsieur. Would you help me write on the cover? I know the words I want to say."

Harper blinked to nowtimes.

He felt something burn in his eyes. He raised the Glock and ejected the bullet from the gun's firing chamber; it chimed hitting the concrete floor. He dropped the gun on the table; it landed with a thud. He reached in his coat pocket and found the plastic egg timer. He dropped it on the table, too. He picked up the Glock by the barrel, aimed the gun's butt, and hammered down.

Riiiinng.

The timer broke open to reveal a rusting winding mechanism and a tiny bell. It was ten times the size of the thousands of nanometer-sized electrical circuits scattered across the table.

"Well, well. What do we have here?"

A few of the circuits landed on top of the lad's storybook. He brushed them off and grabbed the book. He rolled it up and stuffed it in his mackintosh. He walked to Krinkle.

"What the fuck is this place?"

The roadie nodded. *At last, you're asking the right friggin' question.*

"A dark wood, where the true way is wholly lost," he said.

The words popped hot. From the opening line of Dante's *Inferno*.

"That would be a place called Hell," Harper said.

"Check."

"There's no such place."

Just then the earth quaked and spiderlike cracks opened in the walls. Black mist began to seep in and crawl along the floor. Krinkle looked at Harper.

"Yeah, that's what we thought. Turns out we were wrong."

TWELVE

The black train did not stop at Khabarovsk or Chita and passed through those towns unseen. Coming to the Buryatia steppe, the train raced through forests of conifer and larch. The forests were vast, broken only by villages that appeared beyond the windows in ripping flashes.

In the parlor car Komarovsky was alone, sitting in a Chesterfield armchair of burgundy leather. It was the only chair in the sparsely furnished space of oak-paneled walls. There was a mating bed in the corner. The red silk sheets were disheveled and smelled of sweat. The length and width of the floor was covered with a Fereghan carpet from the Markazi province of Iran. The carpet was unique, hand-crafted for Komarovsky in 1918. The border was indigo with shades of green, woven in series of curvilinear patterns that seemed to move with the motion of the train. The central medallion, set in a red field, was a tightly woven pattern of ivory-colored triangles surrounding a cluster of black interconnected circles, three feet in diameter. Like the carpet's border, the circles seemed to move with the motion of the train to take different shapes. Now the inner workings of a clock, now the orbits of the spheres, now the flower of life.

Tinted windows and the single floor lamp near Komarovsky kept luminance levels low in the parlor car. The lamp glowed at 1.0 lux to create a sensation of drifting through moonlight. In this place Komarovsky could remove the dark glasses from his silver-colored eyes.

On the nearby side table was a tombac samovar and a porcelain tea set with polychrome paintings over glaze. The samovar had been handwrought by the gunmaker Nikolay Mailokov in 1837 and presented as a gift to Tsarevich Alexander II of Russia. As emperor, young Alexander started off well: ethnically cleansing the Circassian people from the North Caucasus and decreeing Jews had no place in Russian cities. He later developed absurd notions of himself as "liberator of the serfs." But he was easily disposed of by a bomb in 1881 while riding in his sleigh. A charming scene: legs blown off, stomach torn open, his face disfigured beyond recognition. The tea set had been commissioned in 1883 as part of the Raphael Service by Alexander III, ridiculously dubbed "the peacemaker." In truth his Russian nationalism, carefully inspired by religious fanatics within the Orthodox church, was most helpful in setting the stage for the slaughter of sixteen million souls in the Great War with Germany. The Romanovs were such an amusing family; so amenable to suggestion. The tea set was a favorite of Komarovsky's. The delicate grisaille painting of Cupid presenting a garland to Venus, goddess of love, delighted him. A wisp of steam rose from Cupid's cup and found its way to Komarovsky's nose. It invited him to taste the somniferous potion again.

He took the cup and sipped.

It tasted bitter.

He closed his eyes and dreamed.

"Yes, my goddess, come to me."

She approaches; he smells the scent of her oiled skin. She sinks to her knees before him, opens his robes, takes his penis into her mouth. Her pupils dilate as the potions in her blood release a rush of rapture. She is bewitched and does not turn her eyes from him. She feeds on his pleasure as if it is the source of her own. He touches her long blond hair.

"My goddess, my goddess."

A chime sounded.

Komarovsky opened his eyes and returned Cupid's cup to its saucer. He picked up his dark glasses and set them over his eyes.

"Adjust to one hundred lux."

Light levels in the car increased to the dullish glow of an overcast day.

Komarovsky pressed a button on the side table. The door opened and in came a beautiful man wearing a cutaway coat and pinstripe trousers; the man closed the door gently. Komarovsky watched him cross the Fereghan Sarouk carpet and stand on the center medallion. The chamberlain bowed and raised his eyes, but he did not dare to look directly at Komarovsky. Instead, he maintained an unfocused gaze at the far wall.

"Speak to me," Komarovsky said.

"Lord, the chief physician wishes you to know the child remains in stable condition following the procedure."

"What did he find?"

"A microtransmitter implanted in the child's thigh. It has been removed."

"The child has no pain?"

"No, lord."

"He must not know pain or fear. He must remain in a state of grace until the time of his sacrifice."

"As you command, lord."

A proficient chamberlain, and pleasing to the senses as beautiful creatures should be, Komarovsky thought.

"And the transmitter?" Komarovsky said.

"It has been analyzed by your attendants. It appears to have pinged once when the vessel carrying the boy was opened in Alaska. They have tracked the ping to an Inmarsat communications satellite in geostationary orbit above the Pacific Ocean. Your attendants assume the ping was detected by your enemies."

Komarovsky lifted Cupid's cup and sipped. "Without a doubt."

Of course, the chamberlain thought, *the master knows all things; and all things serve the master's purpose.*

"Yes, lord."

Komarovsky sipped again and closed his eyes. He longed to be reunited with his goddess. The chamberlain stood silently on the center medallion of the carpet until the master returned from his reverie.

"Is there something else that requires my attention?" Komarovsky said.

"The chief physician requests an audience, lord."

"I wish to be alone with my dreams."

"I have expressed your wish to him, lord. He remains most insistent."

"What is the issue?"

"He believes it necessary to discuss the state of your present form, without delay."

"I see."

Komarovsky set the cup in its saucer. He turned, opened the drawer of the side table, and removed a small lacquer-painted jewelry box. He laid it on the table. The chamberlain allowed his eyes the quickest of glances to see the picture on the lid. It was a painting of a Siberian folktale: Tsarevich Ivan, the Firebird, and the Gray Wolf. The chamberlain knew the contents of the box. Inside were potions of pleasure or punishment to be dispensed as the master deemed fit. The chamberlain looked away and focused on the far wall as Komarovsky turned back to him.

"Show him in."

The chamberlain bowed, and in a well-rehearsed move, he stepped back nine steps to open the door without turning away from Komarovsky. On the outer platform the chief physician stood erect and resplendent in his copper-colored robe. In his right hand he held a long staff of polished wood topped with a small carving of a pterosaur skull. It was the ancient scepter of his office. The chamberlain made a gesture with his hand: *You may enter.*

The chief physician paraded in in a manner befitting his high position. He passed the chamberlain without regard. He stepped onto the central medallion of the carpet and made a flourishing bow. Komarovsky studied the physician's face as it was raised to him. He did not think the face as beautiful as it should be. But so far the physician possessed invaluable skills; allowances could be made for his imperfection.

"Speak to me," Komarovsky said.

Unlike the chamberlain, the physician looked directly at Komarovsky. The knowledge that he was granted such a privilege inflated the physician with great pride.

"My lord, I have reviewed the latest reports relating to your present form. I am obliged to come to you with a recommendation. With your permission, of course."

Komarovsky nodded.

"Lord, we are concerned the particular form you occupy will reject your divine being."

"We?"

"Myself, lord, and the council of physicians who attend to your well-being."

Komarovsky placed his hands together and bowed his head as if in prayer. "Did I not command that potions be created to prevent rejection of my form?"

"Indeed, lord. And I did make them. However . . ." The physician searched for the proper words.

"Yes?"

"Lord, the potions are not performing as well as I had hoped. Their efficacy is lessening. Therefore, I am concerned."

Komarovsky signaled the chief physician to step closer. "Explain your concern."

The physician glanced at the chamberlain standing at the door with that look of one who sees nothing but hears all. *Such a presumptuous little turd,* the physician thought, *daring to share the divine presence with me.* He stepped closer to Komarovsky and spoke softly.

"Upon your returning to the world six months ago, the clone has been subjected to physical variables. Cellular regeneration is failing to keep pace with morbidity levels. Stem cell infusions are ceasing to correct the problem."

"What will be the end result?"

The physician hesitated.

"The end result would be unimaginable, lord. You are our Lucifer, our only guide through the darkness."

Finishing his diagnosis, the physician gave an unctuous bow. Komarovsky touched the place over his own heart.

"How wonderful your adoration is to me."

The physician inflated again, this time with self-satisfaction. "I am at your service, lord."

"Yes, you are. How long will I be able to dwell in this form given your diagnosis?"

"Weeks, a month at the most."

"I need more time. I need much more time."

"Lord, the risk is too great. If morbidity reaches—"

"I have heard from other members of the council that new potions could be developed to forestall any rejection. Is that not true?"

The physician appeared uncomfortable. "Lord?"

"Is it necessary for me to repeat myself?"

"No, lord . . . I . . . Well, yes, that is the opinion of some. But it would require introducing the clone to more intense psychoactive potions. We are well advanced in the cloning of soulless human forms, of course, but cloning was developed for the purpose of organ harvesting. A clone, in and of itself, is not a suitable temple for your divinity. I must assert my position as your most trusted advisor and urge you to hear my voice above all others. You must abandon your current form."

Komarovsky stared at him. "And do what, chief physician?"

"Lord, I have taken the liberty of selecting a new form for you to occupy. I brought him on this trip so that you may judge him yourself."

Komarovsky signaled the physician even closer. "What does he look like?"

The physician turned to the chamberlain. The servant was still standing in the open door, still pretending to not notice a thing. *Cretin.* The physician cleared his throat, leaned closer to Komarovsky, and whispered.

"A most magnificent specimen, lord, I must say. He will more than meet your standards of beauty. He is of noble lineage, directly descended from the Rus of Kiev. He is a true epicurean, a creature of the finest breeding and taste. I have seen to it, personally, that his desire for pleasure has been encouraged throughout his life, nothing has been denied him. He is in perfect health, gifted with an excellent physique. And he is, lord, extremely virile."

Komarovsky reached for the jewelry box. He pulled it closer and opened the lid. Inside were six hypodermics containing an assortment of chimeric colors. They glistened in the dim light of the parlor car; as they glistened they changed hue from one forbidden color to the next. The physician was encouraged. He had often received the gift of pleasure by catering to the master's lust.

"Continue," Komarovsky said.

"I have prepared an entertainment in my private railcar for your viewing. Four lovely women, abducted in Vladivostok, are now being induced into a state of the most exquisite craving. I selected the women myself so that the Rus's abilities will offer their best display."

Komarovsky fingered the hypodermics. "Tell me more."

The physician wet his lips. "I am confident, lord, you will find the Rus a fitting temple for your divinity for as long as you require. And once occupied the form will continue to experience all sensations as you know them now."

"Instead of all those new sensations on offer by the council."

"Lord?"

"More intense psychoactive potions to suppress rejection. I must say, they do sound inviting."

"Yes, lord, but—"

"But what?" Komarovsky said.

"We are close to the place of complete and utter darkness in the workings of our craft. The things that are proposed by the council are too dangerous to contemplate. You must accept my recommendation, lord."

"I see. Then tell me more about your magnificent new form. What is the color of his hair?"

The chief physician was confused for a moment. "His hair, lord?"

"Yes, his hair. What color is it?"

"It . . . it is brown . . . lord."

Komarovsky looked down at his own long, silver hair hanging to his shoulders. He lifted a handful and let it slowly fall before his eyes. He sighed.

"I do not think I'm in the mood for brown."

"Lord, the color of the hair is a trivial matter compared to the many pleasurable benefits that will be available to you in the new form."

Komarovsky removed his fingers from the hypodermics. He touched his own face, feeling the texture of the perfect skin. "But what if I accept your recommendation and awake only to find my new face is not as beautiful as the one I have now?"

"But lord . . . you have no reflection. Your face is of no consequence. All that matters is after I transplant your eyes into the new form, you will continue to rule as the divinity you are."

"Are you sure?"

"Lord?"

"Are you sure I would not reign as a less beautiful divinity so that your influence within the council would grow to match mine?"

The physician feigned a combination of surprise and grief. He lowered himself to his knees. He offered his throat to the master as was the custom. "I am your most loyal servant, lord."

Komarovsky stared at him, giving the physician time to see his own reflection in his master's dark lenses. When he thought the physician fearful enough, Komarovsky leaned close to him and breathed deep.

"Then why, dear chief physician, do you reek of mendacity?"

The physician blanched. "No, lord."

Komarovsky grabbed the physician's throat. "Look at my face. I cannot see its reflection, not even in your eyes, but it is a face of great consequence. It is the face a goddess has worshipped and adored. It is my pleasure to keep it, and I will not be seduced by your deception."

"Lord, I have not deceived you."

Komarovsky dug his fingers into the physician's neck and found the rings of tracheal cartilage and primary bronchi. He dug deeper, searching for the man's windpipe and larynx.

"Confess that you find the Rus more beautiful than me, confess that you love the Rus more than me. Confess and I will be merciful."

The physician dropped his scepter and grabbed at Komarovsky's hand. Komarovsky squeezed harder.

"Confess!"

"Lord . . . I . . . adore you."

Komarovsky reached into the jewelry box with his left hand and selected the hypodermic containing a shimmering black-green liquid. He stood from his armchair, and with the physician still in the clutch of his right hand, he raised him from the floor. The physician dangled and kicked. Komarovsky carried him across the carpet and held him above the central medallion.

"Your adoration no longer pleases me."

Komarovsky pulled the physician close and rammed the hypodermic into the back of his neck. The physician was blinded and cast into darkness. He opened his mouth to cry out, but there was no sound.

Lord!

"Receive my divine judgment."

No, lord!

The blinded physician heard Komarovsky chant in *voces mysticae*, secret words only the master was permitted to speak aloud. When he heard the words, a terrible vision unfolded in the physician's mind. He saw himself dangling above the carpet, still grabbing at Komarovsky's hand. Then the border of the carpet swirled clockwise and the curvilinear patterns dissolved into a fast-moving stream of indigo and green, then all color faded away. A single black thread emerged in the center of the medallion. It stretched and weaved itself counterclockwise.

Oh, please, lord!

As it weaved, it grew; as it grew, it weaved faster. Now the size of a coin, now the size of a plate, now absorbing the central medallion and becoming a black hole that opened down into the deepest pit of the earth. The blinded physician heard much weeping and the gnashing of teeth.

Please!

The physician first saw long shadows slithering up the walls of the pit. Then he saw long talons at the ends of spindly hands; then he saw grotesque beasts with hideous faces but no eyes. The beasts were covered in boils and lesions; black drool dripped from their gaping mouths. They sniffed the air and caught the physician's scent. They wailed with hunger and swung their talons at the physician's legs. He kicked frantically.

No, please!

The beasts' talons caught the flesh of his calves and dug in.

Ahhh, no!

The beasts clawed their way higher. They tore through his robe, sliced into his guts, and ripped his soul from its flesh.

I beg you, lord!

Komarovsky crushed the physician's windpipe at the peak of the man's fear and the vision was ended. Komarovsky released his grip and the physician's body fell to the floor. It convulsed atop the central medallion of carpet for a few seconds, then it did not move. It was a dead thing sprawled over the flower of life. Nearby was the scepter of office the physician had cherished with great pride. Komarovsky picked it up and held it out to the chamberlain.

"Present this to the council. Tell them I am in need of a new chief physician. Tell them I am intrigued with the promise of new sensations to maintain my current form, then leave them to their greed. Whichever of them survives may claim the scepter."

"Yes, lord." The chamberlain gestured toward the body. "Shall I dispose of *it*, lord?"

Komarovsky searched the high corners of the train car. *Not yet, but soon.*

"Leave it."

"Of course, lord."

Komarovsky returned to his armchair; the chamberlain bowed to leave.

"The Rus from Kiev," Komarovsky said, "have you seen him with your own eyes?"

The chamberlain felt his mouth go dry with fear; he could barely breathe.

"Earlier, I served him a light supper in the chief physician's private car, lord."

Komarovsky looked at the remaining hypodermics in the jewelry box. He lazily touched them one by one. The chamberlain watched from the corner of his eye; he felt the master's gaze return to him.

"And is he as described? A remarkable specimen? A worthy temple for my divinity?"

Cold sweat dripped down the back of the chamberlain's neck.

"I do not consider him as beautiful as described . . . lord."

Komarovsky closed the jewelry box. The chamberlain calmed.

"Where is he now?" Komarovsky said.

"Presently, he is taking champagne, lord. He awaits to be entertained by the four women abducted in Vladivostok."

"Ah, yes, the entertainment."

Komarovsky turned to his tea service. He opened the sugar bowl and scooped out a teaspoon of brown sticky liquid. He let the liquid drip into the teapot. He set the pot under the samovar and opened its valve. Boiling water poured out and clouds of steam ascended to the ceiling of the parlor car. Komarovsky closed the valve, covered the teapot, and poured the potion into Cupid's cup. He lifted the cup to his face and inhaled the fumes.

"Are the women beautiful?"

The chamberlain nodded. "I have no doubt they would offer your divinity immense pleasure, lord."

Komarovsky sipped slowly and dreamed a moment.

"The women are not to be touched by the Rus or anyone. Continue to induce them with craving potions until we reach the dacha. They may attend to me there."

"As you command, lord. But what shall be done with the Rus? He himself is already in a heightened state of craving."

"Deliver him to my attendants to be flayed alive. Tell them they may feast. You may join them if you wish."

The chamberlain bowed. "You are most generous, lord."

The chamberlain slowly exited the parlor car without turning his back on Komarovsky. On the outer platform he bowed once more before closing the door. Komarovsky drank from his teacup until it was empty. He replaced it in its saucer and settled into his armchair. While waiting for the potion to affect him, he heard a fluttering sound. He removed his dark glasses and rested them on the side table.

"Adjust."

Light levels in the parlor car lowered to moonlight.

He closed his eyes and listened to the sound of the physician's soul flutter about the passenger car, searching for a place of safety like some confused and frightened bird. *Yes,* he thought, *that's the sound.* They were all that way when torn from their flesh; like frightened birds, hearts bursting in their breasts.

As the train reached the southern shore of Lake Baikal and turned north into the Irkutskaya Oblast, Komarovsky sensed the soul was beginning to understand its fate. It would see the dead body on the carpet and know "there was the place I once lived," but now it was lost and adrift.

"Now it begins," he whispered to the soul.

Komarovsky kicked back his head and squeezed his eyelids tighter to release the full force of the potion. There was a burst of dead black in his mind. His hands clutched the arms of the chair, and his entire body became rigid. *Delightful, how delightful!* To add to his joy Komarovsky summoned the night spirits from the forests. He commanded them to dance with the soul, to chase it from corner to corner, to spin it in dizzying circles, to batter it with torment. And so it was as the black train raced unseen through the sleeping land.

At dawn the train passed Yekaterinburg and was not far from kilometer 1776 of the Trans-Siberian Railroad. Komarovsky released the night spirits and listened for the fluttering sound again. When he heard it, he smiled. He opened his eyes to see the frightened thing tremble before him. It was exhausted and falling into despair. Komarovsky raised his right hand and pointed to it as he had done in the beginning two and a half million years ago, when he first created the soul of man.

"I am the lord thy god, thou shalt have no gods before me."

Book III

THE RED HEIFER

THIRTEEN

PEACE ACTIVISTS ARRESTED AT QUMRAN

Israel Interior Ministry confirms discovered scrolls are in ancient Hebrew

PA claims Israel using find to remove Palestinians from their land

Special to *24 Heures* by Julian Magnolly in Jerusalem

In dramatic scenes broadcast worldwide, Israeli security forces have secured Qumran National Park near the Dead Sea after nineteen activists from the Tel Aviv–based group Peace and Justice rappelled into caves where the Dead Sea Scrolls were first discovered in 1948. The activists occupied the caves throughout the day, displaying banners calling for the Israeli government to hand over newly found scrolls to the Palestinian Authority. The activists used their own camera equipment and satellite phones to conduct interviews with the world's news media during their occupation of the historical site.

IDF spokesman Natan Liberman told reporters covering the standoff that all the activists had been arrested and would be charged with criminal trespass.

"It's a disgrace that Jews invaded a Jewish historical site demanding that Jews return artifacts of Jewish heritage to Palestinians. They want peace and justice, good, but let's not be stupid about it."

Liberman added there was damage to the interior of the occupied caves and the activists would face further charges once archaeologists from Hebrew University made an assessment.

The scrolls were first discovered two days ago after American tourists stumbled across the entrance to a previously undiscovered cavern. Adam Schwartz and Nicole Davies from Los Angeles, California, were rock climbing in a mountainous area one and a half kilometers southwest of the archaeological site of Qumran, where the Essenes maintained a settlement until the first century AD.

"We reached the summit and stopped to rest," Schwartz, 27, told *24 Heures.* "We had a view of the Dead Sea and the Jordan Valley, and we could see the Qumran settlement. Then the ground under us began to sink. We jumped away in the nick of time just before a deep fissure opened up. It's a miracle we weren't killed."

The Americans had crossed a thin shelf of sandstone, covered by centuries of dust that gave way. Davies, 23, used a flashlight to see down into the fissure. There appeared to be an opening in a side wall at the bottom.

"It looked interesting, and we love exploring caves," she said.

Schwartz used climbing rope and carabiners to lower his GoPro camera, mounted with a small LED light, down the fissure to film through the opening to see if it would be safe to enter. When he pulled up the rope and reviewed the camera footage, he was stunned.

"It was surreal," Schwartz said. "There was a skeleton on the ground. I thought it was a grave."

The two Americans hurried to the tourist center at Qumran National Park to notify officials. Rangers from the Israel Nature and Parks Authority soon arrived to investigate the scene. Within hours, media outlets descended on the park to report the discovery.

INPA ranger Ofir Segal said in an interview broadcast on Channel 2, "At first, we thought it was a hoax. It wasn't until we got into the cavern that we realized a major archaeological find had been uncovered. Yes, there was a skeleton down there, but it wasn't a grave, it's where someone had lived. Jars with scrolls, writing tools, a table and stool, pottery and wood spoons in near perfect condition. It is an astounding discovery."

Asked if there could be a connection between the man in the cave and the Essenes, Segal said, "Whether the skeleton belonged to an Essene who wrote the newly discovered scrolls, or was only guarding them, or whether he was a wanderer who came along much later and made the cave his home, remains to be seen."

In the same interview, Irit Halevi from the Israel Geological Society explained the Jordan Valley and Dead Sea region's geological significance.

"The Jordan Valley and Dead Sea region has always been a geologically active area. We have evidence of major earthquakes during the early centuries of the current epoch, and one can only assume there were just as many that were undocumented. Any one of these seismic events could have easily shifted the ground in a way as to bury the cavern. It's practically beyond belief that this discovery was made. It's like hitting the lottery."

Not everyone was as pleased. On hearing the news of the archaeological find, the Palestinian Authority claimed ownership as the discovery was made outside the boundaries of Qumran National Park, on Palestinian land illegally occupied by Israel. The Palestinian Authority insisted the cavern and all its contents were the property of the Palestinian people. Demonstrations broke out the same day in Jericho and Ramallah, calling for Israel to surrender control of the site. The next day, Friday, Palestinian youths took to the streets of East Jerusalem following Muslim midday prayers and made the same demand. The situation escalated when Palestinians atop Temple Mount threw stones down onto Jews praying at the Wailing Wall. Israeli police and Israeli Defense Forces entered the Temple Mount compound, called Haram al-Sharif by Muslims, and clashed with hundreds of Palestinians. There were forty-nine injuries, including fifteen Israelis, but order was quickly restored.

Israeli government spokesman Amit Zohar said of the clashes, "It doesn't take much to start a riot in Jerusalem, but this time the Palestinians are barking up the wrong olive tree. If anything, the discovery of these scrolls proves the lands of Judea are not 'illegally occupied.' They are Jewish lands occupied by Jews long before the Palestinians got here. The motivation of the Palestinian Authority in encouraging these riots is to suppress the truth."

PA Chief Negotiator Walid Hadawi, based in Jericho less than six kilometers from the Qumran discovery, responded angrily in an interview broadcast on Al Arabiya, the most-watched Arab-language channel in the world.

"This is typical of Israel. They dig up a clay cup or a pot and say, 'See, this proves this is our land. This proves you do not belong here! Get out of Israel!' If that's the case, then every American in the United States should get back on the *Mayflower* and go back to Europe and return the land to the indigenous people the Americans stole it from. And the Israelis should give the land back to the Canaanites whom the Israelis stole it from. If the Israelis want truth, this is truth: UN Resolution 446, not to mention ninety-four more UN resolutions passed since 1955 condemning Israel's aggressive policies against Palestinians and our Arab neighbors."

It was at this point that the nineteen activists from Peace and Justice became involved by occupying the caves where the Dead Sea Scrolls were found in 1948.

The leader of Peace and Justice, Sarah Ornstein, 47, has long been a thorn in the side of Israeli officials for her headline-grabbing actions. Most recently Ornstein led a demonstration at the Wailing Wall in 2012. Ornstein and six other women dressed as Hasidic men and began to chant, 'Your religion is a crime against women!' The female demonstrators were attacked by Hasidic worshippers and badly beaten in front of news cameras.

Yesterday, in an interview conducted with the BBC during her occupation of Qumran just before IDF moved in, Ornstein said, "If Israel is to survive, we must stop using our religion as a weapon of oppression. Whether against women, Palestinians, or anyone Booboo-

stein doesn't like. If we are the chosen people, then we must choose to be better than this."

Ornstein often refers to Israeli Prime Minister Yossi Borstein by the moniker "Booboostein." On his way to yesterday's morning cabinet meeting and asked to respond to Ornstein's latest taunt, the prime minister laughed it off with "There she goes again."

Lost in the political melee is the fate of the scrolls, as a veil of secrecy has been drawn over them. It's assumed the newly found scrolls will be transferred to the Israel Museum in Jerusalem to be studied. When contacted by *24 Heures*, the public affairs office of the museum said all questions regarding the scrolls should be referred to the Interior Ministry.

Pressed by Israeli media during a news conference discussing the security situation in Jerusalem, Interior Ministry spokesman David Cohen was brief in his comments regarding the scrolls.

"The only thing I can tell you is the only thing I have been told: The scrolls are written in first-century Hebrew, and they are genuine. That fact alone should end any discussion, or illusions, as to the ownership of the scrolls."

Reliable sources within the Interior Ministry have confirmed to *24 Heures* that the skeleton found in the cavern is being studied at the site by forensic experts from Hadassah Medical Center. DNA tests are being conducted to determine the ethnicity of the bones. If found to be Jewish, within scientific probabilities, the bones will be buried before the next sundown according to Jewish law.

The Interior Ministry source also told this reporter that the park's closure will continue and that the hills surrounding Wadi Qumran will remain off-limits to everyone but authorized IDF personnel for the foreseeable future. Asked if the ban included members of the Nature and Parks Authority, the source responded, "It means everyone."

Harper set the newspaper on the leather settee. He watched Krinkle continue with his breaking-and-entering rampage, on a computer this time.

"And this means what?" Harper said.

"What?"

"The article."

"Read the fine print under the headlines," the roadie said.

Harper gave it a glance.

Special to *24 Heures* by Julian Magnolly in Jerusalem

"And that means what? And while you're at it, what are we doing here?"

Here was a posh office perched on a balcony and fitted with glass walls overlooking an aircraft hangar. Two silver Learjet 70s were parked on the hangar floor. They gleamed in the 300,000 lumens of eye-popping brightness cast by a high bay lighting rig. The jets were undergoing maintenance, but at 02:30 hours the hangar was empty. There was a huge banner hanging from the ceiling and stretching the length of the hangar. WELCOME TO ALASKA AND ARCTIC X AIR SERVICES: SERVING PREFERRED CLIENTS AROUND THE WORLD, it read in English, Russian, Chinese, and Japanese. The banner gave the hangar a friendly, happy-to-be-so-damn-rich feel. The fact they had arrived here in the dead of a bitterly cold night and let themselves in (Krinkle picking the locks, dismantling the security system, and turning on the lights with three claps of his hands) raised questions in Harper's head. Not to mention following the roadie through the hangar and up the stairs, where instead of picking the lock to the office, he kicked open the door and marched straight to the Dell workstation on the only desk in the room. He tapped the keyboard, and the screen awakened and asked for a password. Krinkle picked up the keyboard, flipped it over. There was a piece of paper Scotch-taped to the underside.

"Aha."

"Aha what?" Harper said.

"The password to the arrivals and departures files is 'drowssap.' You know how many computers in the world have a backward 'password' as a password?"

"A few?"

The roadie laid down the keyboard. "Three hundred million, nine hundred forty-six thousand, eight hundred twenty-nine, the last time I checked."

"So whoever owns this computer isn't the brightest bulb in the ceiling."

Krinkle pulled out his cell phone and opened an application. He held the phone next to the screen. Harper leaned over the desk and saw the X-rayed innards of the screen displayed on the roadie's cell phone. There appeared to be some extra padding and wiring along the edges. Krinkle nodded respectfully.

"Composition C-4. Nope, they're really smart here. I enter *drowssap*, the screen goes bang in my face."

"Big bang or little bang?"

"Big enough to fuck up the rest of the night." He unbuttoned his navy peacoat, pulled a folded newspaper from the back pocket of his overalls, and handed it to Harper.

"I got stuff to do and Inspector Gobet left orders for you to read the article on the front page. Go sit over there."

Over there was the leather settee at the other end of the office. A nearby window offered a view of Arctic X Air Services' apron, connecting taxiways and the distant runway lights of Anchorage International Airport.

"Right."

Harper walked to the settee, opened his mackintosh, and sat as instructed. He scanned the front page: "Intense Street Fighting in Riyadh; Saudi King Declares State of Emergency." "New Ebola Strain Grips Malaysia; Thousands Die Each Day." "Russian Ruble Collapses as Kremlin Financial Scandal Deepens." There were pictures with the stories: Islamic fighters in black kaffiyeh running through a bombed-out street; a truckload of dead bodies being dumped into a mass grave outside Kuala Lumpur; Russians storming a Moscow bank.

"Which one?" Harper said.

"Huh?"

"Which article am I supposed to read?"

Krinkle was banging at the keys like someone who forgot he said the computer was wired to go boom if annoyed.

"Below the fold," the roadie said, not taking his eyes off the screen. "The one about the peace activists arrested at Qumran."

Harper flipped the paper, saw the headline about the busted peaceniks. He wasn't through the first paragraph when he caught a foul scent coming from his coat. And touching his hair, he felt traces of the oily slop that rained down inside the time warp. No wonder the roadie told him to "go sit over there." Truth be told, Harper felt a bit on the foul side. The trip in and out of the time warp was like riding a cosmic merry-go-round. He couldn't shake the sensation he was still going in circles. He looked at his hands; they were trembling. He heard the dead soldier in his head: *No worries, it'll pass.*

"Sure it will," Harper mumbled to himself. He closed his eyes, replayed the last few hours—more like those minutes of the last few hours in which he was compos mentis.

As they'd come up from the bunker and into the yard with the perfectly set graves, the ash-choked wind howled and jagged bolts of lightning shot from the clouds and stabbed the ground. With each strike there was a deafening *CRACK* and the world did quake. Crunch time had arrived. Krinkle's magic bus was humming and waiting at the end of the driveway, half punched through the warp's perimeter. Krinkle climbed on and jumped into the driver's seat. Harper followed and the door slammed shut behind him. High-pressure seals hissed and it was quiet in the bus. Katherine Taylor was already onboard. He saw her through the open door to the rear compartment. She was half sitting on a bed, propped up by two Swiss Guards. One more was taking her blood pressure, and another was scanning her eyes with a penlight.

"Hang on to something, brother."

Harper grabbed the railing along the steps; Krinkle put the bus into reverse and punched the accelerator. For a moment nothing happened; then came that droning bell hum from under the bus floor. Then the world beyond the windows stretched and snapped and they were surrounded by brilliant streaks of colored light from one end of the electromagnetic spectrum to the other. Then the bus was sitting at mile marker 128 of Carson City Road as night claimed the day. One side of the road was an evergreen forest, the other side a black hole in the ground the size of a football stadium.

"That's what's left of the time warp?"

"No, that's what's left of a fireball event."

"Sorry?"

"A comet fragment that falls to earth. No big deal. Happens all the time. At least that's what the SX guys in Bern are putting on the Internet as we speak. Inspector Gobet has the local police securing the area. This is a no-go zone till we leave."

"When do we leave?"

"Soon as I get clearance to roll. In the meantime we sit."

Krinkle shut down the motor and killed the lights. Harper looked beyond the windshield. He considered the fact that one big, black bus was sitting in the middle of the road with its lights off. And it was dark outside.

"How long was I inside?"

The roadie shrugged. "Well, it was daylight when you went in and it's dark now. So let's call it a lot longer than you should've been. That order to hold on and standby was because one of Gobet's computer geeks at HQ added two plus two again. He came up with how really fucked up time was inside the warp. You were to wait for the tactical squad to get lined up along a new set of exfil points."

"But I was already inside."

"Meaning you were going to end up nowhere where we thought you'd be. You were way lost in the shifting sands of time, brother. That's why we went in."

"Hoping I'd blow by."

"Amen."

Harper looked back at Katherine. Her eyes were open, but she was oblivious to her surroundings. So much so that she didn't object when one Swiss Guard lifted the cat from her arms. The other guards eased Katherine onto a gurney and laid her down. They covered her with a blanket and strapped her down.

"Her forty-eight hours became forty bloody days in there. She went mad with grief. She was burying rotting corpses like some hideous penance for not killing her son before they snatched him.

"And if you hadn't found her before the warp collapsed, she'd still be doing it. I mean it would've been lights-out for you, but for her it would be never-ending."

Harper looked at Krinkle. "Sorry?"

"The enemy juiced her with a new agony potion. It has severe psychotropic effects, the wildest being a local's mind doesn't die with the body." The roadie nodded to the would-be meteor strike beyond the windshield. "She'd still be somewhere in that friggin' hole, trapped in a singularity. Her forty days would have become four hundred years, then four thousand. She never would have finished burying the dead. There would be no end to her grief."

Harper thought about it. "You're telling me the enemy injected Hell into her mind?"

Krinkle shrugged. "You surprised? Till now the bad guys injected the locals with the *idea* of Hell through religion and superstition. Now, with this new shit, they can juice the locals with thirty cc's of the real deal."

Harper checked the action in the rear compartment. One of the guards was fitting an oxygen mask over Katherine Taylor's face while another opened a valve releasing God-knows-what into her lungs. The lad's cat had found his way back to her and curled up next to her on the gurney.

"Hey," the roadie said, "she's in good hands."

Harper nodded. "How long have you known about this new potion?"

"Since you went in with the plastic chicken. As you may have gathered by smashing it to bits, it was more than it appeared."

"What did it do?"

"It was a gizmo from Gobet's biomechanics, the same guys who made your bioskin gloves. It collected and analyzed Katherine Taylor's DNA signature floating around inside the warp. Flakes of skin, hair follicles, exhaled carbon dioxide. The data was uploaded on my onboard computers when I crashed through the perimeter. Results matched trace from—"

"Wait a sec. The egg timer I had to crank every fifteen minutes was a biotelemetry device?"

"And to keep you straight when we thought the time warp was operating at a four-to-one ratio like I told you at EPFL. But yeah, primarily it did other stuff."

"You bastard."

"Hey, don't go there. They didn't know if the thing would work, and I didn't want to bore you with details. You had enough to worry about. And they couldn't use a battery without igniting the ash cloud, so you had to power it the old-fashioned way."

Harper stared at him. "You said you picked it up at a hardware store in Renens."

"That particular hardware store is a front for Inspector Gobet's biomechanics. Needless to say, Gobet isn't pleased you broke his chicken. It was a one-off."

"Too bloody bad."

Just then the high trees beyond the windshield swayed and black dust kicked up from the black hole in the ground. Harper leaned forward, looked up at the starry night. A dark shadow drifted over the trees, then descended through the sky to blot out the stars. It was a Sikorsky-class helicopter landing in black ops mode without anti-collision or position lights. And though the main and tail rotors were spinning furiously, it was almost silent. It touched down in the middle of the road and the side hatch slid open. Red interior lights revealed the unmistakable form of the cop in the cashmere coat. He climbed out of the chopper followed by Mutt and Jeff. They marched toward the bus. Harper looked at Krinkle.

"I guess he really is pissed off."

"He's also Madame Taylor's ticket out of here. There's a hospital jet waiting in Spokane. Gobet's taking her to Switzerland."

"I thought we were waiting for orders to roll, I thought we were taking her. Your bus can get there in three and a half hours."

Krinkle pressed a button on the dashboard. The high-pressure seals hissed and the door to the real world opened.

"Speed isn't the problem, brother. It's getting her out of here without the bad guys knowing she's gone. Besides, you and I got another job. Look out, the squad needs to get by you."

Harper turned around and saw the squad carrying Katherine through the bus. When she got closer, he saw her eyes looking at him. She was going deep, but she was trying to hold focus on Harper. *Please.*

"No, hang on. You can't do this to her."

"Step aside, Mr. Harper. You've done enough damage for one night."

Harper turned to the voice calling from outside the bus. It was Inspector Gobet.

"Let me at least go with her, Inspector. She's in bad shape, she needs me," Harper said.

"You? You're a killer, Mr. Harper, not a guardian angel. Trust me, you're the last thing she needs."

"For Christ's sake, Inspector, she's had enough."

The Inspector glared. "Be that as it may, Mr. Harper, if you do not get out of the way right now, my men will drag you off the bus and remind you of your place. And Madame Taylor will still be put on the helicopter with me."

Harper flashed Katherine in the bunker: *Once upon a time the cop, you, and all your fucking friends crawled out of the same stinking gutter.*

"Get stuffed," Harper said.

Those were the last words he spoke till he came to, lying on the floor of the bus, his head throbbing to a heavy four-four beat. Krinkle was at his control panel with his headphones on; reel-to-reels were rolling and music was blaring through the speakers just like old times. The roadie noticed Harper regaining consciousness. He switched off the speakers, pulled off the headphones, spun around in his chair, and offered Harper a cup of steaming tea.

"What happened?" he said.

"I hit you with a little something to shut you the fuck up, much to the disappointment of Gobet's muscle. They were anxious to beat the crap out of you. The guards carried Madame Taylor off the bus and away they flew, us too."

"Where are we going?"

"Sixty-one north at one forty-nine west. More or less."

"And that would be?"

"Alaska."

Harper's mind had fogged up and it took a couple seconds to work out the location on a map. He felt the back of his neck where the needle had jabbed him.

"You really like to jab people with needles, don't you?"

"Me? Fuck no. Needles give me the creeps. But I needed to shut you the fuck up."

Harper sat up against the wall, took the tea, had a sip. "What's in the tea?"

"Essence of *Ornithogalum umbellatum*."

"Tastes flowery."

"It is. Star of Bethlehem, it's called. I added a spoonful of organic honey to sweeten it. Drink it."

"Orders from the cop?"

"Nope. It's a homeopathic doodah Karoliina whipped up for me once. In the real world it helps dogs adjust to the sorrow of loss."

"The sorrow of loss. In dogs."

"Yup. Drink some more."

Harper did, then he chuckled. "Your dream catcher prescribes you herbal remedies for sorrowful dogs?"

"Karoliina says the closest thing to a genuine angel on earth *is* a dog. Finish it."

"If you say so." Harper downed the brew.

"Feel better?" Krinkle said.

"Arf."

"Good boy. Let's go walkies."

Harper blinked.

He was back in the office of Arctic X Air Services at the end of his sixth trip on the cosmic merry-go-round. He'd been looping through beforetimes, unable to get a lock on nowtimes. Finishing the article on the peaceniks at Qumran for a seventh time and setting the newspaper on the leather settee, he watched Krinkle continue with his breaking-and-entering rampage, on a computer this time, and asked him the meaning of this and that . . . *And while you're at it, what are we doing here?* Harper felt the cosmic merry-go-round slam to a stop, aware of what had been causing him to loop through beforetimes. It was a single frame of Katherine Taylor on his timeline, a twenty-fourth of a second of real time. Not enough to see, but enough to cause a skip in his mental processing. She was staring at him with such agony in her eyes: *Harper?* The frame had lodged itself in his timeline like someone desperately holding on and not wishing to let go. But it was not her holding on, it was him holding on to her. Then the microchip embedded in the hippocampus region of his brain kicked in and began to erase the image so Harper could restart his mental processing and get on with the bloody job. As the image was wiped away, he felt something dig at his guts. The sorrow of loss it was.

"Right."

He lifted the newspaper, read the byline under the headline.

Special to *24 Heures* by Julian Magnolly in Jerusalem

He detected incoming lines of causality.

FOURTEEN

Katherine saw herself as the twelve-year-old girl she once was, wearing the white blouse, blue skirt, white socks, and black patent leather shoes of her school uniform. The noon bell had rung and she was with the other girls of her class, who in two perfectly formed lines followed Sister Superior through a long hall. The old nun wore a black habit and veil with a white coif fitted tight around her wrinkled face. She led her flock with determined steps, and Katherine watched the long rosary dangling from the nun's belt. The black wooden beads and metal links rattled against the silver cross bearing the crucified Christ.

The hall opened to a colonnade running through a garden. It was late in the spring term; the air was fresh and the sun was warm. Katherine smelled orange blossoms and jasmine. In the middle of the garden a stone grotto sheltered the lifelike statue of the school's patron, Our Lady of Peace, the Virgin Mother. She wore a white veil over her hair, and a white tunic with a gold belt, and there was a blue cloak over her shoulders. She held a small wooden cross in her arms. Three letters, *IHS*, were carved into the cross. She stood atop a rocky hill, and her bare right foot was crushing the head of a serpent. The statue's ceramic blue eyes watched all passersby.

"Mother Mary is always watching you," the old nun often said with a tone of admonishment for sins past and yet to be committed.

As she walked by the statue now, Katherine's cheeks reddened with shame. *Does Mother Mary know I touched myself last night? That I like the way it made me feel? Will she tell Jesus?* At the end of the colonnade was the entrance to the chapel. Sister Superior held open the doors and her flock filed in. They walked up the aisle toward the altar where the Holy Eucharist was displayed in a gold monstrance. The girls genuflected and signed themselves, two by two, before taking their places in the front pews. They knelt, folded their hands, and waited to be led in prayer as their stomachs growled for lunch. Sister Superior knelt at the communion rail and made the sign of the cross. She gathered her rosary in her hands and kissed the body of Christ.

"The angel of the Lord declared unto Mary," the old nun prayed.

The girls responded: "And she conceived of the Holy Spirit."

Then together: "Hail Mary, full of grace, the Lord is with thee. Blessed art thou among women, and blessed is the fruit of thy womb . . ."

Katherine jolted awake.

She was in bed in a dimly lit room. She sat up and looked at the lamp on a table in the far corner. It was the only source of light in the room, and she stared at it for long seconds before realizing the light was moving. Then she realized it wasn't a lamp; it was a flame atop a candle, and the candle was standing inside a black lantern. Curled in a furry gray ball next to the lantern was Monsieur Booty. Katherine knew this place. It was the loge in the belfry of Lausanne Cathedral.

"Jesus."

She sensed someone's presence and she looked about the room. Across from her, in the shadows, she saw a small form. The form was dressed in black and had black hair. She stared deeper into the shadows until she saw sparks of candlelight reflected in a pair of almond-shaped and emerald-colored eyes. Katherine couldn't find her breath.

"Marc?"

The form stepped into the light. Katherine saw a young woman in dark fatigues. The woman kicked out her right foot and stood at ease with her hands behind her back. She was of Asian descent.

"Who are you?" Katherine said.

"I'm Corporal Mai of the Swiss Guard, ma'am. I was keeping the watch."

"Oh. I thought you were someone else."

Katherine combed her hand through her hair. What was left of it felt clean, and her skin smelled clean, too. The grime had been cleaned from under her nails, and they'd been trimmed and polished. She was wearing a hospital gown of fine white cotton, like the sheets and duvet cover. Her eyes adjusted to the dim light and she made out the rest of the room. If not for the IV stand next to the bed and the clear tube running to the needle in her arm, she could be in one of the better suites at the Lausanne Palace Hotel. Thinking such a thing, she remembered the place she had been. Grover's Mill and the house. She remembered all the dead. And Anne. Then she allowed herself to remember her kidnapped son. She waited for sorrow to crush her. Nothing. She looked at the fluid running into the needle. It had a purple tint and it glittered . . . *No wonder.* She looked at Corporal Mai.

"Where are the guys in white coats?"

"Ma'am?"

"Where am I?"

"I'm not authorized to answer any questions regarding your status, ma'am. Let me get Inspector Gobet. He's outside."

"Oh, him. Perfect. Should have known. Guess that's why you were keeping an eye on me. Making sure I didn't run away."

Corporal Mai smiled. Embarrassed at her lapse in protocol, she quickly wiped the expression from her face.

"Did I say something funny?" Katherine said.

"I'm sorry, ma'am, I wasn't being rude. There's a controller on the bed. One of the buttons raises the window shades. If you press it you'll see why I was smiling."

Katherine stared at the young woman. The smile was gone, but it hung in Katherine's memory as a gentle thing. And for a quick moment Katherine saw Marc Rochat in Corporal Mai's face.

"Maybe I will," Katherine said.

"I'll get Inspector Gobet."

Corporal Mai turned around and walked to the door. Katherine watched her set the palm of her right hand to the wall just above the lantern. The door slid open.

Swish.

"Wait," Katherine called.

Corporal Mai turned around. "Ma'am?"

Katherine pointed to the lantern. "Is that the same . . . ?" She could not finish the question.

Corporal Mai nodded. "Yes, ma'am. That's Marc Rochat's lantern. The exfil team found it."

"The what?"

"The ones who went into the time warp to get you out, ma'am."

Katherine tried to look beyond the young woman and out the door. It opened to a vestibule and another door.

"Oh."

Corporal Mai left and the door closed behind her.

Katherine stared at the lantern and watched the flame sway from side to side. She sighed again, this time feeling something warm flow through her body. She watched the purple stuff drip into the needle.

"So it goes."

She slid back down under the covers, watching Monsieur Booty sleep. She traced her cleaned and neatly trimmed nails along the sheets. She made little scratching sounds. The beast stretched, sat up, and looked at Katherine.

"Hey, fuzzface, come on over and be friendly."

The cat leapt from the table and landed on the floor with a well-fed thud. It pranced over to her with its tail in the air, jumped onto the bed, and sank into the duvet. The beast stretched again, enjoying the sensation of comfort.

"Three hundred thread count of Egyptian cotton, pal. It's the good stuff."

She reached down and scratched the beast's head. Monsieur Booty purred and rolled over. Katherine gently stroked the beast's belly.

"Wow, looks like I'm not the only one who got a bath and her nails done. So, do you know where we are, Monsieur Booty? Huh? Do ya, do ya?"

Mew.

"Me neither. Let's see."

Katherine sat up, arranged the pillows against the headrest and the duvet around her hips. Monsieur Booty immediately claimed ownership of her lap and tapped his head against her hands for more scratchy-scratch.

"Yeah, yeah. Give me a second."

She picked up the controller and saw four buttons: Emergency, Nurse, Lights, Windows.

"Eeny, meeny, miny . . ."

She pressed *moe*, and a whirring noise sounded as six oval-shaped shades, three to a side, were raised. The room was awash in pale blue light. She leaned over and looked out the closest window. She was suspended between heaven and earth.

"Holy cow, that *is* funny."

She was on a jet, a big one. But the wings reflected the color of the sky and were almost invisible.

"Do you see what I see, Monsieur Booty?"

Mew.

"Good. Then I'm not completely nuts."

Far below was an expanse of blue-tinted ice that did not end. It only fell from view with the curvature of the earth. And in the direction the jet was flying, the sky glowed red, then streaks of light came from the other side of the world and hit her in the eyes.

"Wow."

Swish.

She turned to see Inspector Gobet enter the bedroom with Corporal Mai at his heels. Watching him cross the room, Katherine thought he might be scum, but he was a snappy dresser. The dark gray, double-breasted suit was hand-tailored. Like the shirt and the handmade shoes. Katherine tagged his tie as Roberto Cavalli—one thousand bucks' worth of pure silk. Weirdly, it was the same tint of purple as the liquid in the IV.

The cop stood a few steps short of the foot of the bed. Corporal Mai took her place in the room where the shadows used to be. Katherine watched her adopt that same at-ease stance and tune out. Katherine remembered all the Swiss Guard back in Grover's Mill were like that. Anne was the best at it. Being there and not being there at the same time, Anne called it. Katherine always thought it was like being trained to disappear because, sometimes, that's what they did. And it was always her son who saw them first. Finding one of the guards in a shadow was a game for him. It made him laugh. She could see his face just then. He was smiling. He was beautiful. . . . Max.

"How are you feeling, Madame Taylor?"

Inspector Gobet's voice crept into her consciousness. Focusing on the cop's face, Katherine saw the perfect mix of empathy and compassion. She held up the arm with the IV needle planted in the vein.

"I'm feeling exactly the way you want me to feel, aren't I? I mean, I was just thinking about my son and I could see him in my head. I could even say his name to myself without sinking. Or without acting on the urge to jump out of bed and claw your fucking eyes out the moment I saw you. No, wait. I do want to claw your eyes out. And when I'm done with that, I'd like to strangle you with your pretty tie. But instead, I'm sitting here, thinking all will be well while making conversation with a walking piece of shit. That is how you want me to feel, isn't it?"

"Yes, as a matter of fact."

Katherine nodded to the windows. "What's all that out there?"

"All that would be the Arctic Ocean above the seventy-fifth latitude of planet Earth. We're flying the Great Circle route over the North Pole on our way back to Switzerland."

"You sure?"

"I beg your pardon?"

"Because I've never been on a jet that flew with invisible wings. Maybe I'm on a make-believe jet."

"I assure you, you are on a real jet in the real world. Though it is a jet equipped with certain stealth technologies."

"Okay, I'll buy that. But what if we don't want to go to Switzerland?"

"We?" the inspector said.

"Me and the cat. What if we want to go to Anguilla and get a tan?"

The inspector waited a few seconds before speaking again.

"Madame Taylor, I am heartily sorry for your ordeal and the loss of your son."

Katherine stared at him.

"Only human beings can be sorry for what happens to another human being. You're just faking it, aren't you?"

The inspector nodded. "I am incapable of emotions and feelings as you experience them, yes. They are things that are dangerous to us. But I would like to think that in the long years I have walked this world, I developed a certain mindfulness in witnessing the suffering of the innocent, one that reinforces my efforts in assuring that their souls are comforted at the times of their deaths so that they may pass into new lives. It is with that same mindfulness that I will do my utmost to see that your son is returned to you."

"Is that supposed to give me confidence? Sure, your drugs are making me think everything's peachy keen, but I don't believe a fucking word coming out of your mouth."

"Madame Taylor—"

"I'm not finished."

The inspector nodded respectfully.

"I just spent forty days burying people who had their throats slashed and bodies mutilated. I saw what happened to their souls. They were devoured despite your fucking mindfulness. Now you can talk."

The inspector turned to Corporal Mai. "Would you advise the galley that Madame Taylor is awake? Perhaps they could prepare her morning tea."

"*Oui*, Inspector."

Corporal Mai quickstepped to the door and let herself out. Katherine looked at the cop.

"You like them pretty and young, don't you? Anne was pretty and young. Does this one know what happens to pretty, young girls who get hooked up with the likes of you?"

"Corporal Mai is an excellent soldier, Madame Taylor. She performs her duties with precision and dedication. And yes, she is aware of the risks of working for the likes of me. As did all those killed at Grover's Mill trying to protect you and your son. I simply asked Corporal Mai to leave because she possesses acute sensitivities."

Katherine remembered the young woman's eyes and the gentleness of her smile. "Like what?"

"When she was nine years old, in Ho Chi Minh City, her mother was killed in the same manner you witnessed at Grover's Mill. I saw no reason to subject her to reliving the event in her imagination."

"Her imagination."

"Quite."

Katherine remembered waking up, seeing the lantern and cat on the wooden table and thinking she was in the belfry loge of Lausanne Cathedral; seeing a form standing in the shadows. Seeing the eyes . . . *Marc?* And then she saw him standing before her after he brought her to the loge. A crooked little man in a floppy black hat and a long wool overcoat, a mildly insane look in his pale green eyes.

"Where on earth did you come from?"

"Quebec City. It's on the same line as Lausanne."

"The same line?"

"The line on the globe in Maman's house."

Katherine looked at the place where the young Asian woman had been standing in the room. *Keeping the watch,* the young woman said.

"How did Corporal . . . What's her name?"

"Corporal Mai."

"How did Corporal Mai end up in Switzerland?"

"I was made aware of her situation. I brought her to Lausanne to be raised and educated at Mon Repos."

Katherine remembered seeing that place from her flat on Rue Caroline. It was a huge estate in the woods at the edge of town. Neat gardens and fountains set around a big redbrick house. And there were two wrought-iron aviaries on the grounds, too. She sometimes heard the birds from her balcony at dawn. She remembered one day walking along the high stone wall that surrounded the grounds and seeing the sign on the main gate.

MON REPOS ORPHANAGE AND SCHOOL FOR SPECIAL CHILDREN
A PRIVATE INSTITUTION OF THE ROCHAT FOUNDATION
NO ACCESS TO THE PUBLIC

"That's where Marc Rochat went to school, isn't it?"

"Yes. Why do you ask?"

"Your corporal went to the same school as Marc. She has the same eyes as Marc. Like yours, like Harper's, like that old hippie that showed up in the bunker with the cat."

"Because she, like Marc Rochat, like all the children at Mon Repos, were born as half-kinds bred by the likes of me. The shape and color of the eyes reflect shared genetic traits."

"What?"

"Half-kinds were the result of an experiment at the beginning of the 1990s. Needless to say, it was something that should not have happened. Interbreeding of our two species was a practice begun long ago by our enemy to devastating effect on the world. We wished to bring children of light into the world to counter that effect. But our children were born with abilities and sensitivities that rendered them vulnerable to the terrors of the world as it had become. The experiment was shut down within a generation and I established Mon Repos, as a place where the children, our children, could be protected and cared for."

Katherine remembered Rochat shuffling and limping in his misshapen body, struggling to comprehend the world with the mind of a child, living in a world of angels and bells. And Corporal Mai, trying so hard to be a good soldier keeping the watch, but unable to hold back a childlike smile, as if the same strain of mystic innocence still flowed through her blood.

"How did evil monsters like you get here?" Katherine said.

"That would make our progeny the children of evil, would it not? Do you think Corporal Mai evil? Did you think Marc Rochat evil?"

Katherine saw him in the loge again.

"Why are you helping me?"

"Because you're lost."

Katherine looked down at the cat on her lap. He had heard Marc Rochat's name again and was scanning the room. *Is he here?*

"He thought I was an angel," Katherine said.

"Yes, he did. And he died protecting the cathedral he thought was a hiding place for angels."

She looked at the cop. "Was Harper part of your fucking experiment?"

"No. Nor was I or the old hippie who showed up with the cat. Indeed, when Mr. Harper learned of it during the cathedral affair, his reaction was far more indignant than yours."

"Really?"

"For all his roughness around the edges, Mr. Harper's sense of outrage at the injustices inflicted upon the innocent borders on saintly."

"Are we talking about the same Jay Harper? Cheap sports coat, cheap watch, food on his tie?"

"Indeed." Inspector Gobet stepped closer to the bed. "Madame Taylor, the likes of me are not evil. We do not commit and have never committed an act of violence against a human being. We are, in fact, forbidden to touch a human being without following certain protocols. Indeed, in all but one case our children were conceived without physical contact. We used an advanced method of DNA transfer as yet unknown to the human race."

"What happened in the one case? One of your gang get a little too hot and bothered with one of the Earth girls?"

The inspector shook his head. "It was an act of mutual love, though the one who committed the act was unaware of the true nature of his being at the time. Otherwise, the women involved in the experiment were partisans, like the civilians of Grover's Mill. They were willing participants in the experiment and they were loving mothers."

"Who all ended up dead. That's what happened to Corporal Mai's mother, and Marc's, isn't it?"

"There have been many cases like that, yes."

In the lull of voices, Monsieur Booty realized Marc Rochat had not returned, and the beast settled back to sleep.

"How many are there? Children like Marc?"

The inspector bowed his head. "There were many hundreds. There are only three that we know of left in the world. Corporal Mai, the one half-kind born of an act of love, and a young lady who now calls the hour at Lausanne Cathedral. The rest were murdered."

Katherine felt a chill run through her body. "What?"

The inspector drew a slow breath. "Some lived at Mon Repos, the others in similar institutions around the world. The locations were attacked in conjunction with the strike on Grover's Mill. The half-kinds were slaughtered along with their teachers, support staff, security personnel . . . and those mothers who lived with their children. There were no survivors. Analysis of the crime scenes suggest all victims were subjected to unspeakable barbarity before they died. We managed to comfort a few souls, but most were lost."

"Devoured, you mean. The way they were devoured at Grover's Mill."

"Yes."

"Because of me, because of Max? Because the killers were looking for us?"

"We thought that at first. Turns out they knew your location before the attacks even began. A fact made clear to us when Mon Repos was attacked after Grover's Mill, after they had already taken your son from you."

"The killers murdered the children for nothing? Why?"

"Because, Madame Taylor, these killers *are* evil. They torture and they enslave, they kill and devour souls of the innocent. Frankly, the likes of me are all that stand between them and the complete conquest of paradise."

"Paradise."

"Yes, paradise."

Katherine wanted to tell the cop the same thing she'd told Harper: *You and all your fucking friends crawled out of the same stinking gutter.* She sighed instead and received another hit of comforting warmth. She stared at the inspector.

"Can I ask you something?"

"Of course."

"Why is your tie the same color as the stuff going into my vein?"

"You are receiving a potion to hold at bay the sorrow crushing down on your soul, something to sustain a hope that your son will be returned to you. Corporal Mai suggested that wearing a tie of the same color would increase the potion's effect."

"You're kidding."

"As I said, Corporal Mai possesses acute sensitivities. How is the tie working?"

Katherine looked at the tie, then the stuff in the IV. She sighed. "Not too bad."

"She will be very happy to hear it."

Katherine continued to stare at him. "You know, for a cop, you've got the gift of gab."

"Thank you."

"How long have you been here?"

"Two and a half million years."

"Where do you come from?"

"No idea."

"Who sent you here?"

"Haven't a clue."

"So what do you know?"

"Not much beyond the fact we were sent to save all that's left of paradise."

"There's that word again," Katherine said.

"Yes, there it is."

"I take it back about having the gift of gab. You're crap."

"Perhaps if you would allow me another go."

"Why not? It's your jet. And there's a fat cat on my lap so I'm not moving anytime soon."

The inspector walked to a window, gazed down onto the blue-tinted ice.

"The world you live in, all of you, it's not the way it was supposed to be. In the beginning, given its placement in the solar system, this planet was to be home to a miraculous array of life based on natural selection. That's the way it was planned as best we can imagine it. The first wave of our kind, a reconnaissance team, was sent down to watch over and guide the creation, particularly the early humanoids who were developing a sense of self-awareness combined with a free will that would make them the dominant species on the planet. The recon team had powers of observation and subliminal suggestion with which they could communicate with the beings of this world, but remain hidden from them. Their powers were only to be used in support of the mission and never to the detriment of any life-form. Simply put, the recon team's mission brief was to guide the evolving humanoids to an understanding that *because* they were the dominant species on the planet, they were to be the caretakers of this miraculous world. That understanding would guide the species to the ultimate knowledge that this world was nothing more than a part of the singular living organism that is the universe. From there, it would be an easy step to the stars. Instead, the recon team discovered how easily free will could be manipulated in the humanoids by not just observing human dreams, but reshaping them. They became particularly entranced with reshaping the dreams of women. And in reshaping those dreams, our kind came in contact with pleasures they had never before experienced. They were then overcome with a desire to violate the bodies of women and breed a new race on earth. In this way our kind were made flesh and evil came into the world. Evil that slaughtered the innocent in order to lay wealth and power at the feet of the betrayers. Evil that was rewarded, even after death, with the power to devour human souls. Evil that is now leading to the destruction of your world and all life contained here, for no other reason than it is profitable to do so. Evil that was, in fact, a mutation introduced by my kind."

The inspector walked back to the foot of the bed.

"That is where the likes of me entered the picture with orders to save what was left of paradise. We had no choice but to follow the betrayers into the forms of men in order to eradicate the mutation that had infected the creation. There has been a war between us and them for the soul of man ever since."

"And that's why the world is fucked up. That's what you're telling me."

"Yes, in fact."

Katherine looked down at Monsieur Booty. "You buying this?"

Mew.

"I'll tell him." She looked at the cop. "The cat says he's not buying it because this sounds like a rip-off of the Bible. You know, all that 'In the beginning' stuff with God and the angels."

"The concept of God you speak of is a human imagination, as are angels."

"Then why does it sound like something out of the Bible?"

"The plain truth is, Madame Taylor, everything the likes of me know of our existence comes from the legends and myths and religions of men. That would include the Bible. Which puts us at great disadvantage. You see, the endgame of the paradise mission was classified and known only to the leader of the first wave. And while we all have the same powers, he alone was the keeper of the ultimate knowledge of who we are, where we come from, and why we were sent here. Though it appears, increasingly, that the reason my kind were sent here has everything to do with you and your son."

"Two and a half million years later?"

"Yes."

"You know, for someone who doesn't know all that much, you sure had a lot to say."

"In the last weeks a cache of intelligence was found at a house in Paris. We're still sorting through much of it, but it is directing our attention to a whole new perspective regarding our existence and purpose here."

"And your existence is tied up, somehow, with me and my son. As if, somehow, we're part of your mission to save what's left of paradise."

"That is the truth of the matter. You see, you have been on the enemy's radar from the day you were born. They watched you, they paved your way to Switzerland with gold. It's no surprise you followed them. It's no surprise you became the in-demand escort for the Two Hundred Club. It was a front, providing them women for pleasure and breeding. Simply put, the enemy believed if they raped you and impregnated you with their own seed, then the life that was destined to be created within you would never be born. But you escaped from them after you were raped. They failed, they did not make you pregnant. That did not happen until you took sanctuary in Lausanne Cathedral."

Katherine settled back in the pillows. "So what Harper told me down in the bunker. About the junkie being one of your crowd, and the light through the stained glass at Lausanne Cathedral. Him telling me he was protecting the life within my body. It really happened, it wasn't a dream? Because all this time I thought it was a dream. And even when Harper told me it was real, I was sure he was feeding me another fairy tale. I still am, I think. Because that's what you guys do. And I'm not sure you can make me believe anything else."

Inspector Gobet walked to the IV stand, tapped the bottle. The purple stuff shimmered.

"I cannot make you believe anything one way or the other, Madame Taylor. Not our style, actually. Besides, does it matter?"

Katherine watched a drop fall from the bottle and into the tube. "Is that a trick question?" she said.

"Actually, it would be classified as an evaluative question. Something requiring the examination of an issue from all perspectives, however probable or improbable, to arrive at the truth of a particular situation."

"So if I were to evaluate my particular situation, the truth would be what?"

The inspector held open the palms of his hands as if presenting the obvious. "That whether reality or fairy tale, this is where your consciousness resides."

"Well, that's not confusing. Not one bit."

The cop pulled a penlight from an inner pocket of his suit coat. He pressed a button on the side and a thin beam of lapis-colored light came on. "I'm so glad. And as you're in a more supine position, would you mind?"

"Mind what?"

"If I checked your eyes."

"It's still your jet, and the cat's still on my lap."

The inspector raised the beam to her left eye, panned it to the right. He was close to her, but his presence did not have a scent of any kind.

"Looking for something?" she said.

"Phantom images in the axons of your optic nerves."

"Which are what?"

"I'd have to cite a lot of medical mumbo jumbo. Suffice to say any remaining hidden images could cause a relapse of your condition, preventing you from understanding the dream that awakened you just now, and how that dream relates to your son."

She stretched her fingers, touched the silk of his tie . . . *He'd never see it coming.* She sighed instead and let the warmth rush through her blood.

"I think you'd better step back now. That urge to strangle you is becoming more and more appealing."

"Of course."

The inspector turned off the beam and returned the penlight to his suit coat. He retook his place at the foot of the bed.

"So your evil twins aren't the only ones who like to get inside a girl's head and fuck with her dreams," Katherine said.

"That's not what I was doing, Madame Taylor."

"Then how did you know about my dream?"

The inspector shrugged. "You were talking in your sleep. Corporal Mai heard you and reported it to me."

"What did she tell you?"

"That you were reciting the opening of the devotional prayer known as the Angelus."

Rapid-fire images flashed through Katherine's eyes.

The twelve-year-old girl she once was, on her knees in the chapel . . . *and she conceived of the Holy Spirit.* Then the hooker on the run in Lausanne and Marc Rochat taking her into the cathedral to hide . . . *Why are you helping me? Because you're lost.* Then the bum on the altar walking her into the light, rising into a flood of brilliant colors . . . *to protect the life within you* . . . Then the laughing eyes of her son; then the moment the killers tore him from her arms . . . *"Maman!"* And now the flashing message in the control room and the screaming tone drilling into her brain . . . *ANGELUS, ANGELUS, ANGELUS.* Then Harper in the bunker . . . *a child conceived of light, born into the world to guide the creation through the next stage of evolution*. Then a sharp jolt and she was looking at Inspector Gobet's mug. His familiar-looking emerald-green eyes watching her, observing her, knowing everything she just experienced in less than a second.

"Fuck you and the moonbeam you rode in on," Katherine said.

"Madame Taylor, I am only trying to help you understand what is happening to you."

"Yeah, sure. I got the same understanding treatment from Saint Harper in the bunker when he got into my eyes. It feels like rape."

"Indeed not."

"Hey! Do yourself a favor, do not tell a woman what is and what is not rape. You get inside a woman's head and use her to your advantage, it's rape. I thought that Angelus message on the screen was some kind of code from Anne's troops to you, a fucking distress call. But I get it now, there was more to it. The word, the screaming tone—it was for me. You were rewiring my brain to hook up with a little girl's memory."

The inspector nodded. "It was designed to connect you to the facts of the case in the event you emerged from the bunker and—"

"What fucking facts?"

"That you are who you are, Madame Taylor, and that your son is who he is."

She stared at him.

"Now hear this, Inspector: I didn't believe in that Angelus stuff when I was a little girl. I sure as hell didn't believe in it when I was turning tricks in Lausanne. Honestly, I could give a flying fuck if it's true or not. You want to think my son is the savior of your fucked-up world, you go right ahead. But get this through your head: Max is my child and that's all he is. And I swear on his soul, I will kill anyone who tries to keep him from me. Do you fucking hear me? Am I getting through to your superior fucking intelligence?"

That perfect mix of empathy and compassion was reloaded onto Inspector Gobet's face. "I am receiving you loud and clear, madame. I apologize for disturbing you. I'll leave you to rest now."

He turned and walked to the door. He set the palm of his hand on the wall.

Swish.

A curious thought dropped in Katherine's head.

"Hold it."

Inspector Gobet stopped in his tracks but did not look back.

"Not that I give a shit," Katherine said, "but what I just said about killing anyone who keeps Max from me—that's what you wanted me to say, wasn't it?"

The inspector looked back at her. "Yes, as a matter of fact. Corporal Mai will be returning to keep the watch."

"Just in case I talk in my sleep again."

"Something like that."

He was a piece of shit in a snappy suit when he walked in; he's a piece of shit on the way out, Katherine thought. But if turning a metaphysical trick or two meant getting Max back . . .

"Whatever it takes, Inspector Gobet."

He smiled. "I'm so pleased to hear it. Try to rest. We will be landing in a few hours."

He left and the door closed.

The room was quiet.

She picked up the controller and pressed the button to lower the shades. The room became a place of shadows once more. She slid down into the bed, rolled to her side. Monsieur Booty tumbled in the duvet, righting himself to a sitting position. Monsieur Booty looked at her. *What?*

"Nothing. Go back to sleep."

The beast obeyed, and Katherine stroked its head.

She stared at the flame in the lantern.

She imagined the mothers of the half-kind children, watching their own flesh and blood slaughtered before their eyes. She sighed.

"Pray for us sinners now and at the hour of our death."

FIFTEEN

i

"So what am I supposed to focus on in the article? The name or the location in the byline?" Harper said.

Krinkle was still at the desk, sifting through computer files like he was panning for gold. "Give me a minute."

Harper gave him five.

"Son of a bitch," the roadie said.

"Find something interesting?"

"It's what I can't find. Sorry, what did you ask me, before you just asked what you did?"

"Lines of causality. Intersections. Julian Magnolly or Jerusalem? Or is it that they both begin with *j*?"

Krinkle jumped up from the chair and helped himself to a Vivalto Lungo from Arctic X's Nespresso machine. He added two packs of sugar to the cup and walked back to the desk. He sat and drank the brew in one gulp. He wiped dribbles from his beard.

"He's a partisan working undercover at *24 Heures*. HQ never talks to him directly, and he never talks to HQ except through a one-off edition of the newspaper at LP's Bar."

"The bar is his drop site."

The roadie nodded. "The one-off gets left at LP's every day, by whom we don't know, and we don't ask. Every day, another partisan reads through it looking for anything by Magnolly. The one-off is checked against the print run for any added words. Added words are reported to another partisan, who reports them to HQ as flash traffic level one."

"Old tricks being what they are. His intel is solid?"

"He's the guy who planted the story about the Russian tourist they found in the car on the Gstaad road before the cathedral job went down. You read about it in LP's Bar, even though you almost didn't."

"Sorry?"

"Long story. Someone got hold of it and took it and there was a whole thing about getting it back in time. Anyway, it's what got you on track to cracking the case wide open."

Harper checked his timeline. "I can't see it."

"There's a reason for that."

"Which is what?"

"Fuck if I know. That's what Gobet told me to tell you. And it doesn't matter. That was then, this is nowtimes." The roadie pointed to the newspaper. "You're holding yesterday's one-off in your hands. Gobet planned to give it to you to read before he left with Madame Taylor, but you told him to get stuffed and down you went."

"That one I see. Sort of. So what words would he have told me to look for, had I not told him to get stuffed?"

"Third paragraph from the bottom. The last four words of the first sentence have been added to the one-off edition. They were for our eyes only."

Harper found it: *The scrolls are written in first-century Hebrew, and they are genuine.*

"Define 'and they are genuine.'"

"Magnolly is telling us what's in these new scrolls contains critical intel regarding our kind and the prophecy. And before you ask me to define 'critical,' I'll tell you. The new scrolls may be bigger news than the Book of Enoch."

Harper stared at the roadie. "You must be bloody joking me."

"Nope."

"Who wrote the new scrolls? When?"

"The last scribe of Qumran. When is the unknown. Sometime after anno Domini 73."

Harper flashed through episodes of the History Channel. He landed on *The Destruction of the House of God*. Headline: Rome lays waste to Jerusalem, destroys the Second Temple, and scatters the Jewish people to the wind in AD 70. But something didn't fit. According to the History Channel, Rome had already been on a rampage of destruction across Israel for three years before Jerusalem was leveled. The empire was striking back hard to obliterate the Jewish revolt. Jericho went down in AD 67; so did all the surrounding settlements and towns, including Qumran. And the Romans weren't big on taking prisoners.

"Hang on. How could the scrolls be written in—"

"I know where you're going. The Romans didn't know Qumran even existed until they marched along the Dead Sea to wipe out the Zealots at Masada in AD 73. That's when Qumran bought it. And get this: The Romans may have had some help. It seems they had bad guys in their ranks. In the fifth cohort of the Tenth Legion, to be exact."

"How do you know?"

"Because it's in the new scrolls, and the new scrolls are genuine. Remember?"

"Sorry. I'm still looping a little."

"Her?"

Harper nodded.

"It'll pass," the roadie said.

"So a voice in my head keeps telling me. What else is in the scrolls?"

"That's all we got for now. And it's all we're going to get. The intel went cold in a bad way twelve hours ago. Magnolly had a contact with access to the Israel Museum in Jerusalem. That's where these newly discovered scrolls are now. They scheduled a meet at a café in West Jerusalem. The two of them ended up ripped to shreds courtesy of a suicide bomb. A huge friggin' Claymore strapped to a bomber's chest. Thirty-seven collateral deaths. Hamas, Fatah, all the usual suspects denied responsibility. Gobet's partisans got into the morgue to check what was left of the bomber. Pure goon. Same strain as the killers in the Paris job."

Harper scanned the byline again. The story was getting weirder by the minute.

"That would mean Magnolly filed this story from beyond the grave, no?"

"The real world doesn't know he's dead yet. He was basing himself out of an Arab hotel in East Jerusalem and working under an alias. If he didn't get back to his laptop by a certain time, the story was trip-wired to go. On-the-ground intel says the laptop's hard drive nuked itself. A mirror disc image of what was left was sent to the SX geeks in Bern. They got traces of another story he was working on."

"Any clues on what it's about?"

"Fearful sights and great signs."

Harper thought about it. "Luke 21:11."

"Amen."

Harper scanned the story on the scrolls once more. He felt dizzy and dropped the newspaper. He took a slow breath, rubbed the back of his neck. *Shit.*

"Sorry, could you tell me what any of this has to do with why we're in Alaska?"

"Lines of causality can run rings around the world at the speed of light for thousands of years before they intersect. Each intersection points us to a different direction in space-time."

"And lines may have intersected here?"

"Judging from what I cannot find in this friggin' computer, I'd say that's a big ten-four," the roadie said.

Harper looked at his own watch, happily ticking along in the real world. And the roadie was right. If Harper were in Lausanne at the moment, he'd be in Café du Grütli, sipping an espresso with a wine chaser. The Swiss would have already marched back to work, and if there were no bad guys to hunt down and kill, Harper could waste the afternoon watching the world go by outside the café windows; then, soon enough, it would be happy hour. A line dropped in his head. From the Book of Psalms: *Teach us to count well our days, that we may gain a heart of wisdom.* He let lines of causality run in his eyes, tried to count them like the days. The lines raced by at the speed of light; trying to keep up made him feel like he was taking another ride on the cosmic merry-go-round. But this time the centripetal force pinned his eternal being against the wall and the weight of his form crushed down.

"Oh, bollocks." He reached for his smokes.

"Ah, hold it," Krinkle said.

The roadie reached in the pouch of his overalls. He pulled out a small metal and glass tube and threw it at Harper. Harper caught it, looked at it. Four inches long, thin, mouthpiece attached to a clear chamber containing a silver-colored liquid, black metal housing at the tip. Small button and a smaller LED in the housing.

"What the hell is this?"

"A present from Gobet. It's an electronic smoker with a new blend to get you straight after the Taylor job. Just press the little button, a little blue light comes on, and inhale like your life depends on it." The roadie pulled out his own metal tube. He switched it on, inhaled, and released a cloud of vapor. "I was issued one, too. It takes some serious getting used to."

Harper gave it a go. *Press here, little blue light there, inhale.* Took a few hits for Harper to feel the radiance ease the weight. When the weight disappeared, so did the last trace of Katherine Taylor's face from his timeline. He looked at Krinkle.

"You with me now, brother?" the roadie said.

"I'm with you."

Krinkle sat back and rested the heels of his steel-toed work boots on the posh desk.

"Okay. Unknown to anyone on the ground at Grover's Mill, Katherine Taylor's child had a GPS microchip embedded in his thigh. It was a biotech gadget, powered by a hundred watts of energy drawn from the child's own body and programmed to ping once a minute."

"So if it pings, he's alive. No ping, he's dead."

Krinkle nodded. "One of Gobet's satellites picked up a single ping five hours, fifty-eight minutes after the enemy hit Grover's Mill. The ping emanated from just outside this friggin' hangar. Subtract an hour for battle time on the ground and snatching the child from the bunker, forty minutes for a chopper to make the nearest airport at Portland, three hours and twenty-three minutes from Portland to Anchorage on a private jet . . ."

"Welcome to Arctic X Air Services."

Krinkle nodded again. "Thing is, the microchip requires line-of-sight to a satellite. It'll transmit through most substances, except certain heavy metals. My guess is the child was unconscious and being smuggled through here in a container, something that had been turned into a Faraday cage to block the microchip's signal."

"The container was opened," Harper said.

"Most likely. Gobet dressed a few of his Swiss Guards up as Swiss bankers, put them on a business jet, and sent them through here this morning to see if the place was legit. They arranged to have a bit of engine trouble so they could sit around all day and watch who comes and goes and how they do it."

"And?"

"If slippery shits had an airport, this would be it. Still, in and out of the States, everyone gets processed through a mobile Immigration and Customs unit. And get this: *All* cargo listed on the flight manifest is verified before exiting the States."

Harper nodded toward the computer screen on the desk. "Except the flight that came through here five hours and fifty-eight minutes after Grover's Mill was attacked. That's what you were looking for."

"Dude, I've just hacked through Homeland Security, U.S. Immigration *and* Customs, not to mention the company's own files. I got squat. There is no record of any flight coming through here in the time frame we're looking at."

Harper thought about it. "We're being played by the bad guys."

"Check."

"What's the name of the game?"

"As in did they remove the microchip from the child, send it this way and him another?"

"Makes sense," Harper said.

Krinkle shook his head. "Too sensible for revenge."

The roadie's last four words tripped an imagination in Harper's mind.

"Inspector Gobet knows who was behind the slaughter of the innocents. He knows who snatched the child."

Krinkle smoked, releasing a cloud of vapor that half hid his glassy eyes. "Damn," the roadie mused.

"Feel free to share."

"When Gobet gave me the newspaper and the brief on the microchip and told me to tell you what he told me, he said you'd say exactly what you just said. Which I thought pretty funny until you said it. The man might be in a different form than I'm used to, but he's the same old Boz. I wonder if he still blows a blues harp? That *would* be wild."

The roadie stared with a wide grin on his face. Harper had no idea what the roadie was talking about. *More radiance required. Press here, little blue light there, inhale.*

"Does your mind ever travel in a straight line?" Harper said.

"Not since London '72 on the Dead's European gig. During the load-in my form found a few tabs of Owsley hidden inside a speaker cabinet. We're talking grade-A, premium LSD made by the one and only himself. One tab, you're flying. Two tabs, you see the face of God. I took all three tabs. By the time the Dead led into 'Morning Dew,' I was floating above the crowd and I knew I was an angel come to free all souls from the chains of evil."

"That's how you were awakened?"

"Fuck no. I was awakened after my form OD'd ten years later. But knowing I was already qualified as an angel made it easier to accept what I was when Boz and Monsieur Gabriel came knocking at my door." Krinkle took another hit. "What were we talking about?" he said.

"Inspector Gobet knows who snatched Madame Taylor's child."

"Oh, yeah. Gobet said to tell you: He thinks he knows who snatched the child, and so do you."

"Me?"

"That's what he said."

"How am I supposed to know who the hell he is?"

"Because you saw him during the cathedral job," Krinkle said.

"I saw a lot of faces during the cathedral job."

"There's one that Gobet rates as a high-value face of interest."

"Who?"

Krinkle dropped his boots from the desk. He leaned forward and folded his hands on the desktop like a loan officer from a high street bank about to deliver bad news.

"When you see the lad with the lantern on your timeline, you always see him in silhouette unless someone pronounces his name. And from what you've told me, you always see him going over the railing of the belfry and falling through the sky. He ends up dead on the esplanade of Lausanne Cathedral."

"What about it?"

"Marc Rochat didn't go over the side alone."

The sound of the lad's name sent Harper ripping back through time. Then he was in the belfry the day the cathedral job went down. All the bells ringing and the timbers rocking and humming. Him on the floor bleeding out, barely alive. Seeing a battered Marc Rochat pinned against the timbers surrounding Marie-Madeleine, held in place by a dark form with long silver hair. The lad screaming at the form.

"*Non*, Maman was an angel, the detectiveman told me! And he said I'm the same as him, too! That means if he can kill you, I can kill you!"

Harper can't see the form's face, but he hears its voice.

"You want to kill?" it sneers. Then it pulls a killing knife from its belt and rams the blade deep into Rochat's stomach. "This is how you kill."

Rochat shudders as the steel twists through his guts. He turns his head, his eyes watching Marie-Madeleine swing from side to side, feeling her voice vibrate through the timbers and into his body.

"Don't cry, madame, it's my duty," Rochat tells her.

The form rips the knife from Rochat's guts.

"Uhhh!" Rochat collapses to the floor. The form slowly raises the knife over Rochat's neck for the death cut.

"I bring you forever death!" it cries.

A woman's voice screams. "Marc!"

Harper sees Katherine Taylor cowering in the timbers, reaching for Rochat. Rochat looks at her. "Be not afraid," he tells her . . . and he pushes down on his crooked legs and bursts up from the floor and smashes his fists into the form's throat, forcing it back toward the railing and over the side. Rochat pushes the form away and he opens his arms like perfect wings . . . falling . . . till he smashes onto the esplanade, the light slowly fading from his eyes. The bad guy's form ends up splayed on a spire beneath the belfry as if run through by a brave knight's lance, his entrails like bloody strings snapping in the wind. Harper sees the aquiline face, the long silver hair, the unmoving and lifeless silver eyes.

Harper blinked.

He was back in the office of Arctic X, staring at the roadie behind the desk.

"Correct me if I'm wrong," Harper said, "but the form bearing that face of interest is well bloody dead."

"Welcome to paradise, brother, land of the angels and home of the strange."

Maybe, maybe not, Harper thought. *One thing for sure: Someone with the power to create hell on earth had come this way, and he wanted it to be known. Maybe.* Harper looked at Krinkle.

"That would require him being more than the ordinary, renegade bad guy out to rule the world we tagged him to be."

"Depends."

"On what?"

"Getting a visual ID confirming the guy Marc Rochat took over the side was the same guy who passed through this place somewhere in the neighborhood of midnight, three nights ago."

A blue light skipped across the window next to Harper. He looked outside, saw a four-by-four truck with warning lights mounted on the roof making the turn from the main airfield onto taxiway H. The truck's halogen headlamps sliced through the bitter cold night like wraithlike things. The truck slowed coming onto the apron of Arctic X Air Services. It stopped next to Krinkle's bus, and a man in a parka got out of the truck with a clipboard in his hand. Harper saw the writing on the truck's door: HOMELAND SECURITY MOBILE UNIT. The man with the clipboard looked at the bus, then around the apron. Harper saw the man's face in the glow of the hangar's high bay lights. The man was confused. He opened his parka, took out a flashlight, and pointed it at the blacked-out windows on the bus. Harper saw the man's uniform and gun.

"Someone is here," he said.

Krinkle got up from the chair, walked to the window, and saw the man walking toward the hangar.

"Agent Kerr. He's our visual confirmation guy. He was on duty the night the child was smuggled through this place. If Gobet is right about us being played, then our face of interest is hidden somewhere in that man's head."

"Eyes or brain?"

Krinkle shrugged. "Eyes would be easier. The brain means tracking through six hundred miles of neurons. I'm betting what we're looking for is hidden in his brain, somewhere along the calcarine fissure of the occipital lobe."

"Got it."

They lowered their eyes and looked at the floor.

Four minutes and nineteen seconds later, the man was standing at the threshold of the kicked-open office door. His SIG Sauer P229 was drawn and panning an empty office. He reached for the radio handset clipped to his coat, pressed the transmit key.

"Anchorage Operations, I have a possible four-five-nine at Arctic X Air Services. Request police backup."

There was no response.

"Anchorage Operations, come in."

He looked inside his coat to check the radio on his belt.

"No one can hear you."

The man looked up. He saw Krinkle relaxed in the chair behind the desk, then Harper on the leather settee at the other side of the office.

Both of them looking at him now, both of them puffing on electronic cigarettes. The man raised his weapon to fire, but Krinkle already had the palm of his right hand in the man's eyeline.

"Dulcis et alta quies placidæque simillima morti."

The man froze in place. Krinkle lowered his own hand, looked at Harper.

"See, that's the problem with law enforcement in this country. There's an entire generation of people with badges and guns who think if they don't kill someone at least once in their friggin' life, then it hasn't been a life worth living."

"We broke into the place, kicked open the office door. And when we let him see us, he didn't see two altar boys."

"There is that."

Krinkle got up, walked to the frozen man, and pulled the gun from his hand. He stepped back and ejected the round from the firing chamber and the ammo clip from the handle. He tossed the things onto the floor. He walked slowly around the man, studying him.

"We need him conscious and upright to do what we got to do. But he's not a half-kind, he doesn't have their innate sense of balance. It's going to take him thirty seconds to snap out of it."

"So if we wake him up too quickly . . ."

"He might fall flat on his face and knock himself out. Neither of us has clearance to touch him. We'd be screwed."

"Maybe you should have thought of that before you put him under."

The roadie looked around the office, pointed to the brass coatrack next to the door.

"Get that," Krinkle said, walking back to the desk

"You're not going to hang him up?"

The roadie pulled the chair from behind the desk. It was on wheels, and he guided it just behind the frozen man.

"No, I'm sitting him down, that'll be upright enough. I'll ease the chair into the back of his calves to bend his knees, you hold him in place with the base of the coatrack. We'll wake him up and he'll sit right down."

As bizarre as it sounded, it was a solution, Harper thought. He grabbed the coatrack, flipped it around, and set its base against the frozen man's chest. Krinkle eased in with the chair.

"No, hold it," the roadie said.

"What now?"

"I put him under, so I have to wake him up. Here, give me the coatrack and you hold the chair."

They made the switch, and in position with the coatrack tucked under his left arm with the base against the frozen man's chest, Krinkle said, "I wave, you push."

"Go ahead."

The roadie waved the palm of his right hand before the man's eyes. The man began to come around. Harper eased in with the chair as Krinkle held the man in place. Miraculously, the man was set in the chair. He sat dazed and confused for a bit until focus returned to his eyes. When it did he looked like he would piss himself.

"What the . . . ?"

Krinkle was looming over him, coatrack in hand. The roadie dropped it with a bang, and the man jumped with fright. Krinkle stuffed his hands into the pockets of his denim overalls.

"Hi there," the roadie said. "Mind if I call you Dick?"

"What?"

"You're Agent Richard Kerr of Homeland Security. I'm trying to be friendly."

The man looked behind him and saw a grubby-looking Harper holding the chair. Then he saw his P229 and ammo clip on the floor. The man looked at Krinkle again. "I came to process a flight," he said.

"Yeah, we're it. But there's no flight. We just needed to talk to you."

The man nervously eyed the roadie up and down. "Are you going to kill me?"

Krinkle realized with his hands in his pockets and his peacoat pulled open, the man had gotten a glimpse of the kill kit strapped to the roadie's sides. Krinkle quickly closed his coat.

"Oh, shit. You know what, Dick? I'm great behind a microphone talking to millions of human souls at once. You should tune in sometime. Just go on the Internet and look for the last radio station on planet Earth. But I apologize. I'm so garbage at one-on-one interviews. I'm going to turn it over to Brother Harper now. He's better at this whole apparition thing."

"Who?"

Harper circled around him, stood enough distance away so the man would not feel threatened. He slipped his gloved hands into the pockets of his coat. Harper's ragtag appearance was not reassuring.

"That's me. Relax, we're not going to hurt you. The fact is, we're in the same line of work."

"You're with a security agency?"

"That's right."

"Which one?"

"The one no one is supposed to know exists or ask questions about. Am I clear?"

The man calmed a little and nodded.

"Good. We're on a case. There's a missing child involved and there's not a lot of time. We think the child came through here three nights ago around midnight. You were on duty that night. We'd like you to identify a particular face for us."

The man shook his head.

"Yes, I was on duty, but there was no flight out of Arctic X. I can prove it, there would be records."

"We're not questioning your job performance, agent. And we did check the records, and you're right: No flight was listed coming through Arctic X that night."

"Then why . . . ?"

"Because there was a flight that came in around midnight three nights ago, and you saw it."

"I wouldn't have forgotten something like that."

"It's not about forgetting, agent, it's about something you've seen that the bad guys left in your head for us to find."

"What?"

Harper stepped closer to the man.

"Be not afraid, mate. Look into my eyes, listen to the sound of my voice."

ii

Two hours and ten minutes later, the man was put under again and his reloaded P229 was returned to his hand. His consciousness had been reconnected to the moment in time he arrived at the threshold of the kicked-in office door, saw no one inside, and radioed for backup. Everything since had been wiped, and he'd been primed to repeat the radio call in fifteen heartbeats. Given he was under, his metabolism had slowed to one breath and one heartbeat per minute. That gave Harper and Krinkle enough real time to get back to the bus and gone.

The man would come around and he would radio in and repeat his call that he'd stumbled on a possible four-five-nine at Arctic X Air Services. Arriving police officers would call it a bungled, third-rate burglary. Till one detective would notice something odd on the workstation monitor. That oddity would lead to the uncovering of serious criminal activity involving bank fraud, money laundering, and tax evasion on the part of a dozen well-known corporate honchos who passed through Arctic X. Agent Richard "Dick" Kerr would be hailed as a hero. That's how Krinkle explained it to Harper back on the bus as the world spun beneath its wheels.

"I'm telling you, Homeland Security will make him Employee of the Month," Krinkle said, settling down at the console and getting ready to kick on the reel-to-reels and broadcast to the millions of human souls tuning in. He stopped what he was doing as if he'd hit a thought head-on. He looked at Harper. "Suppose he might be a little confused wondering why he's sitting in the chair instead of standing in the doorway?"

"Maybe," Harper said. "Not like we had a choice to fix it."

"No, we didn't." The roadie kicked the bottom drawer under his console and it popped open. "Time for some of the inspector's single malt."

"Orders?" Harper said.

"Fuck no. I'm just thirsty. Aren't you?"

"Sure."

Harper pulled out the bottle of Galileo, grabbed the coffee mugs, and poured healthy measures. He set one mug on the roadie's audio console and carried his to the front of the bus to have a look at the stars. He drank and felt something gnaw at his guts. He reviewed his timeline, looking for anything he may have missed.

He had found the face of interest hidden in the occipital lobe of Agent Kerr's brain, right where the roadie said it would be. It was buried in a twenty-second clip of the man's memory left by the bad guys. Harper uploaded the clip into his own eyes and let it run. He was seeing the world through the POV of Agent Kerr's eyes.

Around midnight; a cold wind blowing in off Cook Inlet.

Two black Gulfstream G650s sitting on the apron of Arctic X Air Services and lights from the hangar washing over the scene. Four men in black leather jackets next to a metal container on the ground. In Kerr's eyes they are just four men; Harper makes them for goons. The container is open, and Kerr is looking down at a meter-long wooden pole carved with depictions of stars and moons, bears and eagles. It's topped with an oval-shaped head bearing an Asian-looking face. *It's what they wanted him to see.*

Then a paregoric voice wrapped in a Russian accent: "Are you satisfied with your inspection of the artifact?"

Kerr looks up, sees a tall man with long silver hair, eyes covered with dark glasses. He asks the tall man to remove the glasses for a visual identification and looks down at his own hands. They're open, if holding things that are not there. *But he sees something. Passports, must be.*

Kerr speaks: "Excuse me, how do you pronounce your name, sir?"

The tall man takes off his dark glasses and reveals his silver-colored eyes.

"Komarovsky. My name is Komarovsky."

The clip ends on a freeze-frame, and Harper sees the silver eyes he had seen in the cathedral job staring back. Harper added it up: Komarovsky wasn't just another bad-guy chief; he was the *one*. The betrayer of the creation, the source of evil in paradise. He was undead, he was all-powerful, he had Katherine Taylor's child and he wanted Harper to know it. Lines of causality began to intersect in Harper's eyes. Then came a wave, then came a flood. Then the lines ricocheted like bullets, slamming into one another and creating a singular density of mass that sucked in all there was, all there would be. "Fearful sights and great signs" didn't begin to describe it. If Komarovsky succeeded, it would be the end of everything.

"Bloody hell."

That's when Krinkle shook Harper. Told him to get out of Agent Kerr's head; told him it was time to get their skates on and get back to the bus. Message on the roadie's cell phone:

FLASH TRAFFIC

RDP: +E821-65CFR+

EX: DRAGON6/SUTF

EYES ONLY: MAGIC BUS AND BLUE LIGHT

SUBJECT: LIFE STATUS/PATIENT

ASTRUC AWAKENED. RETURN TO BASE.

SIXTEEN

i

Karoliina touched the timbers surrounding Marie-Madeleine. She felt the ancient wood reverberate with the great bell's voice. Marie had just rung for six o'clock in the evening. All across Lausanne people were on their way somewhere. Karoliina watched them, listened to the sounds of their voices and footsteps. Some made their way to bus stops, some to Metro stations; some walked through alleyways, some crossed bridges. Karoliina noticed a curious thing about the people she watched. Coming to the crest of a hill or finding an opening between buildings with a clear view of the world, they stopped and stared. Out there was the silver-gray lake and the shadowy mountains that cradled its shores. Above it all was the leaden sky now glowing firelike by a sun cutting through the clouds and hovering above the horizon for long minutes. The Earth rotated on its axis a few degrees more, the sun disappeared, and the people continued on their way. Karoliina wondered if they realized they had received a blessing.

She pulled the hood of her sheepskin over her head and walked clockwise around the belfry. She checked the shadows in the exterior alcoves of Palais de Rumine, then down on Place de la Riponne. All clear. At the north balcony she could see down into the old city, where people gathered in the cafés along Rue Cité-Devant. At the end of the narrow road the twin turrets of Château Saint-Maire were set against the gathering dark.

In medieval beforetimes the château overlooked the main gates into the city. And in those days *le guet de Lausanne* called the hour every hour. When he did, the guards at Château Saint-Maire would answer, *"Rien à signaler." All is well.*

Funny how the times don't change, Karoliina thought. She pulled an infrared illuminator from her jacket, set it to eye-safe, and flipped in the red filter. She pointed it toward the château, signaled in Morse code: *Side one; track three.* Twin flashes came back at her from the twin turrets: *Black Metallic.*

She walked along the east balcony and checked the shadows along the esplanade where it rounded the lantern tower of the cathedral. Clear. She turned, saw Marie-Madeleine resting in her timbers.

"Hyvää itlaa, madame," she said.

It was her custom to offer a good evening to the great bell, but the bell never answered; not yet. Ella said the bell would answer one day. She said after Marc Rochat died it took a long time for any of the bells to talk to her, too. They were very sad, Ella said. It wasn't until she began to play classical guitar next to Marie-Madeleine, to keep her company through the night as she rested between ringing the hours, that the great bell began to speak again. Marie-Madeleine thanked Ella for the music. And it wasn't long after that that the bell told Ella she thought she might like to hear the cello, because she imagined the sound was rounder. When Ella began to play the cello, all Marie-Madeleine's sisters began to talk to her, too. They liked Bach's Cello Suite No. 1 in G Major very much, Ella said. The quick up-and-down notes reminded them of the way Marc Rochat mumbled to himself as he shuffled around the belfry. Sometimes, in the Prelude, the bells would hum along. That's what Ella said. It made Karoliina smile each time she remembered the young girl saying it; her emerald eyes were bright with belief.

Coming back to the south balcony, Karoliina checked the esplanade below the belfry. The cobblestones, the ramparts overlooking Lausanne, the chestnut trees, the fountain on the esplanade, were all clear.

Beep, beep; beep, beep.

She walked to the top of the steps, looked inside the turret, and checked the bank of monitors displaying the views from the CCTV cameras at the belfry's access points. On monitor three she saw Locomotora's drummer/nowtimes cathedral guard crossing the ramp through the women's choir loft. He was carrying a large shopping bag in one hand and a small white cardboard box in the other. Reaching the sealed door at the end of the ramp, he juggled things about to get the palm of his right hand onto the fifth stone up from the floor. Karoliina waited for him to look up at the CCTV camera, then engaged the retinal scan software. She got a green light, reached into the turret, and set her hand on the first stone to the left. She watched the sealed door ease open and the drummer pass through to the bottom of the corkscrew steps going up on monitor four. When the door sealed itself, she turned to Marie-Madeleine.

"Dinner has arrived, madame."

The great bell was unimpressed.

"More for Ella and me, then."

She heard footsteps wind up the belfry; when they reached the last turn, Karoliina smelled the food.

"Vegetarian lasagna with wild chanterelle mushrooms and béchamel sauce," she called down.

The drummer came into view. He leaned against the central pillar, looked up at Karoliina. "How do you do that?" he said.

"I've got a nose for food."

The drummer held up the small white box for her to sniff. "What's for dessert?"

"Lemon mousse with raspberries?"

"Fuck off. There's a trick to it, I know there is."

He handed up the goods, and Karoliina took them. She gave the top of the Escaliers du Marché a quick check to see if the drummer had been followed. Clear.

"How's the crowd at Café du Grütli?"

"They all miss Ella coming down for her supper. Monsieur Dufaux asked how she is. He says if there's anything she needs, let him know."

Karoliina glanced back through the timbers, saw the light of the lantern glowing against the window of the loge. *Le guet* was inside and hiding from the world. She looked at the drummer.

"She spent the night imagining how each of them died."

"The innocents at Mon Repos?"

Karoliina nodded. "It's the only way she can process her grief. She says it's her duty. She has been sleeping most of the afternoon."

"Poor girl," the drummer said.

He took off his leather jacket and dropped it on the stone steps. He grabbed his kill kit from a hook on the central pillar. Karoliina's was hanging next to it. Except for the band's lead guitarist on the roof with a Barrett Light Fifty, the belfry was a no-weapons zone. He slipped his kit over his shoulders, tightening the straps. Another hook held his UZI submachine gun, fitted with laser targeting and sound suppression. He grabbed it and checked the firing chamber and ammo magazine. It was good to go.

"Caught any dreams yet?" he said.

Karoliina shook her head. "Grief suppresses rapid eye movement. There's nothing to catch. You're in the nave tonight?"

"And the crypt."

"Lucky you. How are the rest of the boys?"

"Looking forward to the gig on the weekend. We're doing the new tunes. Fliers hit the streets this morning, all across Europe. Fans should be coming to town soon."

"Cool."

The drummer reached inside his jacket, found the visual data monocle. He slipped the holding strap over his neck and fitted the monocle over his right eye. "Any word from Krinkle?"

"On the air, on his way back with Harper. They should be crossing Pont Bessières soon."

"Back in the protected zone."

"Yeah."

The drummer tapped a polyrhythmic riff on the central pillar. "Dufaux says the word is the mission took them to hell and back."

"What did you say?"

"I said there's no such place as hell."

"Good," Karoliina said. "No need to panic anyone."

"You must be happy he's back."

"I'm happy they're all back, and in one piece."

"You know what I mean."

"Joo," Karoliina said, "I know what you mean.

The drummer lifted his leather jacket from the floor and put it on. "How do you love someone you can't touch, Karoliina? How does that one work?"

"Ask Krinkle."

The drummer laughed, turned around, and headed down the belfry steps. *"Nähdään."*

"Later to you, too. Say hello to the skeletons."

"I will. You should come down sometime. Some of those old bones have some great stories."

The sound of the drummer's steps down the belfry segued into the half-hour double-tap rising from the bells at the Hôtel de Ville on Place de la Palud. *All's well,* Karoliina thought. She walked to the small wooden door set between the timbers, pressed the iron latch, and quietly opened the door of the loge. She entered carefully so not to knock the cello tucked in the alcove behind the door. She saw Ella at the far end of the oddly shaped room, sitting on the edge of the bed. She held a Mason Pearson brush in her hands. Lantern light lit her face and her eyes glistened.

"Ella?"

The girl didn't speak.

Karoliina set the food on the small wooden table. She walked toward Ella and saw tears in the girl's eyes. With the next step, she realized the girl was half asleep, hanging between two states of consciousness. Karoliina moved closer, opening her arms to catch the girl if she fell forward when told to awake.

"Vakna, litla."

The girl didn't move.

"Can you hear me, *litla*?"

The girl spoke slowly, carefully. "There was a baby cow. The cow was red and it had a pretty red face. Men laid it on a black rock in the City of the Three Gods. They cut open its throat and the cow's blood flowed over the black rock. But the cow did not want to die, and it struggled to live. It tried to cry out, but it had no voice. It kicked its hind legs, its hooves scraped the black rock now covered in blood. The blood became fire and the fire spread and consumed the men, then it consumed the whole world."

Karoliina pulled her japa mala beads from her coat and rubbed them together in the palms of her hands. She held the beads before Ella's face. The girl breathed in the scent of sandalwood, exhaled over the beads. If she was dreaming, the beads would become warm to the touch. The beads remained cool.

"Ella, is this an imagination?"

"No, it's what he said."

"Who?"

The girl blinked slowly. The dream catcher saw she was still half asleep.

"Who was it, Ella? Who told you these things?"

"Marc Rochat. He was here."

Karoliina looked around the loge. The light of the lantern moved in waves and brightened the oddly shaped room. There were only teasing shadows in the high corners.

"Where did you see him, Ella?"

Le guet de Lausanne pointed to the wall at the foot of her small bed. Mounted on a timber was the small console table and matching mirror.

"There."

The japa mala beads warmed in Karoliina's hands; then they began to burn.

ii

Reentry across Pont Bessières had been smooth. Lausanne was quiet and all was well within the protected zone. Krinkle made a quick stop along

Rue Pierre-Viret below the cathedral. He opened the bus door and told Harper to get off, go home, and get cleaned up.

"Then what?" Harper said.

"How should I know?"

"What about you?"

"I'm going to Vevey to have a chat with Brother Astruc."

Harper nodded. "You sure we shouldn't have gone on to Vladivostok?"

"And do what?"

"Find Max, for one."

"We know where Max is."

"Where?"

"To a wrinkle in time where the demons dwell, brother."

"Meaning what?"

"Meaning exactly that. Look, we know Komarovsky has the child. We also know he's going to use him as bait, so we'll wait him out."

"What sort of bait? For what?"

"We're working on it."

Harper got off and watched the magic bus disappear around the bend in the road at Palais de Rumine. Harper looked this way and that down the road; nobody. He wondered if it was a good thing or a bad thing. The headlamps of the number 16 trolley rounded the bend from the same direction where Krinkle had just disappeared. A blazing light blasted Harper in the eyes and blinded him a second. He reached in his mackintosh and grabbed his SIG Sauer from his kill kit. He was set to raise it and fire when he saw an ordinary-looking driver behind the wheel and a load of everyday locals onboard. Given he'd spent time in hell and looked like it, not to mention he had a gun in his hand, Harper thought about disappearing into a shadow. He didn't. He hid the gun behind his back and watched the onboard faces watch him as they rode by. He met their glances, each time releasing a glint of eternal light from his emerald-colored eyes. The locals would see him and not see him at the same time. And in the dark hours to come, they would feel a touch of comfort and would dream of angels. The number 16 was well gone before Harper allowed himself to process the fact he'd just violated rules and regs by revealing himself unto them.

"Sod it."

He turned around, counted his way up the last steps of the Escaliers du Marché till he reached the esplanade where the great façade of Lausanne Cathedral filled his eyes. It had rained earlier and the still-dripping limestone arch above the wooden doors sparkled in the floodlights. Harper walked closer, saw the gargoyles and statues of saints and prophets carved in stone. Closer still, he gave the wooden doors and iron latches a recon. Inspector Gobet was right; repairs had left not a trace of the events four nights ago—or was it three nights ago? Hard to tell. Harper was still having difficulty with the back and forth through time. But what happened on whatever night it was remained clear: The great wooden doors to the cathedral had been locked, so Harper had shot his way in. Then he'd helped Krinkle drag Astruc to the altar square. The renegade priest was to be awakened by Monsieur Gabriel, but *le guet de Lausanne* had been waiting for them instead. And she had a message from a lad with a lantern whom Harper watched die years before: *You cannot carry the weight alone anymore, monsieur. You have fallen two times. The third time will be the last. You must wait.* Harper felt himself go weak at the knees. He fell against a limestone column, grabbed it, and balanced himself.

"Bloody hell."

A chilly breeze came up from the lake and hit Harper in the back. He got a whiff of the foul stench on his clothes and skin. He looked at the gloves on his hands. They were covered with the detritus of mass death. Words on paper flashed through his eyes.

Blessed are the—

The words were gone before he could finish reading them. But he knew the words from somewhere.

Forget it, boyo, keep moving, whispered the dead soldier in his head.

"Right."

Harper stuffed his hands in the pockets of his coat, headed into the old city. He got to Number 27, Rue Charles-Vuillermet. He dug through his pockets, found the keys to the door, and let himself in. He climbed the creaky stairs four floors up, passing two flats each floor, until he reached the top landing with one door. Oddly, the same key that opened the door to the street opened the door to his studio flat. He always meant to ask Inspector Gobet about it. Seemed to be pretty lax security, but he never got around to the asking. There was always something to do. Too much back and forth through time. He unlocked the door.

It was the same scene as the last time he'd been ordered back to his flat after a mission. Laid out on the kitchen table was a takeaway job from LP's Bar at the Palace: club sandwich, side of chips, a bottle of Swiss pinot noir. On the floor was an envelope that had been slipped under the door. It bore the seal of the Lausanne Palace and was addressed to *Notre Cher Client*.

"And I bet I know what's inside."

He picked it up, opened it.

"Bingo."

It was another letter written in perfect cursive script. This time *le concierge du Lausanne Palace* welcomed *notre cher client* back and suggested that before dining he might first wish to bathe.

"Well spotted, mate," Harper said.

Accordingly, please remove all personal belongings from your clothing and dump the filthy, stinking rags in *the laundry bag provided in the lavatory*. And yes, there were a fresh bathrobe and slippers provided for his convenience. *Please be aware,* the concierge continued, *that the reported condition of your current wardrobe* meant there would be a delay in returning the clothes. *Therefore, please find in your closet* a new sports coat, shirts and trousers, shoes and overcoat, *purchased from the Caritas Thrift Boutique on Avenue de Morges in Lausanne and delivered to your residence*. There were also assorted items, including *one necktie, suitable for a gentleman*.

"A gentleman?"

Harper walked to the small closet and opened it. Hanging from the rail, wrapped in plastic, were the items as described. Weirdly, the clothes weren't that different from the stinking rags he had on, just cleaner. Tweed sports coat, white oxford shirt, wool trousers. The one shelf above the rail held an assortment of boxer shorts, white T-shirts, and argyle socks. He pushed aside the hanging clothes, got a look at the overcoat. Right; the black double-breasted trench coat was a definite step up. The inside label read *Burberry* and there was an image of an equestrian knight in full battle array charging ahead with his lance at the ready. A banner flew above the brave knight: *Prorsum. Forward.*

He pushed the overcoat aside, found the tie suitable for a gentleman on its own hanger. Silk it was, with alternating broad silver stripes intercut with narrow black and white stripes. The pattern was woven into the fabric at a descending angle of 140 degrees. It looked like an old school tie, or a tie from one of the gentlemen's clubs on Pall Mall in London. Maybe one of the lesser clubs, the kind that used secret handshakes.

"Swell."

Harper looked at the letter for further instructions.

There was a final paragraph advising Harper that, one, *the bioskin gloves used to cover the seeping wounds on the palms of your hands* needed to be replaced, and two, *your esteemed presence is requested to attend to certain administrative matters on the morrow. Therefore,* his esteemed whatsit would be picked up at 09:45 hours *in order to be transported to the Vevey Clinic to attend to the aforementioned administrative matters.* That would mean being hauled to Vevey by Inspector Gobet's muscle, Mutt and Jeff, whether he liked it or not. The letter ended with the concierge inviting Harper to *enjoy your evening.*

"Cheers."

He headed to the bathroom. The neatly folded bathrobe and comfy slippers from the Lausanne Palace Hotel were waiting on the sink. He pulled off his mackintosh and sports coat, stuffed them in the laundry bag. He pulled off his kill kit and hung it from the hook at the back of the door. He stripped down and dumped the rest of his stinking rags into the laundry bag, too. He turned on the shower and cranked it two stops short of scalding.

He got in the shower and spent a long time scrubbing his form with soap before rinsing off; then he washed and scrubbed two more times. As the shower and bathroom filled with steam, he raised the palms of his gloved hands and stood motionless in the falling water. It rushed from the nozzle at needlelike pressure; it stabbed at his palms. He gritted his teeth against the pain but did not lower his hands until the smell of death was eluted from his form. He rinsed his mouth and flushed his nose and ears three times to get rid of any lingering molecules of human corruption. He watched tiny streams of black mucus and spit spiral down the drain. He considered his two and a half million years of walking the battlefields of paradise. He arrived at a common truth: Mass death could be washed from his form, but it could not be cleansed from his eternal being. Like all the faces of the suffering ones, like the sounds of their cries, the scent of spilled blood and rotting flesh was a forever thing. The spiraling black streams disappeared and the water ran clear. The words on paper flashed through his eyes again, and he pronounced them:

"Blessed are the dead that the rain rains upon."

It was from a poem. Something he had read somewhere. He ran his timeline, came up with nothing. He shut off the water, grabbed a towel, and dried himself. He tossed on the robe and slippers. He thought about shaving, but the mirror was well fogged. He almost wiped the glass but didn't, and he watched a face emerge from behind the fog. The face had blond hair, patrician features, blue eyes. Its expression was one of sadness. So was the sound of its voice.

Remembering again that I shall die,
And neither hear the rain nor give it thanks,
For washing me cleaner than I have been,
Since I was born into this solitude.

He blinked and wiped the mirror with his towel. It was only Captain Jay Michael Harper, late of Her Majesty's Special Reconnaissance Regiment, looking back at him now.

"Right."

Harper grabbed his kill kit, slung it over his shoulder, and walked to the kitchen table. He picked up a section of the club sandwich and took a bite. Odd. He laid it on the plate and opened it. Instead of ham in the middle, there was a healthy slab of Norwegian salmon. *Not bad,* he thought.

He opened the pinot noir, poured a glass. He sipped. He looked around the sitting area for the TV remote. On the floor, under the scratched-up footstool. He grabbed it, pressed the power button, and the TV screen came on. He selected the programming guide. One hundred thirty-nine channels were listed, but on his TV only one channel came in: the History Channel. *Too bad,* he sometimes thought, looking at the forbidden fruit of choices. He read through his one working channel's offerings for the night. Two programs grabbed his attention. *A Walk Through Hell: Dante and the Shaping of Human Consciousness* at midnight. That one was followed by *British Poets of the Great War.*

"What a surprise."

He heard steps climbing the stairwell of his building. The steps stopped at the threshold of his flat. He reflected on the nature of surprises in Lausanne. Most of them weren't surprises at all. After all, how can there be a surprise when nothing in this town was by bloody accident? But in his two years of living in this flat, he had never heard anyone come up the bloody stairwell.

Knock, knock.

Harper pulled his SIG Sauer, put a round in the firing chamber. He walked to the door and set the gun barrel against the wood, chest-high.

"Who's there?" Harper said.

"Just open the door and don't go all Léon the Professional on me."

It was a voice he didn't recognize, but it registered as not a threat.

"Sorry, who is Léon?"

"A French hit man in a Luc Besson flick. He falls in love with a twelve-year-old girl. He also shoots a bad guy through the door. Great scene. But as this isn't a movie and I'm not one of the bad guys, you would be wasting your time."

Harper stepped back, kept his SIG aimed as he opened the door. There was a tall guy in black leathers. He had a monocle set over his right eye.

"You're with Krinkle's band," Harper said.

"No, I'm *in* the band. I'm the drummer. There's a huge fucking difference, sir."

Harper ejected the round from his SIG. The drummer plucked it from the air, rapped the hollow-point tip against the door.

"For the record, this door may look like a cheap piece of wood, but it's bulletproof. Had you pulled the trigger, you would've blown your face off." The drummer offered the bullet to Harper; he took it.

"So how did you know I had a gun behind the bulletproof door?" Harper said.

The drummer pointed to the monocle on his face. "New kit from the Swiss cop. It reads body heat and detects metal shapes through solid surfaces up to nine inches thick. It also works as a night sight, downloads and processes data at nine petaFLOPS per second. Which means I can keep an eye on the cathedral, work on my doctoral thesis on palindromic prime numbers, order a pizza, and read through the complete works of Tolstoy all at the same time. Which is what I was doing in the crypt before I got a message to find you. I was reading *War and Peace* aloud to the skeletons. We're at the part where Bezukhov is force-marched out of Moscow with Napoleon's Grand Army. One of the skeletons told me he was a sergeant in a company of Swiss Grenadiers back then and that Napoleon's army wasn't so grand. And he says the Russian winter of 1812 was an absolute bitch. Any more useless questions, sir, or can I get to the point?"

"Go ahead," Harper said.

"Karoliina needs to see you. She'll meet you after the three o'clock bells on the cathedral esplanade. At the fountain under the chestnut. Be there or be square. *Nähdään.*"

The drummer turned around and headed down the stairs.

SEVENTEEN

i

Marie-Madeleine rang for three o'clock.

Harper stepped back into the shadows of the chestnut trees. He watched the belfry's south balcony, saw a crack of light in the timbers as someone came out of the loge. It was *le guet de Lausanne* making her final rounds of the night. She passed through the southeast turret and was gone from Harper's eyes. He waited, heard her call to the east: *"C'est le guet. Il a sonné trois. Il a sonné trois."* Then to the north, then the west. When she returned to the south balcony, Harper saw her clearly: a small form wrapped in a black cloak, blond hair topped with a black floppy hat, raising her lantern into the dark and calling out once more over Lausanne: *"C'est le guet. Il a sonné trois. Il a sonné trois."* She held the lantern steady and did not move. It wasn't until Karoliina came onto the balcony and touched the girl's shoulder that she lowered the lantern and reentered the loge.

Harper looked around the esplanade. Nobody. He stepped from the shadows, walked to the fountain. He leaned down and drank from the spout. The water was cold. He straightened up and wiped dribbles from his mouth.

"Long time, no drink."

He walked to the rampart overlooking Lausanne. He sensed he was at the target-acquired end of a sniper's night sight. He noted positions offering a line of sight within an effective firing range of nineteen hundred yards. The Bel-Air building above Flon, the belfry of the Catholic church in the Riponne quarter, one of the thirteenth-century row houses along Rue du Rotillon. Each position was far enough away that Harper wouldn't hear the shot when taken. He'd only hear the buzz of a .416 brass bullet drilling through the air at more than three thousand feet per second. Lights-out, then comes the *crack*. But just now any snipers holding him in their sights were under the command of Inspector Jacques Gobet.

"We hope."

A bank of coin-operated binoculars stood next to him. Two Swiss francs for five minutes' viewing, the notice read. *Why not?* he thought. He dug through his trousers pockets; no luck. He'd have to settle for his eyeballs. He looked down over the sleeping town and down the hill to the crescent-shaped lake. The five-hundred-foot drop to the water gave him a rush of vertigo, and he wobbled under the weight of his form. He was carrying more than usual tonight.

"Here we go again."

He leaned against the rampart and dug through the pockets of his trench coat, searching for his electronic fag. The new coat was like the smoker; it took some getting used to. The pockets split into bigger pouches at either side of the coat, and things had a way of getting lost. He dug deeper, fumbled with his keys, some scraps of paper, and the silver-striped tie he had yet to put on. He found the fag and pulled it out. *Press here, little blue light there, inhale.* The vapor seeped deep into his form and he stabilized. *All's well for now,* Harper thought. He flashed the new one, Ella, and her message from the dead lad a few nights ago. *Don't fall for a third time, monsieur, or you won't get up,* was the gist of it. He had yet to track how that imagination was planted in her mind, or by whom. Maybe it didn't matter; maybe all that mattered was the truth of it: Harper's episodes of vertigo and crushing weight were occurring with increasing intensity. His mouth went dry thinking about it. He looked at the fountain.

"Actually, wine would be better. Any color will do."

Kaclack.

He turned around. The narrow red door at the base of the belfry tower opened and Karoliina walked out onto the esplanade. She saw Harper and smiled from under the hood of her sheepskin coat. Her japa mala beads were swinging from her right hand, and promisingly, her left hand held a straw-wrapped Chianti bottle. Harper watched the way she moved. She was as delicate and quiet as a cat. She stopped at the fountain and pulled the hood from her blond hair.

"Hyvää iltaa."

"Good evening, mademoiselle. And good timing."

"Good timing?"

Harper pointed to the fountain. "I was just thinking I could use a bit of wine."

The dream catcher smiled. "I hate to break it to you, but there's no running water in the loge. I told Ella I needed to come down for some. If you're thirsty, you need to stick to water for the moment."

It had been years since Harper had visited the belfry, but the line about fetching water from the well sounded familiar.

"How is she?"

"It was a difficult evening, but she is resting now."

"Good," Harper said.

"Sometimes she wonders when you're coming to hear her play the cello for Marie-Madeleine."

Harper glanced up to the belfry. He sighed, looked at Karoliina. "I'm afraid I got rather busy."

"You want me to tell her that?"

"No."

"Then I guess we'll just have to make it happen."

"Sure."

Karoliina eyed Harper from head to toe. "The clothes look nice on you," she said.

"Cheers. They're from a thrift shop."

"I know, I picked them out. And for the record, only in Lausanne would you find a perfectly fine Burberry in a thrift shop."

"You picked them?"

"Krinkle sent me a test message on a back channel. He said you needed new clothes. He told me to go to the thrift shop, pick some up, and drop them off at the Palace to be cleaned in whatever magic soap it is they use on anything that touches your skin."

"Sorry?"

"Apparently you have sensitive skin as a result of your undefined metaphysical condition."

"You're joking me."

"Really? Which of us is the one wearing the magic gloves?"

Harper looked at the bionic skin covering the seeping wounds on his palms.

"There is that," he said.

"Where is the tie? It's an antique. I thought you would like it."

Harper reached in his coat, dug through the pockets. He pulled out the tie and held it up. "You mean this one?"

"Joo."

"I was having difficulty with it. The tips either came out too long or too short."

Karoliina rested the Chianti bottle on the edge of the fountain, walked to Harper, and took the tie. She laid it around her own neck. She made a couple inverted loops and formed and tightened a well-crafted knot. She pulled it from her neck, handed it to Harper.

"It's a Kelvin knot, named after Baron William Thomson. He was a British physicist, June 1824 to December 1907. He had a wild theory about knots and atomic structure. He also figured the temperature of absolute zero at minus 459.67 degrees Fahrenheit."

"Is that so?"

"*Se on totta.* Here, put on the tie. Let's see how it looks on you."

Harper took the tie, fitted it under his shirt collar, and tightened the knot. The tips were perfect. He looked at her. "Verdict?"

"Nice," she said. "I have to say, it's easier to spruce you up than Krinkle and the boys in the band."

"Sorry?"

"Krinkle's got twelve pairs of denim overalls and twelve pairs of black steel-toed boots, all identical. I once got him a nice woolly jumper. It's still in the box. And the boys? If it isn't black, they don't want to know about it."

Harper didn't quite know what to make of the intel. "Right."

He watched Karoliina walk back to the fountain, grab the Chianti bottle, and uncork it. She held it under the spout and filled it.

"Where is Krinkle?" Harper said.

"What do you mean, where is Krinkle? You know where Krinkle is. He's at the clinic in Vevey trying to get Astruc to spill."

"What I mean is, mademoiselle, why am I talking to you alone? There are comms procedures and clearances, not to mention chains of command."

"I never took you for a stickler on chains of command."

Harper stared at her. "Why isn't he here, mademoiselle?"

Karoliina recorked the Chianti bottle, let it float in the basin.

"He said if you asked to tell you he'll see you this evening in Lausanne. He's setting up for the band's concert at La Cave du Bleu Lézard later tonight."

"A concert."

"You disapprove?"

Harper took a long hit of radiance. "Not long ago, in Alaska, he was babbling about fearful sights and great signs."

"I know."

"He told you?"

"Joo."

"What did he tell you about it?"

"That it looks like it's coming down."

"So he's going to set up for a music festival."

"What do you want him to do, weep? The gig is going live on the Net. It's important. Millions of souls will be tuning in. Besides, when I told Krinkle I needed to talk to you and what it was about, he said I should go ahead because the cathedral was your patch."

Harper shrugged. "Seeing as this is my patch, who will be pulling security while your boys are at play?" Harper said.

"A crew from New Zealand. Call sign Jakob. They're in Berlin this week, but Krinkle has booked them to play Lausanne the night after Locomotora."

"One more post-rock band with guns, I take it."

There was an expression of *ouch* on Karoliina's face.

"I don't think Jakob would care to be described as 'one more post-rock band,' guns included or not. Other than that you are spot-on. Three musicians up front, one sound mixer, one lighting tech, and two roadies behind the scenes. They're an experienced squad and more than capable of holding the ground around the cathedral as things stand. Between us and them, we make a platoon. Over the next few days two more bands will make the scene: one from Sweden, another from Copenhagen. Add in a couple thousand followers and we will be a brigade capable of holding the old city for as long as we can."

Harper took a hit from his electronic fag and huffed on radiance while turning over the dream catcher's words.

"Are you telling me partisans are being redeployed to Lausanne because the shit is about to hit the fan here?"

"Did you hear me say those words?"

"Words have lots of meanings, mademoiselle, depending on which side of the mouth they're spilling from."

Karoliina swung her japa mala beads in a circle. "Then let me be perfectly clear, monsieur. The meaning of my words is that there is going to be some great music in Lausanne over the next week, all of it going out live on the Net. Of course, if you want to imagine an alternative meaning, such as partisans being redeployed to Lausanne to stand between the cathedral and whatever fearful sights and great signs might be coming down while you're in Jerusalem, then go right ahead."

"Am I going to Jerusalem?"

"You might be."

"Depending on what?"

"Depending on whether you believe what I have to tell you."

Harper smiled. "You two are a lot alike."

"Who?"

"You and Krinkle."

"How so?"

"You both know the state of play better than I do. And you both know more about me than I do."

She smiled again, from a deeper place this time. *"Kiitos paljon."*

"You're welcome. But before I believe another word out of your mouth, you need to answer some questions."

"Shoot."

"How did Krinkle know you were a dream catcher? How did he find you?"

"He didn't. I found him. Long story."

Harper had another pull of radiance. "Tell me."

"Is that an order?"

"If need be."

"Or what? You'll take me down?"

"If need be."

"Et luota minuun?" You don't trust me?

Harper touched his perfectly tipped silver-striped tie. "Mademoiselle, this is the regimental tie of the 28th Artists Rifles, a Special Forces reserve unit in the British Army from 1859 through 1945. The regiment was made up of volunteers including architects, painters, writers, and poets. Eight members of the regiment received the Victoria Cross during the Great War. Earlier this evening a second lieutenant named Edward Thomas got into my head to pay me a visit. Which was odd, as he was killed Easter Monday, 1917, while serving with the Royal Garrison Artillery at the Battle of Arras. Thing is, before Edward Thomas became a soldier, he was a poet. And when he first enlisted in the army in 1915, he joined Artists Rifles."

Karoliina folded her arms across her chest. Her manner suggested she was not the least bit surprised at the turn in the conversation. "And what did the poet in your head have to say?" she said.

"He told me my days are numbered. He said it poetically, but that was the message."

"'Blessed are the dead that the rain rains upon.'"

"That's right. And now I'm wearing an antique tie you picked up in a Lausanne thrift shop. What are the odds of this tie having belonged to

Edward Thomas? What are the odds it was given to me to hotwire my brain and reconnect me to a form I once occupied?"

"If I were you, I would bet the farm on both counts."

Harper stepped closer to her. "I already have one dead soldier in my head, mademoiselle. Now there's one more. Granted, the latter came, dropped the good news about my days being numbered, and left. But I can barely stand under the weight he left behind."

"You don't think Krinkle sees that? You don't think I saw it when I met you on the Paris-to-Lausanne train?"

"Then why?"

"You think we're trying to kill you?"

"Are you?"

"No."

"Then what's the game?"

Karoliina leaned into him. "Look into *my* eyes, monsieur, and listen to the sound of *my* voice. Krinkle does what he does because he has no choice. Me? I do it because I believe in your kind, I will die for your kind. Perhaps it might be best if you get beyond being as fucked-up as you are from your undefined metaphysical bullshit and realize I'm trying to help you."

"To do what?"

"To not fall under the weight you are carrying, to not give up on the world. Because without you, every soul on this planet will be lost forever."

Harper laughed a little. "Bit of an epic stretch, isn't it, mademoiselle?"

"Is it?"

"I'd say so. Besides, giving up on anything would require my making a choice. I can't do that."

"Krinkle says you made a choice once, that you changed the course of human history by making it. It's why you were resurrected before the cathedral job."

Harper took a long hit of radiance. "I believe the term is 'awakened,' mademoiselle."

"I meant 'resurrection.'"

"There's no such thing."

"And you thought there was no such thing as Hell until you went there and rescued Katherine Taylor."

Her voice registered as absolute truth. He looked up at the sky. There were fast-moving clouds coming in from the west and crossing the face of the moon. Each time another cloud passed, there was another face looking down on him.

"How much does Krinkle know about me?"

"More than most."

"How?"

"He got into Astruc's files on you long before HQ got ahold of them during the Paris job. He read through your apparitions in paradise all the way back to 70 anno Domini."

That one hit Harper like a .416—*crack*.

"That's funny," he said.

"Funny how?"

"Because earlier tonight he failed to mention it while briefing me on all things anno Domini from 67 to 73. Oddly enough, year 70 fits dead in the middle."

"So?"

"Nothing's a bloody accident in paradise, mademoiselle."

"Then I guess you'll have to ask him."

"I guess I will."

Harper stared at her. He couldn't get a read on the manner of the dream catcher's thinking. Where the hell was she going with this drip, drip, drip of intel? Was she going rogue? Was she trying to warn him of a setup? Was she a traitor? He checked over his shoulder, scanned the locations where snipers were holed up. So far there were no laser threads lining him up. He looked back at Karoliina.

"Does Inspector Gobet know the state of play just now?"

"It's Inspector Gobet's world, we only live in it."

Harper smoked, ran her intel so far. One: The cop in the cashmere coat and the roadie were working a clandestine operation almost two thousand years old. Two: The roadie was the agent provocateur; the cop was pulling the strings from behind a door marked "Plausible Denial."

Three: Harper was the sleeper in the middle without a clue, and just now the dream catcher was staring at him as if he were a thing of wonder. He put it together. This meet wasn't about spilling intel from the cop or the roadie; it was intel from her.

"What about you, mademoiselle? What do you know about me?"

"As of tonight, the works."

"The works."

"*Joo.* And I wanted to tell you before I reported it in. I figure you deserve to know. And I had some interesting help receiving the intel."

Harper nodded toward the belfry. "The new one, Ella, she was your interesting help."

"In part."

"Sorry?"

Karoliina tossed her japa mala beads at Harper. He bounced the beads in his gloved hands, caught a scent of sandalwood.

"They're warm."

"You should have been here a few hours ago—they would have boiled water."

"I take it that is unusual."

"You could say that. Those beads are older than dirt. How they found their way to me is a wonderful tale, but maybe we'll do that one later. Bottom line: When a dream catcher needs to explore someone's dream, that someone breathes over the beads as they sleep. Different dreams affect different beads, combinations and sequences of how the beads are warmed reveal the dream to the catcher."

"And when the beads boil water?"

"Beats me, it's never happened before. But I have a theory. It has to do with the nature of reincarnated souls, one soul in particular."

The words popped hot.

"Those are my words."

"That is so. You said them to Krinkle on the altar square of the cathedral after Ella saved Astruc with the lantern. You wanted to ask Ella about one particular soul she said was in the nave, a soul she said was talking to her from the shadows."

Harper ripped back on his timeline. He saw the girl holding the lantern, refusing to surrender it to him, telling him he was too weak to say the words, telling him that's what *he* said . . .

"For Christ's sake, Ella, no one is here. No one is talking to you but me."

"Not you talking . . . Marc Rochat."

Harper blinked himself to nowtimes. His eyes locked on the patch of stones to the right, just under the belfry, where the lad hit the ground and died two years ago. For half a second, Harper saw him lying there.

"She imagined the lad was in the cathedral, she imagined the lad was talking to her."

"He was."

Harper shook his head. "The girl was juiced."

"Wrong."

Harper tossed the beads back to Karoliina. "Bollocks."

She hooked the beads with the index finger of her right hand and they looped in a circle. She kept them looping, faster and faster. There was an undulating sound, like ancient voices speaking in all the languages of the world. It spread over the esplanade, reflected off the stones of Lausanne Cathedral, rose into the dark; next stop, the stars. The dream catcher grabbed the beads tight, and the ancient voices stopped cold. Harper was impressed.

"You know, in another age you would have been burned at the stake for a stunt like that."

"I was. A few times."

"All those voices?"

"Me, down through the ages."

Harper thought about it. "The lives of your soul were never redacted from one incarnation to the next. You're the same consciousness you've always been. Lucky you."

"Not really, but that's what makes me a dream catcher," Karoliina said. "Don't tell anyone. It's a big secret."

Harper took one more hit of radiance. He dropped the electronic fag into his coat, rested his gloved hands in the pockets.

"All right, mademoiselle, seeing as you're an expert on mystical experiences beginning with the letter *r*, what's your theory on the nature of reincarnated souls? One soul in particular?"

She looked up, scanned the predawn firmament above Lausanne Cathedral. She pointed to a bright point of light rising in the southeast.

"A binary star equals two stars bound by a shared gravity while orbiting a common center. Like that one over there, that's Sirius."

"I know what it is. What's it got to do with Ella?" Harper said.

She looked at him. "Binary star, binary soul."

"You're not seriously suggesting—"

"I'm not suggesting anything, I'm giving you a fact. Marc Rochat's soul is alive and well within Ella. And he's got another message for you."

"I'm listening."

"Via Dolorosa."

"The Way of Sorrows."

"Joo."

"What about it?" Harper said.

"He says you need to walk it one more time."

ii

The bearers raised the container high as they entered the Great Hall of the Two Hundred. It was draped in a black sheet and appeared to float cloudlike through the immense interior of the hall. The gilded gothic vaults and rows of supporting marble pillars sparkled with the candlelight of ten bronze chandeliers marking the procession's path to the throne. Members of the court standing to either side of the hall bowed as the bearers passed. Two rows of priests came next, chanting in low tones:

> "We call to You, Oh Lord of Earth, God of our Souls;
> We submit to Thy will and beseech You to receive us."

A muffled bell tolled nine times, and the priests chanted:

"You who have come from the ages beyond the ages;
We worship You and we pray, Do as Thy wilt with us."

Their voices echoed through the hall and circled the pillars and were consumed by the nine bells again. At the end of the hall, beneath a scallop-shaped dome holding the Star of All Knowledge, was Komarovsky. He sat on a throne of gold atop a marble dais of six steps. He watched the procession approach from behind his dark glasses. At his knees were the four women of Vladivostok, abducted to pleasure the Rus. Komarovsky had found the women pleasing and of good breeding stock, so he took them for his own amusement instead. The four women were dressed in black chiffon gowns, sheer enough to reveal their nakedness beneath. They licked and sucked at Komarovsky's potion-laced fingers. The potions rushed through their blood and washed over the dopamine receptors in the nucleus accumbens regions of their brains. Waves of rapture came over them; they murmured and begged:

"So good, never so good."
"More, give us more."

Komarovsky dipped his hands into the jade fonts standing to the sides of his throne. He soaked his fingers in a viscous liquid, then held his hands above the women. Fresh drops of supreme pleasure fell into their mouths. They received it as communion and shared it with one another in ravenous kisses. When they felt their souls begin to separate from their flesh, they licked and sucked at Komarovsky's fingers again. The women gazed upon him from the depths of the trance that bound them together as one wanton being. When Komarovsky blessed them with a glance, the women were overcome with gladness and cried out:

"Lie with us and devour us,
oh magnificent Lord!"
"More, give us more."

Then did the new chief physician enter the Great Hall of the Two Hundred. He was dressed in resplendent robes of red and gold as he carried the scepter of his office before him. The court bowed to him, too, for they feared him greatly. He alone had survived the night of long knives by slaughtering the entire privy council to assume the role of Komarovsky's most trusted advisor. The chief physician was followed by fifty virgins abducted from around the world as his personal gift to the court. They swirled and swayed and their sheer white gowns flowed about their forms. Like the four women of Vladivostok, the fifty virgins were chosen for their beauty and had been induced into the same state of rapture; their lips were wet with mating potions. They carried silver trays holding hypodermics for the members of the court, who received them with quivering hands. Through these needles flowed the Divinity's gift of supreme pleasure. For this was the Sacred Night of the Frost Moon, when the sacrament of communal mating would be offered to them. Then would they ravish the flesh of the virgins and implant their seed into them. Receiving the hypodermics, the court prayed.

"So shall our seed mingle with our Lord's;
And a new race shall be bred among men."

Then came the chanting voices of the priests.

"For thou art worthy, our Lord and God,
Of all glory and honor; For by Your will
Is the world made ours, now and ever after."

Then the nine bells and all the court calling out their praise again.

"Lord, we salute the Highest!"

As the procession came closer, Komarovsky nodded to his chamberlain, who was nearby. The servant stepped down to the main floor and stopped at the marble altar set in the middle of the Great Hall. The altar was sloped at an angle of 120 degrees, and when the bearers rested the container on it, all the court watched with much anticipation. There were rumors throughout the court that the time of their Divinity's judgment upon the world was near. Another gesture from the chamberlain and the fifty virgins fell to the floor.

Komarovsky raised his left hand and there was the howl of four winds and shadows rushed from the corners of the hall. They engulfed the virgins and they were swept away to the place of mating. The priests knelt before the throne in two rows, creating a passage of honor to the altar. They chanted in low tones.

"Thy name is holy.
"Thy kingdom is come."
"Teach us, Lord, that we may do as Thou wilt."

Silence veiled the hall as Komarovsky rose from his throne and approached the altar.

"Very soon we will set the beasts of ignorance and fanaticism loose in the world, and they will mate with the beasts of fear and greed. Then there will be born such monstrous creatures to feast on the blood of the innocent that all the world will be terrified."

The court was breathless. Ages upon ages they had worshipped him, and he had favored them with untold wealth that yielded unimaginable power over the minds of men. And now, he would favor them with the fulfillment of an ancient promise. A promise first sworn to them when they first took the forms of men two and a half million years ago. And he said to them in those days: "Behold, we will choose for ourselves wives from among the children of men. We will beget for ourselves children, and they will be the instruments of our power over the souls of men."

Komarovsky pulled the black sheet from the container. The lid was opened by an unseen hand, and the court saw the small boy inside. He lay as if sleeping, still connected to the breathing apparatus, still clutching the small toy hammer in his right hand. Sighs and whispers echoed through the hall . . . *the child of the prophecy, the child of the prophecy* . . . Then perfect silence as Komarovsky touched the glass lid, lovingly, as if touching the face of the child within.

"Behold the child delivered to us by the womb of the whore who rots in Hell. Behold her benefaction to us. It is a good gift, a fruitful gift. For as her child is slaughtered on the Place of the Skull, so will all hope of human salvation in paradise be lost. There will be no new life, there will be no evolution for these creatures. We will sit in final judgment over a world that we have fashioned in our own image; a perfect world of gods and slaves. Now come the days when we will glean the wheat from the chaff. Those who have loved us according to our pleasure will drink from the tree of our knowledge. Those who have sought that forbidden knowledge from beyond the stars will be cast down with the whore and condemned to our eternal torment. Oh, we will hear them cry out. Oh, we will hear them call for the man of signs and wonders to save them. And their cries will delight us . . . for the man of signs and wonders will be no more!"

A roar of praise filled the Great Hall of the Two Hundred.

"Lord of Earth!
He will not rise again to poison the world with the virus of his heresy!
Lord of the universe!
He will not deny us the triumph of our divine creation!"

As one, the members of the court ripped open their robes and injected themselves with the Divinity's gift of supreme pleasure. They trembled, their eyes rolled to the backs of their heads . . . *so good, never so good* . . . They fell to their knees and prostrated themselves before their One True God.

"Lord, we salute the highest!"

Book IV

THE PLACE OF THE SKULL

EIGHTEEN

i

Harper climbed down from the train at Vevey station and walked outside. He stared at the buildings and road beyond the parking lot. Having never made his way to the clinic on his own, he had no idea which way to go. He didn't even know which street the clinic was on. He was scheduled for a ten-thirty appointment to have the bioskin gloves on his hands changed. He was to be collected at his flat in Lausanne and driven to the clinic by Inspector's Gobet muscle, Mutt and Jeff. That was the plan; that's the way it was always done. No one was authorized to enter the clinic of their own accord. But after his predawn meet with the dream catcher on the esplanade of Lausanne Cathedral, just after she turned back to the belfry with "I should get back to Ella" and left him standing there with a *no bloody way* expression on his mug, Harper thought, *Sod this for laughs.* He marched down Escaliers du Marché, double-timed it through Lausanne, and caught the 05:46 Intercity to Vevey. He had arrived four hours, forty-two minutes early for his appointment. The bloody sun wasn't even up.

"Swell."

He flashed previous trips to the clinic. Driving the lake road from Lausanne into Vevey, passing the Vevey station on the left and continuing on the main road until reaching the intersection of Hôtel des Trois Couronnes and whatever street it was. Go left one block to a small square. There was a small church on the corner. Next to the church was a nondescript five-floor building that people wouldn't notice unless they were looking for it. Mutt and Jeff would drive into an underground parking lot and, Bob's your uncle, he was there. It was just a matter of going up a lift to the second floor and being delivered into the hands of men in white coats.

"Got it."

He headed for the main road. Rue du Simplon it was. He walked at a fast clip, passing closed shops and offices. Somewhere a boulanger was at work and there was the smell of freshly baked bread. He came to the Trois Couronnes. It was a nice-looking joint set behind a high wrought-iron fence. A doorman in full, five-star regalia stood on the portico. He kept an eye on the Mercs, Ferraris, and Bentleys arranged around a neoclassical fountain that made gentle splashing noises. Harper took a left, found the church on the corner. Église Sainte-Claire it was called. But it wasn't a working church anymore; it was a performing arts center. Currently onstage: Samuel Beckett's *En attendant Godot. Une pièce de théâtre de l'absurde,* the advertising placard read. Harper stared at the words.

"A play of the absurd."

He walked on, passed the entrance of a familiar-looking underground garage, and reached the wide steps rising to the ordinary-looking door of a nondescript building that might be the clinic or not. Except for the church, this was a neighborhood of nondescript concrete boxes. Maybe the underground garage led to another building entirely. Next to the door was a large brass plaque with a picture of a Swiss flag and the abbreviation BCSE. A closer inspection revealed this was the Bureau Central de la Statistique et de l'Étalonnages.

"Must be the place."

He climbed the steps, pulled at the door handle; locked. He looked for a doorbell or intercom; nothing. He knocked. The door was just a door, not reinforced in any way. Harper heard his knock echo inside; no response. There was a mail slot in the door. He leaned down, lifted the flap, and peeked in. He saw a lobby with an empty desk and a long hall beyond that. Nobody was there. *Why would there be?* he thought. The place was a bloody front; not to mention the sun had just now come up in Vevey. He saw a small notice next to the mail slot. It translated as: *In case of emergency please use the emergency call apparatus.*

"An emergency call apparatus. At the Central Office of Statistics and Calibrations. Surely you jest."

He stepped back from the doors and looked around. No button, no switch, no CCTV cameras; but there had to be something. He studied the cinder-block wall around the door casing. He noticed a block three up from the ground and two to the right of the door and flashed his trip to EPFL. Following the little man in the white coat down to the basement and coming to a steel door. Watching the chap tap Morse code against the same sort of stone, in the same sort of placement to open the steel door. Harper gave it a go.

O-P-E-N-S-E-S-A-M-E

Nothing happened.

"Sod it."

Harper kicked open the door and marched in.

He wasn't ten steps in when doors opened on either side of the lobby and two squads of Swiss Guard tacticals came rushing for him. Harper got the palm of his right hand up, did a blinding three-sixty before their eyes.

"Dulcis et alta quies placidæque simillima morti."

The guards dropped into hibernation mode and froze in place. Harper walked by the reception desk and down the hall. He checked the small brass plates at each door. The plaques bore more gobbledygook acronyms for departments of this and that and offices of no idea what. The entire ground floor was a front.

"Second floor. Always took the lift to the second floor."

He marched toward the stairwell at the end of the hall, heard the unmistakable clop of steel-toed work boots pounding down his way. It was

Krinkle, had to be. Harper climbed quickly and made the landing between floors one and two at the same time as the roadie. The dull light of the coming dawn filled a huge glass window and highlighted the welcoming grin on the roadie's face.

"Hey, brother. Karoliina said you might be coming. The new clothes look good on you."

"Cheers."

Harper tore into the roadie with a left jab to the gut. The roadie buckled over and his face met Harper's right fist. The big man flew back into the wall and slumped to the floor. Harper rushed ahead, but Krinkle caught him in the chest with a size-eleven boot and kicked hard. Harper flew down the stairs and hit the lower landing. Something went *crack* and a stabbing pain ripped through Harper's chest. For a second he couldn't breathe. He reached for the railing to pull himself up. The pain flared and he fell back to the floor.

"Fuck me."

Krinkle wiped the blood dripping from his own nose. "Did you break a rib?" he said.

"I think so."

"Good. What the friggin' hell was that about?"

Harper looked at him. "You failed to mention you got into Astruc's files on me long before the Paris job. You've been playing me for a chump."

"Orders from the cop."

"Bugger the both of you."

Krinkle got up, walked down the stairs to Harper. He knelt next to him.

"Where does it hurt?"

"Left side."

Krinkle pulled open Harper's trench coat, pushed aside the sports coat. He touched Harper's ribs. "Breathe slowly, brother, let's see if your lung inflates."

Harper inhaled. It hurt like hell.

"Couple of cracks, that's all," the roadie said. "Nothing a couple hours in the tank won't fix."

"Swell."

Harper came up quick with his right elbow and smashed Krinkle's face. The roadie went over onto the floor. Harper got to his knees, drove his right fist into the roadie's jaw. The roadie spit blood onto the floor.

"For fuck sake, would you lay off the friggin' violence, brother?"

Harper struggled to his feet and braced himself on the handrail. He stood over Krinkle.

"What happened in 70 AD?"

"Jerusalem was destroyed."

"Yeah, I got that on the History Channel. Tell me something I don't know."

"Like what?"

"Like what it's got to do with me."

"We're working on it."

Harper kicked the roadie in the stomach. The roadie gasped for air.

"Hey!"

"Why do I have to walk Via Dolorosa one more time? What the fuck does it mean?"

The roadie coughed up his answer. "Told you, we're working on it."

"Work harder."

Harper went for him again. This time the roadie grabbed Harper's foot and pulled. Harper hit the floor and landed on his side; pain stabbed his chest again. He curled into a fetal position, his back to the roadie.

"Bugger!"

Krinkle got up, rested his shoulder against the wall. He spit blood again and felt his teeth to check they were all still in his head. Satisfied with the count, he looked at Harper and sighed.

"You always were such a pain in the ass, brother. Stubborn, mule-headed, and self-righteous. Come on, let's get you to the tank before you do any more damage to yourself." He knelt down on one knee, slid his big hands under Harper. "Just roll over nice and slow. I'll lift you up," he said.

Harper obeyed till he got on his back. That's when he pointed his SIG Sauer at the kill spot on Krinkle's head. The roadie stood, eased back.

"Did I include 'sneaky as shit' in my list of complaints?"

"Afraid not," Harper said.

Harper kept the roadie in his sights till he got to his feet. They faced off across the landing, staring at each other. Pain throbbed through Harper's form. It was hard for him to speak.

"She told me things. Unimaginable things."

"She's a dream catcher, that's what she does."

"Is it true? Any of it?"

"Maybe. Could be. Probably."

"Has she ever been wrong?"

Krinkle slowly shook his head. "No. But keep this in your head: She is only telling you what Ella pronounced in the belfry loge."

"Pronounced. Like prophecy."

"Like I don't know what the fuck it is yet. It could be allegorical."

"Or it could be the real deal."

Krinkle spit blood again. "That too. But like I said, read my fat lip: We're friggin' working on it."

Harper took a slow breath. "She said . . . She said you told her I made a choice once, that I changed the course of human civilization in making it."

"That would be putting it mildly, brother."

The pain dug deeper into Harper's form; he started to lose focus. He bent over, squeezed his left arm into his ribs. "Bloody fucking hell."

Krinkle moved in a blur, pulling a hypodermic from the pouch of his overalls, shifting toward Harper; Harper snapped up with the SIG. The death end of the gun was under the roadie's chin.

"Don't," Harper said.

"Come on, brother. You're not thinking straight."

"Step back. Put away the needle."

The roadie complied.

"What choice did I make when Jerusalem was destroyed that changed the course of history?"

"It's not like that."

"What was the bloody choice?"

"Brother, you're hurting . . ."

"You're damn right I'm hurting! Tell me."

Krinkle shook his head. "I can't."

"Please."

"I can't."

Then a wheezing voice from above: "Perhaps, if you would allow me to explain."

Harper looked up.

On the higher landing, against the window now flooded with the light of a rising sun, a silhouette loomed as if floating. Harper made out the broad shoulders, the heavy build, the shape of a man who could take care of himself in a barroom brawl, even dressed as he was. Hospital robe, flip-flop slippers, leaning on a walking cane. As Harper's eyes adjusted to the backlight, he saw the head of wild black hair and the wispy Ho Chi Minh beard to match; the disfigured right eye and ragged scar running down the cheek as if clawed by some beast. But it was the spark of light in the form's eyes that grabbed Harper's eternal being. It was as dazzling as the rising sun behind him.

"Well, well. Christophe Astruc. Up and about, are we?"

"Still looking through a glass darkly now and again, but awakened enough to answer your question. Though I doubt it will give you much comfort."

Harper lowered his SIG and laughed to himself. Here gathered at dawn in a stairwell of the Central Office of Statistics and Calibrations, a bloody front for a medical clinic attending to the needs of the creatures men called angels, were three of the last of their kind in paradise: one defrocked priest, one rock-and-roll roadie, and him, a dead soldier late of Her Majesty's Special Reconnaissance Regiment. If only the cop in the cashmere coat walked in, the stage would be set.

"Une pièce de théâtre de l'absurde," Harper said.

"Indeed," Astruc said.

Harper put away his SIG. "All right, Padre, 70 anno Domini. Spill."

Astruc held the handrail and descended the stairs. His cane made tapping sounds on the concrete steps.

"We three were there through the destruction of Jerusalem. There were four more of us then, but they are forever gone from us now. The last of them was Alexander Yuriev. He was lost a few years ago, during the cathedral job. Before you were fully awakened, before you could save him."

Harper glanced at Krinkle. The roadie nodded. "It's true, brother. The Yuriev thing was wiped from your timeline. There was nothing you could do."

Harper looked at Astruc. "Stick with ancient history, Padre."

"In those days we were on the back end of a thirty-seven-year mission. We held out as long as we could, but in February of 70 AD we had to flee. You see, by then the Romans had surrounded Jerusalem and laid siege to it."

Astruc reached the landing where Harper and Krinkle stood. He balanced his cane against the wall, looked at Harper.

"On the ninth day of the Jewish month of Av, the Fifth, Twelfth, and Fifteenth Legions of Rome overran the city, then looted and destroyed the Second Temple, six hundred sixty-six years to the day that the Babylonians destroyed the First Holy Temple of God. Then were released the killers hidden within the Tenth Legion Fretensis, who had been encamped on the Mount of Olives. They entered the city, and in a matter of days they slaughtered more than one million Jews. The Jewish historian Josephus wrote of streets clogged with mountains of rotting corpses."

Harper glanced at Krinkle again. "The Tenth Legion. The same outfit that destroyed Qumran three years later?"

The roadie nodded. Lines of causality sparked and crossed in Harper's eyes.

"But they didn't just wipe out the Essenes for the fun of it, they were looking for something," he said.

The roadie pointed to the priest. "Brother Astruc got inside the enemy's darknet before the Paris job. That's how he got all the intel on you.

Like Karoliina told you last night, I read through it back to 70 AD, but that's all there was. Now that Astruc is fully awakened, he's been spilling the intel he never wrote down. I'm still trying to get my head around it."

Krinkle stopped talking. Harper looked at Astruc.

"They were looking for us, because they were looking for your dead body," the priest said.

Harper stared at Astruc's eyes; they glimmered like emeralds. His form had been cleansed of the homemade potions he'd been injecting to prevent his awakening. But up close, the disfigured right eye and ragged scar running down his face reminded Harper that the priest had tried to kill him in the tunnels under Paris.

"My body. Dead, you say."

"Yes."

Harper smiled. "For a minute, Padre, I thought you were on the mend. But you're still as barking mad as you always were and still obsessed with my being dead."

"You think me mad?"

"I'd say you're well stuck behind the dark glass, yeah. If I was dead in 70 AD, how the hell did I make a choice to change history?"

Astruc looked at Krinkle. "He is very stubborn, isn't he?"

"Always was," the roadie said.

Harper lunged at Astruc, grabbed him by the lapels of his robe, and slammed him into the wall. "Sod off, Padre, and tell me."

"You made your choice in 36 anno Domini. You chose to be crucified."

Harper lost focus and felt himself stagger as he had when the dream catcher dropped the message from the dead lad: *You need to walk Via Dolorosa one more time.* Harper shook his head, regained focus. "Bollocks," he said.

Astruc glanced down to Harper's hands. "Then why do you bear the sign of stigmata?"

Harper tried to back away, but Astruc grabbed him by the hands. He pressed his thumbs into the gloved palms. All at once Harper was seized by bone-crushing pain.

"God, no!"

Harper sank to the floor; Astruc went down with him, never easing the pressure to Harper's palms. Harper was held by Astruc's blazing eyes. Harper gasped.

"Stop."

"John 19:16," Astruc said.

"Sod off, Padre."

"John 19:16. *Intuebitur eam.*"

Images flashed through Harper's eyes.

"It can't be."

"Tunc ergo tradidit eis illum ut crucifigeretur susceperunt autem Iesum et eduxerunt."

Harper saw a suffering man stumbling through ancient streets, his broken hands strapped to the heavy crossbeam on his shoulders. Roman whips ripping at the open wounds on the man's back, his eyes drenched by streams of blood flowing from the crown of thorns rammed onto his head.

"Please!" Harper cried.

"John 19:17. *Intuebitur eam.*"

"No, damn it!"

Astruc dug his thumbs into Harper's palms.

"Et baiulans sibi crucem exivit in eum qui dicitur Calvariæ locum Hebraice autem Golgotha."

"Christ!"

Astruc released Harper's hands; the images vanished from Harper's eyes. He slid to the wall, tried to press himself into the concrete. He looked at his hands. Blood and water were seeping through the bioskin palms of his gloves. He stuffed them inside his coat, hiding them from the others, hiding them from his own eyes.

"Torture a man long enough, he'll see or say whatever you want him to. It won't change the fact I don't believe a word of it."

Krinkle knelt next to Harper. "Listen to me, brother. I'm not going to hit you with the dogma of no choice unless I have to. I'm trying to reason with you. We are living in the realm of some very heavy shit. Astruc got his intel from the bad guys over the last fifteen friggin' years. You know how Karoliina came by hers tonight. Each thread on its own has a probability of point-zero-zero-nothing, and yeah, it's nuts to imagine either one. But together? From two different sources? They form two lines of causality coming at *you*, brother, and they are coming with a friggin' vengeance."

Harper shook his head. "What about the prophecy? Madame Taylor's child. He's the one, he's their savior. It had to be one of his soul's past lives."

"Madame Taylor's child didn't have a past life. "

Harper's mind began to spin, then came a suffocating weight on his eternal being. Astruc rested his hand on Harper's shoulder.

"I had the prophecy wrong," the priest said. "I needed it to be wrong and drugged myself into a stupor until I made it wrong. Because I was the same as you are right now. I couldn't accept the truth."

Harper tried to get up, but they pushed him down. Krinkle got in Harper's face.

"We don't know the reasons the job in 36 AD went down the way it did and who did what. Maybe the message you got tonight is allegory, but so what? We're running out of time. We picked up chatter on the Internet. The bad guys are making a move. We think it means lights-out for Madame Taylor's child. We're not sure where, but Jerusalem is looking good on all counts. That's intersecting line number three coming your way, brother. It's why you need to do what you need to do."

"What, go to Jerusalem? Choose to be crucified again?"

"Maybe. But one way or another, figuratively or literally, you've got to walk Via Dolorosa one more time."

"Sod off."

"Listen to my friggin' voice, brother. Julian Magnolly's last words dropped in today's *24 Heures*. He released a few lines from the first six scrolls from Qumran. Not a lot, but enough for us to know the scrolls are about seven angels of the Pure God passing through Qumran and telling Essene scribes about a man of signs and wonders, a man they said was crucified but would return to Qumran. The scrolls are addressed to that man. His name was Yeshua ben Yosef."

"I'm telling you, it's not me."

"Maybe not, but like Brother Astruc says, you're the one with the bleeding hands."

Harper broke from their grip, scrambled to his feet. Krinkle and Astruc slammed him into the wall. Harper swung his arms and kicked and shouted to the heavens.

"Nescio quod dicis! Nescio quod dicis!"

"Statum!" Krinkle yelled.

Swiss Guard tacticals and a gang of medics broke into the stairwell from up and down. They joined the brawl, throwing Harper to the floor. Krinkle pulled the hypodermic from his overalls. Harper saw it coming.

"Get off me!"

He pushed harder, knocked away the priest. He tried to roll from Krinkle's grip. Two guards fell on Harper, flipped him on his face, and pinned him to the floor.

"Bloody—"

Krinkle hit Harper with the hypodermic, pressed the release button, and the needle jabbed deep into Harper's neck. Numbness rushed through Harper's form. He seized up, unable to breathe. Krinkle leaned down to Harper, whispered in his ear. "Sorry, brother. No choice. The job is yours."

Nowtimes began to break up into alternating patterns of hash and flashes of blue light with only shreds of dizzying time to comprehend. Krinkle pulls the needle from Harper's neck. Hash, blue lights, then black. Lifted from the floor, carried to the second floor; door opens, Inspector Gobet is waiting . . . "Mr. Harper, what is the meaning of this?" Hash, blue lights, then black. In a hallway now, moving fast. Mutt and Jeff drag him through crowds of little men in white coats. Inspector Gobet leads the parade, barks on about being "shocked indeed" to learn Harper had been secretly abusing his radiance allotment by mixing it with synthetic dihydromorphinone. He was ordering Harper into the tank for a three-week dry-out. Hash, blue lights, then black. Mutt and Jeff and a squad of Swiss Guards strip Harper of his swell new clothes down to his boxers, toss him in the tank, slam closed the lid. Hash, blue lights, then black. The lid opens and two men in white coats change the bioskin gloves on Harper's hands. Harper can swear one of them was the light mechanic/artificial-intel geek from EPFL. They slam the door closed. Hash, blue lights, then black.

ii

Beep, beep, beep . . .

"Recovery in forty seconds."

Nothingness.

Beep, beep, beep.

"Recovery in thirty seconds."

Nothingness.

Beep, beep, beep.

"Recovery in twenty seconds."

This time Harper held on to the voice in the pitch dark. It was a pleasant voice; a woman with a bit of an Irish lilt. And the beeps were dead ringers for Auntie Beeb's just before the top of the hour on the World Service.

Beep, beep, beep.

"Recovery in ten, nine, eight . . ."

In the tank.

Time's up.

Lid about to open.

". . . three, two, one."

Harper covered his eyes with his hands. He smelled the new bioskin on his palms. Air pressure seals released: *sishhhhhhhhhhhhh, thunk.*

"Open bloody sesame," he said.

The lid was lifted.

A blast of cleansing air hit him in the face and fresh oxygen filled his lungs.

"You can lower your hands, brother. The lights are made safe."

Harper did. The place was lit like a photographer's darkroom; everything was red. Including the roadie holding open the tank.

"How are the ribs?"

The pain was gone at Harper's side. "Fine. What day is this?"

"Same day it was when you went in. Sixteen hours, fifty-five minutes later, to be exact. That makes it almost midnight."

It would take Harper a full ten minutes to fully reconnect with his timeline. For now all he could see was Inspector Gobet marching him down the hall. *Three weeks in the tank,* the cop said to the passing crowd.

"Same day? Midnight? I don't get it."

"You will."

Harper saw the roadie turn to someone.

"Give me a hand, would you?"

A Swiss Guard in tactical gear came into Harper's red world.

"Let's get him out of this thing," the roadie said.

They reached in the tank, grabbed Harper under his shoulders, and lifted. Harper came up and out. They stood him on his feet and let him stand. He wobbled a bit, but he was okay.

"Read the letters on the wall," Krinkle said.

Harper looked ahead. Five meters away was an eye chart bathed in red. But there were no letters, just patterns of interlocking triangles and circles and squares. They were moving.

"What letters? It looks like a geometry student threw up."

"He's all right," the Swiss Guard said.

The voice was familiar; Harper looked at him. More flashes of time reconnected in Harper's eyes. The guard was Inspector Gobet's chauffeur/special-ops sniper. The one who pulled Harper from the cavern during the Paris job, the one who told Harper it looked like he was trying to raise the dead after Harper sliced open his palms and let the blood fall onto the eyes of the dead man.

"Sergeant Gauer. What brings you here?"

"I'm delivering a pizza. What's it look like?"

Harper looked around the tank room, all aglow in red. There wasn't a pizza in sight. He looked at Krinkle.

"I'm confused."

"It's the potion I hit you with before you went into the tank," the roadie said.

"What was in it?"

"Fuck if I know. Something to help you better understand the nature of your mission."

"It's not working."

"Have faith. You could have just drunk it in a really nice mint tea while you were getting your bioskins changed, that was the plan. But you had one of your episodes and we had to do it the hard way."

Hard to argue that an episode of some sort had occurred, Harper thought.

"What mission?" he said.

"You need to go to the Holy Land, sweep Qumran, then get to Jerusalem and get into the Israel Museum. You need to get your hands on the new Dead Sea scrolls and find out if this is the real deal."

Harper let the words sink in. "What?"

Krinkle nodded toward the Swiss Guard. "Gauer is just back from a recon. Go ahead, Sergeant, tell him."

"The Holy Land has been a no-go zone for your kind and the partisans for the last thousand years. The bad guys consider the one square mile of earth the world calls Jerusalem to be under their sphere of influence."

"Considering the innocent blood spilled there in the name of the gods, not a surprising development," the roadie interjected.

"We went in on a probing mission and they smelled us coming," Gauer said. "I lost five men getting the hell out. It wasn't pretty."

"There is a silver lining," the roadie added.

Sergeant Gauer continued. "I think I found a way to get you in under their radar. It means hoping a few locals on the inside help us. Problem is, as a rule, those same locals don't trust us as far as they can throw us."

"But we've got to get you there within the next twenty-four hours," Krinkle said.

Keeping up with the back-and-forth in a world of red light made Harper queasy as hell. Then one more shred of time dropped in his eyes.

It was murky at first; a little like watching a photograph slowly coming clear in a developing tray. It was a portrait of the man of signs and wonders, crucified and buried in Jerusalem; a man who would return to Qumran nearly two thousand years later. His name was Yeshua ben Yosef.

Harper thought about it.

"I'm still confused."

"You go ahead and be confused all you want, brother. In the meantime, get dressed."

NINETEEN

i

Katherine got up from the chair and pulled aside the curtains and saw the moonrise above the Alps. Fields of high snow looked like clouds in the night. Far below were the lights of cities and towns gathered around Lac Léman. Over there, where the lake began to bend and narrow till it met the marshlands of the Rhone estuary, was Montreux. No doubt about it; she was back in Switzerland. And if that was Montreux, then this was Vevey, she thought. In the clinic, Corporal Mai had told her when she bolted awake, "You're safe, Madame Taylor. All is well. You were having a nightmare."

Katherine looked at the buildings beneath her window. The neighborhood looked familiar. There was another window with the curtains drawn on the next wall. She walked to it while pulling the IV stand along on its wheels. The wheels squeaked and her bedroom slippers made flip-flop noises. She opened the curtains, saw the neo-Gothic building rising above the rest.

"Huh."

It was the Hôtel des Trois Couronnes, one of the *grandes dames* of the Swiss Riviera. A lifetime ago—not really, but it felt like it—Katherine had spent the night in the hotel's Tchaikovsky Suite, overlooking the lake. She was turning a trick with a taipan from Hong Kong. Actually the trick was with his executive assistant. Her name was Michelle. She was British. She had auburn-colored hair, porcelain skin, and the most astounding hashish. The taipan watched the women play with each other while he rubbed himself raw. He had a round face, an effeminate giggle, a wicked smile. Katherine tried to remember his name but came up blank.

What she did remember, staring at the hotel just now, was the client was a member of the Two Hundred Club, the private escort agency out of Geneva that booked Katherine Taylor's jobs. That meant if the cop's sermon on the jet was on the level, then the taipan was one of *them*, one of the bad guys who bred evil into paradise. They had watched her the day she was born, the cop told her. They groomed her, paved her road to Lausanne with gold. They passed her from member of the club to member of the club, making her ready to be raped by the one whose name she now remembered: Komarovsky.

She remembered that name because he had come to her in her last round of dreams. She was locked in the bunker. Max was in her arms, crying. The steel door began to buckle and crack open. Black mist leaked into the bunker and a form began to take shape before her eyes. She put the barrel of her gun next to Max's head; she slipped her finger inside the trigger guard. "Big, brave Max," she said. Then the transmigrating form began to reveal itself. She saw a tall, elegant-looking man with long silver hair tied at the back of his head. She saw his flawless face and the dark glasses over his eyes. He was as stunning a creature as he'd been when she'd seen him the first time, years ago in Lausanne. And in the dream he was reaching for her son.

"The child is ours," he said.

Katherine pulled the Glock from her son's head, aimed at Komarovsky, and fired. The bullet passed through him as if passing through dust. That's when Katherine bolted awake in a cold sweat. "Jesus!"

Corporal Mai rushed from her post and held her. Told her she was safe, told her all was well, told her she was in the Vevey Clinic.

"Vevey?"

"Yes, ma'am," the corporal said. "You were asleep when we landed in Geneva. We transferred you here by ambulance."

"What time is it?"

"Half past midnight, ma'am. You were having a nightmare."

"No. It wasn't a nightmare. It was like it was happening, like I was back there."

Katherine looked at Corporal Mai. There was the most blank expression on the young woman's face.

"But you already know that, don't you?"

"Ma'am?"

"You probably listened to me babble while I was sleeping, huh? Reported it in already, have you?"

Corporal Mai did not answer.

"That's what I thought," Katherine said.

"Let me get you a cup of tea, Madame Taylor."

Corporal Mai got up from Katherine's bed and walked to the door. Katherine looked at the IV attached to her arm. The bag on the stand was pumping her with another potion, pale blue this time. She pulled the sheets and blanket off her body.

"Could you help me over to the chair first? Over there by the window. I don't want to sleep anymore."

"Of course, ma'am."

Corporal Mai helped Katherine onto her feet and dressed her in a silk robe and slippers.

"Okay, let's see if we can do this without breaking anything," Katherine said.

Corporal Mai took Katherine's right arm, and Katherine held on to the IV stand. They moved slowly over the white-tiled floor. Katherine looked around the room. She saw Marc Rochat's lamp on a table in the corner; the delicate flame inside swayed atop the candle. Katherine stopped walking, looked back at the bed. Something was missing.

"Where is Monsieur Booty?"

"They took him into the OR for a checkup."

"What's wrong with him?"

"Nothing, ma'am. The medics just want to check him over."

"Looking for phantom images in the axons of Monsieur Booty's optic nerves?"

"Yes."

Katherine laughed. "I was joking."

"Well, that is what they are doing."

"Why?"

"The cat is a sentient creature. The medics want to make sure it isn't haunted by the things it saw."

"What?"

"The cat was pacing the room and mewing as you slept. It took me a few minutes to realize it was crying, like it was afraid of something it was seeing. I sent for the medics, and they took it. They said they will have it back by morning."

Katherine laughed a little. "Broken-down angels, ex-hookers, and cats who see things that go bump in the night. This really is a one-stop shop of the weird, isn't it?"

"Ma'am?"

"They'll take anybody here."

Corporal Mai smiled. "Even half-kinds."

Katherine remembered more of Inspector Gobet's sermon on the jet. Telling her about the half-kinds like Corporal Mai and Marc Rochat; telling her about the hundreds of half-kind children around the world who had been slaughtered as a diversion to kidnap her son.

"I didn't mean 'weird' in a bad way, Corporal."

"I know, ma'am. It sounded funny, not bad."

"The cop, your boss, told me what happened to the half-kinds. I'm so sorry."

"The wheel is turning, ma'am, that's all. I'm very sure the light will come to us again.

Katherine studied the young Asian woman with the emerald, almond-shaped eyes. The eyes reminded Katherine of Marc Rochat, sure, but so did the almost blank expression on her face. And the cadence of the girl's speech just then, and the innocent words coming out of her mouth. For one wild moment, Katherine thought it was him standing there. She looked at the lantern, watched the flame sway atop the candle, then looked back to the girl.

"Did you know Marc at Mon Repos?"

Corporal Mai nodded. "I was two years under him."

"He was something, wasn't he?"

"*Oui*. He always said the funniest things. We were friends. Sometimes I went to visit him in the belfry. We liked to climb in the timbers and talk to the bells. Once, he let me call the hour."

"Really?"

"Really."

They continued their slow walk to the chair.

"The cop said there were only three of you left in the world. You, the new girl in the belfry of Lausanne Cathedral, and . . . He didn't say who the third one was, actually."

"Goose," Corporal Mai said.

"Huh?"

"That's the name of the third one. His real name is George Muret."

"Was he a friend of Marc's, too?" Katherine said.

"Goose never came to our school. He wasn't part of the experiment like the rest of us."

Katherine remembered the sermon on the jet again. Telling her of the one half-kind born apart from the experiment to replenish the ranks of the good guys. The one child conceived in an act of love, the cop said.

"Where is he? Goose, I mean? What happened to him?"

"He's here, ma'am."

"In Switzerland?"

"In the clinic."

They reached the chair by the window.

"Hurrah. Made it," Katherine said. She rolled the IV stand into place and sat down. "What's the matter with him?"

"Ma'am?"

"Goose."

"He was attacked by a pack of dogs. But they weren't real dogs. They were bad shadows."

"Jesus. When?"

"It was a few days before the orphanages were attacked, before the enemy kidnapped your son. Goose was with his father. They were trying to escape across Heaven's Gate. It's a mountain pass through the Pyrenees."

"Escaping from whom?"

"The bad shadows, and us."

"I don't understand. If Goose is a half-kind, then his father is like Harper. Why was he running from his own kind?"

"The father was not well, ma'am. He thought his kind were as evil as the enemy. He didn't even accept Goose as his son. He imagined Goose to be someone else, not his own son. That way he could turn the world back to year zero. He wanted to reset the clock of creation."

"Who did he imagine his son to be?"

"The child of the prophecy, ma'am, the one born of light into this world to guide the creation through the next stage of evolution."

Katherine hesitated. "Like Max?"

"Like your son."

"And you believe that?"

"With all my heart."

Katherine shook her head and looked away. *No, he's just my little boy. That's all he is.* She focused on the pale blue potion running into her vein. Whatever it was, it was allowing her to imagine her son's face. Not crying; he was laughing. And he wasn't in the bunker, he was in his high chair in the kitchen of the house. He was wearing a bib over his Shaun the Sheep pajamas. Katherine was trying to feed him some of Molly's applesauce, but the goofy kid had other ideas. He had his little blue hammer in his hand and decided at that moment to attack the no-see-ums on the tray. *Boo! Boo! Boo!* Applesauce flew everywhere and splattered Katherine's face. She was laughing with him now. *Yeah, you get 'em Max. It's the ones you can't see that'll bite you in the ass!* Katherine held the image of his laughing face in her mind and she was filled with hope. No, not hope; it was the comfort of knowing she would hold him in her arms again and, yes, all would be well. She looked at Corporal Mai.

"Are you supposed to be telling me any of this stuff, Corporal?"

"I was ordered to answer your questions to the best of my ability, ma'am."

"By the cop, Monsieur le Boss."

"After his initial briefing with you on the jet, he thought it might be easier if you heard things from me while you recover."

"He's got that one right."

Corporal Mai nodded. "Do you have any more questions for me, ma'am?"

"No."

"I'll get your tea."

"Thanks."

Corporal Mai left the room.

Katherine got up from the chair and pulled aside the curtains and saw the moonrise above the Alps. Fields of high snow looked like clouds in the night. Far below were the lights of cities and . . .

"Wait a sec."

She looked at the lantern. It continued to glow, but the flame was still, as if the world had come to a stop. It remained that way until Corporal Mai reappeared with a tray in her hands. The tray held a small teapot, a cup and saucer, and two chocolate chip cookies. The corporal rested the tray on a small table next to the chair and poured the tea. Katherine recognized the aroma: Night Clouds blend. Katherine looked at the flame in Rochat's lantern; the delicate thing was swaying again. She returned to the chair, parked the IV stand, and sat down.

"What's in the cookies?" she said.

"Ma'am?"

"Besides chocolate chips?"

"Nothing. They're from my lunch box. I made them at home. I thought you would enjoy some."

Katherine stared at her. Corporal Mai stared back, looking deep into Katherine's eyes.

"It's called looping, ma'am."

"What?"

"What you were doing when I left the room. It happens sometimes, especially after a traumatic temporal event. We have all experienced it. It goes away."

"'We.' As in Harper's kind, half-kinds."

Corporal Mai nodded.

"You read my mind?"

"I saw it in your eyes."

"Like Harper? Like the cop?"

The corporal nodded again.

Katherine had a sip of tea and a bite of the cookie.

"Um, yummy. So tell me, Corporal, as you've been ordered to answer my questions: I am just an ordinary human being, aren't I?"

"Are you asking me if you are one of them? Like Mr. Harper and Inspector Gobet?"

"I'm asking exactly that."

Corporal Mai smiled. "You are a local, ma'am. That's what we call human beings."

Katherine nodded. "Makes sense." She took another bite of cookie and sipped at her tea. "So, do locals loop through time?"

"No, ma'am. Locals have memories."

More tea in slow sips. "So why am I looping?"

"Nobody knows."

Katherine studied the young woman's face again. Her expression wasn't blank, Katherine realized; in fact, it was completely transparent. Corporal Mai was incapable of not speaking the truth.

"Okay, let's try it this way: What is the purpose of looping, in the fun world of angels and half-kinds?"

"It's a timeline reset to better focus on specific data."

"What specific data?"

"Repressed data. Something we want to avoid or not face."

She wasn't talking like Marc Rochat now. She was talking like a shrink with a gun.

"How do you find out what that data is, Corporal Mai?"

"We reconnect with the point in time we left off before the looping began."

Katherine gave it a try. She was walking across the room with the corporal. The corporal was telling her about Goose. Never went to Mon Repos, never knew him, the corporal said. His father, one of Harper's kind, wanted Goose to be like Max, born of light, not of his own flesh.

"Did Goose think he was the one?"

"No, ma'am."

"Was he attacked because he was trying to protect my son?"

"And his father, and all of us."

Katherine rested her cup on the tray.

"I want to see him. Right now."

"Yes, ma'am."

Katherine got herself up from the chair. She grabbed the IV stand and they started walking.

"You knew I was going to say that, didn't you? You read it in my eyes."

"Yes, ma'am."

ii

Sergeant Gauer was at the wheel of the magic bus. At the moment the bus was acting completely normal on the lakeside road back to Lausanne. A fullish moon was suspended over the mountains above Évian. Its light was reflected in the currents and eddies of the dark water. He watched; he added it up. The light on Lac Léman was actually the light of the sun, currently located at the other side of paradise. The sun's light was traveling ninety-three million miles through space and hitting the moon, currently two hundred fifty thousand miles above Évian. That light was reflected off the moon and was now hitting the lake and bouncing into Harper's eyes. Distance divided by speed of light meant the trip took five hundred seconds. Equals: The light in his eyes had left the surface of the sun at the same moment the magic bus pulled out of Vevey 8.33333333 minutes ago.

Not that the events were connected, but the narrow lakeside road opened to four lanes at the same time and a rush of cars passed the bus on the left and floored it for Lausanne. Harper stepped closer to the driver's compartment. He checked the speed of the bus. Fifty-five mph. The cars were zipping by at eighty. Harper checked his watch: 00:30 hours.

"It's the middle of the night," Harper said.

"What of it?" the Swiss Guard said.

"There's a lot of traffic on this road for the middle of the night. It looks like a parade."

"Perhaps they're trying to make it into town before last call," the Swiss Guard said.

A white VW van came along and matched their speed. The side door opened. There were eight excited faces smiling from ear to ear; they waved. Then the door was pulled closed and the van took off. Harper caught the license plate. EU orange. DSM 5574. The blue flag on the left of the plate was stamped with a *D* for *Deutschland*.

"Drinking buddies of yours on their way to last call, Herr Gauer?" Harper said.

"Why would they be buddies of mine?"

"Because they were bloody waving at you."

Harper felt a tap at his back. He turned around. The roadie was offering him a whiskey with his right hand. His left hand was holding his cell phone as he read a message.

"They're fans of the band. They know the bus."

Harper thought about it. "Because you're having a concert, yeah?"

"Four nights of concerts, brother. It's a festival. It's scheduled to kick off tomorrow night, but I got flash traffic: The music has already begun. Would you take the glass and drink, please?"

Harper took the whiskey and sipped. "You're going live on the Internet. To millions of souls around the world. That's what your dream catcher said."

"Yup."

Harper looked out the windshield. The bus was slowing through the towns before Lausanne: Lutry, Paudex, Pully. At each red light, different cars pulled alongside the bus and windows rolled down and there were more happy faces and bigger waves. A couple of them held large fliers out the windows. Harper focused on one of them: *Older Than Dreams Tour Redux. Locomotora, Jakob, pg.lost, Shaking Sensations. Lausanne, Nowtimes.* There was a picture on the flier, too. Harper recognized it. It was the only surviving photograph of himself jumping from Pont des Arts during the Paris job. The shot caught him hanging between heaven and earth in silhouette against the spotlights of police choppers. A gun in one hand, a knife in the other, the flaps of his long coat flaring above his shoulders like wings. The photographed leaked and went viral with the headline "Was This the Angel Who Fell from the Sky to Save Paris?" Harper looked out the right side window. The A9 highway ran along the crest of the hills higher above the lake. Inbound lanes for Lausanne were packed with cars. He looked at Krinkle.

"They're partisans. The lot of them."

"Yup."

Harper waited for the roadie to spill. He didn't. "You're not going to tell me what all this really is, are you?"

"Not till you get better," the roadie said.

"Why not?"

"Because you're already confused as shit. Relax. The active ingredients in the potion are time-released. They'll kick in soon."

An image reconnected on Harper's timeline as Krinkle spoke. Coming out of the tank. The roadie telling Harper about the needle he'd been hit with. *Something to help you better understand the nature of your mission. Wasn't working then, isn't working now,* Harper thought.

"If you say so."

The bus rolled by Mon Repos. Harper flashed passing the place at night in beforetimes. Beyond the wrought-iron gates, beyond the trees and manicured gardens, there were always candles burning in the windows of shadowed buildings. All through the night the candles burned; different hours, different windows. But there was darkness beyond the gates now. There was a terrible reason for it, but Harper couldn't find it on his timeline. He refocused out the forward windshield. The bus was crossing Rue

Caroline and rolling onto Pont Bessières. Harper saw the cathedral on the hill ahead. And all down the hill and all around the esplanade were camping tents and small crowds of people. Flash: *Something's wrong.*

"Where's the time warp? Where's security?" he said.

Krinkle calmly sipped at his own whiskey. "Lausanne has been an open city since sundown."

"You're bloody joking."

The roadie shook his head. "We're trying to get as many partisans inside as we can. The time warp will go back on line as soon as we cross."

Harper checked the side mirrors. There was still a long line of headlamps following the bus.

"And the ones left outside?" he said.

"Not your concern, brother. It's not part of your mission."

Harper thought about it. "In Jerusalem."

"See, you're getting better already."

Harper triangulated the geography from here to there. "We're going the wrong way. We're going west, Jerusalem is east."

"We'll get there. But first, you've got a date at the cathedral."

Sergeant Gauer turned the bus onto Rue Louis-Auguste Curtat and headed up the steep hill to the esplanade of Lausanne Cathedral. Harper saw Café de l'Evêché on the corner. And scanning the windows he saw the joint was packed with more happy faces. Men, women, old, young, every color. All of them with healthy glasses in their hands, all of them seeing the bus pass by, all of them waving. Then he saw the T-shirts under their jackets and coats. All of them branded with the same bloody picture as the flier. He looked at Krinkle.

"What sort of date are we talking about?"

"The kind you don't miss if you're a gentleman," the roadie said.

"Sorry?"

"You're just keeping the books straight, brother. The parade was extra. You were supposed to be gone by now, but Karoliina called Gobet and told him no way should you leave Lausanne without coming to the cathedral first. The cop begged to differ and hung up. Karoliina called back and told him in no uncertain terms that he would be tempting some fucked-up karma by sending you on a mission without first keeping a promise you made."

"A promise."

"Yup."

"The inspector bought that line?"

"Dude, Karoliina was talking about some seriously fucked-up karma. And she's a dream catcher—the cop didn't have a friggin' choice."

The bus crept up the hill, inching through the tents and crowd. Hundreds of faces were highlighted in the headlamps. Here the people were subdued. No one waved, no one smiled; everyone just stared into the bus with an expression of wonder. Harper saw the same T-shirt under open coats and jackets. The penny dropped; they could see into the front of the bus, they could see the one the world called "The Angel Who Saved Paris." As the bus slowed and stopped next to the cathedral, the people gathered around, but they left a passage from the bus to the skinny red door in the base of the belfry. Sergeant Gauer shut off the motor and opened the door. Harper looked at Krinkle.

"I have no idea what I'm supposed to do."

The roadie took the empty glass from Harper's hand. "You're supposed to get off and find out."

"Right."

Harper stepped off the bus. The people on either side of the passage continued to stare at him. It was quiet; no one spoke.

"Good evening," Harper said.

Then came a swell of soft-sounding *hellos* and *good evenings* in all the languages of the world. As the voices faded, a bittersweet sound resonated through the night. It was a cello. Harper knew the music from somewhere: Johann Sebastian Bach's Prelude from Cello Suite No. 2 in D Minor. All the people gathered on the esplanade looked up at the belfry. Harper leaned back and looked up, too. He saw the shadow of a woman's form wrapped in a sheepskin jacket. She was leaning over the railing and lowering down a skeleton key at the end of a very long piece of string. The key came to a stop just in front of the red door. As the cello finished the Prelude and began the Allemande, a shred of time rolled through

Harper's eyes. In the nave of Lausanne Cathedral on a dark and stormy night. The new one, Ella, had emerged from the shadows with a lantern in her right hand. She was making a circle with her left: *Eins og svo,* she was saying. *Like this.* She was describing the round sound her cello made. The great bell in the belfry liked the sound very much, the new one said.

"Would you like to come to the belfry, monsieur? You can listen to me play for Marie-Madeleine."

"Sure."

"When?"

"Sometime."

"Right. That promise."

TWENTY

i

Harper walked through the crowd and removed the key from the string. There was a young kid close to the door. He was dressed in blue jeans and a leather jacket. He stared at Harper with a curious look. All the faces around the kid were the same. The Angelic Effect had taken hold. The crowd waited for Harper to speak, to reveal something wondrous to them. He couldn't think of a bloody thing.

"Anyone know the time?" he said.

"It just rang for one," the kid next to the door said. His accent was Polish.

"*Le guet* called the hour as you were coming across the bridge," a young woman in the crowd said. Her accent was Greek.

"Then she began to play the cello," said a tall woman with pale gray eyes. Harper could not identify her accent.

"Tell me your name."

"Kaia. I come from Estonia."

Harper looked at her and all of them. As he did, he released a spark of light from his eyes.

"Cheers."

He unlocked the outer door, pushed it open, and stepped into a small vestibule. To the left three stone steps led to a wooden door. He knew that it was the way to the belfry and that he'd been that way twice during the cathedral job. That much he was sure of. The door straight ahead was open and the lights were on. He made it for the cathedral gift shop. A tapping sound was coming from inside.

Harper pulled the key from the door and dropped it in the pocket of his trench coat. He closed the door without looking at the faces outside so he would disappear from their memories. He walked to the shop. The drummer from Locomotora stood behind the counter; his hands were moving furiously. It took Harper a couple Planck units to see the drumsticks in his grip. They hammered down on a rubber pad the size of a dinner plate. Dressed in his kill kit with his UZI slung over his shoulder and the monocle set to his right eye, the drummer had the concentrated gaze of someone who would blow your head off if you interrupted him and then didn't buy enough stuff to make the disturbance worth his while. Suddenly, the drummer's hands froze midhammer. He looked up at Harper.

"Sorry, mate. I believe I'm expected," Harper said.

"*Joo,* you're cleared. Karoliina is waiting. Go on up."

"Right. And good luck."

"With what?"

"The music festival and whatever else is going on in this town," Harper said.

The drummer laid his sticks on the glass counter. "You were wrong when you closed the door on the faces watching you. Those people out there will never forget seeing you tonight. You will not be wiped from their memories. That's the way it's going down tonight. You should know that."

"Sorry?" Harper said.

"There have been a lot of changes in the cathedral since your last tour. There isn't a corner of the place I cannot see from this room on CCTV. I watched you with the closing-the-door trick. I've seen Krinkle do it plenty of times." The drummer picked up his sticks, gave them a twirl. "The cop wants me to tell you you don't have a lot of time up there. Go up, let Ella know you came to hear her play. Tell her it's going to be okay, tell her you'll see her again. That's it."

"Understood."

Harper backed out of the shop and mounted the steps to the wooden door. As he reached for the iron latch, the door opened automatically. The side view revealed it was like the door at his flat: blast-proof, bulletproof. He passed through the opening, saw the CCTV cameras fitted in the curves of the stone ceiling. The cameras covered every angle. He headed up the worn stone steps, round and round to the right. It was the same drill through the back-and-forth walkways in the women's choir loft: Armored doors disguised as creaky wood opened and closed without a key or an "open sesame." He reached the tower steps and climbed round and round again till he felt the night air pour down the stairwell. Then came the sound of a cello finishing the Sarabande movement of the No. 2 and beginning the Menuet. Harper rested against the stone wall and listened to the music, wondering how the hell he knew so much about Bach's No. 2 in D Minor. He looked at his freshly gloved hands. The left hand knew the fingering of each stop; his right hand knew every *sul ponticello* and *sul tasto* of the bow.

"Blimey."

He stuffed his hands in the pockets of his trench coat and continued to climb the steps. He made the final turn of the tower, saw Karoliina the dream catcher at the top of the steps next to a bank of CCTV monitors. Her face glowed in the dull light cast by the screens. She had her index finger over her lips and her japa mala beads hanging from her wrist. She turned and walked slowly along the stone arches of the south balcony.

Harper followed.

He saw the execution bell, Clémence, sheltered in the interior timbers. The huge bell was brooding but still. He scanned the shadows in the dark corners. There was no one hiding there. He gave the world below a quick glance. The crowd of partisans stood quietly, listening to the cello. Harper felt a rush of vertigo and turned away. *Bloody heights.* The door to the loge set between the bells was open. Harper looked in as he passed. It looked the same. The funny-angled ceiling and the wooden beams; the small table in the middle of the narrow room and the bed planted sideways at the end of it. There were tens of small candles hanging from the ceiling and they filled the room with comforting light. Coming to the timbers surrounding Marie-Madeleine, Harper saw the dark shape of the great bell. Seven and a half tons of bronze that could rock the belfry when she called the hour. But like Clémence, the great bell was still.

Hang on.

He listened to the voice of the cello drifting through the belfry. He rested his hand on one of the massive timbers surrounding Marie-Madeleine. The wood was vibrating; all the carpentry was vibrating. He walked by Marie-Madeleine, looked through the carpentry to the east balcony. Ella was sitting on a wooden chair at an angle so the great bell could watch her play. The girl's lantern hung from the hammer that rang the hour; it cast a veil of light over her. She played with her head lowered, the black floppy hat on the girl's head hiding her face from him. He focused on her hands as she played. The long fingers of her left hand found the stops with confidence. Her right hand bowed across the strings with grace. She finished the Menuet and began the Gigue, the final movement of the No. 2.

Karoliina signaled Harper to keep moving. She pointed to the shadows in the arches of the southeast turret. From there they would have a clear view of Ella. Harper watched Karoliina step ahead and slip into the shadows. Harper was impressed. He followed in after her.

"Ella doesn't know you're here," she whispered. "It's a surprise."

No kidding, Harper thought.

He watched Ella play. Her fiery technique easily mastered the demands of the Gigue. Single-voiced notes were punctuated with deep-throated harmonies in three-eight time; she finished with a series of breathless leaps through an F major chord before touching down in triumph on B-flat major. For a moment the girl did not move, waiting for the final note to fade. Slowly, she pulled away her hands from the cello and rested them at her sides. Harper almost pronounced her name to make himself known to her, but the dream catcher raised her finger to her lips again and shook her head. *Not yet.*

They waited.

Harper looked out over the railing and down to the esplanade. The hundreds of partisans below were waiting, too. He heard the creak of a chair. It was Ella, shifting her weight and drawing the cello closer to her body. Without looking at the fingerboard, she wrapped her left hand around the neck and her fingers touched the strings. Her right hand bowed a Louré stroke and the cello came to life. It was a simple theme from B-flat to D-natural, then A-flat to C-natural, and she repeated it three times. Slowly she added the harmonies of an E-flat major chord falling to B-flat major. It fell again to an A-flat major, then rose to complete a phrase. The girl's combination of fingering and bow strokes caused the pitch to slide from one note to the other; slowly the theme became a haunting melody. Harper didn't recognize it, but he felt himself being drawn into the sound.

"This is something she's been working on since you told her you'd come," Karoliina whispered to Harper.

"What is it?"

"It doesn't have a name. She was hoping you would come up with one."

"Me?"

"She wrote it for you."

Harper stared at the dream catcher with disbelief. The dream catcher smiled at his reaction.

"Having fun yet?" she said.

It was then Harper heard voices emerge from the music. Voices that harmonized with the chords from distant octaves. Her fingering added double stops, triple stops, and vibrato to accent the tonic note of theme. It created a droning sound that wound through the timber and echoed off the stones before flowing through the hollows of the bells.

Bloody hell, it's the bells.

B-flats, A-flats, E-flats, F- and C-naturals from the cello were resonating with the strike notes of the bells and setting off a cascade of harmonics.

The ringing sound rounded the belfry and sailed off into the night. Harper imagined the cathedral as some massive radio transmitter broadcasting to millions of souls around the world. Actually, considering the roadie was downstairs with his magic bus/mobile radio station, that's probably what was happening. Harper hoped so. The music pouring from Ella's cello was like a mystical thing rising to the stars . . . then it was finished. Ella lowered her hands to her sides. She did not move for long seconds. Harper stepped from the shadows.

"Bonsoir, mademoiselle," he said.

The girl looked up. "Monsieur, you're here! I'm very happy to see you," she said.

"I'm happy to see you, too. I enjoyed that piece very much, mademoiselle."

"Did you? Did you really?"

Karoliina stepped from the shadows now.

"I told Mr. Harper that you wrote it for him, *litla*. I told him you hoped he could give it a name."

"Oh, yes, monsieur," Ella said. "I would like that very much."

"All right. How about . . ."

The girl's emerald eyes sparkled with lantern light. It was a look of great expectation.

"How about *Meditation No. 1* by Ella Mínervudóttir," he said after long seconds.

Harper saw the wheels spinning in the girl's head.

"That means I must write a No. 2."

"It does. But I think Marie-Madeleine would like it, don't you?"

Ella looked at the great bell in the timbers. She tipped her head as if listening. She looked at Harper.

"Marie says she would like it very much."

"Good. And I tell you what: You can play it for me the next time I visit you."

"Are you going away, monsieur?"

"That's why I'm here. I wanted to hear you play before I left."

"I'm glad you remembered to come."

Harper smiled. "Me too."

"When will you be back?"

"I'm not sure."

Ella looked at Marie-Madeleine again, listened intently. She turned to Harper.

"Marie is very sad you are leaving Lausanne."

"Then you must tell her that I'll be back, mademoiselle. You must tell her every night."

The girl stood from the chair and set the cello in a small stand. She rested the bow on the chair and walked to Harper.

"Before you go, monsieur, may I ask you about the princess in the story?"

"The princess?" Harper said.

Karoliina interrupted. "*Litla*, why don't you get the story and show Mr. Harper what you mean?"

"Allt í lagi," the girl said happily.

Harper watched her scurry away in her black cloak and floppy black hat. She ducked into the loge. He looked at the dream catcher. "The princess?"

"Oops—I didn't see the present thing rising in her consciousness."

"What present thing?"

"Krinkle told her you wanted her to have it."

"Sorry?"

Ella came running out of the loge. She dashed to Harper and held up a book with his own handwriting on the cover:

piratz

Une histoire drôle de Marc Rochat

pour Mademoiselle Katherine Taylor

Quick flashes ripped through Harper's eyes. It was the lad's storybook about silly pirates, a flying caterpillar, and a cat. He helped the lad write the words. And yeah, there was a princess inside. Harper found the book in the bunker after rescuing Katherine Taylor. The roadie snatched it from him, bagged and tagged it as evidence. Seeing the book in Ella's hands just now, Harper guessed it never made it to the evidence locker because . . . because . . . It hit him. Binary star, binary soul. *Marc Rochat's soul is alive and well within Ella*; those were the dream catcher's words not twenty-four hours ago. The book was being returned to its author. Harper blinked himself to nowtimes, stared at Ella's face. He wanted to scan her eyes, find the lad. He shot a quick glance at Karoliina; the dream catcher read Harper's intentions. She moved her head slowly from side to side: *Please don't.* Harper nodded. He looked at Ella.

"I'm very pleased you like the book, mademoiselle. What did you want to know about the princess?"

"I know it's a story. And it's a very nice story. But I imagined the princess is a real thing. Is she, monsieur?"

"Yes. She is very real. Her name is Katherine Taylor."

"You know her?"

"I do."

"Truly?"

"Yes."

"And the cat?"

"The cat is as real as the princess."

"Would you please bring her to the belfry sometime? And could she bring the cat? And could we have tea together in the loge, the way it ends in the story?"

Harper nodded. "I'm very sure she would accept your invitation with genuine pleasure, mademoiselle."

The half-hour bell sounded from Place de la Palud.

"I'll call the hour in thirty minutes, monsieur. Would you like to watch?"

Harper checked with the dream catcher. *Time to leave, sorry.*

"I must go now, mademoiselle. I just wanted to stop by to hear you play. And to tell you that all is well."

Karoliina lowered herself to one knee and took Ella by the shoulders. "Why don't you play something before calling the hour, *litla*?"

Ella looked at Harper. "Is there something you would like to hear before you go, monsieur?"

"You choose, mademoiselle."

Ella smiled and ran to her cello. She picked it up and sat down. She held her hands at her sides for a moment, then began to play the first Largo of Vivaldi's Sonata for Cello and Continuo in B-flat Major. It was a hopeful, joyful sound. Harper watched the girl until she lowered her head and her face was gone from his eyes. She would not notice his leaving now. He looked at the dream catcher and whispered, "How did I do?"

"Pretty well."

"You'll see Katherine Taylor comes with the cat?"

Karoliina stood. "I will."

Harper walked to the tower steps. He looked out over Lausanne and the moonlit lake and the snowcapped mountains on the far shore. *Christ, it's never the same.* He turned to the dream catcher.

"Thanks," he said.

She smiled. "Don't mention it. Leave the key with the drummer. He'll lock up behind you."

Harper hustled down the tower. The drummer was waiting in the small vestibule and he held open the skinny red door to the outside world. Harper dug the key from his trench coat and tossed it over.

"Here."

"Kiitos."

Harper looked outside. There was the bus, there was Krinkle standing on the esplanade. Sergeant Gauer was gone; so were all the partisans.

"Where is everybody?" Harper said.

"Most of them hit the hay, some went for a wander," the roadie said. "Sergeant Gauer had to report to the cop."

"And I need to patrol the nave," the drummer added.

Harper looked at him. "Sorry?"

"I can't close the door until you leave."

"Sure. Cheers."

Harper stepped outside. He heard the door close behind him, heard the key slip into the lock: *click*. He scanned the esplanade. He saw lamps in tents and silhouettes bedding down for the night. He saw people heading down Escaliers du Marché. He looked at the roadie.

"So what happens now? You drive me to Jerusalem and drop me off?"

"Not quite. It's complicated."

"How complicated?"

"The SX geeks are still plotting an infil solution. They should have it sorted by the time we get closer to touchdown."

Harper thought about it. "Is there an egg timer disguised as a plastic chicken involved with this infil?"

"Nope."

"Then how complicated can it be?"

"You'll see when we get there." The roadie pulled his cell phone from the pouch of his overalls to check the time. It was 01:46 hours. He mounted the steps of the magic bus. "I'll crank her up, brother. We're cleared to cross Pont Bessières at the top of the hour. We're going out with the friggin' bells."

"Is that a good thing?"

"If Marie-Madeleine covers our space-time signature through the warp like she's supposed to, then yeah, we'll get out of the protected zone and the bad guys will be none the wiser."

The roadie jumped into the driver's seat, started flipping switches and waving his hands over screens. The bus's blue running lights came on and a low-frequency oscillation sounded from the undercarriage.

"If you say so," Harper said, stepping onboard.

"Not yet, brother. You need to pick up some extra kit."

Just then a pair of headlamps rounded the corner at Café de l'Evêché and lit up the dark of the esplanade. Harper saw the yellow box-shaped vehicle attached to the headlamps. It chugged its way up the hill, weaving around the camping tents. It was a bread van. A yellow, 1971 Citroën H-Type. Four cylinders, forty-six horsepower, top speed of forty klicks per hour. A bloody antique with *Gasca, Boulangerie & Pâtisserie, Avenue Alsace Lorraine* painted neatly on the sides.

As the van pulled closer and stopped next to the bus, Harper saw the passengers. Behind the wheel was a large man with black hair wearing gray overalls. Riding shotgun, and almost as large as the man, was a Great Pyrenees mutt. Shreds of time tumbled through Harper's eyes. The man's name was Serge Gasca; the dog was called Shiva. They came from Montségur in the south of France. They'd helped Harper during the Paris job. The man made somber angels from scrap iron. Turned out the man's family had been in the service of Harper's kind for thirteen hundred years. "Our sacred duty," Serge called it. Serge was also the last Cathar on the face of the planet. And the mutt was . . . well, it was a dog. Though looking at the beast now, Harper suspected there was a very old soul hiding in there. Presently, the great beast held a leather strap in its slobbering mouth. The strap was attached to a reliquary box. Harper knew the box was from the Middle Ages and he knew what was inside it. One copper sextant with the mathematical formula for prime quadruplets embedded in the arc. That piece of junk was at least five thousand years old. Then there was the one-third of a clay cup and the one carpenter nail with traces of blood on it. Those two items were from first-century Jerusalem. During the Paris job, Serge the last Cathar called them the things of the Christ.

"God save us," Harper said.

The bread van stopped near the bus. Serge didn't shut down his motor, he didn't shut off the headlamps. He engaged the parking brake and got out of the van. He walked to the passenger side, opened the door for Shiva. The mutt jumped down with the reliquary box hanging from its mouth; beast and man walked toward Harper.

"*Adieussiatz*, noble lord," the man said. "Nice to see you again. They said I should bring the things you left in Montségur. They said you might need them."

ii

Katherine had been sitting in the starkly lit room for hours while holding the boy's hand. There were no clocks on the walls, so she had no idea of the time. There was a measure of change from one moment to the next in the clicks and hisses from the respirator attached to the boy. There were beeps counting heartbeats, too. The boy lay in a coma, unable to breathe on his own, and his broken body was dwarfed by the medical equipment surrounding him. Monitors and controls; a crash cart; banks of IVs containing potions, nutrients, and hydration supplements; a network of tubes, needles, and wires attached to connections extending from the bandages covering his chest and arms. She could only see half the boy's face through the bandages and the halo traction brace around his skull. His half face was the only part of his skin exposed other than his right hand. The hand lay limp and motionless next to him.

When Katherine first saw Goose she could only stare at him through the window of the intensive care unit. It wasn't the sight of the boy's terrible injuries she noticed first, it was the odd shape of him, made even more odd by the bandages wrapped around him. His legs were too short for his torso; his head was much smaller than normal and it was at the end of a long thin neck. Corporal Mai told Katherine he suffered from a form of paedomorphosis: His head and facial features did not develop with the rest of his body. That's why Katherine thought him a boy; he appeared too small for twenty-six years old. It was thought the boy was deaf, but his hearing was fine, Corporal Mai told Katherine. After the boy's mother died from cancer, Goose was left with a mad drunk for a stepfather. The foul man raped the boy repeatedly. In a drunken rage one night, when the boy tried to resist, the stepfather used a pair of pliers to rip the boy's tongue from his head. He imagined the boy was possessed by the devil and speaking in tongues. His real father, someone called Astruc, murdered the stepfather and ran away with the boy.

"What happened to the father?" Katherine said.

"He is recovering in another part of the clinic," said Corporal Mai.

"Was he as wounded as his son?"

"His physical wounds have healed."

"Then why isn't he here?"

"He comes sometimes. It's difficult for him."

"Difficult for *him*?"

"They are not like you, or me for that matter, ma'am. Emotions and feelings are crippling things to their kind. Also, he isn't allowed to touch his son."

"Why not?"

"Father Astruc is awakened. He is bound by the rules and regulations of his kind. They are forbidden to touch locals, even half-kinds."

Katherine looked through the glass window. A dying boy clinging to life, broken and alone.

"How the hell this crowd can call themselves the good angels with a straight face is a fucking mystery to me." She looked at Corporal Mai. "Could you get me a chair, please?"

"Ma'am?"

"A chair. For me. In there next to Goose."

"You will need to obtain permission to enter the room, Madame Taylor. I was told to let you see him only."

"I don't give a shit. Get me a chair."

"Ma'am?"

"I get the feeling you and I are going to spend a lot of time together, Corporal, and I think I could get used to you. But let's get a few things straight. I'll take the medics' potions and teas to keep from falling off the edge of the earth. I'll eat your chocolate chip cookies, tell you they're yummy, and pretend there's nothing else in them. I'll even play along with whatever supercop has planned to get my son back. But I'll be damned if I will allow that broken child to be alone one more minute."

Katherine could see Corporal Mai was muddled.

"Get me a fucking chair, Corporal. Please."

Katherine blinked, saw the boy's hand in hers now. She looked at his half face and smiled.

"The whole time-loop thing is pretty wild, isn't it? I can't imagine how you lived with it. I can't imagine how you lived with any of it."

She turned around, saw Corporal Mai standing in the hall keeping the watch. The corporal had dutifully gotten the chair for Katherine, called in a few doctors to answer questions about Goose, who then took their leave when Katherine said she wanted to be alone with the boy. Katherine wondered if she had been too hard on the corporal. Then again, maybe the corporal was testing Katherine's progress, seeing if she was capable of thinking for herself. No doubt her progress had already been reported to the cop. Who knew what would happen next? Katherine turned back to the boy.

"They told me you're really smart. Actually, they said you're a genius. They said you hacked a supercomputer and got it talking with a spaceship. A for-real, no-kidding spaceship that's leaving our galaxy right now. She said it's carrying an SOS. That's so damn cool, Goose. My son would love you. He's a full-fledged member of the *Star Trek* brigade. I remember taking him into the back garden of our house on moonless nights. He would stare at the stars, point to this one and that one, gurgle and coo and laugh. Sometimes I imagined he was giving names to the stars. It was only the same two names: 'Goog' or 'Boo.' Those were about the only words he knew. 'Boo' was short for his cat, Monsieur Booty. Actually, it was someone else's cat. He's Max's cat now. And mine. Perhaps when you get better and when Max comes home, you two could meet. He'd love to hear how you're talking to a spaceship. My son's name is Max."

Katherine felt a wave of sadness. She sighed and it receded.

"Corporal Mai said you knew you weren't the child of the prophecy, that you were only trying to protect your father and the half-kinds. That's why you let the world know the comet over Paris was coming. You were telling the world it wasn't you, you were telling the world it was someone else. Did you know it was my son? Did you know it was Max? Did you suffer so to protect him?"

She gave his hand a gentle squeeze.

"I think you did, Goose. I think you were trying to protect him, too.

And I want you to listen to me now, because I'm imagining that you can hear me. I'm going to protect you, Goose. I'm going to stay with you until you wake up. I'm here and I'm going to stay with you."

She waited, almost expecting the boy to respond. He did not. She reached out and touched his cheek.

"Oh, my name is Katherine, in case you were wondering."

She turned the boy's hand and studied the palm. She had done so a few times already sitting with him, each time even more amazed at the number of lines etched in the skin. Maybe he was twenty-six, but the palm of his right hand appeared ancient. Hundreds of tiny lines intersected and crossed over one another.

"I went to a fortune teller once. She looked at my palm and told me I had a wounded love line. Man, was she right. I wonder what she would say looking at your hand. So many lines and crosses and stars."

The respirator stopped. The beeps of the monitors stopped. But there were no alarms or medics rushing into the room. And Corporal Mai stood in the hall as still as Lot's wife.

"What the heck?" Katherine looked at the boy's half face. "Goose?"

Then there was a wheezing voice. *"No temas. El niño va a estar bien."*

Katherine looked at the shadowed corner of the room. A raggedly dressed man stood there. It was the bum from her dream in Lausanne Cathedral. The one who lifted her into the light pouring through the stained glass windows. Harper called him Monsieur Gabriel. Oddly enough, seeing him again, Katherine wasn't afraid.

"Hello again," she said.

"Buenos días."

Katherine stared at him. "Did you speak Spanish the last time I dreamed about you, when you did that trick with the light?"

"Sí."

"I don't speak Spanish. But I understood what you said. You said, 'Be not afraid. The boy will be fine.'"

"Muy bueno."

"*Gracias*. But that's not the point. Where did I learn to speak Spanish?"

"We are not really speaking, Madame Taylor. This is only a dream."

"Okay. I'll buy that."

She looked at the boy. She was still holding his hand.

"What happened? Why did Goose stop breathing?" she said.

"He breathes. I am only visiting you in the moment between one breath and the next."

Katherine looked at Monsieur Gabriel. "How can we be taking the time to have our imaginary conversation if we are in the moment between one breath and the next? Did the cop lower a time warp over the place?"

"There is no need for a time warp in dreams."

"Why not?"

"You are full with questions, madame."

"It's the chocolate chip cookies. Why no time warp?"

"Because dreams do not exist in time, they only exist in the moment."

Katherine nodded. "Okay, I'll buy that, too. How do you know Goose will come back?"

"He was only waiting for you to pronounce your name to him."

Katherine smiled. "So, on top of everything else that's happened to me, looping and linguistics included, I'm a miracle worker, too?"

"You were chosen among women to bear the child of the prophecy and bring light into the world."

"Who chose me? When?"

"Does it matter?"

"Call me curious."

"Call me the one who cannot answer the question."

Katherine tried to stand. "I'm stuck."

"You are."

"Why?"

"Because we are in the moment from one breath to the next."

"And why are we here?"

The bum's eyes were bright now. "So that I can tell you about your son."

Katherine received his words without sinking. "What about him?"

"He will not be safe until the betrayer of the creation is destroyed."

"I take it you mean the slimeball who kidnapped my son, Komarovsky."

"*Sí.*"

"Okay, what are you waiting for? Go get him, and take Harper with you. I've seen him in action, he's good at it."

"The light within him struggles to live. He will draw out the enemy and wound him, but he is too weak to destroy him. It falls to another."

"Who?"

"You, of course."

"Me, of course?"

"It is the simple truth."

"In other words, it should be fucking obvious to me."

Monsieur Gabriel nodded again, scratching at the bend of his arm this time. Katherine recognized the action. She had seen it loads in before-times, back in L.A. The bum was in bad need of a fix.

"Help me out with the fucking obvious. On the jet from the States, Inspector Gobet told me all you guys know about your own existence comes from the legends and myths and religions of men."

"*Sí.*"

"Exactly. Gabriel was God's messenger in the Bible. Pretty face, white robes, big wings, always appears in a heavenly light. He gave the Virgin Mary the good news that she was pregnant. Which in her day wasn't good news at all. But Gabriel convinced Mary she was part of a divine plan, that she was bringing the light of God into the world."

"That is the legend."

"Exactly again. You're a junkie with a bad complexion. You've got a ragged overcoat for wings and you're standing in a dark corner delivering a message to an ex-hooker that she needs to kill *your* bad guy as part of *your* truth. Not that I object to the last part, necessarily. But how is it our legends, our myths, our religions, ended up as your reality? Or is it the other way around?"

"That is the truth of your dream being revealed to you."

Katherine smiled. "I was hoping for something a little more starry-eyed. Something along the lines of 'Your dreams are ours, our dreams are yours.'"

Monsieur Gabriel smiled with yellowed, junkie teeth. "We do not sleep, we do not dream. Your dreams are your own. I can only point to the truth within them."

Katherine laughed a little. "So is that the great angelic riddle? Which came first, our dreams or your truth?"

"You are a creature of free will, madame. You can choose to accept the truth of your dreams or not."

Katherine looked at the hundreds of intersecting lines etched in the boy's right hand. So many lines and crosses and stars.

"What if truth is older than dreams? What if truth is something ancient written in the stars, like the stars in the palm of this boy's hands? Born of an act of love, wasn't he? That is *his* truth, isn't it?"

"¿Perdóneme?"

She kissed Goose's palm, looked at Monsieur Gabriel. "What if the truth is our free will has been so twisted by fear and greed that we're not free at all? What if everything around us is an illusion designed to make us the worst kind of slaves, the kind who imagine they are free? What if the truth of it is, given the suffering and pain in the world, we're no different from you anymore, we don't have a fucking choice if we're going to survive?"

"Exactamente."

Katherine looked at Goose, then out into the hallway at Corporal Mai. Everyone, everything, continued to remain still. She looked at the junkie bum.

"So which of your truths is hidden in my dream? And is it this dream or did you have another, older dream in mind?"

Monsieur Gabriel slowly raised his trembling hand and pointed a long, spindly finger at Katherine Taylor.

"As you gave flesh to the light, so must you crush the head of the serpent."

Katherine tossed the words back and forth in her brain. A memory of a statue at Our Lady of Peace Catholic School popped hot. Katherine walked by it every day with Sister Superior and the rest of her class on their way to chapel to recite the Angelus. The statue always watched Katherine pass with its ceramic blue eyes. The statue held a small wooden cross in its hands. It was standing atop the world; under her right foot was the head of a snake.

"Okay, angelman, you have my attention. But before you say one more word, back up to the part about Harper. What's wrong with him?"

TWENTY-ONE

i

Harper came to the banks of the River Jordan.

South was the Dead Sea; north was the Jordan Rift Valley. Up there was a desert spotted with farms, Israeli settlements, and Palestinian towns. One of them was Jericho, the oldest town on the planet. Down the other way was the lowest spot on the face of the earth and a body of dark, lifeless water. Across the river was open desert till you hit the foothills of the Central Highlands. The hills were falling into evening shadow now. Farther west and higher up the sun was setting behind a cluster of mountains. There was Scopus, there was the Mount of Olives, there was Zion. Against the fading light Harper saw the silhouettes of towers and steeples that marked the Holy City of Jerusalem. He had to admit the view looked familiar.

He pulled his electronic fag from his trench coat and smoked. He waited for evening shadow to cross the desert. When it found him in the palm grove where he had taken cover, the air grew cold. He closed his coat, scanned the geography again.

A mile upriver was Allenby Bridge, the official crossing between the Kingdom of Jordan and Israel by way of Palestine's West Bank. It was modern; it was four lanes across. But it was only the latest edition in crossings at this spot. There had been bridges here since the days of the Ottoman Empire. Before the Ottomans, people simply waded across the river, as did the disciples of Moses, according to legend. It would not have been too difficult a task. The mighty River Jordan had never been all that mighty in width or depth. And these days, with most water run off from the valley being diverted for irrigation, the river barely qualified as a stream.

Harper looked up at the sky.

Heavy clouds were rolling in from the Mediterranean beyond Jerusalem. *Good,* he thought. The clouds would diffuse the full moon's light and give him cover. He checked his watch: 18:05 hours. He had one hour, twenty-five minutes before the Israeli Border Police experienced a glitch in their electronic surveillance capability near Allenby Bridge, courtesy of Inspector Gobet's SX geeks back in Switzerland. All CCTV cameras, fence alarms, and motion and sound detectors within a two-mile radius of the bridge would go offline for ten minutes before the system magically rebooted itself. In the sudden dark Harper would walk across Allenby Bridge. But not by way of the modern, four-lane job. That one would be crawling with Israeli and Jordanian soldiers keeping a lid on things during the shutdown. Harper would take the small abandoned bridge of the same name tucked in the shallow depression just ahead of him. Access to both bridges was cut off by a high-tech security fence marking the beginning of no-man's-land. Thirty feet along the fence was a remote-controlled access gate. This side of the river, the gate was used by Jordanian soldiers to enter and patrol their sector of no-man's-land. There was a similar access gate on the Israeli side. Infil plan was: shutdown hits, gates on both sides of the river pop open, Harper strolls across the bridge and into the Holy Land.

"What could possibly go wrong?" he mumbled while thinking about it.

He looked back over his shoulder, back to the east. He watched evening shadows rise up the slopes of Mount Nebo. That's where Krinkle dropped him a few hours earlier after spilling intel on geography and mission targets, as well as the swell plan to reach those targets. Needless to say, Harper didn't think much of it. Especially after hearing the rest of the plan: hoof it, unseen, twelve miles across the desert and get to Qumran for a recce in the dark. And that was only stage bloody one of the mission; stage two was getting to Jerusalem for "an as yet undefined task."

Harper flashed through his timeline . . .

He locked on the roadie's face during the mission brief. The roadie's expression was serious as he poured a round of Galileo's single malt.

"Stay focused, brother. The entire mission is off-radar. You're not here, you're being dried out in a stasis tank for tweaking your radiance allotment. Now, we're hoping you'll pick up some help on the inside, but we're not sure it will be there. So be wary of any help offered. Which reminds me: Leave your wallet, passport, and watch with me. In the event you're snatched by the Israeli cops, you don't exist, got it? However it plays out, do *not* bother contacting anyone at base until further notice. Not Gobet, not me, not Karoliina, not Gabriel, not nobody. Ever."

"I'm not surprised. The whole bloody infil plan is daft."

"No, it's so friggin' improbable, it's foolproof. Look, things are tense inside. I know that sounds like same-shit-different-day for the Holy Land, but given the lines of causality converging overhead at the moment, it's obvious something ugly is about to fall. And it's like the locals feel it."

"And shutting down Israel's electronic security grid isn't going to start World War Three?"

"Don't worry, we've got it covered. The shutdown will look like a computer glitch, nothing more. And it's only a tiny part of the grid. Nobody will die."

"You are confident of that."

"Reasonably."

Harper rubbed the back of his neck. *Bollocks.*

"You hanging in there, brother?" the roadie said.

"More or less."

"What's on your mind?"

Harper looked at the reliquary box at his feet. The leather strap still bore the teeth marks of the Great Pyrenees mutt, but it was almost dry of the beast's slobber. The sextant, the one-third of a clay cup, the one carpenter nail with faint traces of blood . . . *The things of Christ,* the last

Cathar called them. Something else popped hot as Harper looked at the reliquary box, something else the Cathar said about the pottery shard and the nail: *In pieces and separate, they are the things of men. Rejoined and together, they become things of the gods again.* Harper tapped the side of the box with his shoes.

"It's all daft, because it's not just me crossing a river. It's our kind crossing a line we can't come back from. We are getting ourselves directly involved with the consciousness of the locals."

"Not us, you."

"And I should proceed because?"

"No choice."

Harper downed his single malt. "Humor me, then. Tell me how the plan is so bloody foolproof given the Holy Land will be crawling with Israeli soldiers on high alert."

Krinkle drank his glass and poured again. "Easy. The Israelis will be concentrating on big Allenby, the settlements in the valley, and the Palestinian towns. They'll be looking the other way."

"That's daft, too."

"How come?"

"I'm crossing the river within the shutdown radius. From what I hear, the Israelis are excellent shots in the dark."

"The abandoned bridge you'll take will appear normal at Israeli Security HQ in Jerusalem even though it'll be offline, so things will be cool. All you have to do is get through no-man's-land and get to Qumran. Double-time it and you'll be there in two hours. We hacked a Landsat orbiting four hundred thirty-eight miles up. We used it to reconnoiter the area. Qumran is locked down, officially, but it's not airtight. If you stick to the coordinates, it's easily accessible. Once you're inside the cordon, it's a walk in the park."

"Why not just drop a time warp over the place? That's really easy."

"Too risky. The slightest ripple in space-time would tip the enemy that we're making a move."

Like he said, no choice, boyo.

"Anything else of interest I should know?"

"Actually, Brother Harper . . ."

Seems the spot atop Mount Nebo where Krinkle was letting Harper off was the exact spot from where Moses (who was something of a raving lunatic, Krinkle added) sat and watched the chosen tribes cross into the Promised Land. And the place Harper would be crossing the river was the very place where the chosen tribes did the deed. In relating those tales, the roadie had switched into babbling-like-a-speed-freak mode.

"And not far from that spot, John the Baptist—"

Harper felt his head about to explode with wonderment. He waved the roadie to stop. "Sorry I asked," he said, picking up the reliquary box by the strap and slinging it over his shoulder. "Let's get this funfair on the road."

The roadie opened the door of his magic bus and pointed across the Jordan Valley to Jerusalem. "You'll find the abandoned bridge that way, way down there. Just keep the parietal cortex of your brain locked on a heading of 258 degrees as triangulated from this location. That will take you to a palm grove near the river. From there you'll see the crossing point. You'll find plenty of shadows there to hide in till sundown. Qumran is across the desert in those foothills on a heading of 220 degrees from the bridge. You tracking me?"

"Got it."

"Cool. Power shutdown at nineteen hundred thirty hours."

Harper checked the distance to the river. It was a long hike.

"I've got the crossing no-man's-land part on foot, but how do I get down to the river?"

"You'll figure it out."

"That's very helpful."

"Hey, according to the scraps on intel spilling from Brother Astruc, the whole being-smuggled-out-of-the-Holy-Land-in-70-AD-and-getting-yourself-smuggled-back-in-nearly-two-thousand-years-later plan was *your* idea. We just don't know why you did it, how you did it, or if it even happened. It could be ghost intel. Whatever it is, it's on the other side of the river. Oh, reminds me, this is from the cop."

The roadie reached in the pouch of his overalls, pulled out a leather strap, and tossed it at Harper. Harper caught it. There was a monocle attached to the strap, of the same sort he'd seen on the drummer. The monocle had X-ray vision or something like it.

"This is for what?"

"The Israelis have a shitload of area denial ordnance buried in the border zone and all across the desert till you hit Highway 90. Claymore and fragmentation mines, bounding and directional. Some set to go off by contact, others by trip wire. Get by those and you've got antitank mines laid out in staggered grids. It's a local's version of a time warp."

Harper looked at the monocle. Twenty-four hours ago it was a trip through Hell with a tracking device posing as an egg timer. Now it was crossing the River Jordan into an active war zone with a piece of kit that would rate him as a spy if caught. Unless, of course, he had already taken a head shot.

"How does it work?" Harper said.

"It just does. But we can only get a ping on your location every ninety seconds. It will instantaneously triangulate and update your compass position. Anything more would create an identifiable comms signature. You're reconnoitering the old-fashioned way. Sort of."

"Right." He stuffed the monocle in his coat pocket. He stared at Krinkle; the roadie stared back. "So, I guess that's that," Harper said.

The roadie nodded. "Listen to me, brother, if this is the real deal, we will be there. We will get to you like the last time."

"Sure," Harper said.

He stepped off the bus, took a deep breath of desert air. He looked back at Krinkle.

"Just a thought, but why couldn't you drop me next to Qumran?"

"Because weird as it sounds, this *is* the Holy Land. That means you have to go in by the same way you last came out."

"Way back then, when I was who I was. Maybe."

"Maybe. That's what you're here to confirm or deny. Rock on, brother."

The door closed, and off the roadie went.

Watching the bus head off in a cloud of dust, a question dropped in Harper's head.

"Smuggled out how, two thousand years ago?"

He took a few steps to the ridge atop Mount Nebo to survey the expanse of desert before him. There was a dry hot wind coming up from the floor of the desert. It was then the dead soldier in Harper's head responded to his question. *You'll figure it out, boyo.*

"Sure I will."

He refocused on the long hike before him. It was worse than a long hike. Twenty-five miles to the river, Qumran twelve miles farther, then another twenty-five miles to Jerusalem. It was a bloody steep down-and-up, too. From an altitude atop Nebo of nearly two thousand feet above sea level; down to fourteen hundred feet below sea level at the Dead Sea; back up two thousand five hundred feet above sea level to the Holy City of Jerusalem.

"Just another ride on the cosmic roller coaster."

He headed in the general direction of down. He skirted villages and took cover in any shadows he could find. An hour's walk later, the mountain leveled off at a ribbon of asphalt running parallel to the Dead Sea. Keeping out of sight meant Harper had made a meandering trail. It was still a long way to the river.

"Now would be a good time for a miracle."

There was a mirage where the horizon met the road, and out of the mirage came a dusty vehicle with a Jordanian license plate. Harper saw the driver. He wore a white dishdasha and there was a red-checked kaffiyeh on his head. A Bedouin tribesman who had traded his camel for a clapped-out Toyota, Harper thought.

"Ask and you shall receive."

The tribesman's eyes widened seeing the western man in a black coat standing at the side of the road in the middle of nowhere. The tribesman slowed as he passed, and Harper saw two goats in the back of the pickup. The goats stared at him, too. The tribesman kept driving, but Harper caught the man's eyes in the pickup's rearview mirror. He raised the palm of his freshly gloved right hand into the man's eyeline.

"Stop," Harper said.

The tribesman hit the brakes, and the goats stumbled but quickly regained their footing.

"Come back."

The pickup reversed and stopped next to Harper. He leaned down to the open passenger window. He scanned the man's eyes for traces of dead black; they were clean.

"Hello," Harper said.

"As-salamu aleykum," the tribesman said.

"I wonder if you could take me to the river."

"Shou?"

"I'm a tourist. I'd like to see the River Jordan. Someplace where I could cross into the West Bank. Say, old Allenby Bridge?"

"Khouth jiser al-yahoud."

"Well, yes, I should use the official Israeli crossing, but I seem to have left my passport in Switzerland."

"Ma btigdar tigtah al-jiser. Mamnou. Al-jaish bitukhak."

"The soldiers will shoot me only if they see me. Which they won't, or your truck, or your goats."

"Inta shitan?"

"Am I a demon? Actually, I'm one of the good guys."

"Shou?"

Harper opened the passenger door, climbed in the pickup, and stared at the tribesman.

"What's your name, mate?"

"Abu Salah."

"Abu Salah, nice to meet you. I want you to look into my eyes and listen to the sound of my voice. That's it. Now, take me to the river."

Harper blinked to nowtimes.

Evening had arrived and heavy clouds were thick over the Jordan Valley and the Dead Sea, but darkness had yet to spread over the border zone.

Sodium vapor lamps at big Allenby were blazing. Spotlights along the security fence flooded the BZ with light. He checked his watch: 19:30 hours minus three, two, one . . . The lights went out.

"Here we go."

He reached in his pocket for the monocle, slid the strap over his head, and set the glass to his right eye. The darkness before him became a world of shimmering green light. There was the desert, there was the fence, there was the border zone. Then there was a heads-up display of a compass laid in over the green world. He turned his head from left to right; the compass constantly realigned itself to keep the parietal cortex of his brain focused on a bearing of 220 degrees.

Clack.

And there was the gate in the security fence popping open. Words dropped in Harper's head. He recognized them from Isaiah: *Go through, go through the gates; prepare the way for the people.*

"Through a bloody minefield, no less."

He picked up the reliquary box, secured it over his shoulder. He hurried from the palm grove and slipped through the open gate. He kept his eyes on the ground till he reached an abandoned one-lane trestle of rusting iron and decaying wood. He stopped and looked down at the River Jordan, where prophets slaked their thirst and were overcome with mystic visions. It really was a pathetic stream in nowtimes, Harper thought. From the smell of it, it was a polluted one as well. The foul smell of the water kicked off a vision in Harper's own head.

"The river is dying. The whole bloody world is dying."

Then, according to some daft plan he came up with nearly two thousand years ago, Jay Michael Harper strolled across the bridge and back into the Holy Land.

ii

He cleared the border zone without blowing himself up. And the intel on the desert beyond was solid. The ground was littered with things that went bang if disturbed. He could see them through his monocle. At first it worked as a night sight, allowing him to see the trip wires and aboveground Claymores. Then, as if anticipating his need, the monocle augmented itself with an X-ray function. Harper saw antitank and fragmentation mines buried in staggered rows as far as his eye could see.

"This isn't a local's version of a time warp, this is bloody no-man's-land."

He scanned the ground in a left-to-right arc; it was the same in every direction. Desert, brush, and tumbleweeds, things that went bang. He would never make it across the desert before the moon came out from behind the clouds; then he'd be a soft target on the horizon for a sniper.

"Terrific."

Twenty yards to the left he saw a depression carved in the desert floor. He zigzagged through the minefield toward it. The depression went seven feet down and was two meters wide. It was the beginning of a network of ravines and gullies spreading out in all directions, some of them in the general direction of 220 degrees. There were earthen steps connecting the desert floor to the bottom of the depression. He saw boot prints in the dirt. The prints were military; an Israeli soldier on patrol maybe. Harper got the picture. The Israelis used the natural landscape as a force multiplier. If attacked they could maneuver quickly on foot, leapfrogging from one position to the next and forcing the enemy to hold in the minefields. It was only a matter of calling in air support to finish off the invaders.

Smart, the dead soldier in Harper's head offered.

"Not if it's us they're looking for."

Still, if he was going to get to Qumran before the moon turned him into a sitting duck, he didn't have a choice. He checked the steps and lower ground for trip wires and explosive ordnance; good to go. Harper's eyes followed the prints to a bend in the depression. A dim light was glowing from around the bend.

"Hello."

He went down into the depression and headed for the light. Coming around the bend, he found a six-inch infrared ChemLight in the dirt. Someone was marking a trail. And given the operating life of the Chem-

Light, that someone had been here within the last ten hours. Standard military ops, Harper thought. It would prevent patrolling soldiers from getting lost. He listened carefully: no boots on the ground ahead. He followed the prints till he came to an intersection of ravines and gullies. Boot prints went this way and that way.

Harper plotted the bearing of each ravine and gully to figure his next move. It was a bit like plotting your way through a garden maze. *Like the yew mazes at Longleat or Hampton Court maybe,* he thought. He wondered which of the dead Brit soldiers in his head would have known such gentle places of fair quiet and innocence. Didn't matter. In the Holy Land the maze was made of hardened sand and surrounded by killing things. One ravine clocked a heading of 212 degrees. He walked ten yards ahead, stopped. He flashed the roadie's brief atop Mount Nebo: *We're hoping you'll pick up some help on the inside, but we're not sure it will be there. So be wary of any help offered.*

"Or not."

He walked back to the intersection, scanned the passages again, this time checking for infrared signatures. The monocle read one glowing against the walls of a gully on a bearing of 319 degrees. Northwest, eighty-nine degrees off his course. Could be coincidence, could be bad news.

"Only one way to find out."

He shifted the reliquary box from his right shoulder to his left. He pulled his SIG Sauer from his kill kit, fitted it with a silencer. He walked on, found another intersection of ravines and gullies. There was another ChemLight in a tunnel heading southeast on 170 degrees. Ten minutes later there was one more in a ravine heading west on 270 degrees. He was heading in the right direction, more or less. Maybe the Holy Land was a no-go zone for his kind. But maybe, once inside, it wasn't much different from the rest of paradise. Maybe there was no such thing as coincidences or cosmic accidents in this place. *Only leaves the bad news, boyo.*

Harper continued to follow the ChemLights in wildly different directions. Forty minutes later the depressions flattened out and opened to barren desert. He was only three hundred yards from the Dead Sea. The smell of sulfur and salt hit him in the face. Well behind him was Allenby

Bridge. More good intel: Israeli choppers circled low over the BZ and the lower Jordan Valley searching for incoming threats. He was in the clear, for now.

He checked the night sky over Qumran.

The heavy clouds were thinning out. In another hour the full moon would break through and light up the desert. He scanned the desert floor. Bad news: The ground was loaded with explosive ordnance. More bad news: The ChemLight trail went dark. Maybe he was wrong about the Holy Land being not that different from the rest of paradise. Maybe he'd done nothing more than come across the remnants of an Israeli patrol.

"Bollocks."

He scanned the ground looking for a way out.

He saw a single pair of boot prints in the dirt. Harper followed the track step for step. He walked five yards, came upon a jeep track. A nearby sign, in Hebrew and Arabic, explained the really bad news. He was in a highly restricted military zone and would be shot on sight. The sign also said the ground was heavily mined. In the event he might consider walking closer to the Dead Sea to avoid the mines, he was advised the ground along the shoreline was unstable and frequently collapsed into deep pits, which could cause severe injury and/or death.

"Cheers for the warning."

Harper holstered his Sig, shifted the reliquary box from left shoulder to right. The monocle's night sight highlighted fresh wheel markings in the dirt. The track was clear of explosive ordnance. If you were an Israeli soldier, this was safe passage through no-man's-land. The monocle's compass clocked a heading of 253 degrees, meaning the track probably connected to Highway 90 running along the east shore of the Dead Sea. From there he'd have a clear shot 220 degrees. Maybe. He double-timed it. Twenty minutes later the night sight highlighted the foothills of Qumran. He clocked the distance at less than four miles.

Suddenly a set of headlamps lit up the track and hit him in the back. Three Israeli Humvees were coming his way in a cloud of dust; each Humvee was topped with a .50-caliber machine gun. He searched the ground north of the track with his monocle. One meter in he saw antitank mines beneath the ground and a spider's web of trip wire everywhere else. He had nowhere to go.

"Judas Priest."

He pulled the collar of his black Burberry up around his neck, stuffed his hands into the pockets, and lowered his eyes to the ground.

"Lux transit per circuitum," he said.

The convoy rolled by but the soldiers did not see him. And when the convoy was well gone, Harper looked up. He saw red taillights turn onto another track and head north toward Allenby Bridge. *That one calls for a hit of radiance,* he thought. He dug through his pockets searching for his electronic fag. He found it and had three deep hits. The dead soldier in his head piped up: *That, boyo, makes the second bloody miracle of the day.* Harper shifted the reliquary box from his right shoulder to his left.

"No shit."

He got to Highway 90. He crossed over, checked the ground. Everything in an arc from southwest to northwest was clear of ordnance. The monocle pointed him to 220 degrees. He hustled that way. He went through groves of date palm and fig trees. There was no one around. He crossed a dry riverbed and crossed a patch of barren desert. He skirted an Israeli settlement on his right. Had to be. It was surrounded by a fence and security towers. Harper kept his eyes to the ground as he passed and was not noticed. Five hundred more yards and he came over a rise. He saw the turnoff two hundred yards away. There were two Israeli Humvees blocking the entrance. But there were no fence or foot patrols that he could see. Farther up, atop a hill, were three well-lit buildings. Everything about them said *Welcome to the Qumran Tourist Center and Gift Shop.*

He checked his bearings: 220 degrees took him straight through the tourist center and into the far southwest hills. The cave belonging to that last scribe of Qumran was somewhere up there.

"Yeah, but I can't go that bloody way."

Without warning, the monocle's compass and X-ray capabilities stopped functioning. Harper pulled it from his eye, tapped the side of it. He reset the monocle, but only the night-sight function was working now.

Krinkle's brief had gotten him this far and that was it. Harper was back in the wonderful world of "You'll figure it out."

"Sure I will."

He walked ten yards. The monocle's night sight registered a ChemLight twenty-nine yards off his bearing to the north. He walked that way, found an old goat path heading into the high hills north of Qumran. The ChemLight was next to the path, stuffed under a clump of desert brush. Next to the ChemLight was a piece of paper anchored to the earth by a stone. Harper bent down, pulled the paper free, unfolded it. It was a handwritten message in Hebrew.

סע אחרי האור
תאסוף אותם בדרך
זה גן לאומי
אסור להשליך אשפה

It took Harper eighteen seconds to upload the language:

Follow the light.
Pick them up along the way.
This is a national park.
No littering allowed.

Harper scanned the path for tracks. He saw the one pair of Israeli Army–issue boots.

iii

Harper counted his paces. Nearing a mile's worth now. He had not seen one ChemLight the entire way. Not that it mattered. He was walking through a narrow, winding valley through the sandstone hills. The walls on either side were twenty feet high at least. There was no way to go but ahead. Above the high walls was the night. When the valley wound this way, Harper saw stars; that way, he saw the waning moon. Now and again moonlight poured into the valley and highlighted strange patterns in the sandstone walls. Closed shapes, open shapes; swirls and cubic curves; comets and stars. The patterns appeared deliberate, as if the walls were spilling with high-value, encoded intel. Maybe it was him trying to not imagine he was walking into a trap; or maybe it was the real deal. What he did know was everything about this narrow valley, starting with how he got there, said *unknown to the world.*

He had followed the infrared ChemLights into the foothills north of Qumran, collecting them as ordered in the note. He came to a sandstone outcrop that looked like a dead end. His monocle's night sight spotted a ChemLight through a low opening tucked in a hidden corner. He crawled through the opening, found himself in this hidden valley. He saw the same Israeli Army–issue boot prints in the dirt and followed them. Then he saw fossilized human footprints; some barefoot, some wearing sandals. If he were a trained archaeologist, he would classify the human prints as "really, really old."

Another sixteen hundred winding paces and he came to a crack in the left wall. He stopped to have a peek at the outside world. He was looking down on the tourist center. Without realizing it he had climbed three hundred feet from the desert floor and circled around the center by an angle of sixty degrees. Just beyond the tourist center, on a high plateau blanketed in moonlight, were the ruins of Qumran. Harper saw the low stone walls of what was left of the place. The ruins were neatly laid out in rectangles and squares marking the scriptorium and libraries, dining halls, living quarters, cisterns and baths. From the layout Qumran looked to be a neat and ordered place before the Fifth Cohort of Rome's Tenth Legion destroyed it. That was Harper's first impression. Second was, like the view of Jerusalem from the River Jordan, the place looked familiar . . . *More of those bloody wonders never ceasing, boyo.*

The west side of the plateau dropped hundreds of feet into a huge canyon. There sandstone towers rose from the floor like archipelagos from the sea. Harper saw the mouths of caves at the very tops of the towers. Some of the caves had openings on two sides and the moonlight flowed through like water. An episode of the History Channel raced through Harper's eyes. He didn't bother flashing the title; he knew he was staring at the very caves where the Dead Sea Scrolls were discovered in 1948. In one of those caves, cave four to be exact, the Book of Enoch was found. Once denied as never existing, then discovered at Qumran in '52, then denied again as a "holy book" of the Bible.

Funny that, Harper thought.

The closest thing there was to the truth of Harper's kind on earth was written in something called the Apocrypha, books considered so full of falsehoods, or containing writings so esoteric, they suggested forbidden paths to knowledge that could undermine the authority of any organized religion. The bad guys had done their work well, Harper thought. They had infiltrated the religions of men and with a simple bait-and-switch maneuver . . . *Your soul seeks truth? Follow me and forget about the scrolls in cave number four.*

He scanned the higher hills farther west.

Somewhere up there was another cave, where a scribe had left behind new scrolls more explosive than anything Enoch could have dreamed of. *Maybe, boyo. Keep moving.* He walked another four thousand, nine hundred, seventy-six paces, hit the enclosed end of the valley. There was a hole in the wall with a ChemLight waiting on the other side. He crawled through the opening, found himself in a rocky tunnel with enough overhead clearance for a man to stand up properly.

"Why does there always have to be a bloody tunnel?"

The passage climbed at an angle of eighty degrees. There was a trench carved into the rock floor and water flowed in it. Harper bent over, dipped in his fingertips, and tasted them. The water was fresh, clean. He scooped a couple handfuls, wiped his mouth.

"At least the water is good."

He brushed sandstone dust from his knees and coat. He started to climb. After twenty minutes the angle of ascent was forty degrees; ten minutes later it was ten degrees and the only way up was by way of steps carved in the rock floor. The stream of fresh water continued to flow down the trench, now dropping step by step like a terraced waterfall. The air was as fresh as the water here. *Must be coming close to an exit,* he thought. Then he felt something: lightness, dizziness almost. He worked it out. He was breathing in negative ions from the waterfall; the ions kicked off a flood of serotonin in his form; the serotonin was finding its way to the millions of 5-HT receptors in the raphe nuclei of his brain stem. Result: like downing a couple of glasses of fine wine.

He kept climbing to where the passage leveled off into a cavern. There was a fissure in the rock floor and water flowed up from the ground. The more Harper looked at it, the more he realized he was looking at an ancient well. Here, the negative ions were thick. The sort of place a person might like to rest awhile. Breathe, dream; breathe, dream. He had another handful of water, scanned the cavern. Three shafts opened on the far wall; fresh air was coming in through all three. He walked closer, saw a Chem-Light fifteen yards ahead in the left tunnel.

"Right."

He walked that way. Eight hundred forty-eight paces later he came out on a high ridge overlooking Qumran and the Dead Sea. He saw a Chem-Light ten yards along the ridge. Thirty yards farther there was police tape surrounding a hole in the ground, and dim light was coming from it. The tip of a metal ladder poked out of the hole. Harper walked over, stepped over the police tape, and looked down. The ladder dropped fifteen feet through a shaft that opened to a cave. The source of the light was not in view, but he saw boot prints in the dirt. Someone was down there. Someone who had been pacing the place, waiting.

"Hello?" Harper said.

"Shalom," a woman's voice answered.

Silence.

"Mind if I come down?"

"Why not? That is why you came, *lo*?"

Harper thought about pulling his SIG but binned the idea. After all, someone had been nice enough to lead him here. He pulled the monocle from his eye and stuffed it in the pocket of his trench coat. He drew the strap of the reliquary box over his head, let the box hang across his back.

He mounted the ladder, climbed down through the shaft, and came into a small cave. He almost stopped to turn around and see the someone waiting for him, but he binned that idea, too. No quick or sudden moves. He stepped off the ladder, turned slowly around with his hands out at his sides. Battery-powered electric lamps slapped his eyes. Adjusting, he didn't know what to focus on first: the plaster footprint casts on the hardened dirt floor; the reed mat on the ground like a forgotten bed; the quill pens, unused vellum scrolls, and ink-making tools; the old table and stool in the corner. Everything in the cave was tagged with small, yellow evidence cards bearing Hebrew numbers. Everything except the raven-haired Israeli soldier sitting at that table in the corner. Her uniform was olive green, her eyes were amber-colored. Harper made her for mid-thirties. She held a micro assault rifle in her hands. Harper didn't know the make, but it looked like cracking kit. Laser and infrared targeting, bolt mechanism fitted behind the trigger. The weapon was compact as a carbine but maintained the barrel length of a rifle, and a rifle's muzzle velocity. And just now that chrome-lined barrel was pointed at Harper's chest. Harper heard the click of the safety. The soldier's weapon was fire-ready.

"So, are you the man of signs and wonders, or are you just another false prophet?"

TWENTY-TWO

i

Harper saw a dark blue beret with an insignia pin on the table. The pin held a stylized flower with two sharp leaves set in a Star of David. *Equals plant as weapon,* Harper thought.

"I brought you your ChemLights," he said. "They're in the pockets of my coat."

"Toda."

"What would you like me to do with them?"

"Hang on to them."

Harper smiled jokingly. "What if they explode?"

The soldier did not smile. "They won't, unless I lift my left foot from the remote detonator. If you rush me, knock me over, and the detonator is not double-tapped by the exact same body weight within three seconds, then the ChemLights in your pockets *will* explode."

"Powerful enough to kill us both?"

"Shit happens."

Her voice registered hard truth. If Harper couldn't prove he was who she needed him to be, then the mission was over.

"A lot of false prophets come this way, do they?" he said.

"Many."

"It's the same where I come from. They're everywhere."

"I am not concerned with the false prophets where you come from. I only care about the false prophets who come to this land to destroy it."

The soldier wore an olive green satin jacket with blue lambskin collar over her uniform. No rank or name to be seen. He grabbed a look at the beret again.

"You're with Israeli intelligence," Harper said.

The soldier did not acknowledge the comment.

"That's a lily in the beret pin," Harper said. "A lily blooms in the night, closes in the day. It does its work covertly."

"Or perhaps because in ancient times Hebrews used the juice of the bulb as invisible ink."

"Which is it?" he asked.

The soldier gave it ten, silent seconds.

"My name is Chana."

"Is there more to your name?"

"You do not need to know it."

"Right. I'm Jay Harper."

Five seconds.

"What is in the box you carry, Jay Harper?"

"More stuff from ancient times."

"You remember my left foot is on a detonator? Good. Put the box on the table. Open it. Turn it toward me. Now, very slowly, put the contents on the table so I can see them."

Harper did as instructed. He lifted the first object. It was bound in old leather. He laid it on the table and unwrapped it. The soldier glanced quickly at the ancient copper sextant with the first series of prime quadruplets hammered into the arc. As the soldier's eyes met his again, Harper knew she recognized it even as she played dumb.

"What is this used for?" she said.

"I only know what it was used for last."

"Which was what?"

"It tracked the path of a recent comet over Europe."

"The comet that appeared from the constellation Draco, three weeks ago."

"You know about it?"

"Who doesn't? It was in all the newspapers. So were you. You jumped off Pont des Arts in Paris, then cometh the comet."

Ten seconds.

"How was the sextant used to track the comet?"

"The coordinates were fed into a supercomputer in Lausanne. The computer ran a set of triangulations to build a cosmic clock based on the Cartesian coordinate system."

"To tell the time?"

"To plot the exact position of the planet Earth in the universe."

"Because time is motion and motion is time."

"Sorry?"

"I studied quantum mechanics at Hebrew University. Is there anything else I should know about this box, Jay Harper?"

"There's a false bottom to it."

"More ancient stuff underneath?"

"Yes."

"Let's see it. Slowly."

Harper lifted the false bottom and removed two small leather-covered items. The soldier did not take her eyes off Harper as he laid the items on the desk.

"Nothing else?" Chana said.

"Nothing."

"Take six steps back and open your trench coat."

Harper did. The soldier saw the kill kit strapped to Harper's sides. SIG Sauer, killing knives, small glass vials containing iridescent liquid.

"The vials contain what?"

"Something to help me disappear if required."

"Like invisible ink."

"I wouldn't be surprised."

"Close all the buttons of your trench coat. Slowly. Good. Put your hands on top of your head. Wait. Show me your hands." She saw the bio-skin gloves covering Harper's palms. "Continue to put your hands on your head. Do not move. I am very good at hitting a target while looking the other way."

Harper watched the soldier's left hand unwrap the third of a clay cup and the carpenter nail. She gave them a two-second glance, then back to him.

"What do you know of these things?" she said.

"They're from the first century AD."

The soldier nodded. "This pottery fragment has been precisely cut from a drinking cup," she said. "Judging from the discoloration I would say it was used for wine. There are traces of blood on this nail. It could be because the carpenter was clumsy, or it could be because of something else."

"Maybe."

The soldier leaned into the desk, reset her aim.

"Let us try it from this angle. What do you know of these things? Tell me everything you know. Do not leave anything out."

She spoke English with a European accent. Russian, Harper thought. He nodded to the things on the table.

"They were hidden near the volcanic pluton at Montségur. They had been in one family's possession for more than thirteen hundred years. The last descendant of that family told me the things had been given to them by creatures men call angels. In 1244 the sextant was carried to Paris and hidden in a cavern by someone named Bernard de Saint-Martin. The cup and the nail were left in Montségur."

"Who is Bernard de Saint-Martin?"

"A lord from pre-French Occitania. It's the land north of the Pyrenees near the Mediterranean."

"I know where it is. I want you to tell me about Bernard de Saint-Martin."

Harper flashed the Paris job, after he was hauled from the cavern beneath Paris. He was dragged to Christophe Astruc's hideout on Rue Visconti in the 6th. That's when Inspector Gobet hit Harper with intel.

"He fought to defend the Cathars from slaughter at the hands of

French Crusaders. He had two hundred fighters with which to defend two hundred civilians at the fortress above Montségur. He held off ten thousand French Crusaders for nine months. In the end the Crusaders won out. Saint-Martin was condemned to burn at the stake as a heretic with two hundred Cathars. He received the Cathar sacrament the night before. It's called Consolamentum. He survived the fires."

"Nice trick, surviving a heretic's fire, *lo*? Or was it because he was one of those creatures men call angels?"

"That's what I was told."

"Were you Bernard de Saint-Martin in 1244?"

"That's what I was told."

The soldier nodded to the pottery fragment and carpenter nail. "And these? What is the provenance of these things?"

"The provenance?"

"Their origin and ownership since the time of their origins. Art history was my minor at university."

He sensed she already knew the bloody provenance.

"All I know is an archaeologist from la Sorbonne passed through Montségur in the nineteenth century. He was shown the cup and the nail. The archaeologist said the pieces were at least two thousand years old. Brought to Montségur from the Near East by Roman soldiers during the occupation of Gaul, most probably. He said the nail may have been used in a crucifixion."

The soldier shrugged. "The Romans crucified people all over the empire. It was their preferred method of dealing with troublesome locals."

Harper smiled. "That's what I told the man in Montségur when he showed me the cup and the nail. In fact, those were my exact words."

Five seconds.

"Do not get ahead of yourself," the soldier said. "Get one answer wrong and you're dead. *Atta mevin?*"

"I understand."

"The sextant used to track the path of the comet, how old is it?"

"I'm not sure. I would guess thousands of years old. It may come from Persia. From the time of Zoroaster, 1000 BC maybe."

"It is a little older that that. It does not come from Persia, but Zoroaster did possess it when he lived. And that was in the sixth century BC."

Harper stared at her. *New intel,* he thought, *and rather interesting at that.* His own kind had not known it. Or maybe they did and did not tell him.

"You don't say?" Harper said.

"I do. Which raises the question: What was Zoroaster's sextant doing in Montségur with a clay cup fragment and one carpenter nail, both from first-century Israel?"

"I was told the sextant was carried from Persia as a gift to a child born in Bethlehem."

"In the time of Herod the Great."

"Yes."

"That sounds very much like the legend of the three wise men and Yeshua ben Yosef," the soldier said. "That would have been between 6 and 3 BC."

"It does at that."

The soldier waved her left hand over the sextant, the pottery fragment, and the nail. "Then all these things, together, could be things belonging to Yeshua ben Yosef."

Harper thought about it.

"That is what the man from Montségur told me. But he called them the things of Christ."

"That is not all he told you. You saw him in Lausanne just before you traveled to the Middle East. He told you you might need them again," the soldier said.

Harper stared at her. She did not blink. "You are very good at your job," he said.

"Toda."

"Seeing as you know so much about me, perhaps I could lower my hands from my head," Harper said.

"False prophets are very tricky. If I am to believe you are not one of those, then you must first perform a sign or a wonder that will keep me from killing you where you stand."

"Is that what you do? You kill false prophets?"

"If they come to harm this land, yes."

Harper nodded. "Right. Well, do you have any particular sign or wonder in mind?"

"How about raising someone from the dead?"

Harper flashed slicing open the palms of his own hands, draining the blood onto a dead man's eyes.

"I tried that once."

"Where?"

"In Paris. In the cavern where I found the sextant. A man, an innocent man, was killed."

"How did it work out? Raising him from the dead?"

"Not well."

"Then perhaps we should try something less difficult."

Harper ran the odds in taking her down. They came up slim to none.

"Like what?"

The soldier reached in the pocket of her satin jacket with her left hand; her right hand kept the death end of the assault rifle targeted at Harper's chest. Her left hand reappeared rolled in a fist. She held it out, offering something to him.

"Take this. And remember, my foot is on a detonator."

Harper lowered his arms. He stepped forward and held out his hand. The soldier opened her fist and a small rectangular box dropped into Harper's gloved palm. It was dark purple with silver lettering. It was a bloody matchbox from LP's Bar in Lausanne.

"Now, Jay Harper, step back to where you were and tell me what is inside the matchbox."

Harper stepped back, looked at the matchbox. He shook it. Something small and solid slid back and forth. "Am I supposed to guess?"

"You are supposed to open it, look at it, and tell me what it is."

Harper opened the matchbox. Inside was a Swiss five-franc coin; it was dented along the edge. Images flashed through his eyes and vertigo hammered him hard. He stumbled back into the wall. *Time is motion, motion is time; no shit.* Harper found his balance, looked at the soldier.

"How?"

He couldn't find the rest of the words.

"It was taken from you without your knowledge, and all memory of it was wiped from something called a timeline. Seeing it now, you are supposed to reconnect to the events regarding the coin. That would be proof of your identity. Or so I was told."

"By whom?"

"A Swiss Guard who came this way two days ago on a recon mission. He was trying to escape across the Jordan River when I caught him. He told me a story. It took most of the night for him to tell it. The highlight was that the man of signs and wonders would soon return to the Holy Land. If you have my job, something like that grabs your attention."

"Sergeant Gauer."

The soldier nodded. "One thing led to another. A deal was made."

"What sort of deal?"

"One you will never know about if you cannot tell me about the coin. So, stranger, are you the man of signs and wonders or are you just another false prophet?"

Harper looked at the coin. He touched the dented edge.

"I did a job at the Lausanne Cathedral a few years ago. There was a lad who spent his nights in the belfry; *le guet de Lausanne*. He called the hour from the belfry through the night. There were bad guys who wanted him dead. They wanted a lot of people dead. The lad had found a key in a titanium box. He called it lunch box. He was funny that way. He would say things; brilliant things. He found the box in an old well under the altar square of the cathedral. He took me down to show me. We found an opening to a shaft at the bottom of the well. There was a ladder built into the side wall that went down, but it went deep and it was dark. I had the coin in my pocket. It wasn't dented then. I was about to drop it down to see how deep the shaft was. The lad stopped me, asked me if I had anything smaller."

Harper stopped talking. He saw the lad's face by the light of his lantern, with an expression of disbelief that Harper would toss away five francs.

"What was your answer?" the soldier said.

"Sorry?"

"What did you say to him when he asked you if you had anything smaller and what happened then?"

Harper stared at her. "I said nope and I dropped the coin. It fell a very long way. We went down the ladder. The lad found it at the bottom of the shaft. It was sorely dented. He wanted to give it back to me."

"What did you tell him?"

"I think I've said enough to verify my identity, thank you."

"You told Marc Rochat to keep it for good luck. By the next sundown he was slaughtered as the bells of the Christian Sabbath rang out over Lausanne. He was slaughtered saving the cathedral, a pregnant woman named Katherine Taylor, and you, a creature some men would call an angel, who may or may not be the man of signs and wonders. Is that what happened, Jay Harper?"

Harper stared at the soldier.

"Sod off."

Ten seconds.

"Right answer," she said.

The soldier made her weapon safe and double-tapped the detonator on the floor to deactivate it. She rose from the stool. She was five feet six, special-ops fit; she moved with the poise of a cat. Harper ran her name: *Chana*. A Hebrew name meaning *grace*.

"I am with a special unit of Israeli Military Intelligence."

"Israeli MI has a unit for angels and ancient stuff?"

"We have a unit for everything. Empty your pockets of the Chem-Lights, leave them on the table. Then we will go to Jerusalem."

"And do what?"

"That you will find out."

"How do we get there?"

"I have a jeep. We will take the scenic route."

"Would the scenic route include checkpoints?"

"Of course. This is Israel."

"It's only I'm afraid I don't have a proper entry stamp in my passport."

Chana tapped her shoulder tag. "No problem. And I was told you can keep the coin."

Harper looked at it a second, closed the matchbox, and almost dropped it in the bottomless pocket of his trench coat. He slipped it in the pen pocket of his sports coat instead.

"Cheers," he said.

Chana headed for the ladder, got two rungs up, and looked down at Harper.

"Is it true what that Swiss Guard said? About what you found under the cathedral? A burning bush?"

"Yes, actually."

"And you call it the first fire of creation?"

"Yes."

"Sababa."

She slung her rifle over her shoulder and climbed out of the cave.

ii

Chana drove west through open desert. She drove without headlamps, but the moon cast enough light to see the way. She knew the terrain well and made sharp, fast moves. She came to a dirt track running north, turned onto it, and picked up speed. Harper had the sensation of rising higher. A few dips and turns later, the jeep passed a large sandstone building with white domes along the roof. There was a minaret at one corner.

"Al-Nabi Musa," Chana said.

"What?"

"The place you are looking at. It is a place of Muslim pilgrimage dating back to the fourteenth century. From there they could look across the Dead Sea to where Moses was buried on Mount Nebo."

Clearing the building, Harper got the view of the far mountain and the expanse of dark water beneath it. *Impressive,* he thought. *One minute you're somewhere in the real world, then* wham, *you've crossed into the Holy Land.*

"Right."

Chana cut left, drove down into a small valley, and joined a military-only track. It wound around and connected to a four-lane highway. The road was empty. She turned on the jeep's headlamps, hit the gas, and sped into the lanes heading up the mountain.

"This is the same road Yeshua ben Yosef would have taken in his final days. He would have done it on foot. A two-day journey at least. He would have slept in this desert."

Harper gave the scene a quick scan, then he looked at the dashboard. It was a rather stripped-down vehicle for a spook, the sort of thing a nobody in the Israeli Army would drive while safely tucked inside a military base. Harper looked at Chana. *A bit like invisible ink herself,* he thought.

She felt his eyes but kept her own on the road. "You wish to ask something?" she said.

"Would I get a direct answer?"

"Depends on the question."

"Did you believe what Sergeant Gauer told you?"

"About what?"

"Signs. Wonders. Me."

She did not answer. But he sensed she was thinking about it, winding her way up the Jericho-Jerusalem road. At one bend a sign was mounted in the side of a hill.

SEA LEVEL   פני ים   البحر سطح

Now and again they passed Bedouin camps in small valleys. The people lived in tents, their goats hobbled nearby. Climbing higher, the hills were spotted with scrub, wild grasses, and acacia trees. Then the road met an interchange with cloverleaf exits, and there was traffic coming and going. To the left were long rows of identical apartment buildings. There were tree-lined streets and playgrounds. The buildings stretched over two hilltops, and there was new construction on a third hill.

"The Alamo."

"Sorry?"

"Ma'ale Adumim. It is a settlement of more than forty thousand Israelis. It is either an illegal occupation of Palestinian land by Jews or a Jewish birthright from God Himself. It depends on who is doing the talking."

"No room for maneuver between the two?"

"There was, but those days are gone from us. These days in the Holy Land the blind lead the blind."

To the right were stacks of razor wire set between the road and a cluster of rough-looking buildings on a hillside. There were no tree-lined streets or playgrounds to be seen; flats were crammed together.

"That is a Palestinian town called Al Za'im," Chana said.

There were similar buildings dotting the hills left of the road now. Then Harper saw a massive concrete wall snaking from the north along a high ridge. It stopped at the Jerusalem-Jericho road but began again on the south side. It cut through the landscape, sometimes through the middle of Palestinian towns.

"And that scar on the land is either the Israeli Security Fence or the Wall of Jewish Apartheid."

"Depending on who is doing the talking?"

"Ken."

"Which is it to you?"

"Both. That is the tragedy of it."

Chana eased off the gas. They were approaching a checkpoint of bright lights, Israeli flags, and individual lanes like tollbooths. Israeli Border Police in green uniforms, green flak jackets, and green berets stood battle-ready with M16 assault rifles in their hands. They waved through cars with Israeli license plates after a quick check of the passengers. Cars with yellow Palestinian plates carrying passengers of darker complexions were pulled over for inspection. Chana stopped at the checkpoint, rolled down her window. She had a speedy conversation in with policeman.

"Shalom."

"Shalom, Rav Seren," the policeman said.

One: They knew each other, Harper thought. *Two: Chana was a major in Israeli MI.* The conversation continued after the policeman gave Harper a visual once-over.

Who is your passenger?

A security consultant for the International Olympic Committee. I am giving him a tour to convince him Jerusalem will be safe enough to host the 3052 Summer Games. So far it is a tight race between us and Mogadishu.

Good luck with that, ma'am.

We live in hope, no? Is my escort here?

Other side of the security fence. Near the roundabout on Al-Hardub Street.

Thanks. A quiet night to you.

You, too, the policeman said. *I will hold traffic for you.*

Thanks.

Chana passed through the checkpoint, turned on her headlamps, and cut across oncoming lanes onto a small road. The road got her inside the wall. She pulled onto Al-Hardub Street and stepped on it. Harper saw the roundabout ahead and the Israeli jeep parked there. The jeep's headlamps came on and it took the point down the dark road. Chana followed. Soon the convoy was driving through Arab neighborhoods. There were old men in dishdasha and kaffiyeh drinking Arabic coffee outside their homes; there were teenage Palestinian boys in sweatshirts and blue jeans playing football in the street; there was a donkey tied to a telephone pole. Small grocers, mosques, falafel joints, Arabic pop music. The place was full of life. The lead jeep made rights and lefts and passed through poorer Arab neighborhoods.

After one more left the jeeps slowed.

They passed a high chain-link fence topped with razor wire and security cameras. Behind the fence was a new four-floored building with an Israeli flag flying above the roof. Three civilian guards out front. Kippah on their heads, tzitzit tassels hanging from their waists. They were armed with M16s and sidearms. None of them looked pleased to see the jeeps. One of the guards spit at the lead jeep as it crept by. The lead jeep hit the gas; Chana followed.

"An odd greeting, considering," Harper said.

"Considering?"

"Those were Jews spitting at Israeli soldiers, even as they are surrounded by Palestinians. Not to mention you slowed down to receive the compliment."

"The Jews living on this street are members of the Third Temple Movement. They believe God gave Jews all land from the Mediterranean to Mount Nebo and all the Jordan Valley in between, from the Golan Heights to Sinai. Full stop. And they want the land cleansed of Arabs, living and dead. Jews only, even the graves. Then they will destroy Al-Aqsa Mosque and the Dome of the Rock on Temple Mount to make room for their Third Temple. Then comes the Mashiach, then comes the end of the world. That is their peace plan. We just like them to know we are watching them."

Harper looked around the neighborhood. "At the moment they would appear to be surrounded by Palestinians."

"*Ken.* And many of those Palestinians, like millions of Muslims surrounding Israel, think all Jews should be drowned in the sea." She glanced at Harper. "I said I would take you by the scenic route."

Harper looked around. The hills seemed to fall away; there was a dark and strangely glowing sky.

"Where are we?" Harper said.

"The Mount of Olives. Welcome to Jerusalem, Jay Harper."

The jeep rounded a wide turn, just skirting the edge of a cliff above the Kidron Valley. Buildings and trees disappeared and the entire descending slope of the mountain was covered with thousands of Jewish graves. Then he saw it: Across the narrow valley, high atop Mount Moriah, almost floating in the night, was the gleaming Old City of Jerusalem. It was dominated by the glimmering Dome of the Rock on Temple Mount. A Muslim shrine sitting on the holiest place in Judaism. At first glance it was a beautiful sight, then the incongruity of it took hold; then it looked like a mountain of never-ending trouble. Beyond the gold dome were the low roofs of stone houses and church steeples and minarets, the lot of it packed together by high stone walls. There was a world beyond the Old City, a world of skyscrapers and modern suburbs west and south, but Harper's eyes stripped them from his vision. He imagined beforetimes, when an ancient traveler would have walked up the Jericho–Jerusalem road and come to this place in the midday light. The trip would have taken days, and the traveler would have been tired. From here he would have seen the Second Temple sparkling in the sun like some beatific vision. Then he would see the Court of the Women; the Nicanor Gate leading to the Western Court; the twelve steps leading to the entrance of the Holy of Holies. The scent of burned offerings would rise from the Altar of Sacrifice and drift across the Kidron Valley to meet the weary traveler. A line ripped through Harper's head: Isaiah 2:3. A line about people coming to the mountain of the Lord, to the House of God so that He could teach them His ways and they could walk in His path.

"Lo and behold," Harper said.

"You got that right."

iii

Chana cut a sharp right, but the lead jeep continued straight on. Harper got a glimpse of a small blue sign on a stone wall: MA'ALE HO-KOHANIM STREET. By the time he read it, Chana had turned left down a narrow lane with high stone walls on either side. She stopped near an iron gate, shut down the jeep's motor, and turned off the lights. Harper looked through the gate. There were olive trees and gardens and neat stone walkways. He looked at the soldier.

"Mind if I smoke?" he said.

"Go ahead. It is going to be a long night."

He searched through the pockets of his trench coat, found his electronic fag. Switch on. Blue light. Inhale. *Bloody hell.*

"What happened to your escort?" he said.

"They did what they needed to do."

"Guide us through the scenic route, yeah?"

Ten seconds.

"You asked if I believed what the Swiss Guard said. About signs, wonders, you."

Harper nodded.

"Let me tell you what I believe. I believe this land is holy. I believe it was holy before the Canaanites came, and the Jews and the Caliphate, and the Crusaders and the Ottomans and the British and the Arabs. I believe it is holy because it is a place of sacred light. I believe through the ages the sons of darkness have risen up again and again, taking form as king or conqueror or false prophet, and they have reduced this city to dust in an attempt to crush all the light left to us. I believe the final battle is upon us and if we fail then the sons of darkness will rule the world."

"Hell of a story. Sacred light, sons of darkness."

"Yes, it is. It is not particularly a Jewish belief unless, like me, you have an interest in the Kabala. But keeping it at the forefront of my life makes me a better Jew, and a better soldier to defend this land. I do not judge anyone by religion or race, I judge according to the light in their souls."

"You can see people's souls?"

"The manner of a human being's life is the measure of the light in their soul. Take Yeshua ben Yosef of Nazareth. He was a devout Jew, the son of a carpenter who learned his father's trade. Contrary to the born-in-a-manger story, the ben Yosef family was quite well off, enough to travel to Jerusalem from Galilee every year for Passover. Ben Yosef had a comfortable life ahead of him, but he gave it up to become a healer of the afflicted and a consoler of souls. He was between thirty-three and thirty-six years old when he died. That would make him an old man in a world where half the population never made it to eighteen."

She pointed beyond the windshield and through the iron gates.

"The night before he was crucified he came to this place, Gethsemane. Christians say he came here to pray, knowing he was about to die. In fact, as a Jew, he would already have done his praying within the walls of the Old City, at the temple and in the upper room of an inn during his last Passover supper. He came to Gethsemane to sleep, as many Jewish pilgrims did. These olive groves were inexpensive campgrounds in the first century. More than that, ben Yosef was trying to keep a low profile. He was the cousin of Yochanin, the one Christians call John the Baptist. Herod Antipas had the Baptist beheaded two years earlier for arousing the people against him. Yeshua ben Yosef was preparing to assume his cousin's followers by incorporating baptism rituals into his own healing rituals. He had every reason to live out the last years of his life doing good works as a devout Jew. He did not come to Jerusalem that Passover to announce he was the Son of God and die; he came to worship his God at the temple, then carry on with the mission of making straight the way of the Lord."

Chana started the jeep, drove ahead. They passed an onion-domed Orthodox church, then a neoclassical church with huge Corinthian columns. In the pediment above the arches there was a depiction of Jesus praying to God, asking for the cup to be passed from him. He was surrounded by his apostles and seven angels. Chana made a sharp left down into the valley and up the other side. She drove under the east wall of the Old City now. There was a graveyard stretching beneath the wall; Muslim this time.

"Back then Jerusalem was seething. Between the false prophets and the rebels, the Romans were having a tough time controlling their Jews. And Passover was a time when the city's population quadrupled. Hundreds of thousands of Jews came from all across the Middle East. Jerusalem was on high alert. The Romans had already put down two rebellions in the weeks before Jesus arrived. They slaughtered hundreds of innocent Jews doing it."

Chana rounded the southwest corner of the Old City. The world fell away into the Kidron Valley again. There were more compounds flying Israeli flags, all of them surrounded by Palestinian homes. There was also a wide swathe of ground under excavation. Chana stopped in the middle of the road. She kept the motor running, her foot on the brake.

"Down there is the Lower City, the City of David. Jerusalem's walls in Yeshua ben Yosef's time would have included all this. There was a gate at the bottom of the city where the Kidron Valley meets the Hinnom Valley. Inside the gate was Siloam Pool. That is the entrance Jewish pilgrims used to enter the city. They would ritually cleanse themselves in the pool, then climb the steps to temple. You can see the gates in the wall up there."

Harper looked out his window, saw the massive south-facing wall of Temple Mount. There were double- and triple-arched gates, all of them sealed now.

"In his final days ben Yosef spent time at the Siloam Pool. There were always beggars, widows, and sick ones there. Ben Yosef had compassion for them. He performed his healing rituals upon the sick and told stories of comfort to the rest. If someone offered him food or drink, he gave it to the poor. Crowds began to gather around him, rumors of miracles began to spread. When the High Priests of the Temple heard the cousin of the Baptist was in Jerusalem, they grew nervous. When the words *Mashiach* and *Yeshua* began to be heard in the same sentence, the High Priests panicked. What happened next is unclear. Christians tell of a conflict with money changers in the Royal Stoa outside the Temple. But such a conflict could not have happened. The Romans oversaw everything on Temple Mount from Antonia Fortress on the north side of the compound. Any disturbance, by anyone, was put down quickly and brutally. Suspicious persons were arrested and disappeared."

"What's your guess?" Harper said.

Chana shrugged. "Ben Yosef? He was a Jew of the Semitic race. He was a product of the culture. I can see him telling the money changers, and the High Priests, and everyone gathered around him that the Temple was the House of God, a place of prayer, that the very priests who professed to be doing the work of God were turning it into a den of thieves. Ben Yosef would know a subtle dig like that would carry much more weight and cause far more humiliation than simply kicking over a few tables. Plus throwing a tantrum in the Temple courtyards would have gotten him arrested instantly. Whatever happened, whatever was said, severe offense was taken. As today when men of religion are insulted, the temple priests cried "Blasphemy." A few nights later, ben Yosef was arrested at Gethsemane by the Temple police. They brought him to Jerusalem by the same road you just drove from the olive groves. They entered the city by the same gate into the Lower City, passing the same pool where he performed his acts of healing."

"We're on his final path."

"This is the true way of sorrows, not the one made up by Constantine's mother in the Middle Ages."

Chana's foot came off the brake and she drove on. The road eased down a hill.

"Everything to the right would have been within the walls of ben Yosef's Jerusalem, too. This section was called the Upper City. It's where the privileged and wealthy lived. There were many of them. The rich did very well under Herod Antipas. Like the High Priests, they would disapprove of anyone who might upset their security. Yeshua ben Yosef did not have many friends in the Upper City. The Temple guard brought him here for a face-to-face with Caiaphas, the Highest of the Priests. There were probably a few members of the Sanhedrin there too. Enough to give ben Yosef a hearing. If found guilty of blasphemy, he would be condemned to death by stoning, beheading, burning, or strangulation. Those were the only methods of execution sanctioned under Jewish law."

"Jesus was crucified."

"*Ken*. And as Caiaphas wasn't shy about ordering blasphemers killed, it seems he did not have enough evidence to condemn ben Yosef. That did not mean Caiaphas did not wish to get rid of him. After all, ben Yosef was the cousin of the Baptist. He could only bring chaos to Jerusalem. Caiaphas feared chaos above all else. To him, chaos was God abandoning Jerusalem."

Chana rounded the bottom of the hill and drove north along the west wall of the Old City now. There was a steep drop to the left, a narrow valley rising on the far side to modern-looking buildings along the ridge. Chana slowed, cut right, and drove onto the grass beneath the wall. She parked near two stone outcrops. They looked like the ruins of a stairwell.

"This wall runs along the site of the original walls from the first century. There was a gate here then. It was the gate of closest access to the praetorium of Pontius Pilate, the Roman overlord of Israel. His neighbor was Herod Antipas, the Jewish king. It was called the Essene Gate."

"The scribes from Qumran?" Harper said.

"According to the historian Josephus, they were everywhere and nowhere all at the same time in ancient Israel. And they were far more than scribes. They were healers, too." She pointed across the narrow valley toward the modern buildings. "They had a camp over there somewhere. Herod Antipas liked having them in the neighborhood. He called on them for their medical knowledge. That's how the gate, in its day, was tagged with the name."

Harper scanned the valley and the modern buildings along the ridge. Nice-looking modern flats, hotels, commercial buildings. His eyes drifted south to where the house of Caiaphas once stood, then to the west wall where there was a gate named after the Essenes. A line dropped in his head: Luke 23:1 . . . *Then the whole body of them got up and brought him before Pilate.*

"They brought him here?"

Chana pointed to the wall. "Inside the Essene Gate was a courtyard. It was the place of judgment where Pilate conducted public meetings and trials. Once ben Yosef was taken through those gates, he was as good as dead. Pilate is painted as a sympathetic character in the Christian Bible. Conflicted, fretting, not wanting to kill the sad-looking prisoner before him, forced to submit to a ravenous Jewish mob. Pilate was a monster so renowned for his brutality and incompetence that the emperor removed him as prefect of Judea. So seeing ben Yosef would not raise an ounce of mercy in Pilate, especially when he heard the prisoner was attracting crowds. Someone was even heard hailing him as 'King of the Jews.' That was all Pilate needed to hear. He ordered ben Yosef to be crucified at first light. Roman soldiers dragged him to a prison near the praetorium. They flogged him until his skin was torn from his back, they pressed a crown of thorns down on his head, they dressed him in a purple robe. Tradition decreed that a condemned man's crime be written on a plaque and carried before him on the way to his death. In a slap at the population he despised as much as he ruled, Pilate ordered ben Yosef's plaque to read '*Iesvs Nazarenvs Rex Ivdæorvm.*'"

"Jesus of Nazareth King of the Jews."

Chana nodded. "At dawn the soldiers laid a heavy crossbeam across his shoulders and strapped his arms to it. They marched him through the streets of the Upper City. When he fell, they kicked him and forced him to his feet again. A few of his disciples followed at a distance. The wealthy of the quarter watched from their rooftops."

"You seem to have an inside knowledge of events."

"Nothing a study of archaeology and history based on fact cannot show anyone who cares to look."

"And you? Why do you care to look?"

Chana put the jeep in gear, but did not press down on the accelerator. She looked at the wall as if imagining the Essene Gate was still there.

"Millions of Christian tourists come to Jerusalem each year. They come because they wish to be close to the places the man they call Jesus spent his final hours . . . and they drive by this place without so much as a glance. It is not the fault of the believers. Things haven't changed much in this city since ben Yosef's time, religion is still a big business. Where else but Jerusalem would you find a Sixth Station of the Cross Souvenir and Gift Shop?"

"You're joking."

"I wish."

She pulled onto the road, continuing north, and they passed towers in the west wall and a wide gap with access into the Old City.

"Jaffa Gate," Chana said in passing.

Harper felt dizzy. The bum's rush through two thousand years of history was mind-bending. He had been holding his electronic fag throughout the tour. He switched it on again, took deep hits.

"What is it you smoke?" Chana said.

"Radiance."

"What is it for?"

"It prevents me from falling down."

"You have a problem with falling down?"

"Not particularly. It's the getting up I'm finding difficult."

"I am not surprised."

Harper looked at her. "Meaning what?"

"Meaning it is a difficult trip across the desert. The abrupt altitude changes, the emptiness, coming to this city. It affects a person. The Jerusalem police keep a lookout for people who suddenly think they are Yeshua ben Yosef or Miriam or the Baptist. The police collect them, get them help, send them home."

Harper wondered if that's what she was doing to him. She turned right at the northwest corner of the Old City's walls, then another quick right through a stone arch barely wide enough for the jeep to pass.

"New Gate into the Christian Quarter," she said.

She made a series of turns down narrow lanes, came to an open courtyard. She shut off the motor, turned off the headlamps. There was no one around, but Harper heard distant voices. He smelled cumin, cardamom, and sumac. His eyes adjusted to the dark and he saw two great domes above the rooftops. They were gray and topped with Byzantine crosses.

"Over there is the Church of the Holy Sepulchre. It is where Christians believe ben Yosef was crucified and buried."

"Big business or historical fact?"

"Strangely enough it is where business and fact meet, partly." She waved at the surrounding buildings. "All this around us was outside Jerusalem's walls in the first century. It was a rock quarry called Golgotha, the Place of the Skull. There was a well-traveled road east of where the church stands now. It was a first-century roundabout connecting the Jaffa and Damascus roads. It made the ground under the church an excellent killing ground. The sight of seditionists hanging from crosses provided Jewish passersby with a healthy reminder of Roman power. Ben Yosef would have been marched out of the city through Gennath Gate. It was near that mosque over there, meaning he would have been led through Jerusalem on a completely different path than tourists are shown today. From where the gate stood it was a short walk to the killing ground. Roman soldiers laid ben Yosef on his back and stripped him of his clothes. They nailed his hands to the crossbeam and hoisted him onto a post. Then they nailed his ankles to the post, one on each side. They did not need nails. He was already lashed to the cross. Nails were used to drown the victim in pain. Ben Yosef died a miserable death."

"But he wasn't buried within the church."

"Jews would never bury a Jew in a place of execution. And before you ask me where he was buried, I do not know."

"Does anyone?"

"Lots of people. American radio preachers, Internet sites specializing in alien abduction, filmmakers for cable channels. Or you could just come back tomorrow and ask anyone in the Christian Quarter. They will be happy to show you where the true grave is for one hundred shekels. Then pay someone else another one hundred shekels and he will take you to another true grave. You could spend a fortune doing that. Some people do."

"Right."

Harper had a final hit of radiance. He switched off the fag and dropped it in his coat. He looked at her.

"An enlightening tour, but you haven't answered my question."

"Signs? Wonders? You?"

"That's right."

"Ask me if I think you are the second coming of Yeshua ben Yosef, the answer is no. He was a vessel of sacred light who sought to heal the sick. You? You're a warrior who kills as required. Very efficiently, from what Sergeant Gauer says. But for someone like me, that particular talent means there is a connection."

She started the jeep's motor, turned on the headlamps. She backed up and headed through the narrow lanes, toward New Gate.

TWENTY-THREE

חמש

Now when Jerusalem fell into the hands of Titus Flavius, the sky beyond the Mount of Olives was lit with a great fire. It burned with fury and rage as we gathered for our evening meal. We sat in silence and meditated on the meaning of the flames, knowing that it was Jerusalem burning on this ninth day of Av, as had the Babylonians burned the city on the same day more than six hundred years before. By this sign we accepted the end of the world was at hand.

For many weeks before the fire, small caravans of suffering came down from Jerusalem and passed near the ruins of Jericho to seek refuge in the lands across the Jordan River. They staggered as they carried bundles of meager possessions. Many camped not far from us. We went to them with food and healing. In this way we learned of the evil into which Jerusalem had fallen.

Jew had taken up arms against Jew. Zealots and warlords battled each other for a finger's breadth of ground. Bandits and murderers prowled the streets. Women and their daughters were violated without mercy. The weak fell in their steps and died where they lay. Then came disease; then false messiahs appeared and caused the disease of madness to spread within the city. Each day did a new messiah lay claim to the Holy of Holies. One of these slaughtered children as a sacrifice to YHWH; and so were many children slain. Not since the days of Manasseh at the Hinnom Valley had such evil passed through Israel. As these things were done, Rome tightened her grip on Jerusalem, and those within the city walls starved. Every animal was devoured for its flesh. Even the rats that fed on the dead in the streets were consumed. When the rats disappeared, so did the living fall on the dead to devour their flesh before it was corrupted. When the starving outnumbered the dead, so did the people begin to slay one another for food. There were stories of mothers who slaughtered their youngest children and ate them.

Now three nights after we first saw the great fire, having watched it burn for all those nights, the caravans of suffering ceased. Then the fire ended and there were only steep columns of black smoke. For some days we wondered if all the people of the world had been killed.

Ten days after the destruction of Jerusalem, as evening shadows moved over the commune, six men appeared near the shores of the Salt Sea. It was the twenty-second day of Av and was recorded in the book of Community Rule by the Teacher of Righteousness.

The men who appeared were Jews by their dress, but the spears in their hands and swords at their sides said they were bandits, too. Four rode on horses and two drove a cart. The cart was heavily laden and bound closed with oryx skins and lengths of rope. From the distance, and as the last of the day's sun rolled over them, many of the brethren saw glints of light in the metal joints of the harnesses binding the animals, the sheaths of swords and the tips of spears. One of the order said that the horses and weapons must be stolen from the Romans. Another wondered if the bandits were not servants of Rome, seeking to betray their fellow Jews for pieces of silver.

As shadows engulfed them one of the riders approached. He carried his spear upright as he rode up the plateau. He stopped within a two spans of us, quickly spinning his spear and driving the tip of it into the sand. He made his horse move three steps to the left, away from the spear. There, the bandit waited.

By now all the order had come from their residences. With them came the Teacher of Righteousness. He regarded the rider, seeing the bearded and fierce-looking face, but also that the rider's weapon had been set in a sign of surrender. The Teacher of Righteousness called to the bandit.

"What is it you desire of us, stranger?"

שש

The bandit dismounted and walked to us, stopping at the low stone wall that separated us from the rest of the world. There was a breeze from Mount Nebo across the sea. It brushed the bandit and carried his scent of smoke and sweat to us. He bent down, inspected the ground, and gathered seven small stones. He stood and looked over the community. Then, gently and one by one, he tossed the stones into our world.

"Be not afraid. This is not the time of your destruction, not yet. But it will come."

"And will you bring it to us?"

"Not me. Not any of us. But it will come."

"When?"

"I'm not a prophet, Rabbi."

The Teacher of Righteousness bowed his head and spoke softly. "We are surrendered to the end of the world."

The bandit tossed the last stones. He brushed his hands of dust. "No, this isn't the end of the world. It can't be, it mustn't be."

The Teacher of Righteousness studied the bandit, as we all did. Though dressed in a tunic bound with blue ribbon, though speaking our language, he was not one of us. It was with the teacher's words that we understood he, too, shared our fear of the bandit.

"The manner of your words is dark," the teacher said.

"Yes, I'm sure. But like I said, be not afraid." The bandit turned to his fellows by the sea. "We've brought you scrolls from Jerusalem, from the ones like you."

Having once gone up to the city to deliver messages to our community that were encamped in the valley to the west, I called to the bandit. "And our order, what of them?"

There were murmurs among those gathered that I had spoken before our teacher, but he did not reprimand me.

"Yes," the teacher spoke, "what news of our order?"

"Slaughtered. All of them."

There was silence. Down by the sea I saw the men making camp and lighting six fires at six points about them. It appeared they were setting themselves behind unseen walls drawn by the fires, and the light crossed the desert and pierced my eyes. Two of the men limped as if wounded. The bandit spoke to us again.

"We were protecting a tomb from bandits. It was not far from your brethren. After the Romans took the city, a cohort came from the Citadel and made camp at the Essene Gate. They found your brethren and charged. The Romans were too fast, too many. We couldn't save your brethren, but two of my men got in and smuggled out their library. We also have scrolls from the Temple. Not all, many have disappeared. You need to save them, protect them."

The Teacher of Righteousness became confused. "But if this place is to be destroyed—"

"You won't keep the scrolls down here," the bandit said. He pointed up to the caves in the west hills. "Up there. With everything from your scriptorium, too. We'll set up block and tackle above the caves so we can rappel down and hide the Jerusalem scrolls. Then your scrolls, the ones you think are important first, then the rest."

"But we have years of transcriptions yet. Our work is not finished."

"Then finish it," the bandit said.

His voice was sharp and filled us with dread. He regarded our faces. He spoke with a sense of calm.

"The killers won't find this place for a while. They'll follow us for a year before they realize we don't have what they want."

Those of the order looked to one another, wondering at the meaning of the bandit's words. The Teacher of Righteousness silenced us.

"You speak as if it is not the Romans we should fear," he said.

The bandit tossed the last of his stones onto the ground.

"The worst a Roman can do is kill you, Rabbi. It's the ones hiding in the fifth cohort of the Tenth Legion Fretensis that have the power to devour human souls. They are the sons of darkness, we are their sworn enemy."

Then did the bandit reveal the light within his eyes, and the Teacher of Righteousness was overcome with awe. He fell to his knees and lifted the palms of his hands to the bandit.

"Truly, you are an angel of the Pure G-d. Command us, lord."

The bandit drew his sword, lowered himself to one knee before our teacher, and laid the sword on the ground.

"We carry one of our own in the large cart."

"Does his body need healing?"

"No, there is nothing you can do for him. The soul of his form has already been delivered to the stars."

This caused the Teacher of Righteousness to wonder. "I do not understand your words. If he is passed and he is a Jew, he must be buried at once."

"Rabbi, some of my kind need healing, all of us need food and drink. We would be grateful for your help. Then, perhaps, we can talk. There are things you need to know about the world."

ii

Harper walked back along the display tables to the section holding scroll number one. He tapped the glass cover. The glass was three inches thick and the scroll inside was in an atmospheric environment that matched conditions at Qumran. He had to admit the scrolls looked pretty good for being nearly two thousand years old. So good that when he first saw them he wondered if the whole thing was a hoax. Even on the second run, scrolls one through four read like the ravings of a madman. And even if they contained an awareness of Harper's kind, it would not be the first time a madman imagined the truth.

Then came scrolls five and six.

He felt a chill reading them through the first time. On the second go he felt a rush of ice-cold fact. He was reading the only written account of an encounter between the creatures men call angels and locals. Harper had no doubt it was genuine. There was just one problem. He leaned over scroll number six and read aloud:

"'Receive, then, these seven scrolls to know of the seven angels of the Pure God who appeared to us in the days after Jerusalem was destroyed; to know of the crucifixion of Yeshua ben Yosef and the man who is called the man of signs and wonders.'" He looked at Chana. "Where is the seventh scroll?"

"Not here at present."

"What's in it?"

"Ask me after I read it."

Harper rubbed the back of his neck. Chana watched him.

"Am I missing something?" Harper said.

"Only the obvious."

Harper looked around the room. Computers, two electron microscopes, large-format scanners, multispectral imaging kit. All locked in a room with regulated temperature, humidity, and filtered airflow.

"What is this place, anyway?" Harper said.

"A document research vault for an agency of the Israeli government."

"The sign out front says this is a prosthodontics laboratory. Implants, dental bridges, and such."

"We saw no reason to change the sign, we only redecorated the interior. The new scrolls were first taken to the Israel Museum to be analyzed with the rest of the Dead Sea Scrolls. After a particular anomaly was discovered, the scrolls were brought here."

"What anomaly?"

"Footprints. The police looky-loos made a *balagan* of the scribe's cave before we got there. We managed to brush away layers of dirt and found footprints dating from 10 BC to 125 AD. Those would have belonged to the Essenes who worked there, including the scribe who wrote these scrolls. We also found one more set of footprints made five hundred years later."

"That's fairly precise intel, even for Israeli MI."

Chana did not respond.

"Do you think that someone took the seventh scroll?" Harper said.

"*Ken*, but my guess is he was not a thief. A thief would have taken everything. My guess is someone of education found the scribe's cave, read the scrolls, and believed every word, because he believed in the sacred light of Yeshua ben Yosef."

"I'm listening."

"An educated man of the time would have known that Jerusalem and the Holy Land had become the fault line between East and West. The land was being poisoned in the name of gods. Never-ending war was coming."

She knows what happened, boyo.

"What else would an educated man of the time have done, besides taking the seventh scroll?" he said.

"He gathered the things of the Christ. He carved a piece from the cup and divided the nails. Three nails and the greater part of the cup were hidden somewhere in Jerusalem with the seventh scroll. The sextant, one nail, and a piece of the cup were sent away for safekeeping."

Harper thought about it. As a logical proof he was connected to the man of signs and wonders it was shaky, but who the hell knew? He ran his timeline for hits; nothing. He blinked.

"Is that how it works?" Chana said.

"What?"

"The thing Sergeant Gauer told me about. Your eyes lost focus for a fraction of a second. I was watching you. So what happens? You go to the past, then you blink back to now?"

"More or less."

"An interesting way of doing things."

"I'd settle for an ordinary memory. As far as where I've been, nothing pops hot with your theory."

"It is not a theory. It is fact."

That's when he saw something in her eyes. Not a light connecting her to his kind, but something connecting her to some ancient knowledge.

"Where are you from?" Harper said.

"Where do you think?" Chana said.

"Russia would be my guess. Second generation."

"My mother was from Moscow. She taught me English, so the accent is hers. My father, however, was descended from Persian Jews who first came to Israel in the time of Herod the Great. Just before the Hebrew king died, to be exact."

"When, exactly?"

"Nine years after the birth of Christ."

"And what did this descendant of yours do for a living?"

"He was a scribe in service to one of the Magi, the one who was the astronomer. The family kept up the blogging-on-parchment tradition in Israel."

Harper flashed back, saw the soldier at Qumran glancing at the sextant and telling him it was thousands of years old. *Zoroaster did possess it when he lived.* When he blinked himself back to nowtimes, she knew where he had gone.

"Figure it out?" she said.

"The astronomer's scribe would know the provenance of the sextant. And so do you."

"*Mazel tov.* It dates back to the eighteenth Egyptian dynasty. From the reign of Akhenaten. In the neighborhood of 1350 BC."

Harper scanned the History Channel. Akhenaten came to the throne as Amenhotep IV. He had a vision: All the gods of Egypt were reflections of the one God called Ra, and Ra was the blazing disc of the sun. Monotheism was born on the Nile. End of the Pharaoh's reign: Monotheism was forgotten and Egypt's gods returned en masse. He blinked. Chana was staring at him.

"Are you up to speed?" she said.

"I got it," Harper said.

"Akhenaten had visions. There was one about a sextant. He described it and his astronomer made it for him. In his vision, the sextant would guide its bearer to a savior who would bring perfection and eternity to the world. However, the savior would be made known through three souls conceived by Ra's sacred light and born to three different women over thousands of years. So the sextant and instructions on how to use it had to be handed down through the generations."

Chana gave it a second to sink in. Harper appreciated it.

"Just out of curiosity, is this part of the official Israeli MI briefing?"

"What official briefing? I am only telling you old family stories. It is all part of the tour. There was a comet over Thebes, I am not sure when. It was a comet the bearer of the sextant was waiting for. He had also been given coordinates that triangulated a position in Persia near today's Tehran. The sextant was carried there and presented to soul-born-of-light number one: a monotheist named Zoroaster. With him the savior was called Saoshyant. With the name comes the concept of the savior's role on earth: He is here to benefit humanity. Jump ahead a few thousand years and a new monotheistic faith called Judaism takes shape from Babylonia to the Mediterranean Sea. Despite its bloody history getting started, it is the first religion on earth to codify works performed in the name of the One God to benefit humanity. And they have a savior, too, he's called the Mashiach. Jump ahead a few thousand years again and there is another comet that someone with a sextant has been waiting for. This time triangulation guides the bearer, one of the Magi, to Israel. The sextant is presented to soul-born-of-light number two: Yeshua ben Yosef. The final entry in the family blog tells of ben Yosef's crucifixion. No details. Just that his death occurred. End of story."

It took Harper fifteen seconds to realize she had nothing more to add.

"Sorry?"

"Forty years after the crucifixion, Rome would destroy Jerusalem and scatter the Jews to the wind. The family blog disappeared. Everything I am telling you has been handed down orally over two thousand years. It was considered too dangerous to write it down. But according to Sergeant Gauer, your commander found them in Paris among a treasure trove of ancient documents and secret writings."

"Your family history? In Astruc's hideout on Rue Visconti?"

"That is his name, Astruc?"

"Yes."

Chana nodded. "Good name for an angel."

"I'll be sure to tell him."

She stared at him. "But a child was born, *ken*?"

"Sergeant Gauer didn't tell you?"

"I said I saw the comet after seeing a photograph of you jumping off a bridge in Paris. I told him it looked to me like a child had been born. He told me the sextant was used to track a comet. I said, 'So what?' We left it there. But I need to tell you this: The sons of darkness need to slay the child, as they slayed both Zoroaster and ben Yosef."

"Both?"

"Zoroaster was slaughtered while praying at his altar. The one you call Jesus was slaughtered on the cross. Slaughter soul number three and the sons of darkness will inherit the earth. That is what will happen, or so said an Egyptian pharaoh in 1350 BC."

Harper had to admit it thread the needle rather neatly. Almost.

"Did you leave something out?" he said.

"Such as?"

"My connection to Jesus."

"Lo," she said. "But so what?"

"It's the bloody reason I came to Jerusalem. And from what you've told me and shown me, it's the same bloody reason you helped me get here. Or does it take the seventh scroll to find out?"

Chana pointed to the scrolls in the display. "Even without the seventh scroll, the connection is obvious."

Harper felt himself wobble. He leaned back against the scrolls. "What is it?"

She recited from memory: "'To know of Yeshua ben Yosef and the crucifixion of the man of signs and wonders; to know how through him the world may be saved.' At first glance one would think the scribe is talking about one in the same person. What if it is two beings in the same body?"

Harper flashed his meet with the dream catcher on the esplanade of Lausanne Cathedral. *Marc Rochat's soul is alive and well within Ella . . . Binary star, binary soul.*

"Maybe. But it requires the two beings having souls. I don't have one."

"What if it is two separate beings in the same body at two separate times? That is how it works with angels, isn't it?"

Harper did not answer. She read his mind.

"Do not worry, your Swiss Guard friend did not tell me your secret. I discovered it when I read the scrolls. Six angels in the form of Jewish bandits appeared at Qumran, one more was being carried in the cart. One for whom nothing could be done, one whose soul had been delivered to the stars. Question is, if his soul was gone, why save the body? Why not just leave it where it was buried to await the return of the Mashiach, according to Jewish custom? After all, Yeshua ben Yosef was a Jew. That would be his belief. Answer is, an angel was still using it."

She was better than very good at her job; she was brilliant.

"Trust me, taking human form isn't something we do on a whim," Harper said. "It's a complicated process. And there are rules and regs; starting with, we are forbidden to intervene in the manner or time of someone's death."

"Unless you had no choice but to make a choice."

Harper flashed the dream catcher again: *Krinkle says you made a choice once; that you changed the course of human history by making it.* He blinked to nowtimes. Chana was watching him come back again, her assault rifle slung over her shoulder, leaning on the large table holding the electron microscope. The reliquary box was on the table, too. Chana's hand was resting on it; her fingertips tapped it softly.

"What choice?" Harper said.

"You knew who Yeshua ben Yosef was. You saw him suffering and you intervened. You delivered his soul to the stars and you died in his place. Except you did not die, you only appeared to die. You were laid in a grave by ben Yosef's followers, then quickly moved to a second grave by your angels. There you were hidden for forty years, until the fall of Jerusalem meant that you had to be moved. In doing so you gave ben Yosef resurrection."

Harper felt dizzy. He took a slow breath to steady himself. "I'm . . . I'm not sure."

"Says the warrior angel bearing the stigmata on his palms, who this night of nights crosses the River Jordan carrying the things of the Christ on his back."

Harper stood in perfect silence, looking at the bioskin gloves on his hands.

The real deal has landed, boyo.

A numbness washed through his form. He felt the urge to slip into hibernation mode and stay there.

"My turn," Chana said.

It took Harper 17.4 seconds to reconnect with nowtimes.

"Sorry?"

"My turn with a question."

"Go ahead."

"What do you call the child who was born, the one you are trying to save?"

"Why do you ask?" Harper said.

"Why not?"

Harper smiled. "You think he's the third soul born of light," he said.

"Don't you?"

Legends, myths, religions. All we know of who we are and why we are here, Harper thought. *The locals, us; it's all the same.*

"We call him the child of the prophecy. His mother named him Max."

"For Maximilian or Maxwell?"

Harper shrugged. "As far as I know it's just Max."

Chana nodded. "This is a good name for him. Excuse me." She reached in her satin jacket, removed a vibrating cell phone. She swiped the screen, held it to her ear. *"Halo?"*

She listened for thirty seconds, then closed the phone. She slipped it back in her jacket.

"*Yalla*, time for you to make good on your end of the deal I made with Sergeant Gauer."

"The deal?"

Chana lifted the reliquary box by its strap and held it out to Harper.

"I show you the real Via Dolorosa and let you read the scrolls. In exchange, you help me save Jerusalem."

TWENTY-FOUR

i

Sirens. Flashing blue lights. Ambulances and police cars racing through the streets. Chana was three minutes into the drive before Harper realized it was no longer night. The blazing disc of the sun was set in a midmorning sky, its light ripping across the Jordanian desert, skimming Jerusalem and slicing into Harper's eyes.

"Three Palestinian terrorists have attacked a settler preschool in the Arab Quarter. Two Israeli guards were killed, one teacher. Eleven children and three more teachers are being held hostage. The terrorists hacked the school's CCTV system and got onto the Internet. They said they would kill the hostages and themselves unless a list of prisoners is released from Megiddo prison."

"Are the attackers known?"

"Three teenagers from Silwan. They were dressed as Israeli students."

"If they're human beings, I can't help you."

"For better or worse we are accustomed to this sort of thing. The security forces will deal with it. But there may be something else, something more along your line."

She made a hard right onto a wide road, swerved around an oncoming tram. Civilians lined the road. Secular Jews, Hasidic Jews, worried-looking Palestinian workers. Coming into downtown West Jerusalem the road narrowed, and two trams occupied the rails in both directions. Ambulances were trapped in a bottleneck.

"Hold on," Chana said.

She drove onto the pavement and through a sidewalk café. Table and chairs went flying; luckily no one was sitting at them. All customers were inside the café watching the breaking news on the telly. The ambulances followed Chana's lead. She drove fast and furious; she talked slow and calm.

"My telephone call before? It was your Swiss Guard sergeant. He said Bern HQ was tracking suspicious intercommunications between radical Jewish and Islamic Web pages. Hold on again."

"Let me guess, more deals in the works."

"I was tracking encrypted traffic on Israeli Internet servers. It was embedded in both Hebrew and Arabic Web pages."

Chana came to an intersection, hit the brakes, and skidded to a stop. A long line of traffic—ambulances, police cars, and four-wheel drives with the letters "TV" gaffer-taped to their windows and doors—passed from west to east. She pulled onto the pavement again, let the ambulances behind her pass to join the caravan. Harper saw a blue sign on a stone wall: TZAHAL SQUARE. This side of the intersection was modern West Jerusalem; on the other side were the walls of the Old City. *Like sitting at the crossroads of nowtimes and beforetimes,* he thought.

"Did he tell you what sort of comms?"

"He said they were working on it. He said to get you inside the Old City for a recon."

Traffic cleared and Chana sped through the intersection and drove alongside the Old City. Harper clocked it as the same road he'd been on last night. He was about to ask her where they were headed, when she cut left and raced up the hill for Jaffa Gate. A barrier was set across the road. She crashed through it, and drove on to Omar Ibn Al-Khattab Square. Israelis, Palestinians, and tourists scattered. She went right down a street barely wide enough for the jeep to pass. Hasidic women pulled their children into doorways to protect them. The street followed the interior of the city's walls, cutting left then running east, then rising to the top of a hill. Chana turned the wheel, jumped the curb, and hit the brakes. Fifty feet down was a great plaza laid out before the Wailing Wall, all that was left of Jerusalem's Second Temple. Just now, all across the plaza, Israeli police were battling an angry mob that ebbed and flowed like water. Harper identified the rioters as Jews.

"Right-wingers," Chana said. "They must be here to avenge the preschool attack." She pointed to an enclosed ramp rising from the ground. "They are trying to get the ramp over there. It leads to Temple Mount and the Dome of the Rock."

Harper watched the scene, heard the curses of the mob.

"The police are Nazis!"

"Jewish traitors!"

"Death to Arabs!"

There were TV crews on the fringes of the riot, broadcasting the mayhem live to the world. Chana looked at Harper.

"So far it looks like the usual suspects from my domestic watch list. The police can handle this. You see anything?"

"I'm too far away to get a read on anyone's eyes. I need to get closer."

"Your Swiss Guard said to hold here for orders."

Small explosions sounded from the plaza. Harper watched tear gas canisters skip over the stones and into the mob. Riots in one part of Jerusalem, a terrorist standoff in another.

"The traffic on the Internet," Harper said. "Gauer is running it through the SX grid looking for lines of causality, connections."

"*Ken*, that's what he called it. But it does not make sense."

"Why not?"

"Hard-core Islamists and radical Jews intercommunicating? The only thing they would say to each other is 'Fuck your mother.'"

Harper added it up: Attack in the Arab Quarter, riot at the Wailing Wall. All of it being broadcast live to the world.

"Everything that's happening just now, it's all a bloody diversion. It's cover for something bigger and worse."

Chana watched the riot. She whispered to herself. *"Shema Yisrael, Adonai Eloheinu, Adonai Echad."*

She reached in her jacket, grabbed her vibrating cell phone. She swiped it and listened. She looked at her wristwatch, a digital job. *"Rav toda."* She closed the phone, stuffed it in her jacket.

"What is a time warp?" she said, pressing buttons on her watch.

"Hard to explain. Why?"

She showed Harper the watch. It was counting down minutes and seconds.

"Your Swiss Guard says one is about to drop. He said we have less than seventeen minutes to get inside the target zone or we are fucked. Those are his exact words. He said you would know what they mean."

"It means whatever is coming down requires blowing my cover to stop it. Where's the target zone?"

"East end of the Arab Quarter, near Lions' Gate."

"How far?"

Her eyes followed the road. It curved around to a gate to the outer world; it was jammed with police vehicles.

"Too far to drive with this chaos. We need to run through that," she said, nodding to the riot. She pulled her beret from her jacket, set it on her head, and grabbed her assault rifle. Jumping from the jeep, she said, "Stick close to me, do not get lost. And you should bring the reliquary box. Empty government vehicles have a habit of getting torched by right-wingers."

Harper reached in the backseat, grabbed the box. He pulled the leather strap over his shoulder and got out of the jeep. Chana was already running down the road.

"Right."

He took off after her.

At the bottom of the road she headed for the security checkpoint blocking access to the plaza. The gates had been shut; no one in or out. But a couple of coppers saw Chana coming their way and quickly opened one of the gates. Harper was close enough to hear the chatter on police radios.

Man in trench coat with suspicious package approaching checkpoint. Do we take the shot? Repeat: Do we take the shot?

Swell, snipers, Harper thought. He watched Chana grab a radio transmitter from a policeman's bulletproof vest.

Negative. Man in trench coat is NOT a target. Repeat: Man is NOT a target.

Harper got to the checkpoint and squeezed by the police, following Chana through the metal detectors. *Beep, beep, beep, beep.* She called to one cop as she ran by him:

Radio the north checkpoint. Tell them I'm coming through with someone. Advise everyone on the plaza I'm coming through.

Yes, ma'am.

They came onto the plaza and into a cloud of tear gas, then a crush of rioters backing away from the gas and moving sideways across the plaza. Harper's eyes and lungs burned. It was the same with the mob. Then no one could see and bodies began tripping over one another. He saw Chana go down, but she wasn't falling; she was scooping up an onion one of the rioters dropped on the ground. She straightened up, saw Harper, nodded to her right. Her eyes were red and swollen and wet. He was damn sure he looked the same.

"Follow me," she said.

She forced herself through the mob, taking a few punches along the way. She found a patch of clear ground behind an army jeep.

"Over here."

They crouched down. Harper watched her smash the onion against the butt of her rifle. It broke in two. She handed a half to Harper.

"Over your nose and mouth and breathe," she said.

Harper did; so did she. The fire in his eyes and lungs subsided; his vision cleared.

"Always take an onion to a riot," Chana said.

"Old Jewish saying?"

"Teenage Palestinian. From the West Bank."

She pointed toward an arch at the north end of the plaza, two hundred yards away. It was a staging area for the police. Just now hundreds of them were kitting up in gas masks, making ready for a final push against the rioters.

"We go that way." She took off.

"Of course we do." He went after her.

She shouted in Hebrew at Israeli Border Police dead ahead.

Get out of my way! Move!

One look at her running toward them and the police parted like the sea before Moses. They ran through the arch and into a tunnel, through another security checkpoint. Out of the tunnel, into a maze of narrow cobblestone lanes and sixteen-hundred-year-old buildings. Arab shops, Jewish yeshivas, Arab barbershops, Hasidic Jews, old Palestinian men in dishdasha and kaffiyeh. Everyone panicking, closing shops, shuttering windows, trying to get away. Chana cut right, then left, then right. She stopped at a fountain built in a wall. She quickly washed the tear gas from her hands and face. Harper did the same. They leaned against a stone wall to catch their breath. She checked her wristwatch.

"Eleven minutes."

"How far to the target zone from here?"

"Twelve minutes."

"Know a shortcut?"

"*Ken.*" She took off.

"Of course she does."

Harper followed her along a straight and narrow lane. She cut left at a corner. When Harper got to her she was running up a set of stone steps. There was a small sheesha pipe and tobacco shop in an alcove; an old Arab man was lowering metal shutters over the windows.

"Abu Marwan," Chana called to the man.

He turned to her.

"*Aamo, ana bihajeh la musa'adatak,*" she said in Arabic.

"*Inti bitu'mori.*"

She turned to Harper. "Give me the box. Abu Marwan will keep it."

"You sure?"

"He believes what I believe."

Harper pulled off the box, handed it to Chana. She gave it to the old man, spoke to him again in Arabic.

If I do not come back, you know what to do with it. Do you understand?

He bowed his head to her. *The Pure God be with you,* he said. The old man ducked under the shutters and into his shop.

"This way," Chana said.

She ran back to the lane; pulling her cell phone as she ran, tapping out a text message, then shoving the phone back in her jacket. She picked up speed, cut right into a vaulted arcade lined with shops selling Arab sweets and spices. Here, too, locals gathered their goods and dropped metal shutters. There was a large arch in the wall at the end of the arcade; it held a massive green door, and Chana was heading straight for it. She shouted in Hebrew:

Open it! Open it!

That's when Harper saw the two Israeli soldiers on either side of the door. They had their weapons trained on Chana. One of the soldiers called back:

Orders are no access to anyone!

Chana kept running, shouting, "Alpha X-ray! Noveniner, noveniner, nadazero!"

The two soldiers instantly got up and threw open the green door. The arcade was flooded with flashes of gold light. Dead ahead, perfectly framed in the arched doorway, was the Dome of the Rock. Chana charged through, stopped, and stepped aside as Harper cleared the passage. She looked at the soldiers.

Radio the soldiers at Bab al-Asbat. Tell them to open the gate and leave the area.

Ma'am?

Do it.

Yes, ma'am.

Who is here?

Only the Grand Mufti and his entourage. They are in Al-Aqsa.

Where is everyone else?

Evacuated.

Okay. Close this door and don't open it. Anyone asks, you did not see us.

Yes, ma'am.

The soldiers pulled the door closed with a loud bang. The cacophony of sirens and mobs was gone. Harper scanned the compound. A completely leveled space of thirty-seven square acres. The space was trapezoidal in shape and walled in on all sides. The Dome of the Rock sat atop a raised platform in the center of the compound; to the south Al-Aqsa Mosque stood beyond the fountains; there were places for ablutions, there were gardens and trees. *A picture of peace,* Harper thought. *Too bad about the war raging around it.* Chana's voice snapped him back to reality.

"Lions' Gate is that way," she said, pointing to the far northwest corner of the compound.

"Right."

They ran up the steps, cut across the platform, and ran through the shadow of the dome. Down another set of steps and through the garden. Ahead, another green door in the wall; it was open. They got to the doorway, stopped, looked through it. There was a small courtyard leading to a stone arch. Chana checked her watch.

"Four and a half minutes to spare," she said breathlessly. She pointed to the arch at the end of the courtyard. "Lions' Gate is just beyond that arch and to the right. Your Swiss Guard said this courtyard was the target zone."

"From the arch to the door."

"Ken."

"What is it called?"

"El-Ghazali Square."

"What is it—what was it?"

"A cistern in Roman times, then a rubbish dump, then a vegetable garden. Now it's a hot spot for clashes between Palestinians and Israeli soldiers. Could this mean something?"

Harper thought about it. "Not yet."

He scanned the layout. High wall to the right, alleyways off the courtyard to the left. "Where does that lead?"

"Via Dolorosa. The tourists' version."

"You're joking."

She shook her head. "It is strange, as if whatever is happening with your infiltrators is a copy-and-paste of an Israeli–Palestinian clash. Young Palestinians came in through Lions' Gate and into this courtyard heading for Al-Aqsa. They were trapped here. The Israelis had Via Dolorosa cut off, like today."

"Today?"

She nodded toward Via Dolorosa. "The preschool under siege is down that way, near the Third Stage of the Cross. Like I said, strange."

Third Stage of the Cross, Harper thought. *Jesus falls for the first time. What the bloody hell are they up to?*

"Trust me, it isn't strange at all," Harper said.

Chana's cell phone vibrated and she pulled it from her jacket. *"Halo?"* She listened for ten seconds, then handed the phone to Harper. "It is for you."

He took the phone, put the receiver to his ear. "Yes?"

"Good morning, Mr. Harper. Time is short so I will be brief. Intel suggests six of the enemy will materialize very soon. They will appear as Israeli civilians. Their mission is to film themselves using explosives to damage the building behind you. They plan to transmit the event live on the Internet."

Harper looked back, saw the Dome of the Rock through the trees. "Got it."

"Mr. Harper, the situation is extremely grave."

"Just get the time mechanics to drop the warp at the right moment and keep it in place. I'll take care of the rest."

"That is the problem, Mr. Harper. There are undefined radio waves emanating from the location that make it all but impossible. Indeed, it is the same reason the enemy is being forced to materialize at your current location instead of closer to their target. But it's our only chance at blocking their live transmissions of the event. As it is, we are not sure the warp will even hold. If it does fail, you will only have sixty seconds before enemy cameras reconnect with their comms satellite. If they succeed, as I said, the fallout will be biblical in its proportions."

Harper flashed his meet with the dream catcher on the esplanade of Lausanne Cathedral. She was telling Harper of Ella's dream. A baby cow with a red face; men slaughtering the beast on a black rock in the City of the Three Gods. But the beast struggles to live as its blood drains away. Its hooves catch the blood on the rock, it sparks, and a great fire consumes the world. Harper blinked to nowtimes. Chana was watching him with her amber eyes, knowing he had just gone somewhere.

"Will you be able to contain the fallout in Jerusalem, Inspector?"

"I am afraid not."

"Understood."

He closed the phone, handed it back to Chana. "Do you have children?"

Her face was Israeli MI blank, but her eyes flashed a touch of fear. "Two daughters, twins," she said.

Bloody hell.

"You should leave," Harper said.

"Why?"

"There is every chance this will go the wrong way. If it does, then war will engulf this place, completely, utterly."

She looked to the ground, shook her head. *"Lo."*

"You have no idea what is coming."

She lifted her eyes to him. "And you still have no idea what is really going on in Jerusalem. Look behind you again, look through the gate. Good. Forget the Muslim holy places you see now, forget the Jewish Temples that once stood there, forget Yeshua ben Yosef prayed there. That ancient ground is what is left of Mount Moriah, the most sacred ground on the face of the earth, not because of what men have built on it, but because of what men have forgotten about it. *This* is where heaven and earth collide. *This* is the shortest distance between the Creator and mankind. If I will not abandon Jerusalem to fanatics of any religion, what makes you think I would abandon it to the sons of darkness? That is what is coming, isn't it?" Fierceness flared in her eyes.

"Actually, we call them goons," Harper said.

She nodded. "Good name."

"How much time left?" Harper said.

Chana checked. "Ninety seconds."

Harper pulled his SIG Sauer from his kill kit, loaded a round in the firing chamber.

"There will be six of them. They will appear as Israeli civilians, like the right-wingers at the Wailing Wall. But make no mistake, these are not human beings. One will be carrying a bomb, probably in a backpack. One will have a camera of some kind. Bomber is primary, then the camera, then the rest. They can only be killed with a head shot between the eyes or by slicing their throat and separating the spine from the brain."

"I don't have a knife."

Harper pulled his killing knife with his left hand. "No worries. If you only wound them, they will get back up again, so don't miss."

Chana raised her assault rifle, flipped off the safety, set the weapon for single fire. She switched on the laser targeting.

"This is a modified TAR-21. It fires a single sixty-two-grain M855 round at three thousand feet per second. By 2018 every Israeli soldier will have one. Until then there is me and the Special Forces, and I never miss."

"Glad to hear it."

They backed up to the open gate to Temple Mount and waited.

"Do you smell smoke?" Chana said.

"No."

"I smell smoke. Twenty seconds."

Harper started counting them down in his head: *Nineteen, eighteen, seventeen . . .*

"Amini," she said.

"Sorry?"

"When we met at Qumran you asked if there was anything more to my name. It is Amini."

Harper ran the name. Amini: Sanskrit in origin, meaning *priest*.

"It's a good name," he said.

"Toda."

Just then a swell rolled through the ground under their feet, and for a moment, the walls and buildings surrounding them wobbled.

"What was that?" Chana said.

"Look at your watch."

She did. "It stopped with two seconds to go."

"Welcome to a time warp, Chana Amini."

She looked up. She saw the sun moving through the sky; she saw wisps of clouds and birds racing by at high speed. It all shuddered to a stop.

"Sababa."

ii

"BBC World Service. I'm Will Austin, with *The World Tonight*. Some Israelis are calling it the 'Day of Judgment.' So far eighteen Israelis including six members of the Israeli Defense Forces are dead and scores more injured, some critically, after a day of violence and rioting. Three Palestinian teenagers involved in a terrorist act have also been killed. And as the day ends, the Middle East is on the brink of all-out war. Islamic leaders from Saudi Arabia, Pakistan, Iran, and Iraq have issued a joint communiqué calling for the annihilation of Israel. The terrorist organization Da'esh has said a million-man army will march on Israel in three days. Turkey, Egypt, and Jordan have severed diplomatic relations with the Jewish state and put their own armed forces on high alert as a protective measure against mounting civil unrest in their respective countries. Severe rioting has broken out throughout the Muslim world, claiming more than fifteen hundred lives. Overnight in Kuala Lumpur, the American embassy was under siege by more than twenty-five thousand protestors. Malaysian troops fired into the mob to keep the protestors from gaining access to the embassy compound. Sources say more than two hundred people are dead. All across Europe, governments are on high alert for terrorist strikes. And in the last hour, rockets have been launched into Israel from Lebanon, Gaza, and Syria, but there are no reports of casualties as yet. In Jerusalem, Prime Minister Yossi Borstein held a press conference this evening announcing the general mobilization of Israeli forces. All ports, borders, and commercial airspace above Israel have been closed. Mr. Borstein stated in clear terms that if at-

tacked, Israel would respond with every weapon in its arsenal. Israel has never admitted to possessing nuclear weapons, but is believed to have up to four hundred strategic and tactical nuclear systems. There have been frantic efforts by the United States, Great Britain, and the European Union to defuse the crisis, and a meeting of the UN Security Council is scheduled for later tonight. And from the Vatican, Pope Francis has asked people of all faiths to pray for peace.

"The crisis began when three Palestinian teenage girls dressed as Israeli students attacked a preschool in the center of the Old City. Two guards and a teacher were killed outright, while eleven children and three more teachers were taken hostage. The school's CCTV system was used to show the hostages bound together and surrounded by explosive devices. The Palestinian teenagers, who claimed to be from the Arab village of Silwan, demanded the release of prisoners from the Israeli prison at Megiddo and threatened to detonate their bombs if the demand was not met by seventeen hundred hours GMT. The hostage-takers cut the CCTV feed and said there would be no further communication. Israeli Special Forces mounted a counterstrike in the early afternoon, and after a short firefight all the hostages were released unharmed. A government spokesman has confirmed the three hostage-takers are dead.

"Shortly after the preschool was attacked in the morning, violent clashes erupted near the Wailing Wall when hundreds of right-wing Jewish activists stormed a ramp leading to the compound known as Temple Mount. The area within the compound is revered by Jews and Muslims alike and is under the control of the Waqf, the Islamic trust overseeing Al-Aqsa Mosque and the Dome of the Rock. Jewish activists involved in the clashes claimed they were taking back Temple Mount in retaliation for the kidnapping of Jewish children. It is not clear what happened next, but a fire broke out on the ramp and the flames quickly spread. Nine activists and five Israeli policemen were burned to death. Nineteen more Israelis, including three policemen, sustained serious burn injuries.

"But it is today's third event that has taken the region to the brink. The BBC's Sophie Orr is in Jerusalem and joins us by telephone to talk us through what happened. We must warn viewers that these images are disturbing. Sophie?"

"Good evening, Will. Exact circumstances surrounding what happened on Temple Mount are unclear. Both the Israeli government and the Waqf are not commenting on the details. All we know is what was seen in ninety seconds of video footage first broadcast by French television earlier today. A TF1 cameraman gained access to a high location near Temple Mount to transmit live pictures of the ongoing riot at the Wailing Wall. His footage suddenly pans to the interior of the Temple Mount compound as a man with a backpack is seen running from the north gardens toward the Dome of the Rock. The footage is shaky, and by then smoke from the fire at the Wailing Wall was drifting across Temple Mount, so the man's identity is unknown. Unconfirmed sources say he was an Israeli activist with the Third Temple Movement. Chasing after the man is a female Israeli soldier with an assault rifle. She appears to be badly wounded but manages to shoot the running man in the legs before he can get anywhere close to the Dome of the Rock. The soldier then shoots the man once in the chest and once in the head, point-blank, as if executing him. Then two more unidentified men with backpacks run into the frame and attack the soldier from behind with knives. Despite being wounded, the Israeli soldier manages to kill one of these men, but the second man stabs her in her throat. As the soldier falls, a man in a trench coat hobbles into the picture. He fires his handgun and kills the soldier's assailant. He hurries to the backpack, cuts it open with a knife, and appears to disconnect something. Now, he did this with the two other backpacks as well, and an independent munitions consultant on Sky News has said this looks very much like someone defusing a bomb in a desperate and hurried situation. The man then limps to the Israeli soldier and kneels next to her, leaning close to her face. He removes his coat and covers the dead soldier. The footage then pans wildly and stops. TF1 has told the BBC that it was at this point the Israeli police burst onto their live location and shut down the broadcast. But the damage had been done. The shocking footage has been seen around the world, and it set off a firestorm across the Middle East. Earlier today, the President of the United States appeared in the Rose Garden of the White House and pleaded for calm, saying it is important for the world to remember an Israeli soldier lost her life defending an Islamic holy site. The coming hours will tell if the President's plea has fallen on deaf ears. Will?"

"Sophie, we are showing the pictures as you talk to us, and they are quite shocking. If this was a plot to destroy the Dome of the Rock, it's obvious the Israeli soldier and the man in the trench coat, as you call him, were working together. Do we know anything more about him? And does the manner of his dress suggest he is a European?"

"Will, I spoke with an Israeli police spokesman, who says there is no evidence—"

"Sophie? Can you hear me, Sophie? We seem to have lost the line with Sophie Orr in Jerusalem, but we'll try to get her back as soon as we can. She was telling us of the disturbing footage shot on Temple Mount in Jerusalem today. She was telling us there appears to have been an attempt by an Israeli citizen to bomb the Dome of the Rock. Actually, I have just been handed a note advising me that the Israeli Minister of Internal Affairs has announced that all civilian telephone and Internet communications in and out of the country have been suspended until further notice."

TWENTY-FIVE

i

In a dark, silent room. Naked on a concrete floor. His wrists bound together in front of him; no idea where he was or how he got here. He sat up, leaned against a padded wall. Pain flared in his right leg. He touched his thigh, felt the tightly wrapped bandage around it.

He scanned the dark. Not a speck of light. Images fell through his eyes. When it was over on Temple Mount there was a rush of Israeli Border Police. They knocked him to the ground, tased him with fifty thousand volts, then came a whack to the back of his head. The last thing he saw before lights-out was Chana's dead body on the ground. She was covered with his coat. He rubbed the back of his neck.

"Please, no."

He ran his timeline.

Eleven goons, not six, taking form at the arch across the courtyard. Each of the goons looking like one of the Third Temple crowd, except for the killing knives in their hands. Each one with a large pack on its back and a body camera strapped to its chest.

"Which one is the primary?" Chana says.

"All of them. Don't fire until they completely materialize."

Harper waits until he sees the dead black swell in their eyes.

"Now," Harper says.

Chana lets off three rounds and drops three goons in two seconds; Harper nails goon number four with two rounds to its head. Brains and black blood splatter against Jerusalem stone. The standing goons charge, and Harper puts a round in the lead goon's body camera. The punch knocks the thing back, and Chana finishes it off with a head shot. The surviving goons stall and sniff the air. Black drool drips from their mouths as they turn to Chana and spread out.

"They've got the scent of your soul," Harper said.

"Tell them to come and get it."

"They'll come on their own. Draw them away from the gate. I'll sort backpacks."

Chana eases to the side of the courtyard. The goons prowl after her. Harper flies to the dead goons, slices open their backpacks. Each pack crammed with blocks of Semtex connected to digital timers counting down: *06:46, 06:45, 06:44*. Basic kit, no trip wires. Harper pulls the detonators, tosses them away, puts a bullet in each body camera. Back to Chana. The goons whirl around her in a blur, dropping her in a trance. Harper runs, pulls a vial from his kill kit. He hits the ground, slides over the cobblestones under the goons.

"Cover your eyes."

Chana does.

Harper smashes the vial on the ground.

"Et facta est lux."

There is a blinding flash of blue light. The goons squeal and fall back. Harper flies at one, slices open the goon's throat, and rams his killing knife deep—*crack*. The thing goes down, and Chana drills a bullet through its body camera. Harper's form seizes with pain as a goon's knife cuts across his right thigh. "Argh!" Harper falls, feels himself being hauled back up to his knees. A blade is set at his throat, there is hissing voice in his ear.

"I bring you forever death."

Harper hears a shot. A bullet from Chana's rifle rips by his head—*whoop, whoop, whoop*—it hits the goon in the jaw, blows off half its face. Harper knocks away the goon's knife, spins around, swings his own knife, opens the goon's throat. It goes down. Harper presses the barrel of his SIG against the goon's head.

"Sod off."

Bang.

He defuses one more bomb.

Chana screams; Harper turns to her. She's on her knees now, bleeding from her left arm. She's taken a bad slice above the elbow and her rifle is on the ground. A goon rises behind her, lifts its knife for the death cut at the back of Chana's neck. Harper plugs two rounds through the goon's body camera. The thing staggers back, charges again. Chana scoops up her rifle with her right hand; her left arm dangles from her side. She puts sixty grains of lead between the goon's eyes, and the back of its head explodes with brains and black blood.

The ground swells; Jerusalem's walls shake.

Sirens, faraway screams; thick smoke, a blackening sky.

Chana looks at Harper.

"What is happening?"

"Time warp didn't hold. We're back in real time."

Chana looks through the gate to Temple Mount. Three goons running through the gardens and breaking into three different directions. Chana goes after them, stays on the trail of the goon making a straight run for the Dome of the Rock. Harper hobbles after her, gets through the gate, keeps moving. He watches her take down the goon with leg shots and finish it off with a bullet to the head. He sees two goons rushing at her.

"Chana!"

Light exploded in the dark room, scorching the rods and cones at the back of Harper's eyes. He put his hands over his face for long seconds, not wanting to be dragged back to nowtimes. *Please, no.* When he lowered his hands, he saw he was in a nine-by-twelve room. No windows, a small vent, a camera built into the high corner of the wall. It took him a few more seconds to see the door. It had no handle or window, and it blended in with the soundproofing covering the walls and the ceiling. He looked at the cable tie binding his wrists together. *Wherever this place is,* Harper thought, *bad things happen here.*

The door opened and a wall of sound flew in. Footsteps and voices, copper radio traffic and distant sirens. Then came a stocky man with gray hair. He wore an Israeli uniform with an Israeli Military Intelligence tag on his left shoulder and the rank of major general on his epaulets. He was unarmed, but he looked tough enough, even behind his wire-rimmed glasses. Two more soldiers followed, each of them with a Jericho 941 semiautomatic pistol strapped to their belt. One of them carried a wooden stool; the other held a gray wool blanket. In quick moves the stool was set in the middle of the room and Harper was lifted from the concrete floor then dropped on the stool. Pain flared through his leg again.

"Fuck!"

The blanket was tossed over Harper's shoulders and the soldiers left the room. When they closed the door it was quiet again. The general walked across the room, rested his back against the wall, facing Harper. He reached in his breast pocket, took out a pack of American-made fags and a Zippo lighter bearing the ensign of the Israeli Paratrooper regiment. He went through the ritual of lighting up. He inhaled deeply and exhaled a cloud of smoke, all the while staring at Harper.

"What did you say to her?"

The general spoke with an Israeli accent of East European descent from the sound of it. Lithuania maybe.

"Sorry?"

"What did you say to Major Chana Amini as she lay dying on Temple Mount?"

Harper got a read on the general's eyes; they were clear. Harper ran rules and regs: It had always been forbidden to reveal truths of the soul to locals. He looked at the bioskin gloves on his hands. *But those days are gone from us. These days in the Holy Land the blind lead the blind.*

Harper cleared his throat. "I told her to look into my eyes and listen to the sound of my voice. I told her it doesn't end for her kind, I told her it never ends. I told her, *'C'est le guet, il a sonné l'heure.'*"

The general smoked. "Not that I understand the English any better, but the last part was French."

"Yes."

"What do these words mean?"

"They mean, 'This is the watcher, this is the hour.'"

"Is it a prayer?"

"No, it's not a prayer."

"Then why did you say these words to Major Amini as she died?"

Harper flashed Chana's amber-colored eyes. She was trying to stay with him, but she was slipping away. He opened his irises, flooded her eyes with light . . . but she was already gone.

Harper blinked and looked at the stocky man in olive green. "It's a translation of ancient words of comfort."

"From where? What is the root language."

"I don't know."

The general smoked. "The wound is not serious."

"Sorry?"

The general pointed to Harper's thigh. "Where you were stabbed. It is not critical, but I'm sure it is painful. I chose not to give you any pain medication. For the moment I thought it best if you remained clear in the head. We were not sure about the gloves on your hands, so we left them. We took X-rays and found gashes on your palms. From a previous wounding, I take it. The gloves are an exceptionally advanced medical technology. May I ask where it was done? I only ask because I assume it was done by the same people who made sure there is no trace of your identity in any fingerprint or facial recognition database anywhere in the world. Do you even have a name?"

Harper did not answer.

The general walked in a wide circle around the room.

"Major Amini had a good way with people, no matter their religion or race. She spoke eleven languages fluently. She worked alone, apart from the rest of the intelligence section. She kept an office next to the boiler in the basement. She ran a network of Palestinians in the Old City. *'Al the'ab,'* she called them. It is Arabic for 'the wolves.' She never told me their names, only that they wanted to protect Jerusalem from evil as much as she did. She said those very words to me once. Most officers here did not appreciate her. They found her odd and could not understand why I kept her on. The fact is she knew more about the history of this city than anyone I know. She had an uncanny ability to put intelligence in a historical context. We would share a bowl of hummus for lunch sometimes. She would tell me stories full with visions. My grandmother often said it is a wise man who listens to a woman of vision, and our history has many of them. Miriam, Deborah, Huldah, and Anna."

Harper ran the women's names. "Those are the names of prophets from the Bible."

"True."

"Are you telling me Chana Amini was a prophet?"

The general was at Harper's back now and stopped. He did not answer the question. Harper listened to him smoke, exhale, then continue his slow walk around the room.

"She had two daughters, you know. Identical twins. They are ten years old."

"She told me."

"Really? In our business we have a practice of not revealing personal information to strangers."

Harper pulled the blanket tighter around his shoulders. "What will happen to them? Her daughters?"

The general came full circle now. He retook his position against the wall facing Harper. He smoked again.

"Her husband died of lung cancer six years ago, and both her parents are dead. But she has, or had, an identical twin sister. Her name is Batya. She paints desert landscapes, very well known in Israel and New York. Major Amini told me identical twins ran in the family like an old joke. Chana and Batya were close. They lived in the same building in the German Colony. The daughters are with the sister now, sitting shiva. I was there before I came here. I am curious: When did Major Amini tell you about her daughters?"

"Just before the job at the courtyard near Lions' Gate."

"The job?"

"Stopping the attack on the Dome of the Rock."

The general nodded. "Stopping the attack, yes. Messy, wasn't it?" he said.

"It always is. Sometimes less than others."

"But this was not one of the lesser times."

"No."

The general tapped a long ash from his smoke. Harper watched it fall to the concrete floor.

"Do you know what is happening in our world tonight?" the general said.

"How would I? I've been locked up in here."

"Yes, you have, so I will tell you. Six million Jews living within Israel are facing annihilation at the hands of tens of millions of Muslims who believe God has commanded them to annihilate Israel and wipe Jews from the face of the earth. Think about it. Less than a hundred years ago, six million Jews were slaughtered by the Nazis. How can it be that the world is burdened with this hideous number again? If I were a religious man I might say God is punishing us for our sins. After all, in the eyes of some of our best friends, we have committed many sins in Gaza and the West Bank. But I am not a religious man, I am a realist. And this is reality: Times have changed since the last time fanatics tried to annihilate the Jewish people. Right now Israeli rockets, jets, and submarines are being armed with nuclear-tipped munitions. One word from the Prime Minister, and Tehran or Baghdad or Damascus will disappear and six million Jews will have annihilated tens of millions of Muslims in the blink of an eye. And it is not just the Middle East. In America, tens of thousands of Christians are praying in their churches; not for peace but for the end of time. I saw it on CNN this afternoon. And Fox News conducted a poll of its viewers. Seventy-five percent believe the end of the world is at hand. Fifty-nine percent of those people think this is a good thing. Can you imagine it?"

"Yes, actually," Harper said.

The general stared at him. After a moment he shook his head and smiled a little.

"You know, when Major Amini told me about a joint mission with someone she only identified as 'the stranger,' I did not know what to think. But as I said, she was a very good storyteller, so I gave her the go-ahead. Besides, she said if you turned out to be a false prophet then you would be disappeared. That was her specialty: tracking down false prophets and making them disappear. Do you know what she told me to really convince me to allow her to go ahead? She said she had received solid intelligence that your enemies were the enemies of this ancient land. She said if this was true, then your enemies were our enemies."

"The enemy of my enemy is my friend," Harper said.

"But Major Amini was not your friend, was she?"

Harper pulled his blanket tighter. "I don't follow you."

"She went off radar seventy-two hours ago, chasing after one of her false prophets. Then strange things happened. The power outage at Allenby Bridge, for one. That is how you got in, isn't it? And she helped you."

"She wasn't a traitor, if that's what you think."

"I do not think she was a traitor. I think she was used."

"I still don't follow you."

"Don't fuck with me, asshole. I have eight bodies at Lions' Gate and three on Temple Mount with no fingerprints. And the three terrorists at the preschool from Silwan? Bullshit. I know every Palestinian in Silwan and I have never seen those girls before. I went to the morgue to check. None of the girls had fingerprints, either. Then I checked the burned corpses from the Wailing Wall. Guess what? Two corpses with no fingerprints. Do I need to mention the black blood, or do you get the fucking picture?"

Harper gave it ten seconds.

"You forgot the bomber in West Jerusalem a few days ago, General. The bomb killed a Swiss newspaper reporter and an Israeli who worked with the Dead Sea Scrolls. The bomber had no prints," Harper said.

The general gave it five.

"I did not forget about him. I only wished you to prove my point."

"Which is?"

"Major Amini is dead because of you."

Harper nodded. "You're right."

The general dropped his cigarette on the concrete floor and stepped on it. "So, what should I do with you? Kill you? Throw you in a hole so deep no one would ever find you? Or should I let you make a phone call to your superiors to clear up the situation?"

Harper laughed quietly to himself.

"Something is funny?" the general said.

Harper looked at him. "I wouldn't know how to call."

"You do not know how to use a telephone?"

"I don't know any numbers to call. They always call me."

"I see," the general said. He reached to his back, pulled a small combat knife from inside his belt. He walked toward Harper. "Hold out your hands."

Harper did. The general cut the cable tie binding Harper's wrists, then resheathed the knife. He looked up at the camera in the high corner and snapped his fingers. He went back to his wall, did not speak. Ten seconds later, the cell door opened. A soldier walked in carrying Harper's clothes and two cell phones. The phones he handed to the general; the clothes he gave to Harper. He took two steps back and stood with his hand resting on his sidearm, watching Harper with a bitter glare.

"Leave us, Seren," the general said.

He waited for the officer to exit and close the door. The general lit another smoke, looked at Harper.

"Your trench coat was badly stained with her blood. It was dealt with according to Jewish religious practices. The rest of your clothes were examined for traces of her blood, found clear, then cleaned. Dress quickly."

Harper wondered about his weapons, but decided it would be a wasted question. He stood, keeping the blanket around his shoulders as he dressed in his boxers and trousers. He sat on the stool, put on his socks and shoes. He stood again, dropped the blanket, put on his shirt and sports coat, shoved his still-knotted regimental tie in the pocket of his coat. He tapped his pen pocket; the matchbox with the dented five-franc coin was still there. Harper looked at the general.

"Why are you doing this?"

The general held up one of the cell phones. There was dried blood on it.

"This is Major Amini's encrypted cell phone," the general said. "Like everyone in MI, her calls were recorded by an agency of the Israeli security services. Every communication on this phone in the last seventy hours has vanished. There is not a trace of a call or text message to her or from her anywhere in our system. Our computer experts called it an unexplained glitch. That would be the second unexplained glitch in twenty-four hours."

"It happens."

"Yes, that is what I was told by the head of signals, right before I ordered him to shut down Israel's links to the outside world."

He pulled another cell phone from his other pocket, swiped the screen.

"This evening, more than five hours after Major Amini was buried, I received an encrypted message from her. Do you know when I received it? Two minutes after I left the Prime Minister's office to come here. Until today Israel could hack any computer in the world, and believe me, no one could hack us. But Allenby Bridge and these two phones tell me someone has breached our firewall. That someone used that power to make sure Major Amini's last words were delivered to me at a moment of their choosing, presumably when it would have the greatest impact. Which would be now. You see, I was coming here to torture you until you explained things. Her message saved you from that fate."

For a second Harper didn't know what the hell the general was talking about. Then he flashed the race through the Old City. Dropping off the reliquary box with the old Arab man, running again . . . Chana pulls her cell phone, types a text as she runs. The general was right; Inspector Gobet was pulling strings as only he knew how.

"What's the message?" Harper said.

The general swiped the screen of his phone, turned it around, and held it out for Harper to see.

"Do you know what these words mean?"

Harper read the Hebrew script.

ירושלים נופלת. אם אמות לזרוק אותו לכלבים.

"It says: 'Jerusalem falling. If I die, throw the stranger to the wolves.' More or less."

The general shook his head. "'Means' and 'says' are two different things. You would not make a good Israeli intelligence officer. Do not bother to apply."

"Sorry?"

"These words mean the sons of darkness have brought the world to the eve of destruction and that you may be the only person to stop it. Though if I were a betting man, I would say you are already too late."

ii

In the back of an Israeli jeep, speeding along a four-lane thoroughfare through West Jerusalem. Two soldiers up front: one behind the wheel, one riding shotgun. Both of them wearing Israeli MI tags on their blue jackets. The one riding shotgun was the same officer who'd drilled Harper with a bitter glare. Just now he was following Major General Somebody's orders to throw the stranger to the wolves.

Harper looked out the side window. The world ripped by in a rain-soaked haze at first, then he could see it. Rows of apartment buildings, lights burning in windows. But except for army jeeps and police vehicles, the streets were devoid of life. The driver made a right and went down a hill, and they came to a traffic circle. There was a small mosque across the road. Even with the jeep's windows closed the Muslim call to prayer was blaring. The driver turned right, drove by a joint called the American Colony Hotel. Looked swell. The kind of place that would have a decent bar. *A drink would go down well at the moment,* Harper thought. *Too bad about the end of the world.* Then he was in a neighborhood of rough-looking buildings, then he was passing piles of trash in the street where scrawny cats clawed for food. The driver made a fast left. There was something called the Tomb of the Kings on the left and Saint George's Cathedral on the right. Harper looked for the cathedral but could not see it through the rain. Then came two Israeli government buildings protected by riot-proof fences. There were squads of Israeli Border Police behind the fences. Rocks and broken glass in the street said the coppers had had a tough day. Harper saw a sign on a wall: SALAH AD-DIN STREET. The street was lined with shuttered shops. All the signs above the doors were in Arabic. There were stones and sticks and rubble everywhere. Harper saw fresh graffiti on a wall in Arabic: *Islam is the solution!* Then there was a long line of Israeli Army jeeps and police cars. At the end of the street Harper saw the walls of the Old City across another traffic circle. He realized that he had returned to the border of nowtimes and beforetimes. Then another bunkered government building on the corner. An entire company of Border Police mustered outside. The building was an Israeli cop shop, and it looked like it had been used as target practice for most of the day. Stones, steel bars, and broken glass lay scattered at the policemen's feet; there were scorch marks on the walls from Molotov cocktails. *Like a bloody combat outpost in Afghanistan, boyo.*

"Swell," Harper said.

The jeep slowed, rounded the circle, and pulled onto the pavement beneath the city walls. The soldier riding shotgun got out of the jeep and told Harper to do the same. He walked to an open arch in the wall; Harper limped after him.

"You go through there," the soldier said.

"And do what?"

"Maybe one of Major Amini's wolves will find you. Good luck. This is the roughest end of the Muslim Quarter. There are a lot of angry Palestinians inside who would love to kill a Jew today. But frankly speaking, any Westerner would do. There are also a few hundred Israeli settlers living in the Arab Quarter. They are armed, and tonight, they are very dangerous. They could mistake you for someone they want dead."

The soldier pointed to the hundreds of kitted-up Border Police gathered across the street. They were attaching extensions to the barrels of their M16s.

"Over there the Border Police are fixing their rifles to fire rubber-coated bullets. As soon as they get the order, they're going into the Muslim Quarter. Here, through Lions' Gate and Damascus Gate. The PM is under pressure from the Americans to keep our jets on the ground. He's also under pressure from radical nationalists in his cabinet. And they want the

Old City locked down and all Arabs confined to their homes as a show of force. It is going to go to shit in there."

Harper checked the kitted-up cops across the road. They were securing their helmets, lowering thick plastic face shields.

"Any clues on getting myself found?" Harper said.

The soldier shrugged mockingly. "None of us have seen one of Major Amini's wolves in the Old City. It always sounded like bullshit to me. No one but the general listened to her stories. Who knows? Perhaps the general knows how bad it's going to get, so he'll try anything. Personally, I was surprised he let you go. I would have put a bullet in your head. We don't have time for bullshit. We have a war to fight."

Harper looked at the gate. It was different from the other gates he had seen in the city walls. This gate was smaller, darker. The soldier was already heading for the jeep.

"Hang on," Harper called.

The soldier stopped, looked back.

"Seeing as you didn't shoot me, maybe you could answer a question. Does this gate have a name?"

"Does it matter?"

"Everything matters in this place, doesn't it?"

The soldier looked at the gate. "Arabs call it Flower Gate, Jews call it Herod's Gate."

If Harper had the energy, he would have laughed himself silly.

"Which one? The Great or Antipas?"

"Antipas," the soldier said.

The soldier jumped in the jeep. The driver looped around the traffic circle and headed for West Jerusalem. As Harper limped toward the Gate of Herod Antipas, a line dropped into his head from Luke's Gospel: *Now when Herod saw Jesus, he was exceedingly glad; for he had desired for a long time to see him.*

"Here we go."

Harper stepped through, keeping his eyes on the uneven cobblestones, checking the shadows. Inside the gate he came to a narrow, wet lane. He went left till it rounded south. Farther on was a fenced-in compound with an Israeli flag hanging from coils of razor wire. Security spotlights flooded the lane, and security cameras watched everything that moved. All that was missing was the sign on the fence: ARABS OUT OF JERUSALEM!

Harper backed up to the gate, went right this time. The lane turned south like the other one. No Israeli flags this time; just a long stretch of lane filled with the detritus of a riot. A sign on the wall tagged the street as Aqabat el-Rahbat. A few feet on there was a road to the right. SA'ADIEH, a street sign said. He went that way, came very close to Jerusalem's interior walls, then went toward a street marked IBN AL JARRAH. The street sign also had an arrow pointing the way straight on to Damascus Gate. Just now there was a platoon of Border Police marching down it, coming Harper's way. The lockdown of the Muslim Quarter had begun. Harper ducked into a shadow, lowered his eyes, and the Israelis turned the corner down Ibn al Jarrah without seeing him. He raised his eyes just as Arabic curses and stones rained down from rooftops onto the police. The cops answered with rubber bullets. A police helicopter cruised in low overhead. It lit up the rooftops, and the rock throwers scattered. Harper backed up to Aqabat el-Rahbat and went right. Then the sound of more heavy boots over the cobblestones, from behind him this time. Harper worked the geography. The oncoming boots were from Salah Ad-Din Street. They were double-timing it.

"Bollocks."

Harper ducked into another shadow, waited for the coppers to pass him by. His wounded leg was slowing him down. Best to be behind the cops than trying to outrun them, he thought. He stepped into the lane and followed after the police. They broke into two groups at a four-way intersection of narrow lanes, one group going left, the other going right; then the wet night exploded with violence. Screams, stones, gunshots, tear gas, an Israeli officer shouting commands through a bullhorn, Arabs shouting, *"Allah akbar! Allah akbar!"*

Harper limped ahead, got to the intersection, and checked the lanes running left and right. Palestinians had set up barricades of carts and garbage bins in the middle of both lanes. The Israelis were trapped. Rocks came over the barricades, Molotov cocktails and burning tires were dropped from rooftops. One of the Israeli cops caught fire. His squad threw him to the ground and beat out the flames. Another police helicopter swooped in over the rooftops. Harper saw a sniper hanging from the chopper's side door. His weapon was not fitted for rubber-coated bullets. The pilot switched on the searchlight and lit up the rooftops; the sniper opened up.

Crack, crack, crack.

The lit-up night dripped with rain and human blood.

Harper hurried across the intersection. Another Israeli squad was charging toward him. Harper looked for cover, but there were more choppers in the sky now. They panned the scene with searchlights and obliterated the shadows. There was no place to hide. He saw a small alleyway ten feet ahead. He limped toward it, ducked in. He was navigating a warren of alleyways going this way and that way. It was the same drill as before the job at Lions' Gate, but without Chana, Harper knew he was lost. A rock slammed into his back and he fell.

"Fuck!"

He rolled onto his back, saw a gang of Palestinian men charging at him. They had rocks and iron bars in their hands. One of them pointed at Harper and shouted, *"Khalles allaih hada ameel!" Finish him, he's a spy!*

More rocks flew at him. He had no time to get the palm of his hand into their eyeline to take them down with a spell. He scrambled to his feet, caught another rock in his back, fell again. He crawled around a corner, got to his feet, ran as best he could. He ended up in a dead end.

"Shit."

He saw a flimsy piece of plywood blocking access to an abandoned building. He kicked it down, jumped inside. The place smelled like rotting garbage and cat piss, but it was full of shadows. He slid in one, lowered his eyes. He heard the Palestinians coming down the dead end. They stopped at the opening to the abandoned building. They did not see him and left.

He stood still. Feeling the wet cold of the night, listening to the sounds of battle raging in nearby streets. Sirens, gunshots, choppers, and screams. And now the air was heavy with burning rubber and cordite. He looked up. Three hollowed-out floors, old timbers crisscrossing all the way up to keep the walls from caving in. The tin roof covering the place was peppered with holes. Threads of light seeped through the holes and hung in the dark.

Suddenly, Harper flashed the old man to whom Chana had given the reliquary box. *He believes what I believe,* Chana told Harper. And then she told the old man, *If I do not come back, you know what to do with it. Do you understand?*

The old man knows the wolves, Harper thought. *Need to find him . . . but where?* It was then Harper sensed he was not alone. He spun around. No one there, just the dark. Then he heard steps through the shadows.

"Hello?" he said.

A police chopper flew overhead, and spotlights blasted the tin roof. Fast-moving streams of light washed through the shadows. Harper saw garbage and rats, then three human forms in silhouette. The chopper banked away and the light quickly disappeared, taking the three human forms with it. Harper stepped back to the wall and scanned the ground for a stick or a piece of scrap iron. Then sniper rounds cracked overhead. He looked up, saw tracer rounds flying through the night. The Israelis had taken up positions on rooftops to get at the Palestinians. The chopper flew overhead again; this time its searchlight dripped into the dark and lit up the three forms head-on. They had Mohawk haircuts, hard faces, and brown eyes. They wore running shoes, blue jeans, and leather jackets over black sweaters. The one in the middle had the reliquary box hanging from his shoulder. *Bloody hell.* The chopper banked away and the men disappeared. Then came an Arabic-accented voice calling to him:

"Are you the man of signs and wonders, or are you just another false prophet?"

It was the same bloody question Chana Amini asked him at Qumran.

"All I know is what Chana told me," he said.

Harper heard the steps of the three Palestinians move away. They were abandoning him to the stinking dark.

"Wait . . ."

Outside, wild automatic weapon fire opened up like jackhammers. Palestinians had brought out AK-47s, Harper thought. Then came an Israeli Army chopper, a bloody Apache; then a *whoosh* and a blinding explosion of light. The abandoned building shook, bits of stone and timber tumbling down. The Israelis were answering the AKs with air-to-ground rockets. For a moment the battle was quelled. Then came the cries and screams of the wounded; then fires rose over Jerusalem and a malefic glow filled the dark of the abandoned building. Harper saw the wolves standing at a low opening in a wall. A way out of this place maybe.

"Yes," Harper said, "I'm the man of signs and wonders."

"Right answer. Come with us."

TWENTY-SIX

i

"*Bisur'a, bisur'a." Quickly, quickly.*

The wolves guided Harper through hidden alleyways connecting one narrow lane to another. They used shadows well, Harper thought. They came to a long arcade of shuttered shops.

"Here we cross into the Christian Quarter," the one with the reliquary box said.

A street sign marked the road as Suq Khan ez-Zeit. And two more signs on corners: one marking the Sixth Station of the Cross, the other marking number Seven. They darted across the street, hurried down El-Khanqa to an Arab barber shop. The place was closed and dark, but the door was unlocked. They entered quickly with a limping Harper in tow. At the back of the shop two of the wolves pushed aside a heavy wooden cabinet. There was a low opening in the wall four feet by four feet.

"Tell me we are not going underground," Harper said.

"Not underground, but between the walls," the wolf with the reliquary box said. He whispered to his pack in Arabic; they nodded. He pulled a penlight, switched it on, and looked at Harper.

"Bisur'a."

"Sure."

The wolf ducked and entered the passageway. Harper followed, hearing the wooden cabinet being shoved back against the wall.

"Turn sideways and stand. Watch out for rats."

Harper did. The passage was barely three feet wide and the ceiling varied in height: here ten feet overhead, then forty feet, then into darkness. Their steps echoed in the stone-bound place. The wolf led the way, going left and right at uneven intervals. There were places where the passage tightened and they had to squeeze through. At one tight spot, the wolf stopped. He pressed his ear to the wall.

"People are talking. Electricity has gone out across Jerusalem and Israelis say terrorist cells from Da'esh are operating in the Old City now. The government has imposed a curfew everywhere. Anyone in the streets will be shot on sight."

"You can hear people through the walls?"

"Can't you?"

"Not a bit."

"Pity."

They continued down the passage and came to a round stone shaft. Harper did a slow three-sixty. It was a center point where eight passageways branched off like the cardinal and ordinal points of a compass. There was ancient script carved into the walls; Aramaic from the look of it. Without stopping for bearings, the wolf crossed the circle and continued down the third tunnel to the left.

A few minutes later he stopped at a steel door. He pulled it open carefully, silently. He slipped out, and Harper followed. It was another narrow passageway, but it was open to the sky a hundred feet up. The rain had stopped, and with electricity out, Harper saw a dense cluster of stars high overhead. The stars came and went as fire smoke drifted in the wind. The wind carried the sounds of guns and screams and cries.

The wolf made a few twists and turns, then squeezed around a set of Corinthian columns. When Harper made the same move, he found himself standing in an open courtyard of high limestone walls and well-worn stones on the ground. It felt like an ancient place. He did another three-sixty. There was a minaret beyond the walls at one end of the courtyard; a collection of mismatched windows and façades; then a massive stone edifice of Gothic arches, Corinthian columns, and stone stairways. Darkened windows and small doors were built into the walls to the left and right, and a Byzantine cross was carved into the wall above one door. But it was the two great arches, weirdly tucked in the corner of the courtyard, that held Harper's eyes. The high walls above the arches were supported by eleven tall columns. One of the arches had been bricked closed; the other arch framed two huge wooden doors.

"What is this place?" Harper said.

The wolf turned off his penlight, put it in one pocket of his leather jacket. He pulled a very old key from another.

"This is the entrance to the Church of the Holy Sepulchre."

Harper looked at the key. "You have the key to the Church of the Holy Sepulchre?"

"Muslim families have been the guardians of these doors for eight hundred years. My family now has the duty of protecting the key."

"Muslims hold the key to the most important Christian church in the world?"

The wolf smiled. "The priests of this church are from all different sects, and they detest one another. Inside they argue over pieces of dust like children. Often it becomes violent and the Israeli police must come in to restore order. This happened today after the killings on Temple Mount. The Israeli police already had enough trouble on their hands and ordered the church cleared and closed until further notice. Truly, it is a rare night when this church is empty of all priests and pilgrims. There are always a few who stay locked in through the night to be close to their God."

There was a blast of light in the dark sky, then a deafening crump rolled over the rooftops. The Israelis had sent another rocket into the Old City. The battle was spreading and coming this way. The wolf lowered his head.

"Nad'o khaleq kula shay' an yahmi al-abriyaa." We pray to the Creator of All to protect the innocents.

He looked to Harper for an amen. Harper pointed to the doors of the church instead.

"Get me inside," he said.

The wolf hurried to the doors and worked the old key into the old lock. Harper limped after him. With the right leaf of the doors open, the wolf stepped aside and waited for Harper to cross the threshold. He went in after Harper and closed the door with a dull clacking thud that echoed away.

Klaboom, klaboom, klaboom.

Harper listened for the sounds of war through the thick stone walls. Like the distant thunder of an approaching storm it was, and it rumbled through the darkness. The air was musty, scented with incense and candle wax. Except for the eight lamps hanging above a rectangular stone slab on the floor thirty feet ahead, there was no light of any kind. The lamps glowed on the slab and blinded him for a moment. His eyes adjusted quickly, and he saw he was in an immense hall where columns upon columns held up a dizzying number of stone vaults in the ceiling. Beneath the ceiling were blue stone arches opening to a great room with a domed ceiling. There was a huge icon of a Byzantine Christ painted in the center of the dome. On the wall beneath the arches, two huge mosaics depicted the anointing and burying of Jesus. Harper lowered his eyes to the slab on the floor again. This time the hanging lamps were not as bright and he saw it better. It was reddish in color, eighteen by three feet; it was smooth and highly polished. There was something lying on it, something wrapped in old calfskin and bound by ropes.

Harper looked at the wolf. "For me, I take it?"

The wolf pulled the reliquary box from his shoulder and offered it to Harper.

"Cheers," Harper said.

He took the box, slung it over his shoulder, and limped over the well-worn floor stones toward the slab. Coming closer, he saw the lamps were suspended by chains made of small crosses. And directly above the lamps the hollow of a tower rose at least a hundred feet. *Like the lantern tower of Lausanne Cathedral,* Harper thought. To the right was the ambulatory and it disappeared into the dark; to the left was a huge arch opening to a stone passageway. He stepped closer to the slab. There were tall silver and brass candle stands at the head and foot of it. He took hold of one, lowered himself to one knee, and rested the reliquary box on the floor stones. He pulled the calfskin something closer; he untied the ropes, opened it. There were three items, all wrapped in calfskin, too. He unwrapped each of them.

A vellum scroll. Two-thirds of a clay cup. Three bloodied carpenter nails.

Harper opened the reliquary box. He removed the leather-bound sextant and laid it on the slab. He lifted the false bottom from the box. He removed the two things hidden there and laid them out. Those things, like the sextant, were wrapped in old leather. And damn if the old leather did not match the calfskin protecting the scroll. Harper looked up at the mosaic of the dead, anointed Christ. Words dropped into his head from the Gospel of John: *There was a garden; and in the garden a new sepulchre, wherein no man had ever been laid.*

"Right."

He unwrapped the sextant, the bit of pottery, the one carpenter nail. The bit of pottery completed the cup; the nail was a perfect match to the other three.

"Blimey."

He heard a single set of steps coming from the great dark space around the corner; then came a woman in black boots, black jeans, and a black leather jacket. She was raven-haired; she had amber-colored eyes.

"Chana?" Harper whispered.

The woman stopped. "No. I am Batya."

Harper grabbed the candle stand again, used it as a crutch to pull himself to his feet.

"Her sister. Sorry, I forgot a moment."

Batya walked to the slab on the ground, stood opposite Harper. They watched each other through the haze of the hanging lamps. Harper ran rules and regs on apologizing for the death of a local's twin because you were not fast enough to save her. Batya watched him thinking about it. She looked down at the slab.

"This is called the Anointing Stone. Christian pilgrims and tourists are told by the priests that it was on this stone that Yeshua ben Yosef was washed and anointed after his crucifixion. The tourists take pictures, the pilgrims fall to the ground and kiss it. They weep, they pray. They laid things on it to be blessed: rosaries and crosses, bottles of water, teddy bears. They believe in the holiness of this stone with all their hearts. The truth is the legend of the anointing was carried to Jerusalem by the Crusaders in the thirteenth century, and this stone was only added in 1810 when the church was renovated. The truth is ben Yosef was a Jew, killed by Romans for being a unruly Jew. His followers were Jews. They probably buried him without washing or anointing his body. In that way he could stand before God and bear witness to the manner of his death."

Everything about her was the same, Harper thought. Her appearance, the sound of her voice, her eyes reflecting the same ancient knowledge.

"Sorry, I don't mean to stare. I just . . . Your eyes."

He looked back at the Palestinian. He was sitting on a stone bench to the right of the doors now. One of Chana's Palestinian wolves he was. In the faint light, his brown eyes had shifted color and Harper saw traces of amber in his irises. *My family now has the duty of protecting the key.* He turned to Batya, ran the meaning of her name: *daughter of God*. Harper rubbed the back of his neck, laughed to himself.

"'An educated man,'" he said.

He looked at her. She had one eyebrow raised in curiosity.

"Chana said she was only telling me family stories handed down through the generations. One story was about an educated man who stumbled across the scrolls in Qumran five hundred years after it was destroyed. She didn't identify him, and I completely missed it. You, her and her twin daughters, the wolves, that old man in the Old City she dropped the reliquary box off to . . . she called him *Aamo*, it means 'uncle.' You're all related, descended from the Magi of Zoroaster. One of those descendants was the educated man who found the scrolls because it was his job to keep tabs on the sextant. As in who might come for it. That means he knew it had been taken to Qumran by my kind. I'm guessing that means he knew where the body of Jesus was hidden until the fall of Jerusalem, when my kind carried it out of the Holy Land. That's where Chana's educated man hid the seventh scroll with the other things. He knew they would never be found by strangers, because only the direct descendants of the Magi knew where the grave was. And that's where the scroll has been until tonight, until you went to get it to bring it here with the things of Christ."

Batya smiled. "Chana told me you were wise," she said.

Harper ran his timeline, but couldn't see a frame where the sisters might have communicated.

"When?"

"When we were teenagers. She dreamed she would meet you one day and together you would save this city in the name of the sacred light."

Harper looked at the things laid out on the Anointing Stone. He stood silently for a long time. Outside, the thunder of war drew closer. Batya watched him.

"Do you not wish to read the scroll?" she said.

He looked at her. "Why don't you just tell me what is in it?"

"You know what is in it."

"Tell me."

"An eyewitness account of what happened during the crucifixion of Yeshua ben Yosef. It tells how the man of signs and wonders returned ben Yosef's soul to the stars and died in his place to spare him great suffering."

"You've read it."

"No, nor Chana."

"Then how do you know that's what happened?"

"Stories handed down in the family, remember? We were never told the details of how the switch was done. All we were told was the seventh scroll records everything, including the final sayings pronounced from the cross, and that the scroll was to be kept hidden until the man of signs and wonders returned. We were told he would know what to do with it next."

Harper thought about it. He had no bloody idea of what to do. *The final words pronounced from the cross.* It took him three and a half seconds to scan the New Testament.

"The Gospels record seven sayings from the cross," he said.

"Ken."

"Are those sayings recorded in this scroll?"

"Only one, the last one. The rest are legends."

"Do you know the true sayings from the cross?"

She shook her head. Intersecting lines of causality raced through Harper's eyes. He looked down on the seventh scroll, his mind working the intel.

"Whatever the words were, whether they were said or not doesn't matter. It's what the words mean. They make up a message, don't they? After all, 'says' and 'means' are two different things, yeah? Odds are you were told it's a message for the third child conceived of light, born into the world to lift mankind to the stars."

"So goes the story," Batya said.

Harper looked at the gloved palms of his hands. *Two and a half million years of hiding in the forms of men comes down to this: standing in a land of sacred light where heaven and earth collide. The shortest distance between the Creator and mankind; that's what Chana said.* Harper bent down, wrapped the scroll in calfskin, and lifted it from the Anointing Stone. He limped around to Batya, handed over the scroll.

"Take it," Harper said.

"Why?"

"I've spent a long time bouncing from myth to legend looking for answers to who I am and where I am from. I have yet to find an answer that makes sense. Maybe that's the way it is for someone whose existence is defined by the grace of human imagination. The wonder is we're both trying to get to the same place. Locals call it salvation, my kind call it the point of knowing. Chana brought me as close to my point of knowing as I'll ever get, and it's close enough. Just now I have a job to do with no idea of what that job is. That's why you have to take the scroll. Put it back in the grave where it will be safe. If the world rights itself, someone like me will come looking for it. Give the scroll to them. Everything I'm supposed to know in this scroll will come to me in flashes when I need it. That's the way it works with my kind."

"But the message for the third child born of light?"

"Actually, we call him the child of the prophecy. Whatever he's called, he's too young to read just now, and I'm utter crap at storytelling. It's best left to someone else."

"Who?"

"I don't know. Maybe it's supposed to be you."

Batya glanced at the things on the Anointing Stone. "You will keep the things of Christ?"

Harper gave the things a quick look. An ancient sextant, a broken cup, four carpenter nails. *The sextant to find our way through the stars, the cup to give us drink when we thirst, the nails to kill.*

"I'll keep those for now. I've been told I might need them. I'll see they get back to you."

"To be returned to ben Yosef's grave with the scroll?"

"Yes."

"It will be done, noble lord."

Harper stared at her a moment. "Did you and your sister ever take a holiday in the south of France? Say, somewhere near Montségur?"

Batya smiled. "When we were teenagers. It was there Chana dreamed about you. After visiting the ruins atop the pluton."

"It's a small world."

"It is."

Batya left Harper at the Anointing Stone. She walked toward the Palestinian wolf who already had the great doors open to the night. The sounds and smells of battle seeped in.

"Sorry. One more thing," Harper called.

Batya turned to him.

"Your sister said Jesus was crucified somewhere within the walls of this church."

"Ken."

"Do you know where?" Harper said.

She looked about the place. "All this was deep in a mountain of black rock in the time of ben Yosef. It was leveled to make way for a Roman Temple when they expanded the city." She pointed to a set of stone steps near the entrance. "Those stairs lead to a Chapel of the Crucifixion atop a high point of the rock. The priests say it was there. Archaeologists say the site was closer to the Aedicule, perhaps very close to it. At the Place of Mourning, perhaps, from where the priests say the followers of ben Yosef watched the crucifixion."

"Sorry?"

"The shrine in the rotunda under the great dome. It is through the arch and down the passageway to the Place of Mourning. From there it opens to the rotunda. However, the priests insist the shrine is where ben Yosef rose from the dead. Other Christian sects say the site of the crucifixion was farther from the Old City, in a place now behind the bus depot on Sultan Suleiman Street. There is a hillside there with small black caves. When you look at the hill, it looks like a skull."

Harper smiled, almost relieved. "So no one knows the truth."

He watched Batya look up into the tower, then down to him.

"The truth is, Jay Harper, at this very moment you are standing as close to the place of the crucifixion as anyone can get."

Harper pointed to the Anointing Stone. "Here?" he said.

She pointed up. "Where the roof meets the tower, to be exact."

It was her turn to watch him look up into the tower then down to the stone slab.

"You are thinking of something?" she said.

He looked at her. "Did you talk to your sister in the last seventy-two hours?"

"My sister was involved in a mission. She would never communicate with me in those times."

"Then how do you know my name?"

Five seconds.

"Good question," she said.

She stepped outside and the wolf followed her, but he did not close the door. The war in the streets gave no sign of easing; fire and cordite smells drifted into the church and mixed with the scents of incense and candle wax. Harper saw a pool of light move over the outer floor stones, then three silhouettes appeared in the courtyard. They took form, crossed the threshold of the church, and walked toward Harper. The largest silhouette kicked closed the doors behind him.

Klaboom, klaboom, klaboom.

They marched over the floor stones, took form and their faces came into the light. Krinkle the roadie with a duffel bag balanced across his shoulders; Astruc the defrocked priest pulling a black metal suitcase on wheels; an ex-hooker named Katherine Taylor. Closer to Harper, she pulled Marc Rochat's lantern from the folds of her black cloak.

"Hey, brother," Krinkle said. "Told you we'd be here if this was the real deal."

ii

"What the hell is this?" Harper said.

Krinkle lowered the duffel bag to the floor. "Nice to see you, too," he said. He pulled the zipper and opened the bag. Inside were killing knives, SIG Sauer pistols, ammo magazines, injectors, and explosives. He handed Harper two SIGs. "Here."

"How did you get into the Holy Land?"

"Would you take the friggin' guns?"

Harper grabbed the SIGs. The roadie tossed him a few magazines of ammo.

"Here, these too—we're using spark rounds."

Harper looked at the top round in the magazine. Brass casing, but the bullet was a transparent acrylic and it contained an iridescent liquid.

"What's in it?"

"Fuck if I know. Liquid light or some shit. They told me we're going up against killers who date all the way back to the fifth cohort of Rome's Tenth Legion. They're immune to lead, they just heal up in seconds. Spark rounds are the only thing that will bring them down. Fries them from the inside out."

Harper slammed a magazine into one of his SIGs. "How many and when?"

"Unknown. Intel says Komarovsky will arrive once the fifth cohort secures the ground. They say he'll be bringing Max with him. First wave will materialize in seventy-five minutes, at twenty-three hundred hours. They're up against the same clock we are—we're all counting down to the midnight hour."

"Does the enemy know I'm here?"

The roadie shrugged. "That video on Temple Mount pretty much let that friggin' cat out of the bag, don't you think? They don't know you have backup, though."

Harper looked at Astruc. The priest was on his knees and his black metal suitcase was open. Inside was a laptop, a small satellite uplink, and connecting cables.

"You appear rather fit for someone who was using a walking cane the last time we met, Padre."

"Yes. Remarkable what medics can do when they put their minds to it."

He lifted a small JBL speaker and clamped it to a block battery. He switched it on, pulled a long black antenna. He stood and faced Harper.

"Besides, I'm only insane and not the one suffering from an undefined metaphysical condition, am I?"

True, Harper thought.

"So what's the speaker for?"

"To receive comms, hopefully," Astruc said.

"Comms. From whom?"

The priest did not answer. He hurried to an alcove in the ambulatory, hid the speaker between two pillars. He came back and closed the case. He fitted a monocle to his right eye, grabbed the sextant, and headed down the colonnade.

"I'm going to the roof to connect with the satellite."

"What satellite?" Harper said.

The priest called back as he disappeared into the shadows. "The one we moved into geosynchronous orbit twenty-three thousand miles over Jerusalem, ten minutes ago."

Harper turned to Katherine Taylor. She was looking at him with a familiar half smile. He flashed seeing it in beforetimes at LP's Bar, a lifetime ago it seemed.

"Madame Taylor, why are you here?"

She rested the lantern on the stone slab. It cast warm light over the things of Christ. She grabbed two SIG Sauers from the duffel bag and slammed mags in the handles. She stuffed the guns in her belt, grabbed extra mags, and stuffed them in the pockets of her cloak. "What's it look like? I'm here to get my son back."

Harper limped around the Anointing Stone, stood in front of her.

"You can't stay."

"Overruled."

"By whom?"

The roadie got to his feet. "Inspector Gobet, brother."

"He's in Jerusalem?"

"We all slipped just after the time warp crashed near Temple Mount. The cop is at the Amini house in the German Colony now. He stayed with Chana's daughters while Batya came here."

"What the hell is he doing anywhere near Chana's daughters?"

"Last I saw he was pulling imaginary blue bunnies out of thin air," Katherine said.

"Sorry?"

"They're children, Harper, and they had a lousy fucking day. The cop is comforting them, helping them understand the nature of death."

Harper felt a sharp jab to the back of his neck. "Bloody hell." He spun around and saw Krinkle with an injector in his hands.

"A little something to help you with that undefined metaphysical thing," the roadie said.

Harper rubbed the back of his neck. In quick seconds the pain in his leg was gone, but the madness around him was no clearer.

"How about a simple explanation instead?"

"Simple, no. Quick, yes. Brother Astruc finally came around and laid out the whole story. Us, the bad guys, and the locals are all chasing down the same legend."

"I got that intel from Chana."

"And he got it from the written histories her family kept from the days of the Magi and before. Gobet's been at them since we found them in

Astruc's hideout during the Paris job. It's been slow going because they were written as sacred hymns. That made them both easier to hand down through generations, aurally, *and* incredibly difficult to crack unless you speak Zend, the language of Zoroaster. Hasn't been used as a written or spoken language for four thousand years, except between the descendants of the Amini family and, weirdly enough, Brother Astruc. Bottom line: We've been players in the salvation game since way before the time of Christ. A black ops job all the way back to 1350 BC, when the concept of One God first took shape in Egypt. Gobet didn't know about the mission, no one at HQ knew about the mission. But according to the hymns, the sons of darkness knew, and they cast a two-thousand-year spell over the world to hide the truth from the sons of the light. The Amini family has been handing down the secret, waiting to be contacted by the man of signs and wonders."

Harper thought about it. "Sons of light and darkness, a man of signs and wonders. Those names are in the lost scrolls from Qumran."

The roadie nodded. "I know. Gave me friggin' goose bumps just hearing about it. Dig it. I ran tactical, infils and exfils. Astruc was the keeper of the sextant and chief comet man tracking the birth of the three children conceived of light. You were the guardian of their souls, you made sure they didn't end up forever dead."

"You sure? Zoroaster was murdered as he prayed, Christ was crucified, Max was . . ."

He looked at Katherine. He had forgotten she was there. She filled in the silence.

"Max was kidnapped by the sons of darkness. They need to slaughter him on the same coordinates where Jesus was crucified, and they need to do it before the midnight hour ends. Then the goons erect a temple to their One True God and fuck up the world for good."

Harper flipped his eyes to Krinkle. "Solid intel?"

The roadie nodded. "The SX geeks cracked the enemy codes while you and I were heading to Mount Nebo. They were screaming with glee on the dark side of the Internet."

Harper stepped closer to him. "Did you know what would happen in Jerusalem today while we were on our way to Mount Nebo?"

"I knew something would happen, not what," the roadie said.

"And you didn't bother giving me a heads-up?"

"Orders."

"What orders?"

"When Sergeant Gauer got back from the recon, we ran Chana Amini through the SX grid. She came up listed."

"You knew she would die?"

"Would, yes. How or when, no. But you know how it is, brother. We are forbidden to interfere with the time or manner of a local's death, full friggin' stop."

Jerusalem's war echoed through the church. Harper seethed.

"Innocent people died today. Innocent people are dying in this city tonight."

"Yeah, and we smuggled in a few hundred comforters with us. They're in the streets right now trying to cope. But get this, brother: Locals are dying all across the Middle East, and it's getting worse. A renegade Iranian Army group moved Scud missile launchers into eastern Iraq. Twenty minutes ago they put themselves on the Internet loading chem-weap warheads and fueling the missiles. Israel saw that and scrambled her jets—they're in the air and circling above the Med Sea right now. If we don't stop this shit pronto, a third of the world will go down in flames and take a few billion more locals with it. So, Brother Harper, do you want to get with friggin' Plan B or not?"

Silence. Katherine moved close to Harper, spoke softly.

"Inspector Gobet told Batya everything about your kind, me, Max, and why you came to the Holy Land. He even told her he knew Chana had been listed to die. He said he was forbidden to stop it, but he made sure you would be with her. He said that was the best chance for Chana's soul to be returned to the stars according to their belief. He said that's what you were doing when you knelt next to her on Temple Mount. That's why Batya went to collect the seventh scroll and bring it here."

Harper looked at her. Her eyes scanned as pure truth.

"And as you're scanning my eyes, Harper, there's one more thing you should know as truth. Before we left the house, Chana's twin girls asked me if I would come back with the man who helped their mother's soul get back to the stars. They'd like to thank you in person."

"What did you tell them?"

"I told them I was very sure you'd accept their invitation with genuine pleasure."

Harper had a strange sensation, as if he had heard those words before. They were comforting words, but he could not find them on his timeline. He blinked, looked at the roadie. "What's the plan."

"One: Get you into Jerusalem and chase down the scrolls, see if this was the real deal. If so, get you in position to head the enemy off at the pass."

"Done," Harper said.

"Two: Spread the first fire of creation across the world."

Harper looked at the lad's lantern on the slab. "By bringing it to Jerusalem?"

"This is only one spot on the map, brother. The music festival in Lausanne? It was cover. Thousands of partisans got into Lausanne and left with shreds of flame from the first fire. They passed right under the noses of the enemy, who were too busy screaming with glee to notice. As the partisans got to their bases across Europe, Sergeant Gauer started making drops around the world like friggin' Santa Claus."

Harper looked at the lad's lantern, watched the way the light pulsed in the polished surface of the Anointing Stone.

"We're lighting up the planet."

"Bingo, brother."

Harper looked into the tower. Up there the pulsing light gathered in small pools.

"Astruc is setting up for the same trick he pulled at Montségur with his son. He's using a comms satellite to upload a new set of triangulations into Blue Brain. This time he's using the sextant to plot the coords of the crucifixion and the million fires spread around the world. All he needs is a third point of reference."

He looked at Krinkle and Katherine.

"All he needs is another comet."

Silence.

"Is there another comet coming?"

Astruc's voice from the shadows now: "Yes. Emanating from the constellation Pleiades as soon as you give the all-clear that Madame Taylor's child is safe."

Harper turned as Astruc stepped into the light. "Sorry, Padre?"

The priest walked to the duffel bag, grabbed three SIGs, twenty mags of ammo, and two killing knives. He talked as he sorted his kit.

"The triangulations based from Montségur plotted the Earth's exact position in the universe. The triangulations centered from this site will confirm the next stage of evolution has already begun in paradise. At least that's how it reads in the sacred hymns of the Amini family. In the hymns, this conflation of scientific knowledge and human imagination is called 'the Night of Nights,' from which either the sons of darkness or the sons of light will triumph in battle during the midnight hour. Though in the hymns the process of using cosmic triangulations as comms is called 'the True Alignment of the Heavens,' you are called the man of signs and wonders, Max is the third child conceived of light, and saving paradise from mass extinction is called attaining 'the wisdom of the angels.' *Et voilà*, the locals are ready to be contacted from the other side of the universe."

Harper glanced back to where the priest stashed the audio speaker. "Contacted. By whom?"

"By someone who answered our SOS aboard Voyager 1 as it crossed into interstellar space."

"What?"

Astruc tucked his weapons in his belt and pulled a cell phone from his coat. He swiped the screen, then tapped it. The church filled with a hissing sound, then a high-pitched screech for half a second; the hissing sound and the same high-pitched screech again, for two seconds this time. Silence. The priest dropped the phone in his coat.

"Those are sounds recorded by Voyager 1 from interstellar space and beamed back to Earth over a period of six months. The first burst was discovered in November 2012, the second in May 2013. They have not been repeated or heard again. Scientists at NASA called the sounds vibrations of plasma clouds or ionized gas. Six months ago, Goose began analyzing the sounds, looking for mathematical structures that might suggest intelligence. He discovered phonology, phonetics, syntax."

"Language," Harper said.

"Not only language, but a voice. The voice was using Voyager 1 as a transmission device, asking for confirmation that all was well in paradise and that the next stage of evolution had begun. If confirmation was not received during the midnight hour, the voice said another attempt would be made in one thousand years of Earth time. One more thing: The voice chose to communicate in Zend."

Harper checked with the roadie. The roadie already knew the question in Harper's head.

"I know what you're thinking, brother. The little guy in the white coat in the basement at EPFL in Lausanne."

"Peabody. Professor Peabody."

"That's him. He ran the research through Blue Brain. It's solid."

"Does this voice from the other side of the universe have a name?" Harper said to Astruc.

"The Amini hymns have a thousand names for the voice. The most common is 'Creator of All.' And according to the hymns, He is watching the world this Night of Nights, waiting for the man of signs and wonders to guide Him in with an all-clear."

"Just like that. Say the magic words and presto. How's that work exactly?"

The priest shrugged. "I tell you how it works, as soon as you tell me why just now there are massive bursts of gamma rays and X-rays radiating from dead center of the Milky Way, twenty thousand light-years above and below the galactic plane. For lack of a better term, scientists are calling them Fermi bubbles. I would call it one more mystery of the universe, no more odd than the man of signs and wonders giving the all-clear to hail the arrival of a comet."

Harper scanned the priest's eyes. Insane he still might be, but his eternal being was fully awakened, calm and steady. Harper looked down at the Anointing Stone. He rubbed the back of his neck.

"You need a hit of something again, brother?" Krinkle said.

"No. I don't want anything. Just trying to wrap my head around the mysteries of the bloody universe."

The roadie sighed. "Yeah, and if we had time to think about it, we would. But listen to me, brother, right now we've got end-times crashing down in the real world. We are losing this war—in fact, it's friggin' lost if the enemy slaughters Max. A thousand years from now, when the Creator of All comes around again, there won't be a soul left to save—paradise will be a lifeless rock. This is it, brother. This is the sharp end of our two and a half million years on earth. We're flying into our last battle on the back of myths and legends, but it's all we've got."

Harper looked at Katherine.

"None of this explains why you're here, Madame Taylor," he said.

"I told you. I'm here to get my son back."

"Right."

Harper scanned her eyes. She was telling the truth, but not the whole truth. He turned to Astruc. "Anything else in the hymns I should know, Padre?"

The priest pointed to the things of Christ. "That you will use the cup to resurrect the third child of salvation, and the nails of the crucifixion to wound evil unto death."

"Rather poetic."

"Beautifully so. Which is why you will need these," the priest said. He held out two metal vials.

"For Max?"

"They need to be mixed in the cup at least sixty seconds before they are administered or they will have no effect."

"Why not just use injectors?"

The roadie shook his head. "We tried—the efficacy of the mix disintegrates in the injectors. Besides, we're skating such a fine line between us and the real world, we don't know if we're coming or friggin' going. HQ says we stay with myths and legends to be on the safe side."

Harper took the vials and dropped them in his trouser pockets. "Makes sense. But just so I'm clear, how do I use the nails to wound evil unto death? And while we're at it, how do I give the all-clear and call in the comet? Anyone know the magic words?"

Astruc traded glances with Krinkle and Katherine.

"What's wrong?" Harper said.

"Well, brother, we thought you would've figured that out by now. That intel was in the seventh scroll."

"I didn't read it."

"Oh shit. Why not?"

"What's in the seventh scroll is for Max, and Max alone."

Katherine's mouth hung open. Krinkle spoke the words she was thinking. "No friggin' way!"

Astruc raised his hand. "Peace. Our warrior angel will know what to do and when to do it."

"How?" Katherine said.

"Comme ça."

Astruc took Harper's gloved hands. He laid his thumbs over the wounds on Harper's palms. He did not press down, he just looked Harper in the eyes. "Feeling stubborn, or will you see him again?"

Harper flashed the Vevey Clinic before coming to the Holy Land. The priest had dug his thumbs into the wounds to send shock waves of pain through Harper's form . . . then, for a Planck unit of time, Harper had seen a suffering man fall under the weight of the crossbeam lashed to his shoulders. He blinked, saw Astruc waiting for an answer.

"Lead the way, Padre."

"Passover eve, 36 AD, Jerusalem. In the dungeon of Pontius Pilate's praetorium. *Intuebitur eam.*"

Harper ripped back on his timeline. It locked and rolled. He heard pitiful screams.

iii

The suffering man's arms are wrapped around a stone pillar, his hands bound with ropes and hooked to a wooden peg. He dangles like a broken thing. The man's robes are stripped from his back and his flesh has been torn open by the cat-o'-nine-tails in the hands of the soldier who takes great pleasure in torturing the prisoner. The suffering man cries out each time the iron nails in the leaded tips of the whip strike and rip at his flesh. The five soldiers watching laugh at the man's anguished cries.

A Cyrenian slave attends to the soldiers and fills their cups with wine. He will wash the stone floor of blood after the suffering man is taken away to be crucified. It has been his job for more than ten years, and he has witnessed the art of inflicting pain many times. He knows to scourge a prisoner is not to kill him; it is part of the ritual. It is designed to break his will and prepare him for sacrifice. The slave watches the whip tear at the suffering man's flesh again. The man cries out in despair, and his head falls to the side. The slave can see the man's eyes. The light of his soul is dying, but the soldiers are too drunk to notice and the torturer brandishing the whip is in a trance now. The smell of the suffering man's blood, the sound of his cries raises the torturer to a place of wicked joy, and the soldiers are lifted with him. They praise the gods of Rome with each scourge and tearing of flesh.

The slave shuffles to the commander, freshens his cup with wine.

"Centurion," the slave says. "Pilate will not be pleased if the man dies before he is to be crucified. You know the Governor's temper at such things."

The commander recovers his senses. "Enough," he calls out.

But the torturer continues to flay the suffering man. The commander rushes at him, pulls the whip away.

"Enough, I say!"

The commander drops the whip to the ground, examines the prisoner.

"Throw salt water on the Jew's back."

The torturer obeys. The suffering man writhes in agony as the salt burns his wounds. The commander shouts at his men.

"Stop! He has had enough for now, we will let him rest. There is plenty of life left in him yet. We will all have a turn at the whip, but he must live long enough to be slaughtered properly. One of you go to the gate. There is always one of the Essenes nearby waiting to attend to Herod if needed. Tell him there is a Jew in need of healing, tell him to be quick. The rest of you go into the garden, make a crown of thorns. That will freshen the prisoner for his crucifixion."

The soldiers dress in their armor and collect their swords. The commander falls onto a stool and leans against the wall. He dozes, but then snaps awake.

"Be sure one of you makes his death plaque for the cross. Make it read 'Jesus of Nazareth, King of the Jews.' Those are our orders, do you hear?"

The soldiers acknowledge their orders and leave the dungeon. The commander reaches into the leather pouch on his belt. He takes out three pieces of silver, holds them out to the slave.

"You are wise, old man."

The slave knows the commander is a ruthless executioner who enjoys inflicting pain on the weak and making it last as long as possible. The slave takes the coins, bows his head.

"As you are generous, Centurion."

The commander is unaccustomed to such familiarity from the old Cyrenian. "What is your name, slave?"

"I do not know my name, Centurion. I only know I am here."

"You dare to mock me?"

"No, Centurion. I fear you for the terrible death on the cross you will bring to me. But know that the instruments of my crucifixion will be used to wound evil unto death. Then shall it be, with my final words, that the light of the Pure God is revealed in paradise."

"What . . . do you say? Are you a sorcerer?"

The slave passes the palm of his hand before the commander's eyes. *"Dulcis et alta quies placidæque simillima morti."*

The commander becomes like stone. The slave takes the cup of wine from the soldier's hand and dumps the wine onto the stones. He shuffles to the suffering man, searches his eyes for light. The man is delirious, his consciousness sinking into darkness.

"I thirst," he murmurs.

The slave reaches in his cloak and removes a small calfskin pouch. He opens it and pours iridescent liquid into a cup. He raises it to the suffering man's lips.

"Drink this. It will ease the pain."

He offers the cup. The liquid spills from the man's mouth.

"Drink, you must drink."

The suffering man raises his head and sees the old slave before him.

"My God has forsaken me," the man says.

The slave shakes his head. "You are not forsaken, and your suffering is at an end. This day your soul will take its place among the stars."

The man's head sinks, death is taking him. The slave moves closer to him and holds the man in his arms.

"Look into my eyes, Yeshua ben Yosef, listen to the sound of my voice. The light of your soul will *not* die, it must never die. Drink of this cup. Drink so you will escape forever death, drink so your name will be remembered." The Cyrenian holds the cup to the suffering man's lips again and he drinks . . .

iv

Harper blinked.

The priest let go of his hands.

"Am I supposed to thank you for that trip through beforetimes?" Harper said.

"In fact, it is we who should thank you. After all, you're the one who lived it, and you're the one who must live it again."

Harper looked at the broken cup on the Anointing Stone. The same cup he held to the lips of the suffering man. *Drink so you will escape forever death*. Harper bent down, picked up the pieces of the cup and the four carpenter nails. He handed the cup to Krinkle.

"You don't happen to have any glue in your duffel bag, do you?"

"I'm a rock-and-roll roadie, I got gaffer tape."

"Do it. Then keep the cup in the pouch of your overalls."

The roadie fitted the pieces of the cup together and secured them with tape. Harper stared at the four carpenter nails. He wrapped them in a piece of calfskin, tucked them in his belt. He lifted the lad's lantern from the Anointing Stone, stared at the delicate flame atop the wick.

"We need candles. Lots of them."

TWENTY-SEVEN

i

There was a gift shop at the end of the passage leading to the Place of Mourning. It took Krinkle 4.5 seconds to pick the lock. Inside was a cavernous room with religious postcards and calendars, crosses and icons, bottles of Holy Water from the Holy Land, and thousands of candles laid out on a long table. The smallest candles were five shekels each—a dollar and a quarter. A small cardboard sign announced the shop also took euros and Jordanian dinars. Harper did the math: *A dollar and a quarter times twelve million tourists a year equals money changing is still alive and well in Jerusalem.*

"Stuff your pockets with candles," Harper said.

They grabbed them by the handful and loaded up.

"Let's go," Harper said.

"Wait a sec," Katherine said. "Who's paying for the candles? We can't just steal from a church."

Astruc made the sign of the cross over Katherine's head. "You are forgiven, my child."

They ran to the rotunda. Harper lifted the lantern and a cloud of light filled the space under the great dome. It was like the inside of a layer cake. Four rings of gothic arches supporting a dome sixty feet in diameter. A hundred feet up, the ceiling was decorated with stars and golden rays of light emanating from the dome's center. Harper stared at the peak of the dome, saw a dark circle at the center and small points of light within it. *A window framing a star-studded Night of Nights,* he thought. He lowered his eyes to the shrine beneath the dome. It was an odd-looking thing. The stone was darker than the Jerusalem stone of the church's interior walls, and the structure seemed bound together. He stepped closer, held the lantern close to the shrine. Red marble, not Jerusalem stone; all enclosed in a cage of steel beams and crossbars to keep the thing from falling apart. Lamps hung along the sides, but with electricity to the Old City cut off, the lamps were dark. Harper saw trays of sand attached to the side of the shrine and candle stubs standing in the sand. He saw thousands of scorch marks burned into the red marble. He could imagine the scene: pilgrims buying candles, lighting them, then snuffing them out against the red marble of the shrine. The candles would be wrapped like holy things and carried back into the real world. Harper scanned the rotunda. Pillars and arches, open passageways in walls, and old wooden doors. He looked at Astruc.

"You know this place, yeah?"

"I was a priest. What do you think?"

"If we draw them into the rotunda, can we cover our flanks? Reach an escape route if needed?"

Astruc scratched his goatee and thought about it. He pointed to the opening between two walls facing the shrine. Light from the rotunda spilled into a large rectangular room. Harper saw the Byzantine Christ in the ceiling looking down.

"That's the Catholicum," Astruc said. "At the far end, beyond the two thrones, there are two doors leading into the ambulatory. Just across are steps heading underground. They lead to the Chapel of Saint Helen. In the corner is a stone alcove, the Chapel of the True Cross it's called. It's protected on three sides and there is no getting above us."

"And getting out?"

"Very close to the chapel there is a passage to the quarries beneath the church."

"Let me guess: You know of a hidden tunnel that leads back up to the streets."

"Yes, but it was walled up in the nineteenth century. We will need to blow through the wall."

"I got what we need in the duffel bag," Krinkle said.

"Right. First, we light up the shrine and set up candles at all the doors and passageways in and out of here. Stand the candles in six-point formations, keep the formations close together."

"Why?" Krinkle said.

"Tell you later."

Harper opened the door of the lad's lantern; they all reached in with their candles. At first the wicks would not light, then came a bright spark and four new flames were born. They moved quickly. When they were done, Astruc and Katherine met Harper at the entrance to the shrine, each holding a lighted candle in one hand and a bunch of candles in the other.

"Done. Krinkle's doing the doors and passageways."

Harper studied the shrine. The door was shut and locked; the path leading to it was lined with towering candle stands topped with dead electric flame-shaped lamps. But their own candles had lit up the red marble stone of the shrine and it glowed with a flickering light. So did the rays of gold light in the dome high overhead, and there were still stars in the dark center of the dome.

Flash.

Roman soldiers ram a crown of thorns down on the head of their prisoner. His scalp is sliced open, and blood drips in his eyes and down his chest. The soldiers cut the prisoner down from the pillar; he falls. They drag him into the courtyard, load a heavy timber across his shoulders, lash his hands to it. They haul him to his feet, march him through the narrow streets of the upper city. People on balconies and in the streets spit on the prisoner, curse him. Coming to Gennath Gate now, falling to his knees once more. The prisoner raises his head. Through the blood in his eyes he sees the black stones of Golgotha. Two prisoners had already been crucified. One was hanging from his cross; the other, his hands nailed to a crossbeam, was being hoisted up onto a post. *Give me strength . . .*

Blink.

"Let's keep moving," Harper said.

He hustled along the passageway to the entrance hall; Katherine and Astruc followed. He pointed to the ambulatory ahead and the stairs going up to the Chapel of the Crucifixion.

"Those two places next. Madame Taylor, take the ambulatory. Astruc, take the stairs and the chapel inside. I'll do the Anointing Stone."

Astruc ran up the stairs, and Katherine headed into the ambulatory. They laid walls of fire across the access points. Harper set the lad's lantern on the stone slab and built a wide oval-shaped firewall around it. He called to Astruc.

"Can you jump down from there into the ambulatory and get around the rotunda, Padre?"

"Or I could take the second set of stairs at the side of the chapel."

"Whatever, you're up there for now."

Krinkle was approaching from the passageway. Harper pointed to the floor stones. "Set candles at the crossing into the entrance hall."

Krinkle dropped to his knees, started arranging candles and lighting them. "You want to tell me why I'm doing it while I'm doing it, brother?"

Harper gathered the calfskins from the Anointing Stone, rolled them up and tied them closed with rope. "Something I read in the scrolls. The scribe wrote he saw six angels set fires in six-point formations around their camp. He wrote it looked like they were setting themselves behind unseen walls drawn by the fires. He wrote the light of the fires crossed the desert and pierced his eyes."

Harper saw *bingo* race through the roadie's eyes.

"We used the first fire as cover," Krinkle said, "because goons couldn't jump the first fire. Why the hell wouldn't we know that in nowtimes?"

"You said it yourself, the savior mission was a black ops job. No one knew about it, not even HQ. Everything about it was wiped from our timelines, including that bit of intel."

"Perhaps the enemy's fear of the first fire is only superstition," Astruc mused aloud, tugging at his beard.

Harper shrugged. "Who cares, Padre? If it works, it works, and we've got ourselves a kill box."

"What if it isn't superstition?" Katherine said. "And what if you guys can't jump the fire, either?"

Harper looked at Astruc and Krinkle; they were both looking at him.

"Madame Taylor makes a good point," Astruc said.

Harper grabbed the roadie's duffel bag, stuffed the calfskins inside, and zipped the bag closed. He picked it up and faced the candles on the floor, staring at the haze of light rising before him.

"Here goes."

He passed through the firewall.

"Impressive," Krinkle said.

Harper walked toward him, tossed the duffel to him through the roadie's firewall. The roadie caught it.

"Careful, brother. It's full of things that go boom."

"Sorry. Here's the deal: The goons will come through those doors in waves."

"You sure?"

"Father Astruc's priestly touch is causing me flashes. This hall lines up along the last steps of the Way of Sorrows. Just now, the goons are like me, they've got no bloody choice but to walk the walk, including Komarovsky. When the first wave materializes, wait for them to charge so we know they're not apparitions. We take as many down as we can with head shots."

"Oh," Krinkle said. "I forgot to tell you. The new ammo is for body shots. Anywhere within a five-inch circle of dead center."

Harper looked at him. "But a head shot will do just as well, yeah?"

"Oh yeah. We just have more kill for the bullet on this job."

"Good to know. Astruc and Madame Taylor—"

"For God's sake, Harper. Considering we're about to go to war, do you think you guys could just call me Kat and save your breath?"

Astruc and Krinkle were looking at Harper again.

"Your call, brother. Command protocols in back-to-the-wall jobs come under the heading of 'your friggin' job.'"

"Fine. Komarovsky is on the same clock we are. He needs to kill Max in the midnight hour. We hold the entrance long enough for Komarovsky to know he's got a fight on his hands. When I give the call, Astruc and Madame Taylor fall back to the rotunda through the ambulatory. Krinkle falls back from the passageway. Set up at the shrine, establish a fire line, and hold."

"Then what?" Katherine said.

"That depends on Komarovsky. Our mission is to secure your son by any means that will buy me enough time to give the all-clear."

"What do you mean 'buy enough time'?" Krinkle said. "You do it as soon as we get Max."

Harper shook his head. "There is no all-clear until Komarovsky is finished. He does not get away this time. Otherwise Max will never be safe. Sorting Komarovsky is my job. Is that understood?"

Harper checked the nodding heads: one, two . . . Katherine did not nod. He stared at her through the glow of their firewalls. She had that same *I'm just here to get my son back* expression on her face.

"Is that understood, Madame Taylor?"

Her emerald-colored eyes sparked in the light. As he watched her, a thought dropped in Harper's head. A voice calling from the other side of the universe asking for confirmation that all was well in paradise and if the next stage of evolution had begun; that was the brief from Astruc. Looking at Katherine Taylor just now, Harper sensed the next stage of evolution *had* begun. Katherine Taylor wasn't just the mother of the child conceived in light or the child of the prophecy or just an ordinary little boy called Max; she was the mother of a new life-form on the planet. Question: Then why the hell did Inspector Gobet send her into a battle zone with minimal chance of survival? The dead soldier in Harper's head dropped an answer: *If the cop wanted you to know, he would have bloody well told you, boyo.*

"Yeah, I understand, Harper," Katherine said. "What I don't understand is why the walls are moving."

Harper scanned the massive space of the entrance hall. He saw it: walls bending outward, ceiling rising, the floor stones stretching and widening like some insane hallucination.

Astruc called down from the top of the stairs. "Komarovsky is creating another dimension of space-time within the walls of the church so he can fit in as many goons as he wants."

"You mean he's making this place bigger?" Katherine said.

"It won't be bigger in reality," Krinkle called from his position. "But it will sure as hell feel like it."

Katherine looked at Harper; he was staring at her again. "What?"

"Sorry?"

"Is there something else on your mind besides space-time? Or are you just making eyes at me?" she said.

Harper pulled one of his SIGs from his belt and loaded a round into the firing chamber: *ka-clack.*

"There was something on my mind, but I think I figured it out."

"From what I'm told, you always do," Katherine said.

Harper turned, faced the doors of the church. *Flying into our last battle on the back of myths and legends,* the roadie had said . . . *Hang on.* He reached into his sports coat, found the matchbox from LP's Bar, and dropped it in his trousers pocket. Then he dug through the coat again and pulled out the regimental tie of the 28th Artists Rifles. It was still knotted, and he slipped it over his head and fitted it around his neck.

"Nice tie, brother," Krinkle called from beyond his firewall.

Harper looked at him. "Cheers, mate. How much time left?"

The roadie looked at his watch. "None."

Then came the tolling of a single bell in the tower, tolling in threes and sixes. *They're dying; the children are dying . . .* Like Clémence, the execution bell in the belfry of Lausanne Cathedral. *Swell,* Harper thought, *just what the world needs: a One True God with a fucked-up sense of humor.* Harper picked up the lad's lantern, held it at his side.

"They're here."

ii

The great doors of the church were opened by unseen hands, and the sounds of Jerusalem's war rushed in. The dark sky above the rooftops sparkled with stars and tracer fire. On the ground, sixteen shadows appeared in the outer courtyard. They floated toward the church and held at the threshold. Slowly, they crept across and floated over the floor stones. They wandered like blind things feeling their way. When they neared the firewalls, they pulled back.

"What do you know? It works," Harper said.

The shadows gathered in the center of the floor in a wedge formation. One at the point, then two, then three, then a line of ten; then there were sixteen goons in black jumpsuits and balaclavas. They were crouching low to the floor. They rose to their feet with heads bowed and revealed the lances in their hands. The weapons were ancient and well-used things; wood staves, iron pyramidal tips and shanks. They raised their faces and opened their dead black eyes. The goon at the point scanned the faces behind the firewalls. It locked its dark eyes on Katherine Taylor for a long moment before addressing Harper.

"Surrender the whore," it said.

Harper looked at Katherine. "I guess it means you, Madame Taylor."

"I guess it does."

"Do you feel like being surrendered?"

"Not at the moment."

"Fine." He turned to the goon."Sod off."

He put a bullet into the goon's head. The thing glowed like being set alight from within and it dropped; its dead black eyes melted and dripped from its skull. The rest of the goons charged; Katherine, Krinkle, and Astruc opened up. The goons whirled like dervishes; they deflected the bullets with the flat sides of their lances. Harper held the lad's lantern high.

"C'est le guet! Il a sonné l'heure!"

The flame in the lantern and all the flames in the church flared with the light of the sun and the goons were truly blinded. SIGs emptied. Five seconds later, the floor stones were littered with brain-fried goons; fifteen seconds later their forms turned to ash. A menacing wind rushed through the doors and scattered it. The firewalls dimmed as the ash tried to choke out the candles. Harper held the lad's lantern high over his head.

"Transit umbra, lux permanet!"

The firewalls held and the ash dissolved into oblivion. The wind died away. Except for the war in the real world, there was no sound.

"Reload," Harper said.

Clicks and clacks sounded as ammo magazines were swapped out. Katherine Taylor's voice echoed off the stone walls.

"Okay, that's sixteen less of them."

"That was only a recon unit," Astruc said. "Probing our defensives, reporting our numbers, seeing who is who."

"But they're dead, they won't be reporting anything," Katherine said.

Krinkle called from beyond the firewall at the passageway. "Komarovsky can see the world through their eyes. Before their eyes melted in their heads, I mean."

Harper stared at Katherine. "And he sure as hell saw you."

She stared back. "I guess he did."

Bloody hell, so that's it, Harper thought.

He lifted the lantern from the Anointing Stone, passed through his firewall, and walked to Krinkle. "Take the lantern, stash it quick. If they kill this fire, they kill the rest."

"Roger that."

Harper returned to his position. He faced the door.

Flash.

. . . the prisoner staggers through the killing fields of Golgotha; he cannot support the crossbeam on his shoulders any longer. He falls a third time, this time on his back. The crossbeam hits the back of his head and drives the crown of thorns deeper into his skull. The prisoner cries out in agony, and blood spills onto the black rock. The Roman commander stands over the man, kicks him in the side. The commander is not pleased with the prisoner's dulled senses. He turns to his soldiers, calls for the Essene healer attending the crucifixion. The commander wants the prisoner conscious when the nails are hammered into his flesh . . .

Blink.

Fifteen goons in black now, all taking form in the entrance hall of the church. They were tall, powerfully built. This time they stood in a Cannae formation behind bloodred shields; three sets of two to the left and the right, three soldiers in line at the middle, inviting Harper to attack at their weak center. The goons drew short swords, slapped them against their shields, and marched ahead.

"Let 'em have it."

Harper fired three rounds into the goons, one went down. Katherine, Krinkle, and Astruc opened up and two more goons dropped. The rest raised their shields and formed a shell. Spark rounds ricocheted off stone and ripped through the hall. Harper charged, hit the ground, and slid into the middle of the formation. He pulled one of the goons to the ground, pressed his SIG point-blank against the thing's body mass, and fired. The goon skidded back and broke open the formation. Harper pulled a shield over himself as bullets rained down on the goons. The bullets stopped, and Harper tossed the shield aside. He was surrounded by goons bleeding dead black from their eyes.

"Fall back."

Astruc charged down the chapel's back stairs; Katherine got up and followed the priest down the ambulatory. Krinkle called to Harper.

"Hey, brother, you sure about this?"

Flash.

. . . the Essene touches the prisoner's bloody lips with a sponge soaked in myrrh. The prisoner revives a little, looks into the Essene's eyes. "Remember these words, healer, pass them to those who will take me down from the cross." The prisoner's voice is weak and he speaks in a whisper. The Essene leans close to him and listens . . .

Blink.

"I'm sure," Harper said. "We're about to have a visitor."

Krinkle, Astruc and Katherine retreated. Harper got to his feet. He kicked the dead goon closest to him. The thing turned to ash. He walked around the floor stones kicking each of them; they all turned to ash. He waited for the rush of wind to come through the doors, but it did not come, and for the moment the courtyard was clear of incoming shadows. Harper smiled to himself. Komarovsky was out there thinking things over, unsure of his next move. The real world reflected the pause, and the sounds of war in the Old City quieted.

"Right."

He stuffed his killing knife in its sheath, leaned down, and picked up one of the swords from the floor stones. He crossed back behind his firewall at the Anointing Stone. His right thigh throbbed, and he saw blood seeping through the bandage. The roadie had hit him with an injector jet and he felt no pain, but the wound had broken open.

"Swell."

Outside the church a grinding roar echoed off the stone walls of the courtyard. Harper scanned the real world beyond the doors. He saw the attack chopper, hovering low over the rooftops now. Its nose stooped into a firing position and a Hydra rocket fired from its left wing—*whoosh*—and then came a mighty crump as the rocket found its target. The thick walls of the church trembled as a fireball rose into the night.

"Really, really swell."

He knelt on one knee. He laid the SIG and sword on the ground. He tightened the bandage to stop the bleeding. When he finished, he looked at his hands. For a second he thought it was blood smeared from his leg; then he saw droplets of blood seeping through the bioskin gloves covering his palms.

Flash.

. . . the commander orders two of his soldiers to step on the prisoner's wrists. When they do, the commander kneels near the prisoner's head, leans over him, and presses the point of the first nail into the prisoner's left palm. The commander raises a hammer, swings down hard, and drives the nail through the prisoner's hand. *My God!* The commander presses the point of the second nail into the prisoner's right palm and swings down again with the hammer once, twice, thrice. *Ahhh!* The prisoner is suspended in a place of crushing pain. He sees the commander's face; black drool drips from the corners of his mouth and his silver eyes are wide with rapture . . .

Blink.

Then a paregoric voice wrapped in a Russian accent: "Now the dog of war raises his angry hackles to fight for the stripped bones of majesty and snarls in the gentle face of peace."

Harper looked up and saw a tall man standing in the entrance hall. He had long silver hair and wore a black overcoat. There was a black scarf around his neck and dark glasses over his eyes.

"Well, well, what do we have here? If I didn't know better I'd say you're the spitting image of Komarovsky. I was just thinking about you, I think. Can't be sure, there's a lot of looping going on in my head just now. I suppose that's to be expected, yeah? How about dropping the shades so I can get a positive ID."

Harper saw the slightest of smiles form at the corners of Komarovsky's mouth.

"Give me the whore," he said.

"You can't be serious, pal. You've already drugged her and raped her, kidnapped her son, and condemned her to hell. Hard to top all that for a night out, isn't it?"

"She belongs to me."

Harper smiled. "Well, well, what do you know? You're as surprised to see her here as I was, aren't you? I'd say you're smitten in your own sick way. I get it, she's rather special. In fact, she's more than special, she's one-of-a-kind."

"I will have her."

Harper picked up his SIG and got to his feet. "Over my dead form. And by the way . . ." He fired a round into Komarovsky's skull. The bullet passed through as if passing through a cloud. ". . . sod off with the apparition shit and send in the clowns."

Komarovsky disappeared.

"Everything A-OK out there, brother?"

Harper turned, saw Krinkle, Astruc, and Katherine standing behind the firewall at the passage to the Place of Mourning.

"No worries. I thought I saw a ghost. Is the lantern safe?"

"Yup."

Out in the real world, automatic weapons cracked and another Israeli rocket found a target. The outer courtyard flared with a burst of light, and the Church of the Holy Sepulchre shook again. Harper watched the light spark on the Anointing Stone.

Flash.

. . . the soldiers haul the prisoner from the ground, drag him to the post standing between the two crucified men. They tie a thick rope around the crossbeam, toss it over the top of the post, and haul up the prisoner from the ground. One soldier grabs the prisoner's legs and lifts him so the hole in the crossbeam lines up with the top of the post. The crossbeam drops into place and the prisoner's weight pulls against the nails in his hands. *God!* The soldiers grab the prisoner's dangling legs and hold his ankles to either side of the post. The commander sets the third nail to the prisoner's left ankle bone, swings the hammer, and drives the nail through flesh and bone. The prisoner lifts his head to cry out, but there is no sound. The commander sets the fourth nail to the prisoner's right ankle and hammers it into place. *Dear God, the pain!*

"Harper, look out!" Katherine cried.

He blinked, saw a goon with a spear charging through the doors.

"I bring you forever death!"

Harper dived to the side, raised his SIG, fired a round into the goon's chest. The thing flew back, but it had anticipated Harper's move. The spear caught him in the stomach.

"Ah, fuck!"

"Harper!"

iii

Krinkle jumped through the firewall. Katherine made the same move, but Astruc grabbed her cloak and held her back.

"We stay and kill anything coming through the doors," he said.

"Understood."

The two of them crouched into firing stances and targeted the doors. Near the Anointing Stone, Krinkle checked Harper's wound.

"How bad?" Harper said.

"Sliced your side. No organ damage."

"Incoming," Astruc shouted.

Two more goons with spears now. SIGs opened up and the goons went down. Krinkle pulled a pressure bandage from his overalls, ripped it open, and set it over the wound.

"Press down on this, brother, and keep your head up."

The roadie jumped up, grabbed Harper by the ankles, and dragged him over the floor stones toward the firewall at the passageway.

"Make a hole!"

Astruc and Katherine moved out of the way and Krinkle crashed through the firewall.

"More company at the door," Katherine said.

She crouched behind the left corner; Astruc took the right. Three goons crossed the threshold with spears, then five more. They spread out in the entrance hall forming two lines of four. They spotted Astruc and Katherine.

"Give us the whore!"

"Drop dead," Katherine said.

The first line let go with their spears. Astruc and Katherine ducked behind the stone walls and the spears whipped by. The first line of goons was marching forward with swords drawn; the second line followed with lowered spears. Astruc and Katherine jumped out from behind the walls and fired. Muzzles flashed as SIGS exploded in rapid fire. Bullets caught skulls and body mass; goons squealed and dropped. The floor stones and walls of the entrance hall were splattered with dead black. Out beyond the doors hundreds more shadows descended into the courtyard.

"Holy crap. That's a hell of a lot more than fifty," Katherine said.

"Let's fall back."

"Wait. Where is my son? He's supposed to be here. What's happening?"

Astruc looked out the doors once more for a recce of the ground.

"That's what we need to figure out, Madame Taylor. Come on."

They hustled into the rotunda. Harper and Krinkle were in an alcove behind a firewall. Harper's sports coat had been pulled off. His shirt and regimental tie were stained with blood. Krinkle was next to him, pulling long bandages from his duffel bag and wrapping them around Harper's midsection. Astruc and Katherine passed through the firewall.

"What's happening out there?" Harper said.

Astruc leaned against the wall, swapped out magazines in his SIG.

"Looks like the entire Fifth Cohort is arriving now, four hundred more players at least. The word must be out they had the man of signs and wonders and his accomplices cornered."

Krinkle snorted. "Stupid shits. Only took them two thousand years to track us down."

Harper thought about it. "With that many goons, we've got five or six minutes until they all materialize."

"How is the wound?" Astruc said.

"Ask Krinkle."

The roadie was wrapping up Harper's shoulder now. "It took a chunk out of his external oblique muscle. I cauterized the wound with healing potion, but the tip was coated with snuff," he said.

"How much?"

"Almost enough to do the trick."

Katherine didn't like the expressions on the angels' beat-up faces. "What the hell is snuff?"

"Here, let go of the pressure bandage, brother. I got it now," Krinkle said.

Harper lowered his hand, and the roadie did a quick mummy job around Harper's midsection.

"It's what it sounds like, Madame Taylor," Harper said.

"Well, there's an antidote, isn't there? You have the antidote in your bag, don't you, Krinkle? You've got enough for everyone, don't you?"

The roadie shook his head. "Snuff is expressly designed for specific targets based on intel picked up from previous encounters."

"What the fuck does that mean?"

Harper shifted his weight to ease the pain. "It means the bad guys had a crew scouring the battlegrounds in Lausanne and Paris looking for any trace of my DNA. Once they found it they could develop a potion to slowly destroy the platelets in my blood. All they had to do was get it inside me."

"So what do we do about it?" Katherine said.

"It's all right, Madame Taylor," Harper said. "It won't kill me, not unless they get me again. In the meantime I need to duck a bit faster."

Silence.

"Madame Taylor was asking about her son," Astruc said.

Harper nodded. "I've been sitting here asking myself about him, too. How much time till midnight?"

"Thirty-eight minutes."

Harper looked at Katherine. "The ghost out there before I was hit. It was an apparition of Komarovsky. He's smitten with the brand-new you. He wants to kiss and make up, make you a goddess in his temple."

"Bullshit," Katherine said.

"Of course it's bullshit. But it's bullshit we can use. Padre, how long will it take to get out of this place if we blast our way out through the quarry?"

Astruc pulled at his goatee. "If we move before the next attack, five minutes. Otherwise we'll have to fall back in stages."

"Right. We wait for the next attack. Madame Taylor, you'll stay here in the alcove, the rest of us position ourselves around the rotunda. We're going to stage it so the goons cut you off from us and force us to run for it."

"Then what?" Katherine said.

"You surrender."

Katherine stared at him. Harper read she wasn't that surprised at the suggestion.

"And do what?" she said.

"Tell Komarovsky you saw me take another spear or a sword, or whatever the hell they use this time. We'll fake it for their bloody viewing pleasure. Tell him you heard someone yell something about snuff potion. Tell him you thought it was over and you want to make a deal: you for your son. Make him believe he can have you as long as he lets Max live. Make him believe he can have whatever he wants from you. Make him believe you'll make all his dreams come true. After all, that's why Inspector Gobet sent you on this mission, isn't it?"

Silence again as Krinkle tied off the bandages. Katherine stared at Harper, waiting for Krinkle to hit him with an injector jet for pain.

"Feeling better?" she said.

"Good as new."

"Then fuck you, Harper. And as you seem to have a problem figuring it out, I'm the one on this crew who's going to confirm that evil piece of shit ends up forever dead."

"No worries. Took me a little time, but I did figure it out. What I haven't figured out is if you know what it means."

"Harper . . ."

"Do you what it means to confirm forever death?"

"Yes."

"And do you have the power?"

"Yes."

"How? Did the cop juice you with potions or cast a spell?"

Astruc rested his hand on Harper's shoulder. "Monsieur Gabriel gave it to her."

"Why?"

The priest did not answer. Harper grabbed the roadie's arm. "Why?"

Krinkle shook his head. "Sorry, brother, you know how it is."

"More orders? More orders to not tell me the truth?"

"Check."

Harper looked at Katherine.

"That leaves the truth-telling to you, Madame Taylor. Why are you the one to confirm his forever death?"

Katherine drew a slow breath. "Gabriel said you were too weak to do it."

"To do what? What did he tell you about me, exactly?"

Krinkle coughed. "Brother, you're asking her to spill things from the messenger. That's a huge no-no. Brother Astruc and me aren't even clued in to his exact instructions."

"But Madame Taylor can choose to tell me anything she bloody well wants. Isn't that true . . . Kat?"

Katherine nodded. "He said, 'The light within him struggles to live. He will draw out the enemy and wound him, but he is too weak to destroy him. It falls to another.'"

"You."

"Yes. But is doesn't mean you'll die in your form. Gabriel told me . . ."

"Stop, don't say anymore. You've told me all I need to know. Now I'll tell you something. Komarovsky will get inside your head. When he does, he'll know you're lying to him and he'll punish you. You must hold on until we get back."

"I understand."

Harper stared at her; the dead soldier in his head piped up. . . . *Good soldiers always understand their orders; many of them die anyway, boyo. Doesn't mean they won't end up dead anyway.*

"Good. Krinkle, get a bandage and wipe blood on Madame Taylor's cloak and my coat. Leave my coat here. Get me the lantern and let's get into position, smear blood over the floor stones along the way."

"Should we reset the firewall?"

"No, let them come."

TWENTY-EIGHT

i

Two minutes later bad shadows gathered at the passage to the Place of Mourning. When the shadows took form, twenty-five goons were lined up in rows of five; they carried bloodred shields. The first line drew swords, slapped the fronts of their shields, and marched through the gap in the firewall. The second line bore spears.

SIGs fired. A few bullets caught skulls and those goons dropped; most bullets hit shields, sparked with fire, and fell to the floor stones. The goons formed a wall across the rotunda and spears came flying over the shields at Harper, Astruc, and Krinkle. They drew back behind corners and the spears crashed into stone walls. Harper watched Krinkle reach into his duffel bag and pull two stun grenades. The roadie pulled the pins, reached around the corner, and tossed them across the floor stones toward the goons. Just under the shields the grenades detonated with deafening bangs. The goons staggered and tripped. SIGs opened again and nine goons fell before they reset their shields, then came another wave of spears. One was coming for Harper, and he went hyperspeed: dropping his gun, catching the spear, and pulling it to his stomach.

"Fuck!"

Astruc and Krinkle rushed to him. Krinkle broke the shaft from the tip, wiped it against Harper's bloodied shirt, and dropped it on the floor; he stuffed the tip of the spear in his overalls.

"You ready, brother?"

"Make it look good."

The roadie yelled toward Katherine. "They've got him with snuff! We need to get him out of here! Madame Taylor, fall back!"

"I can't, I'm surrounded!"

Krinkle shouldered his duffel bag and Astruc grabbed the lantern; they hauled Harper into the Catholicum and passed under the gaze of the Byzantine Christ.

"And the friggin' Oscar goes to our sneaky butts," the roadie said with a laugh.

They got to the far end of the room before nine goons appeared at the entrance. Krinkle pulled his second SIG and fired both his guns at the bad guys; Astruc fired through the locks of the doors and kicked them open.

"Let's go," he said.

They carried Harper through the doorway and into the ambulatory. It was dark at this end of the church, and the lantern filled the space with hallowed light. A wide set of stone stairs was dead ahead. Harper got to his feet and took the lantern from Astruc.

"Hold them for five minutes, then catch up, Padre."

"Avec plaisir, mon ami."

Harper and Krinkle charged down the stairs. Harper leaned back into a wall and pressed his hands to his sides.

"You doing okay, brother?"

"For someone too weak to finish the job, you mean? Like the last time?"

"What are you talking about?"

"Me. Golgotha. The last time. I was too weak to finish the job then, too. That's the truth of it, isn't it?"

"What you did the last time was give our kind a way out when we were trapped. What you did the last time was reset the cosmic clock, brother. BC became AD. That bought the human race two thousand years of hope, and our kind one more chance to deliver some cosmic payback."

"You sure about that, mate?"

"Ask me if we get through tonight in one piece. But yeah, that would be my guess at the moment."

"Fair enough. What else do you have in your bag of tricks?" Harper said.

"Enough to bring down the house."

"How about just enough to slow down the goons until we get them into the tunnels? Then we bury them."

Krinkle nodded. "I can do that."

Krinkle dropped the bag, opened it, and pulled out six small IEDs, all of them radio-controlled.

"These charges won't damage the church, but they will fuck up any goon walking by. At least that's what Gobet told me."

"Go to work."

Krinkle gaffer-taped the charges to the pillars at the bottom of the stairs. Harper panned the lantern through the dark. It was a huge underground cavern with hundreds of Armenian lamps hanging from the domed ceiling. Icons and paintings on the walls, a large mosaic on the floor, an altar across from the stairwell.

"This must be the Chapel of Saint Helen. Where is the Chapel of the True Cross?" Harper said.

Krinkle was setting two more charges in the middle of the cavern. "To the right of this place, a small set of stairs going down, Astruc said. I think."

Harper walked ahead, panned the lantern, and found the stairs. He called back, "It's over here."

"Cool. I'm coming with Brother Astruc, soon as we—"

Gunshots and flashes of fire exploded from the Catholicum and rotunda. *Another wave of goons closing in,* Harper thought. Then it went quiet. Thirty seconds later, Krinkle appeared at the entrance to the Chapel of the True Cross.

"—kill a few goons."

Astruc came with the lantern in hand.

"What's happening in the rotunda, Padre?"

"They're closing in on Madame Taylor, but being very careful about it. It's obvious their orders are to not harm a hair on her head, not yet. Another platoon is coming after us, they're regrouping in the ambulatory now."

Harper looked at Krinkle. "Give me the detonator."

Krinkle handed it over. "Just flip the switch," the roadie said.

"Got it. Same setup here as the other place, on the same detonator. Shape the charge back into the Chapel of Saint Helen. Then Astruc shows you where we need to blow through the wall."

It took a few minutes to rig the charges, then Astruc took the lead and headed down the stairs. They came into a low-ceilinged, rock-cut alcove with a simple stone altar and cross. There was a brown mosaic in the floor; it held an image of a plain wooden cross. Harper scanned the place. He saw chisel strikes in the ceiling and remnants of frescoes on the walls.

"Where is the way out?" Harper said.

Astruc pointed to a low archway. "There."

Harper ran over and looked in. Small set of wooden stairs going up. Under the stairs was a low steel door built into the wall. Weirdly enough it was one of those things no one would notice if they were not looking for it; there wasn't even a lock on it, just a cross brace.

"Through the door?" Harper said.

"Yes, the sealed-up wall is only a hundred feet in."

"How the hell did you know about it?"

"I spent two years here doing archaeological research while I was in seminary."

"Lucky for us."

"Luck had nothing to do with it. It was always part of the plan."

'Whose plan?" Harper said.

The priest smiled as if he knew but wasn't telling. "Does it matter?"

"I suppose not. How long till you're ready to blow the wall, Krinkle?"

"Couple minutes more."

Harper pulled a candle from his pocket, lit it from the lantern, and stood it on the floor stones. He pulled his second SIG from his belt.

"Right, get to it and take the lad's lantern. I'll hold off the goons."

Krinkle and Astruc headed for the way out. The roadie stopped.

"Oh, did I mention when you set off the charges to close your eyes really tight? And don't stand in the open or anywhere within the target zone?"

"No worries," Harper said.

He headed back up the small steps. He heard boots on the ground. He eased around the wall, scanned the cavern of the Chapel of Saint Helen. The platoon was marching down from the ambulatory now and coming into the cavern. They had abandoned their shields and were holding short swords now. They were ready for close-quarters fighting. Harper crouched down, flipped the switch on the detonator, and set it on the floor stones. He stood and gently rested the sole of his left shoe atop the magic button. He loaded a round into the firing chamber: *kaclack*. The metallic sound caught the attention of the goons, and when they turned to it, they saw Harper standing in the open with the death end of his gun pointed their way.

"Come to say a few rosaries, boys?"

Harper emptied his magazine. Two goons dropped, the rest charged. Harper stepped back behind the wall, closed his eyes, flipped the switch. There was a muffled crump and a wave of sizzling heat. Even with his eyes shut tight he saw a red glow against the backs of his eyelids. Then quiet. Harper leaned back out around the wall. Nothing, not even piles of ash.

"Blimey."

He headed back to the Chapel of the True Cross. He picked up the candle from the floor and rushed to the now open steel door. He holstered his SIG and held the candle through the opening. It was a half-walking, half-crawling job through a black hole.

"Bugger."

He ducked in and scurried like a rat on the run. He went left and right before reaching Krinkle and Astruc at a small bricked-up alcove in the wall. Krinkle was finishing with setting charges, and Astruc was holding the lantern.

"Everything good back there, brother?"

"Yeah. What the hell was that stuff?"

"No idea, it's a prototype. You see the light blast, you're vaporized.

That's all Inspector Gobet told me. Other than he wanted a full report telling him if it works or not."

"It works. You have more of it?"

"Enough for one more blast. We're good to go here. Where is the closest cover?"

"There's a quarry fifty yards ahead," Astruc said.

Krinkle handed him an electric wire and a detonator. "Take these. I'll be there in ninety seconds with the lantern. Can you haul the bag, brother?"

"Sure," Harper said.

Harper led the way with his candle, dragging the duffel bag behind him. Astruc followed, laying out a line of wire along the ground. A small arch opened to a lightless quarry. They scooted in and put their backs to the wall. Their breathing echoed off black stone. It felt like one of those moments of silence that demand to be filled by voices. The dead soldier in Harper's head chimed in: *That's the way it is in a foxhole when you're staring death in the face.*

Harper rubbed the back of his neck. "No shit," he muttered.

"Did you say something?"

Harper looked at Astruc. "What?"

"Did you say something?"

"No, not really. I was just thinking."

"Yes, it is curious what one thinks about at times like these."

"That trick with the laying on of hands, making me see him again, how did you do it?"

"It's just what I do, what I have always done."

"Right."

Silence.

"Goose . . ."

"My son."

"Is he going to make it?"

"Yes, by the grace of a miraculous intervention."

"What sort of miraculous intervention was it?"

"Madame Taylor."

"What?"

"She held his hand, pronounced her name to him, and he was awakened. He immediately filled us in on everything that needed to be done with the triangulations tonight—as if while at edge of death, his subconscious never ceased to function."

"Impressive."

"Very much so."

Harper thought about it. "Bloody hell. Madame Taylor has come a long way from LP's Bar."

"And she has a very long way to go. It's good Madame Taylor and Goose have become close. They will need each other, I think."

Pain stabbed Harper's side and pressed his arms to his side. "Mind if I ask a question, Padre?"

"Such as?"

"What's it like? Having a child, I mean."

Harper heard the priest breathing in the dark, thinking about it maybe.

"I saw him before leaving for Jerusalem. He had come out of his coma and was sleeping comfortably. I was full with shame for what I had done to him, burdening him with my guilt. I sat near him and I wept. He heard me. I felt his hand on my shoulder and looked up to him. He signed, 'I love you, father.' In two and a half million years, that moment is the one genuine confirmation of my existence. It changed everything."

"How so?"

"You and I and that renegade back there fixing the explosives, we are without free will. We are only extensions of the will of another. All we fight for, all we do, we do not do it in the name of humanity or paradise. We do it because we have no choice. How empty we are, how without purpose and meaning. But not this time. This time I do it for my son."

Harper listened to the sound of the Astruc's voice.

"I'm sure he'd be proud of you, Padre."

"In fact, those were the last words he signed to me when I said good-bye to him."

"Good-bye?"

Harper heard the priest laugh softly to himself.

"Surely, you must have figured out that there are two possibilities tonight. We fail and fall into forever death ourselves, or we win and this war is over. Either way our time in paradise is at an end."

It was Harper's turn to laugh.

"You know, Padre, I never gave it a bloody thought."

"Of course not. That is why we are here. We do the thinking for you."

"Cheers."

The quarry filled with brilliant light as Krinkle ducked inside with the lantern.

"Hey, brothers, went back and did a quick recon. The goons are filling up the Chapel of Saint Helen and coming our way. I think they're a little confused as to what happened to the forward platoon. Give me the detonator," he said.

Astruc handed it over. Krinkle connected the wires to the contacts, primed the detonator. Now the roadie burst out laughing.

"What's so funny?" Harper said.

"Dude, it's only been, like, a hundred and forty friggin' hours since I was giving you shit for shooting your way into Lausanne Cathedral so we could get Brother Astruc to the altar square. Look at us now. We're like the friggin' Three Musketeers from Outer Space, blasting our way out of the Church of the Holy Sepulchre so we can circle around and come at the backs of all the king's men. That's our plan, right?"

"That's our plan."

"Cool. Cover your ears."

ii

Katherine felt the rotunda shake.

She dropped her weapon, got to her feet, put up her hands.

"I surrender!"

The goons who had hunkered down behind shields quickly snapped to attention. They saw Katherine was unarmed and withdrew their spears. They watched her with dead black eyes as she stepped through the firewall. She stopped three steps from the goons.

"Which one of you is in charge?"

The goon in the center of the line stepped forward.

"Hello, handsome. Take me to your leader."

Except for the one standing still in front of her, the goons moved in a blur and reformed as parallel lines running by the shrine and out of the rotunda. Katherine followed the lead goon through the lines. She counted sixty-four of them.

"Good luck, boys," she mumbled to herself.

Approaching the entrance hall, she heard faraway gunshots and furious explosions. The war outside had spread beyond the walls of the Old City and it was intensifying. Closer to the hall, the double-tap cracks of a sniper's rifle said anyone in the Old City's streets gets shot on sight. And while she was thinking all that, she was staring at the sword at the goon's side.

The goon stopped Katherine before crossing into the entrance hall. She leaned around the thing and saw lots more goons with spears and shields on either side of the space. She shook her head; the space appeared ten times as big now, almost as big as the nave of Lausanne Cathedral. The goons stretched from the Anointing Stone to the doors, two rows deep, fifty goons to a row. Between the rows, two hundred men in silver robes formed a semicircle facing the Anointing Stone. Another inch to the side and Katherine saw what the men were looking at: an oblong-shaped silver container lying on the floor stones outside the firewall and perpendicular to the Anointing Stone. Two massive goons stood guard on either side of the container. Katherine stared at it. *Like a fucking casket . . .* then she was overcome with a terrible imagination.

"Max!"

She lunged forward, but the goon guarding her knocked her to her knees. She reached out.

"Max! Jesus, Max!"

The goon's fist hit the back of her neck and she went down hard. She rolled on her back, reached for the goon's sword, and got her hand around the grip. The goon spun around in a blur, kicked her back to the floor stones. By the time she blinked, the goon had the tip of the sword at her throat.

"Noli spirare," the goon said.

Katherine did not breathe; she did not move. *Keep it together.*

A voice echoed through the hall.

"Now comes the One True God!"

The two lines of goons marched past Katherine into the entrance hall. They formed a V-shaped honor guard on either side of the Anointing Stone. The goon with the sword at Katherine's throat moved behind her, touched the point of the sword to the back of her neck. She watched the two hundred men in silver robes fall to their knees and prayed as one:

"For thou art worthy, our Lord and God,
Of all glory and honor; For by Your will
Is the world made ours, now and ever after."

In the outer courtyard the darkest of shadows appeared. They formed into a procession and moved toward the doors. First came a scar-faced goon with a sword at his side and an ancient piece of wood in his hands. It was a plaque, and Katherine saw the script written on it.

IESVS NAZARENVS REX IVDÆORVM

The twelve men in silver robes lifted their eyes to see the plaque. They raised their hands in supplication and prayed again.

"Now, Lord, return to this place of glorious death
Where we may witness this new sacrifice of blood
And thereby proclaim Your kingdom to the world."

The goons smacked the floor stones with the heels of their spears three times, like three mighty claps of thunder that rumbled through the cavernous church. Then there was silence as another shadow took form and crossed into the hall. Katherine saw a tall, elegant man dressed in black-on-black robes. He had long silver hair pulled tight to the back of his head with a silver clasp. He had a sculptured face and wore small, dark glasses over his eyes. She knew it wasn't a ghost this time . . . it was Komarovsky. The two hundred men cried out.

"Lord, we salute the highest!"

Behind Komarovsky came six bodyguards and two more men in resplendent copper-colored robes. One of the men held a wooden scepter in his right hand; the other carried a golden dagger resting on a pillow of black silk. The silver-robed men parted for the procession to pass. The goon with the plaque stood at the foot of the silver container and turned to face the court. Komarovsky stopped in the center of the hall, his bodyguards forming a tight arc at his back. The two men in copper-colored robes came to Komarovsky's side. They bowed to him, and the goons pounded the floor stones to summon the sound of thunder again. The two hundred men rose from the ground and bowed to their One True God.

There was silence except for the echoes of war in the real world beyond the church. Komarovsky turned his head a little, as if listening to the sound. The sound was pleasing to him. He looked through the haze of the firewall and lamps to see the giant mosaic of the dead Christ on the wall; then his gaze lowered to the arrangement of the Anointing Stone and the container. Perfect lines running east to west and north to south; at the foot of the container stood the goon bearing the plaque of crucifixion. The One True God was pleased, for here was the true cross of Golgotha, where the third precious savior of the creation would be slaughtered.

"I have promised you the riches of my kingdom and eternal pleasure and joy. Let it begin."

The man with the golden dagger stepped toward the casket.

"Wait, High Priest."

The man stopped and turned to Komarovsky and bowed. "Lord?"

"We have been visited by a goddess this night. We will welcome her back into our fold. Bring her to me," Komarovsky said.

Two goons from the honor guard ran to Katherine and took positions at her sides. The goon behind her grabbed her by the shoulders and hauled her to her feet. Katherine felt the tip of its sword poking at her back. She walked forward, biting her lip to resist the urge to rush to the silver container near the Anointing Stone and rip it open. She heard the whispering voices of the Two Hundred . . . *The mother of the child . . . How is she here . . . The Lord commands all things . . . How joyous . . .* The goons led Katherine to Komarovsky and threw her to the ground before his feet. She looked up at him.

"Is that my son in there? Is he already dead?"

"The child lives, but tonight he will be sacrificed."

The court murmured with anticipation.

Katherine's heart pounded in her chest.

"Why, because of some silly prophecy? Surely the One True God isn't bound by the myths and legends of men. Surely the One True God creates his own prophecies."

A goon marched from the rotunda. He carried the broken staff of a spear and Harper's sports coat. He offered them to Komarovsky.

"We have found angel's blood, Lord."

Komarovsky signaled the splendidly robed man. "Chief physician," Komarovsky said.

The man called the chief physician approached the goon and held his scepter over the dark, wet stains. The scepter glowed with purple light. He walked to Katherine, passed his scepter over her coat, and it glowed purple again.

"It is the blood of the warrior angel, Lord. The potion has entered his form."

Komarovsky looked at Katherine.

"Is he forever dead?"

"He was as good as dead the last I saw him. He was hit twice with spears, once out here, once in the rotunda. And I heard something about 'snuff.'"

Whispers rose in the court . . . *Did you hear . . . The warrior angel is wounded . . . Our Lord is great.*

Komarovsky raised his hand for silence. "Where is he now?"

"The two with him said they needed to fall back to bandage him up. I don't know where they went."

Komarovsky regarded Katherine through his dark glasses. "And you chose not to go with him?" he said.

"I didn't have a choice, I was cut off from them. Besides, I didn't come here to die with them. I came here to get my son back, that's all. I saw how it was playing out. Harper was dying, and you're looking like a winner to me. So you give me what I want, I'll give you what you want."

Komarovsky smiled. "And tell me, my goddess, what is it I want?"

"Me. You know what I am. You said it yourself: I'm your goddess. That means I can read you like a book, even with your eyes hiding behind the dark glasses. You remember how good I was, and now, you're imagining how good I'll be. You know I can give you thrills and chills like nothing you've ever experienced. I'm telling you, you can have it, all of it. All I want is my son to live. We'll be one happy family."

"Do you give yourself to me of your own free will?"

"I do."

"Then kneel before me, my beautiful goddess, and pledge your troth."

Katherine pulled herself from the floor and stood. She walked close to Komarovsky and knelt again. She rested her hands on his thighs; his entire form stiffened. Slowly, she raised her eyes. She could see herself reflected in his dark glasses, giving him the blank, mesmerizing gaze she'd mastered long ago—a gaze that allowed men to worship themselves through a hooker's eyes. It was the oldest trick in the book.

"You won't be sorry, Monsieur Komarovsky. I swear it on my soul."

He touched her cheek. "I accept the offer of your soul. Now receive your gift, lying whore."

The chief physician moved in a blur, pulling an injector from his robes and slamming it against Katherine's neck. *Click.* A needle shot into her; she felt a powerful rush in her blood.

"Jesus."

She arched her back and froze in place for long seconds. *No, please no.* Then, as if she were an empty vessel, darkness began to fill her form. *Jesus, no, fight it.* Sensing she was resisting, the darkness wrapped itself around her soul and squeezed. Watching her, Komarovsky smiled with pleasure.

"There is no one to protect you now. And there is nothing you can give me that I do not already own. Your flesh, your mind, your soul belong to me."

Katherine could barely speak. "Please . . . my son."

"Stand her up," Komarovsky commanded.

The goons pulled Katherine to her feet, balanced her like a doll. Komarovsky leaning close to her and walking around her, smelling the flesh of her neck.

"I will chain you to the altar of my temple and you will be my unholy sacrament. You will never grow old, you will never die, you will never see the light of day again. You will have no thoughts, no will, no sense of self. You will only crave my presence, my scent, my flesh. When I come to you, you will fall to your knees and wash my feet with your hair and attend to my every pleasure. Your only purpose will be to breed a race of creatures who will carry my divine seed to the ends of the universe."

Fuck you, fuck you!

He came around to her face, saw her struggling to resist. He traced his fingers across her mouth, then down her neck. He touched her breasts and caressed them.

"When you have serviced the last of my desires, you will be passed on to my court for the sustaining of their seed. This will be the manner of your existence as the lost souls of paradise are devoured. And when this world becomes barren and there are no more souls on which to feed, we will leave this place for a new world, and you will remain chained to the altar of my temple. For all time you will be raped by the soulless beasts and demons who will inherit the earth. Through your eternity of suffering you will cry my name and beg to be saved, such is the depth of your love for me that you will do all this, and more."

God, no!

The darkness rising within her clawed into her soul now and began to rip it from her flesh. She could feel the darkness feeding on her.

Don't! Don't fucking say it!

"Yes, my truest love," Katherine said.

Komarovsky turned to the chief physician. "Open it," he commanded.

From the corner of her eye, she saw the chief physician bow and step solemnly toward the container.

No, please! Don't hurt my son!

Komarovsky came close to Katherine again, breathing deep the scent of the fear rising from her flesh.

"Profess your adoration for me. Swear that I am your only love."

Fucker! You fucker!

The darkness clawed deeper into her soul.

"I adore you, you are my only love," she said.

Komarovsky turned and sat on his throne of bloodied wood. He nodded to the man behind him holding the golden dagger. The man stepped to Katherine.

No . . . no.

"Receive the instrument of sacrifice."

Katherine looked at the dagger. The blade was polished gold, twelve inches long; the grip was hand-painted in blues and reds; the pummel was rock crystal.

Fuck, no!

But the darkness had pierced her soul and was beginning to feed. She was helpless.

Please . . . no.

She took the grip in her right hand and lifted the dagger from the pillow. The golden blade was mirrorlike, and she saw a face in the reflection. *Jesus.* The dead-eyed bitch from the bunker was staring back at her with a knowing smile. *No!*

Komarovsky smiled watching her sink into a new torment.

"Since I tore your son from your arms, he has slept in a perfect state of grace. He has known no pain or suffering. I have loved him and protected him from the mother who would have killed him to deny him his glorious fate. But on this Night of Nights you will take him in your arms. You will carry him through the firewall and lay him on the Anointing Stone, then you will perform the act of sacrifice. Go, my goddess, my slave, go and slaughter your son in the name of the One True God."

iii

"Time."

"Twenty-one minutes till midnight."

"How long to go with the charges?"

"Two. Give me the motion sensor and gaffer tape."

Harper dug the things from the duffel bag and handed them over. The roadie hooked the sensor to the detonator, set it on the floor. He pulled a strip of gaffer tape, made an inside-out circle, and flattened it into a double-sided sticky strip. He pressed the motion sensor on one side of the strip, pressed the other side against the stone wall.

"That'll hold it. When the point comes around the corner, they'll set off the sensor. The first thirty or so will be hit with the light blast. The rest of them will be buried alive when the C-4 detonates. The fuckers will rip one another to shreds trying to get out."

"Works for me. Let's go."

They followed the candles Astruc had set along the tunnel. Two minutes more and they ran into the priest, who was coming back at them; he was holding the lantern.

"The tunnel going forward collapsed. Looks like excavations on the surface caved in."

"Oops, because it's too damn late to go back," Krinkle said.

The priest shook his head. "No need. I felt fresh air coming from somewhere, so I pulled away some of the debris, and I found a hole in the wall leading to a vertical shaft. It is a scramble, but it goes up to a passageway."

"To where?"

"A chamber with seven more passages leading in different directions, like a compass."

Harper flashed being led through the Old City by one of Chana's wolves. "I know that place. It's part of a network that runs between the walls of buildings in the Christian Quarter. One of those passages is only four or five minutes from the main entrance to the church."

"That's what Inspector Gobet said. He's there and asks if you would be so good as to get a move on."

Astruc turned around and headed off with the lantern. Harper looked at Krinkle. The roadie smiled.

"Guess he's done pulling imaginary blue bunnies out of thin air."

"I guess so," Harper said.

They hurried through the tunnel, followed lantern light around a turn, and came to the pile of rubble blocking the way forward. Astruc was already crawling through the hole in the wall. By the time Harper and Krinkle got through, Astruc was looking down at them from the top of the shaft. Krinkle scampered halfway up, tossed his duffel bag to the priest, reached back down, and grabbed Harper's shoulders.

"Up you go, brother, try not to tear open the stomach wound."

Harper climbed, then came a rush of air pressure from the tunnel beneath him.

"Oh, shit, hold on," Krinkle said.

Then the earth shook as the C-4 detonated. The walls of the shaft began to crumble. Harper slipped; his stomach slammed into the rocks.

"Fuck!"

He dangled in midair at the end of the roadie's grip.

"Come on, brother, work at it," Krinkle said.

"I'm trying."

"Trying ain't friggin' good enough—do it!"

Harper kicked his feet, found his footing, and steadied himself. Krinkle hauled him up.

"Brother Astruc, can I pass up one broken angel?"

"Absolument."

Astruc's mighty hands reached down, grabbed Harper, and pulled him up into the passageway. The priest dragged him away from the shaft and dropped him on the stone ground. Harper curled up in a ball.

"Oh, bloody Christ."

Krinkle cleared the shaft, rushed to Harper. "Your side is bleeding, your leg is bleeding. I need to redo the bandages."

"No time. Just pull them tighter."

"The snuff is turning your blood into the consistency of water, brother. You'll bleed out if we don't stop it."

"Just give me something for the pain and tighten the bandages."

Krinkle pulled at the bandages around Harper's stomach and thigh. Harper gritted his teeth against the pain until the roadie hit him with an injector jet. Numbing relief came in a half second.

"That's all I can do. And for the record, your form can't take any more painkillers. You're at the lights-out mark."

"Understood. How far to the cop, Padre?"

"Three minutes."

"That puts us at . . ."

"Eleven minutes to midnight," the roadie said.

"Get me to my feet."

Astruc lifted Harper from the ground, looked deep into Harper's eyes.

"Remember, you're the only one who can awaken the child and set up Komarovsky to die."

Krinkle pointed his finger in Harper's face. "So do *not* take another spear until you save Max and deliver some cosmic payback to the head goon. Then you can take all the spears you want."

"Got the message. And thanks for caring."

'No problem, brother."

Astruc led the way with the lantern. Two and a half minutes later they came to the radius and Inspector Gobet; the cop in the cashmere coat was not alone. His muscle, Mutt and Jeff, were at their usual positions to his left and right. The three of them were armed to the teeth: Micro UZIs, killing knives, stun grenades. The cop was wearing a comms kit, too, and just signing off.

"Ah, good evening, Mr. Harper. So glad to see you could make it. You'll be happy to know we have a mobile hospital bus standing by outside the city to attend to your wounds. The sooner we complete this mission, the sooner you will be made well. Father Astruc, as you have the lantern, would you take the point? It's the passage just behind you. And do be sure to hide the lantern in your overcoat when approaching the outer courtyard."

"Yes, sir."

Astruc turned and ducked into the passage. The inspector looked at Harper and Krinkle

"I have already briefed Father Astruc. Corporal Mai and two snipers have just taken positions in the shadows near the church with a view of the courtyard. There are six goons outside standing guard. Our snipers will put them down as we enter. We will then charge into the church on my signal and clear a path for Mr. Harper to reach the boy."

"What's happened to Madame Taylor?"

"Corporal Mai reports Komarovsky has seized her soul. He has just commanded her to slaughter her own son. I am afraid she is weakening under his spell."

"Then what the hell are you waiting for? Order the snipers to take the shot," Harper said.

"Negative. Komarovsky's bodyguards have him covered."

"For fuck sake, Inspector, the snipers use fifty-mil rounds—just shoot through his bloody bodyguards."

"Mr. Harper, if we fire, we tip our hand. The boy will be slaughtered in a rain of spears. Our only chance is to proceed as you had planned: Come at their backs and take them by surprise. Shall we?" The inspector headed for the passage; Mutt and Jeff followed.

"How did you know that was my plan?" Harper said.

The inspector looked back at him. "I had every confidence that once you understood Madame Taylor's purpose in being here, you would do exactly as you have done."

"You think she's up to it?"

"It is my fervent wish that she is. But it all depends on getting her into the right position at the right time. That bit of trickery, as I trust you know, is up to you. So the proper question is, Are you up to it, Mr. Harper? Have you sorted a means of wounding him unto death?"

Harper tapped the calfskin-wrapped nails in his belt.

"More or less."

"Good. Now, do hurry along, the witching time of night beckons."

iv

Katherine approached the silver container as the two hundred men in silver robes chanted in a language she did not understand. Their deep tones and rhythms were hypnotic; the sound got deep into Katherine's mind, and the meaning of their unholy words was made known to her.

"So did the mother slaughter the fruit of her womb;
And all light in the world was diminished."

Jesus, stop, Kat!

But her feet continued to carry her on. The chief physician was waiting for her and raised the scepter of his office. Two goons stepped forward and undid the latches of the container. They pulled the top open and pressure was released—*shisshhhhh*. And when Katherine came around the back of the chief physician, she saw through the glass lid. She saw the circuits and wires, the breathing tubes and air tanks, the blinking monitors labeled HEART RATE, BLOOD PRESSURE, BODY CORE TEMPERATURE. She saw the little boy with black hair strapped to a small hospital bed and the oxygen mask over the boy's face, his eyes closed as if he was sleeping. She saw the small blue rubber hammer in the boy's right hand.

Jesus, Max. Please, wake up. Stop me!

"Raise the glass!" Komarovsky commanded.

The chants of the Two Hundred intensified with fervor.

"Then did the One True God ascend to the throne of judgment;
And all the world fell down to worship Him."

The glass lid was lifted and carried away. The chief physician disconnected the leads and oxygen mask from the small form within the casket. Komarovsky commanded Katherine again.

"Mother, take your son in your arms!"

Katherine slid the golden dagger in her belt. The court of Two Hundred shuddered with joy watching the goddess lift the sleeping child into her arms.

"Mother, lay him on the Anointing Stone!"

Max, I'm sorry. Please forgive me.

Katherine passed through the firewall and circled around the Anointing Stone to face Komarovsky. She laid her son down on the stone.

"Mother, now kiss his brow and slay him!"

She hesitated. *Please, no . . . please.*

"I command you! Slay your bastard child!"

I'm sorry, Max. Mommy is so sorry.

She leaned down and kissed his brow. She straightened up, pulled the dagger from her belt. She stared at the razor-sharp blade, saw the dead-eyed bitch from the bunker smiling back at her in triumph.

No . . . I can't.

You will.

"Slay him and prove your love for me!"

Hearing Komarovsky's voice, Katherine raised the dagger over her head.

Kill yourself, just kill yourself.

You cannot kill yourself, you can only obey the will of the One True God!

Katherine squeezed the grip of the dagger. As much as she tried, she could not turn the blade on herself.

I love you, Max.

She stared at the throat of her sleeping child and she slipped into darkness.

"Lord, we salute the highest!" she cried.

V

Six sharp cracks sounded from the outer courtyard, and a warrior angel's voice rang out through the Church of the Holy Sepulchre.

"C'est le guet . . ."

Stun grenades detonated, SIGs blasted, spark rounds exploded, goons dropped. All the court turned to see the small band of angels and Swiss Guards rushing through the doors. The fifth cohort tried to form a line of shields, but thirty dropped instantly with shots to their backs. The unarmed men in silver robes had no cover, and they went down in a hail of bullets. Komarovsky's bodyguards pulled their God to the side of the hall, and a platoon of goons rushed to defend them with shields. Komarovsky saw Katherine frozen in place behind the firewall at the Anointing Stone desperately holding on to her soul to keep from drowning in darkness; he saw a flicker of remembrance in her eyes. He followed her eyeline to the doors of the church and saw the bandaged, limping angel crossing the threshold with a gun in one hand and a lantern in the other.

"He lives!" Komarovsky howled.

Harper fired two rounds, blowing open the heads of the chief physician and the high priest, then he raised the lantern high.

"Il a sonné l'heure! Il a sonné l'heure!"

A wave of spears came at Harper as the flame in the lantern flared, and a thread of firelight shot through the hall and into Katherine Taylor's eyes. The light picked her up and pinned her against the stone wall beneath the mosaic of the dead Christ. Her body trembled and glowed like a faraway star. Then the thread of light ceased and Katherine fell to the ground. She got to her knees, suddenly aware of the battle around her. She saw the unmoving child on the Anointing Stone.

"Max!"

She dropped the dagger, crawled to her son. She pulled him into her arms.

"Max, it's me. It's Mommy."

The child was limp, lifeless.

"Max, honey, wake up."

She felt his chest; it was still.

"He's not breathing. Jesus, he's not breathing. Harper! Max isn't—"

She saw Harper on his back; one of the spears had lodged in his chest. He was conscious, reaching for the lantern next to him. The lantern lay on its side, the glass shattered and the flame inside dying in melting wax. All through the church the firewalls began to dim.

"Harper's down!" Katherine called.

One hundred goons formed into two lines and marched toward the attackers in a wedge formation. They lowered their spears and rushed ahead. Katherine saw the faces of the ones trying to save her son. The cop, Krinkle, Astruc, Corporal Mai, and the rest . . . all being forced back to the doors now. Three more stun grenades rocked the church. Astruc broke right, flew through the firewall at the ambulatory. Corporal Mai and two Swiss Guards, one of them with Krinkle's duffel bag on his back, broke for the Anointing Stone. Goons fell on them; a sword caught one of the Swiss Guards across the throat and he went down. Corporal Mai and the remaining Swiss Guard fired between shields and dropped the goons, then jumped through the firewall. They moved to either side of Katherine and her son.

"Cover them!" Corporal Mai said while swapping out magazines and opening fire again.

The Swiss Guard pulled a ballistic blanket from Krinkle's bag and tossed it over Katherine and Max; he reloaded his Micro UZI and opened up. Goons with their backs exposed went down; heads of goons exploded as Astruc picked off targets from the ambulatory. Komarovsky and his bodyguards were pinned behind shields. Mutt and Jeff took positions at the passage to the Place of Mourning and laid down cover fire as Krinkle grabbed Harper and dragged him behind Gobet's muscle and into the rotunda. Inspector Gobet followed, grabbing the lantern on the way. They hunkered down in the shadows of the Shrine of the Resurrection. Inspector Gobet held the lantern over Harper's face. Blood oozed from his mouth. Krinkle checked the angle of the spear embedded in Harper's side.

"Sort of jumped the gun, didn't you, brother? It was 'one-two-three-go,' not 'one-go.'"

Harper coughed and spit blood. "No choice."

"Yeah, yeah. Well, it's a standoff for the moment."

"The child . . ." Harper said.

"Stay put, brother," the roadie said.

". . . not breathing."

"Komarovsky has him suspended between life and death," the inspector said. "But the longer he's under, the less chance you have of reviving him."

"Hang on, brother, this is going to hurt," the roadie said, breaking the spear at the tip.

"Oh, Christ," Harper hissed through gritted teeth.

Krinkle checked the entrance wound. The steel head of the spear had broken through the fifth and sixth ribs on Harper's left side. The lack of blood loss said Harper was bleeding internally; the blood on his lips said blood fluids were seeping into his lung. Harper saw the expressions on the faces looking down on him. He smiled.

"No worries, lads. Not dead yet."

Inspector Gobet heard a signal in his comms rig. "Do what you can for him, Mr. Krinkle. I'm receiving flash traffic."

"Roger that." Krinkle pulled a vial of cauterizing potion from his overalls and poured it around the edge of the spear tip. The wound sizzled.

"Holy fuck."

"Shit, brother. I can't pull out the head of the spear, it's plugging the hole in your lung."

"Just cauterize it the best you can and wrap a bandage around me."

Inspector Gobet signed off on comms. "HQ reports that tens of thousands of the enemy have descended on Jerusalem. They are sweeping through every street, secret passageway, and tunnel in the city and coming our way. We are surrounded, gentlemen."

"Time to midnight?" Harper said.

Krinkle finished the wrap job, looked at his watch. "Ninety seconds."

"Get me up," Harper said.

"Easy, brother."

"Sod it with easy."

They picked Harper up, and Krinkle pulled Harper's left arm around his own shoulder to steady him. Harper looked at Inspector Gobet.

"So what's my plan now, Inspector?"

"As soon as Corporal Mai sees us in the passage, she will break to the edge of the firewall and establish a forward line. I will break right with my men and hit them with blue fog."

"We won't be able to target the enemy in the fog," Krinkle said. "We'll be shooting blind."

"Affirmative. We will establish our lines of fire before detonation to keep from shooting ourselves. It's all we can do to get Mr. Harper to the child. When the potion is administered, everyone falls back to the rotunda, except for Mr. Harper." The inspector touched Harper's shoulder. "I believe you have an all-clear to deliver."

Harper smiled, blood dripping from the corners of his mouth. "Good plan, if I do say so myself." He looked at the roadie. "Give me the cup, mate," he said.

Krinkle took the brittle, gaffer-taped thing from the pouch of his overalls.

"Now take the vials from my pocket, and pour them in the cup."

The roadie did it. The liquids were dark and thick. But in the cup they formed a clear potion that sparkled with beads of light.

"Do try not to spill it along the way, Mr. Harper," the inspector said.

"Yes, sir."

vi

"Now!"

Corporal Mai and the Swiss Guard jumped to the front of the Anointing Stone and laid down suppressing fire. Inspector Gobet and his muscle charged to the center of the hall, established a crossfire line. Gobet pulled a glass vial and smashed it on the floor stones.

"Et facta est lux!"

The hall filled with a burst of light and a thick cloud of blue fog.

"Let's move," Harper said.

The roadie hauled him through the firewall surrounding the Anointing Stone. They hit the ground next to Madame Taylor and her son.

"He's not breathing," Katherine said.

Krinkle checked Max's eyes. "He's going fast."

"Bring him to me." Harper said.

Katherine scooted to Harper, held Max to him.

Harper stared at him a moment. His jet-black hair, his round face. *Like any child in the world,* Harper thought. He tipped the cup; the potion touched the child's lips.

"Drink, Max Taylor."

Just then the midnight bells began to toll over Jerusalem and a cry of ecstasy rose from the goons.

"Lord, we salute the highest!"

Then Komarovsky's voice: "Bring me the head of the bastard child!"

The sound of shields hitting the floor stones and swords being drawn echoed off the stone walls. The goons marched slowly forward, slashing their swords through the fog. SIGs and Micro UZIs exploded, goons shrieked. Their hideous sounds were answered with another volley of fire. Harper's hands began to shake, and the cup slipped. Katherine grabbed his hand and steadied his grip on the cup. He stared at her hand wrapped around his, felt an energy emanating from her flesh. He looked at her. There were tears in her eyes.

"Harper, please."

He tipped the cup and poured the potion into the boy's mouth.

"Drink, Max Taylor. Drink that you will escape forever death."

When the last drop had been taken, Harper slumped and dropped the cup; it fell on the floor stones. He rolled onto his side and stared into the fog. Patches of clarity appeared. The place was littered with dead goons, but at least a hundred were still standing. They formed into four lines of five, raised their swords, and charged the Anointing Stone. Komarovsky was watching with pleasure from behind his bodyguards. He didn't give a shit about losing goons; he knew thousands more were on the way. Corporal Mai and the Swiss Guard ripped the front line apart with automatic fire, emptying weapons, swapping mags, firing again; spark rounds lit up the entrance like intersecting lines of causality on speed. Goons fell like bowling pins, two of them skidding over the floor stones and hitting the candles of the firewall to break it open. Then the third line went down, then the fourth . . . The goons kept charging.

"Fall back!" Inspector Gobet shouted.

Krinkle grabbed Max, threw him over his shoulder, pulled Katherine from the floor with his right hand, and grabbed the lantern with his left. Katherine reached for Harper.

"Come on," she said.

Harper struggled to his feet, holding his bleeding side.

"Find a shadow and hide in it, Madame Taylor. Wait until he's wounded."

"Harper, please, you can barely stand. C'mon, we'll find another way."

"This is the only way. It's your world now, it's down to you."

"Harper!"

He turned from her and stumbled toward the fog. The space within the church was still expanding, and he began to wander in a circle. When he became lost in the fog and could walk no farther, he fell to his knees. He pulled the calfskin from his belt, unwrapped the four carpenter nails. He tossed the calfskin away, reached behind his back and tucked two nails in his belt. The remaining two he held in his hands.

"You are not forsaken," he whispered silently to himself, crossing his arms across his chest.

SIGs and UZIs quieted, and when the fog cleared, Harper was on his knees in the middle of the hall and facing the open doors of the church. His arms were wrapped tight around his chest, blood seeping from his wounds. He was surrounded by hundreds and hundreds of fallen goons, spears, and swords; the floor stones were soaked with dead black dripping from empty eye sockets. But Harper did not notice them; he only stared out the doors of the church. He saw stars and tracer fire above the rooftops. It was heavier now, racing through the night from every direction . . . or maybe it was just the world racing through the universe at two million miles per second, he thought. He heard the sound of guns, sirens, and screams, then heard words in his head. *Bellaque matribus detesta. Wars, the horror of mothers.*

"Hold on, boyo, not long now," he whispered to himself.

The bodyguards opened their shields and the One True God emerged to claim his kingdom. Four of the guards moved in a blur to set walls of shields blocking off the rotunda and ambulatory. They remained at those posts with swords drawn. The remaining two guards escorted Komarovsky to the suffering man kneeling once again on Golgotha, waiting to die.

"What a wondrous entertainment this has been," the One True God said, walking around the bodies and instruments of war. "Godly, was it not? Playing with the souls of men, giving them a taste of hope then stealing it away? And we still have more to come before the end of this midnight hour."

Komarovsky stopped, signaled his guard to pick up some things from the floor and give them to him.

"Your fellows are trapped with the whore and her child near the Shrine of the Resurrection now. A wondrous image, I think: the last hope of humanity cowering in the shadow of such a thing. In the gospels of the new religion that shall be carried to the ends of the universe, this holy night will be long remembered as the final victory over the souls of men in paradise."

Harper continued to stare out into the courtyard, refocusing his eyes and seeing hundreds of shadows descending and taking form. He heard thousands more clawing at the walls of the church, breaking through glass windows and wooden doors. They knew the child was inside; they could smell his flesh and blood, and they craved to devour him. *Not long now, not long now.*

Komarovsky stood before Harper, dropped the wooden plaque on the floor stones. It broke apart in two pieces. Harper's eyes pieced together the Latin script: *Jesus of Nazareth King of the Jews*. Komarovsky spoke again . . .

"The sons of light are vanquished this Night of Nights. You will not win by deceit this night as you did with Zoroaster and the Jew. It is why I selected this ground to slaughter the child of the whore. I thought you would appreciate the irony of your defeat."

Harper squeezed the hidden nails in his hands while staring at the two pieces of ancient wood on the floor stones; like splintered shards they were . . . *Know that the instruments of my crucifixion will be used to wound evil unto death. Then shall it be, with my final words, that the light of the Pure God is revealed in paradise.* Then he stared at the One True God's shoes. Expensive, Italian maybe. Komarovsky reached out his hands to lift Harper's chin. Harper leaned away from him and stared at the smooth flesh of the One True God's palms; the long fingers, the perfectly manicured nails.

"Raise your dying eyes to me," Komarovsky said.

Still, Harper did not move.

One of the bodyguards grabbed Harper's hair and forced back his head. The second guard laid the blade of the golden dagger at Harper's throat to keep him in place. Harper saw himself in the dark glasses of the One True God: broken and beaten, bleeding from his nose and mouth. Komarovsky studied the face.

"I loved you the most, you were my favorite. Why did you not submit to me? Why did you force me to chase after you through the ages? To trap you finally in a form from which you could not escape?"

Harper tried to speak but coughed up blood instead. He settled, and when he did speak, he could barely recognize the raspy whisper that was his voice now.

"Is that what happened?"

"Through our time in paradise you have fought me, from the very beginning when I first created the soul of man."

"Can't think why at the moment. Probably because I knew what you planned to do with the souls you created. It wasn't supposed to be this way."

"And how should it have been?"

"No idea, but it sure as hell isn't this."

Komarovsky laughed. "You are so like the creatures of this place in your innocence. Such faith and belief that there is a god beyond the stars more powerful and beautiful than me, and that somehow, I would allow such a god to be found."

Harper felt fluid filling his lung. *Not long now, not long now.* He coughed and shivered from pain and cold. He leaned over, watched blood drip from his lips and onto the floor stones. He scanned the hall from the corner of his eye. He saw something moving through the shadows by the Anointing Stone, then in the high arches above the mosaic of the dead Christ. *Here we go, boyo.* He coughed up blood again and spit.

"Bollocks. What's out there waiting for these creatures is the point of knowing, becoming one with the whole of the universe. What waits for them is something bigger than any god imaginable in the minds of men or me even, or you, you worthless piece of shit."

The guards kicked Harper in the back, hauled him to his knees. Komarovsky grabbed Harper's throat and squeezed.

"Confess your sins and I will be merciful."

"What fucking sins?"

"Confess your treachery to your God."

Harper spit in Komarovsky's face. Komarovsky removed his dark glasses, smashed them to the floor, and wiped his sleeve across his face. He leaned close to Harper, his silver eyes flaring with rage.

"You dare to mock the one who has ruled this world for two and a half million years?"

"You're not a god, you're nothing but a false prophet. And in case you haven't heard, Jerusalem is where false prophets come to die."

Crack, crack; crack, crack.

The four bodyguards at the shields fell dead. Harper pulled his arms from his sides and held them high; Komarovsky caught a fleeting glimpse of the two carpenter nails in Harper's hands. Horror raced through his eyes as Harper summoned the last of his strength and pounded down with his hands to nail Komarovsky's feet to the floor stones.

"Ahhhhh!" Komarovsky fell to his knees.

Crack, crack.

The guard closest to Komarovsky went down dead; the other fell on Harper, drove the dagger into Harper's back.

"Fuck!"

The guard pulled out the dagger, raised it for a death cut.

Crack.

The guard's head exploded and his body flew off Harper. Harper rolled to his side, forced himself onto his knees . . . fading, slipping . . . *Not long now.* He was face-to-face with Komarovsky and staring into the eyes of a creature that had never known pain. The One True God appeared confused, not knowing what to do or think; his perfectly manicured hands were shaking, hovering over the nails in his feet.

"Hurts, doesn't it?" Harper said.

Komarovsky tried to speak, but before a sound was uttered, Harper rammed two more nails down onto the tops of Komarovsky's hands and pinned them to the floor stones.

"Ahhhh!"

Harper looked deep into Komarovsky's silver eyes.

"Still not feeling it? Let me help."

Harper picked up the two shards of ancient wood and stabbed them into Komarovsky's sides. Komarovsky gasped and shuddered.

"You . . . would kill . . . me?"

Harper smiled. "Not my job, pal."

Just then Komarovsky felt familiar fingers moving slowly through his long beautiful hair, twisting it into clumps. Then his head was yanked back and he saw Katherine Taylor looking down on him.

"My goddess?"

"That's right."

Katherine lifted her right hand to reveal the golden dagger. She eased it into Komarovsky's mouth.

"And a little advice from an ex-hooker whose son you tried to kill: Fuck off and die."

She rammed the dagger down his throat. She let go of him. He wavered a moment as gurgling sounds rumbled from his mouth. Katherine moved in a blur, picking up a sword from the ground, spinning in a wide circle, and slicing the blade across Komarovsky's shoulders before his body hit the ground. The head of the One True God hit the floor stones and rolled out the door.

The shadows in the outer courtyard disappeared; the clawing at the walls and doors ended; Komarovsky's form dissolved into quicksilver and spread over the floor stones; it bubbled and burned, then vanished from the face of the earth.

For a moment nothing moved, as if the world had come to a stop.

Then explosions and gunfire from the real world rushed into the Church of the Holy Sepulchre. Harper heard the sound of military jets flying low over Jerusalem, heading east.

"Must give all-clear . . . Stop the war."

He fell. Katherine dropped her sword and jumped to him.

"Harper."

"Must give . . . all-clear."

Crashing sounds echoed through the church as Inspector Gobet and his gang broke the shields and ran toward Harper. The cop held the lantern; the roadie had his duffel bag. The inspector knelt next to Katherine and passed the palm of his right hand before her eyes: "Madame Taylor, your mission is over. Go to to your son now, we'll take care of this."

Katherine looked back, saw the cop's muscle holding firing positions at the passage to the rotunda. Then she saw beyond them to the Place of Mourning. Corporal Mai and the Swiss Guard were fitting an IV into her son's arm. "Jesus." She got up and ran. "Max! Max!"

vii

Krinkle and the inspector knelt next to Harper.

The roadie pressed his hand over the dagger wound on Harper's back. Watery blood oozed through his fingers.

"Oh shit, brother."

The roadie cauterized the wound and stuffed a bandage into the hole. The watery blood slowed but did not stop flowing. They eased him over onto his back. Krinkle pulled his penlight and scanned Harper's eyes with the lapis-colored beam. Harper's face was pale now, his eyes losing focus, and he was only half conscious.

"Brother, you with me? Come on, talk to me. What do we do now?"

"Time."

Krinkle looked at his watch. "Two minutes till the end of the midnight hour."

"Get me to the stone. Bring the lantern . . . Must stand there for all-clear."

"You know what to do, what to say?"

Flash.

Hanging on the cross, the weight of his form pulling down on the nails in his hands and lashings around his wrists. Gasping for air now, unable to breathe. Raising his head, seeing Jerusalem through the blood in his eyes. Raising his head higher to the sun in the sky. He can see it burning, bursting, washing the world with light. A sign, a sign. Yeshua ben Yosef's soul was safe amid the stars, and this Passover night, he would look down on the Holy City. All is well. He lowers his head and releases his final breath. He whispers . . .

Blink.

"Last words."

Krinkle and the inspector looked at each other, not sure if Harper was hallucinating. The inspector held the lantern close to Harper's face.

"Look into my eyes, Mr. Harper, listen to the sound of my voice. Komarovsky is dead, the child is safe. There will be contact in another thousand years."

More jets roared over Jerusalem, heading east.

"Earth is dying. Must make contact now."

Krinkle let out a sigh of relief. He grabbed Harper's hand. "What a friggin' relief. For a second I thought you'd gone AWOL. Come on, brother, let's do it."

They lifted Harper from the ground. He coughed and blood sprayed from his mouth. They carried him to the Anointing Stone.

"Astruc?" Harper said.

"Already on the roof, Mr. Harper."

"Good man," Harper said.

The lamps above the stone had all been shattered in the battle. The polished surface of the stone was covered with pieces of broken red glass and tiny metal crosses.

"Here, facing east," Harper said. Then he slumped between his bearers.

"Come on, brother," Krinkle said, "stay with us."

They pulled him back to his feet.

"The medics are on their way, Mr. Harper. You just need to hold on," the inspector said.

"Lantern . . . Must lift it high. Help me."

Krinkle and Gobet put the lantern in Harper's hands, raised it over his head. Harper breathed as deep as he could, but the watery blood was gathering in the back of his throat. His hands began to slip from the lantern.

"Mr. Harper . . ."

He recovered, balanced himself. "Stand back."

"You'll fall, brother."

"Stand back."

Slowly they pulled their hands from him. He wobbled but did not fall. He stood alone before the Anointing Stone with the lad's lantern high over his head. He looked up to the great mosaic of the dead Christ being carried to his tomb. *You are not forsaken.* He stumbled, but regained his balance. His hands trembled as he raised the lantern one more inch.

"Consummatum est!"

And he smashed the lantern down onto the Anointing Stone.

There was an explosion of light, and the earth began to tremble and groan. The Church of the Holy Sepulchre rocked and swayed. Windows throughout the church shattered, cracks appeared in the walls, chunks of stone fell from the ceiling. Harper fell hard onto the floor stones. Krinkle lay over him to protect him from falling debris. The inspector crouched next to them; he was receiving flash traffic through his comms set.

"It's an earthquake, all through the Jordan Valley."

Krinkle looked at Harper. "You sure those were the right last words, brother?"

Harper smiled through bloodied teeth. "I'm sure."

Inspector Gobet stood. "Into the courtyard, everyone!"

Corporal Mai was already leading her team from the rotunda. Max was in the Swiss Guard's arms, while Katherine held the IV. The earth shook again and she tripped. Inspector Gobet ran to Katherine to help her. Krinkle lifted Harper into his arms and they all stumbled outside. Inspector Gobet ordered his muscle to take positions to cover the high walls, and the Swiss Guard covered the doors of the church.

"There may be a few renegades hiding in the shadows of the city, take them down."

Krinkle got to the center of the courtyard. "Here, away from the walls," he said.

They laid Harper and Max on the ground, side by side. They all got to their knees and leaned over them to protect them. Krinkle opened his duffel bag and pulled out bandages and an IV of shimmering liquid.

"Here, Boz, run this," he said to Inspector Gobet.

The inspector found a vein on Harper's arm, inserted the needle, and opened the fluid. Krinkle dug through the bag and pulled out two shock blankets. He tossed one at Corporal Mai; the both of them tore open the wrappers, spread the blankets over Harper and Max, then tucked them under their backs and wrapped them in cocoons. Katherine pulled Max into her arms and lay over him. Krinkle did the same with Harper.

Then the earth calmed.

All sounds of battle ceased.

Inspector Gobet received flash traffic on his comms kit.

"Message received," the cop said. He looked at Harper. "Reports are flooding into HQ that enemy shadows are disappearing," he said.

"From Jerusalem?" Krinkle said.

"From everywhere in the world. They are gone, our war is over."

Harper looked to the stars in the sky. There was Orion, there was the North Star, he thought. Then, slowly, he raised his trembling hand and pointed to the seven-starred cluster of the Pleiades.

"Incoming," he whispered.

They all looked up, as all the world looked up to see a great slash of fire and light arc across the sky. It hovered and shimmered and turned night into day. Then from inside the church came a deep-throated droning sound: *Ooooommmmmm, oooommmmmm, oooommmmmm*. The tone rose and fell in pitch, searching for a specific resonance within the walls of the church, and when it found it, the entire massive thing began to hum as if the stones themselves had come to life and were singing to the heavens. Then came the one o'clock bell ending the midnight hour.

Krinkle leaned down to Harper, got close to his face. "You hear, brother? That's contact. You friggin' did it."

Harper coughed up blood. Krinkle lifted Harper's head and torso to rest on his lap.

"You listen to me, brother. We got you through this once, we'll do it again. But you've got to work with me. You hold on, friggin' hold on."

Inspector Gobet touched Harper's shoulder. "Yes, hold on, good fellow, the medics are a few minutes out. We will get you help."

Harper watched the comet until it faded; then the drone quieted and the stars returned with the silent night.

"Maman."

A child's voice.

Harper turned his head as Inspector Gobet shifted aside. Harper saw the profile of a young boy with black hair. Wrapped in a shock blanket and peeking out from under his mother's arms. Katherine was still huddled over him. Slowly she straightened up and looked down on her son.

"Max?"

He reached for her face and touched her cheek. *"Maman."*

"Hello, Max, hello, honey."

She leaned down and kissed him. The child played with his mother's hair.

Astruc came running from the church; he knelt at Harper's feet. "Primary triangulations are in. Blue Brain is running the show now. All is well."

Harper lost focus and faded for a second, but Krinkle called him back. "Hey, stay with us, brother." Harper came back and tried to raise his arm. Krinkle loosened the shock blanket, helped him lift it. Slowly Harper signed to Astruc, *The nails, the cup. Must go back to the grave with the scroll.*

The priest lowered himself to one knee. He touched Harper's shoulder. *It will be done, mon ami.*

"Flash traffic reports the medics are two minutes out now," the inspector said.

Harper crunched over and coughed blood. "No."

"Brother?"

"The locals . . . not me." He looked up at Inspector Gobet.

"Mr. Harper, our war is over and we will be withdrawn from this world very shortly. The medics have a new technology to separate you from your form. It's experimental but it just might work. You only need to hold on a little longer."

"No more. I want to stay awhile and rest . . . please."

Inspector Gobet bowed his head a moment, whispering to himself as if in prayer. Then he stood erect, radioed through his comms unit. "Baker Six to all units. Medics not required on site. Attend to the locals. That is an order."

Then a woman's voice.

"Harper?"

Harper turned his head, saw Katherine staring at him. Max was lying across her lap, holding out his hand and pointing his way.

"Max wants to touch you," Katherine said.

Krinkle checked with Inspector Gobet; the cop nodded. Krinkle turned Harper's arm toward the child. Harper opened his bloodied hand, and Max touched his finger to Harper's gloved palm.

"Want to watch the stars with me, kid?" Harper whispered.

"Boo," the boy said.

Harper looked at Katherine.

"That's what he calls Marc Rochat's cat. And a lot of other things. In this case it means 'yes.'"

Harper watched Max lay back in his mother's arms. The little guy watched the stars a bit and went to sleep. *See, it's easy, boyo. All you have to do is close your eyes.*

"If you say so, mate," Harper whispered to himself, then choking and gasping for air, grabbing at his legs.

"What is it, brother? What do you need?"

"Matchbox . . . in pocket."

Inspector Gobet pulled aside the shock blanket and dug through Harper's pockets. He found the matchbox, showed it to Harper.

"Inside," Harper whispered.

The inspector opened the box, removed the dented five-franc coin. Harper held out his hand. "Please."

"Of course, my dear fellow. Of course." The inspector said, laying the coin in Harper's palm.

Harper flashed beforetimes. He saw Marc Rochat in Lausanne Cathedral. He was smiling, happy, giving Harper the coin for good luck . . . *Thank you, lad.* Harper blinked slowly, opened his eyes. Katherine was watching him now and her eyes were full of tears, but they were not tears of sorrow. Harper showed the coin to Katherine. "For Max, yeah."

Katherine smiled. "Yes, Harper, for Max. You rest now. Just close your eyes and rest."

"Yeah. I'm so . . . very tired."

Harper closed his fist around the coin and held it tight. Krinkle eased him to the ground and rested his head on the duffel bag; he put Harper's hands together and covered them with his own.

"I'm with you, brother, we're all with you."

Harper nodded, looked at the stars again. There were the Pleiades and there was Sirius, he thought . . . there was the galaxy stretched across the sky . . . there was the edge of the bloody universe. *You see that, boyo?* Then fast-moving clouds rolled in from the Mediterranean Sea and the stars were hidden from him. Harper closed his eyes; he felt tiny drops of rain fall from the heavens and touch his face.

"Blessed are the dead . . ."

INSPIRARE

The black Mercedes turned onto the esplanade of Lausanne Cathedral and stopped near the chestnut trees. Corporal Mai alighted from the shotgun seat and scanned the scene. It was a warm evening with deep blue skies. Dozens of locals strolled around the cathedral; a hundred more were camped along the ramparts with blankets, picnic baskets, and bottles of wine. They had come to watch the sunset over Lac Léman and listen to the music that would soon fill the cathedral. Corporal Mai opened the Merc's right passenger door.

"I'll go inside and check our seats," she said.

Katherine Taylor tied a white silk scarf over her hair and tossed the tails back over her shoulders. "We'll wait for you on the esplanade, yeah?"

Corporal Mai pulled a cell phone, tapped in a code, and hit send.

"You're covered. I'll be back in a minute."

Katherine checked the fading light outside. It was still too bright for her eyes. She put on her Ray-Bans; the funny kind from the clinic in Vevey. The lenses cleansed each particle of daylight in the 4000°K to 8000°K range before the light hit her eyes. That's what the little man in the white coat had told her, anyway. She stepped from the car, reached back.

"Come on, Max."

The little boy climbed down from the backseat and stood on the cobblestones. He had been dressed for the occasion. His black shoes were polished, and he wore a new pair of dungarees and a new white sweater. Katherine leaned down, licked her fingers, and combed her son's mop of black hair. She eyed him from head to toe.

"You're growing like a weed."

Max stood on his toes.

"Soon, I'll be this big."

"Don't rush it, buster. One day you're playing whack-a-mole in your high chair, saying 'Boo' and 'Goog,' the next day you're reading books and talking like a pro. You need to be a kid for as long as you can, and I want to be a kid's mom for as long as I can. *Tu me comprends?*"

"Oui, Maman."

"Now, this is a concert, so there are a few rules. No blowing your nose, no tapping your heels on the chair, no 'I have to pee' until the intermission."

"May I drink from the fountain before we go inside?"

"Can you keep from being a big Mr. Dribble Face on your new sweater?"

"I'm not a big Mr. Dribble Face, I'm a weed."

She poked the tip of his nose.

"And a pretty funny one at that."

Katherine stood, took Max's hand, and walked toward the fountain. She looked over the locals along the ramparts. There were Swiss Guards hiding among them; probably a few more amid the crowd strolling on the esplanade. She had no idea who they might be. But she knew they were out there watching her, watching her son. She lifted Max onto the stone basin and held him steady.

"Just a sip so we don't have to break the no-pee rule, okay?" Katherine said.

"Okay."

Max leaned under the iron spout and sipped from the cold stream. He straightened up.

"Done?" Katherine said.

"Uh-huh."

She lowered him to the ground. He stood very still a moment, watching the faces in the crowd.

"*Bonsoir*. Are you coming inside the cathedral for the concert?" he said to them.

The locals answered with hellos as the well-spoken little boy wiped his mouth with his sleeve. One of the locals explained that, no, they liked to be outside for the "resonance." Max did not know the meaning of that word, but he would remember it and read about it tomorrow.

"Bonne soirée, messieurs et mesdames," he said.

"Et vous, le petit monsieur."

Katherine rescued Max's sweater from further dribbles with a handkerchief. She wiped his mouth, gave his hair one last comb with her fingers.

"All set?"

Max patted the pockets of his trousers.

"Oops, I dropped it."

He dashed for the Mercedes. The passenger door opened automatically and he jumped onto the backseat and looked around.

"Looking for this?" a voice from the driver's seat said.

Max saw Sergeant Gauer staring at him in the rearview mirror. He was holding a dented five-franc coin. Max reached for it, Sergeant Gauer pulled it back.

"What's the magic phrase?"

"$E = mc^2$."

"No, the other magic phrase."

"Planck time is the smallest measurable unit of time."

"No, the other other magic phrase."

Max thought about it. "Please, sir, may I have my lucky coin back?"

"Bravo," Sergeant Gauer said, handing over the coin. "Be careful with it, Max. You never know when you may need it."

"Yes, sir. Thank you."

Max jumped from the car and ran to his mother.

"Got everything now?"

"Yes, *Maman*."

Katherine led him across the esplanade toward the cathedral. They weaved between the evening's strollers. At the great limestone arch of the entrance Katherine saw the placard mounted on the plinth between the old wood doors.

Ella Mínervudóttir
Les Meditations 1–6
Cathédrale de Lausanne, 20.00

Max busied himself with the funny creatures carved in the arch. His favorite was Jack and the Beanstalk, but it took time to find him. The fellow was always hiding somewhere new. Max found Jack just as the cathedral doors opened and Corporal Mai stepped out.

"We need to go in by the belfry entrance," she said. "There is nothing but standing room in the aisles."

Katherine shook her head.

"But I booked seats weeks ago."

"There was a mixup with the reservations. The concierge said to use the belfry entrance. He'll find us a place in the back of the nave through the gift shop."

"But . . ."

"Come on, Kat, it's the best we can do."

They hurried to the red door at the far side of the belfry. Max ran with them, thoroughly enjoying the confusion. Corporal Mai pressed the palm of her hand against the red door and it popped open. They went into the alcove, the red door closed behind them. For a moment Katherine was confused. The entrance to the gift shop and the back of the nave was shut, but the security door to the belfry was open and there were candles on the rising stone steps. Katherine took the sunglasses from her eyes and watched the flames. She had been up and down the tower with Max many times since Jerusalem. But just now, seeing the candles lighting the way to the belfry, Katherine flashed beforetimes . . . half naked and bleeding, running across the esplanade, hiding from Komarovsky's goons. A misshapen man jumps from the shadows, grabs her, and drags her into the cathedral. *You can hide here until you can find a way home,* he tells her. That's how Marc Rochat came into her life. Katherine blinked herself to nowtimes, looked at Corporal Mai.

"What's going on?"

Corporal Mai gave Katherine a nudge.

"Would you just try and have some fun, Kat?"

Katherine looked at Max. "What do you think, buster? Shall we have some fun?"

"Will there be any teasing shadows?"

Katherine pulled the scarf from her long blond hair. "Maybe."

"Okay."

They made their way up the first turns of the tower, then back and forth through the women's choir loft; candles lit their way and Max spotted teasing shadows in the high corners. Climbing the corkscrew stairs to the bells, they came to a low wooden door in the side of the curving wall. The door stood open, and burning candles lined the inside of the tunnel.

Katherine flashed Marc Rochat again.

He was leading her through the same tunnel after she had taken sanctuary in the cathedral. Rochat said he wanted her to see things to help her remember she was an angel who was lost in Lausanne . . . *I'm very sure you'll like it*. Katherine blinked to nowtimes. "Wow," she whispered to herself. Max was staring into the tunnel, too; his emerald-colored eyes sparkled with candlelight.

"What's in there, *Maman*?"

"Something from once upon a time, I think. Let's go see."

Katherine bent down and scooted through the tunnel, Max following after her. She came out in the tribune, a forgotten balcony hidden from public view by the massive wooden cabinets housing the organ's pipes and horns. Katherine straightened up, saw the secret space was lit by a lone candle standing on the floor stones, just the way it was with Marc Rochat. She looked up, saw the crucified Christ in the darkening stained-glass window embedded in the cathedral's west wall. Max emerged from the tunnel and saw the image too. He moved close to his mother and she stroked his hair.

"Be not afraid, Max. This is a safe place."

"Is that the angel who died, *Maman*?"

Katherine saw the face of the suffering man nailed to the cross.

"Yes, honey, that's him."

Corporal Mai came through the tunnel now and stood next to Katherine. She pointed to the metal ramp leading to the organ console platform. "Your seats are that way."

The ramp was set between the massive cabinets. They framed a partial view of the nave beyond, and a familiar-looking cloud of light hovering in the high vault. Seeing it, Katherine lost her balance. Corporal Mai held Katherine's arm and steadied her.

"Ça va, Kat?"

"Just a lot of looping hitting me at once. It's hard to keep up."

"It's all fine, Kat. I promise."

I'm very sure you'll like it.

"Yeah, I know."

Katherine picked up the lone candle from the floor and offered it to her son.

"Before you were born I was brought here by Marc Rochat."

"*Le guet* before Ella."

"That's right. He gave me a candle just like this one, and he asked me to lead the way to the organ platform. He said if I did I'd see something wonderful in the nave. Since you're such a big boy now, I think you should lead the way this time."

Max thought about it and liked the idea very much. He took the candle, turned, and walked along the ramp, careful not to spill melting wax. He stepped down onto the cantilevered platform that jutted out over the back of the nave. He stood very still. Katherine trailed slowly after him, stopping when the great expanse of the nave was revealed. She saw candles hanging from the pillars and arches of the aisles, lining the triforium and upper balconies running all round the cathedral, in the giant chancel dome and at the edges of the altar square beneath the lantern tower.

"Oh, my."

She remembered seeing it with Marc Rochat in beforetimes. It was like beholding a mystic vision, as if a cloud of firelight had lifted the cathedral and the great gothic thing were now unconnected to the earth. She wondered what effect the vision would have on her son, but she realized he wasn't looking at the cloud of light. He was looking to his left on the platform, to something hidden from Katherine's line of sight. She watched him tip his head from side to side as if studying a new word in a book.

"Max?"

He turned to her, his face aglow with excitement. "There are two of them, *Maman*."

Katherine looked at Corporal Mai. "Two of what?"

"I guess you'll have to find out for yourself."

Katherine walked to the end of the ramp and was about to step onto the platform when a woman in a sheepskin jacket, smiling and flipping japa mala beads in her right hand, stepped out in front of her. "Hello, Kat," the woman said.

"Karoliina, you're here! Did the band make it, too?"

"They're playing the Église de Saint-Germain-des-Prés tonight. But driving into Paris before the gig, they let me off at Gare de Lyon and told me I had ten minutes to make the TGV to Lausanne. So here I am. Surprised?"

"Unbelievably so. I mean, I don't understand this. No one was here when Marc lit up the nave for me in beforetimes. It was just him and me and—hold it. You had something to do with this, didn't you?"

Karoliina nodded. "Marc's soul rose again a month ago, while Ella was rehearsing for the concert. He told her all about that night with the candles. He said he was very sure you would like to see it again, with your son this time. She contacted me, I contacted the Lausanne partisans, *et voilà*. Like it?"

"I love it. And I love seeing you."

"Me, too. It's been too long."

Katherine kissed Karoliina's cheek. "How are you doing on the road?" Katherine said.

"Oh, you know. It was difficult at first, heading out without Krinkle. But when the Swiss Guard took over security around the cathedral, I knew it was time. Besides, it's what he wanted me to do. 'Keep on keeping on, sister,' was the last thing he told me before he left for Jerusalem. That's what I'm doing, that way he's always with me. And it's kind of fun traveling the world in his bus, hosting his radio show. There are more than a billion followers now."

"That's so great. And really, thank you for all this, thank you for coming. How's Goose? Does he like being a roadie?"

"Ask him yourself," Karoliina said, easing to the right a bit.

Katherine saw Goose sitting on a stool at the far end of the platform. He wore a white ski cap, and a white scarf around his neck. He looked swell in his denim overalls. Katherine signed:

Goose!

Hello, Madame Taylor. I would not miss this concert for the world. Hello, Max. How are you?

Max signed, too.

I'm very happy to see you, Goose! We're going to the belfry for tea after the concert. Would you like to come?

Goose held up a bag from Blondel's on Rue de Bourg.

I would love to. Otherwise I'll have to eat all these chocolates by myself.

Oh, my favorite!

Katherine shook her head. "Man, this is all such a huge surprise."

"It isn't finished, Kat."

"What?"

Karoliina swung her beads and stepped aside again. Katherine saw a raven-haired woman with hazel-colored eyes. Next to the woman were two identical girls sitting on the organist's bench.

"*Shalom,* Kat," the raven-haired woman said.

Katherine drew a sharp breath. "No way."

Max tugged at his mother's hand. "Who is this lady? Who are the two of them?"

Katherine knelt next to her son. "Honey, this is Batya Amini and these are her nieces. They're from Jerusalem."

Max bowed to them. "Welcome to Lausanne, Madame Amini and her nieces from Jerusalem."

"Thank you, Max," Batya said. "I have looked forward to meeting you."

The two girls jumped down from the bench and took turns shaking Max's hand.

"My name is Niloo. It means 'water lily,'" the one on the left said. "And I'm Nikoo. It means 'beautiful,'" the one on the right said.

"I like your names very much," Max said.

"Toda," the twins pronounced as one. It was the third new word Max had heard this evening. He would read about it tomorrow after *shalom* and *resonance.*

"Goose and I are having tea and chocolates in the belfry after the concert," he said. "Would you like to come? You can see the bells and watch Ella call the hour. And she has a picture book about my mother when she was a princess. And there's a big flying caterpillar in it, and funny pirates with paper hats and wooden swords."

"Oh, yes, please," Niloo said. Nikoo pointed to the organist's bench. "Come sit with us, Max, so we can be friends."

"Okay," he said.

The twins took Max's hands and lifted him onto the bench and sat on either side of him. The three of them watched the cloud of light. Batya stood and hugged Katherine.

"It is so nice to see you, Kat. I hope you don't mind that we crashed your evening. Chana's girls so wanted to come and see the cathedral, and it seemed like a good time, three years on and all."

Three years, Katherine thought. *Three whole years since you left us.*

"No, it's wonderful you came. I've been thinking about you a lot."

"I have been thinking about you, too."

Karoliina checked her watch and clapped her hands like a schoolmistress. She rushed to sit next to Goose. "Grab a stool and sit down, everyone, it's almost eight o'clock. The concert is about to begin," she said.

Katherine sat with Batya, and Corporal Mai took a position on the ramp, three steps behind Katherine. Mai scanned the triforium and upper balconies. She keyed the microphone of her comms kit.

"Control, Vega and Moonstone are secure," she whispered.

But Katherine heard it. Those were the new code names for her and her son. "Everything good back there, Mai?"

"Just checking in, Kat. Enjoy the concert."

Katherine read the corporal's eyes. "Thanks," she said, and turned back to the nave.

The place really was packed. Every seat taken, people standing in the aisles and the north and south transepts; even the area beneath the chancel dome was filled with people sitting on the floor stones. All eyes were on the altar square, where two chairs were set directly under the lantern tower. One chair was empty, the other held a bow for the Cremona cello in the nearby stand. Just then Marie-Madeleine rang from the belfry. Her muffled voice rolled through the nave. Batya Amini grabbed Katherine's hand.

"Are you all right, Batya?"

"Loud sounds make me jump sometimes."

"Me, too."

"Still?"

"Still."

With the toll of the eighth bell the nave fell quiet and the sacristy door near the Lady's Chapel opened. A slender form wrapped in a black cloak and black floppy hat stepped out. The form pulled aside its cloak and raised an old lantern lit with a bright but delicate flame. And when the form lifted its head, the audience saw the pretty face of Ella Mínervudóttir, *le guet de Lausanne*. She weaved through the crowd and climbed the three steps to the altar square, followed by a fat gray cat. She rested the lantern on the floor between the chairs, then picked up the bow from the chair next to the cello and sat down. The fat cat took the empty chair and promptly went to sleep. The attending hush was broken by the voices of children echoing from the back of the nave.

"What a funny fat cat, Max."

"That's Monsieur Booty. Sometimes he lives with me and sometimes he lives in the cathedral with Ella. He'll join us for tea and chocolates, too."

"Sababa."

Laughter rolled through the nave, now.

Ella looked up and saw Max waving from far away, and she returned the greeting. She took the cello from the stand and stood it between her knees. When she lowered her head, her face was hidden from view. She curled her left hand around the cello's neck and pressed down on the fingerboard. She drew a slow breath and pulled the bow across the strings with a legato stroke. Then came a low, droning harmonic that rose into the lantern tower, slowly ascending in tone and pitch until melody took flight like some broken angel leaving the world.

Three years since you left us, three whole years.

Katherine closed her eyes and let the music carry her to a recurring imagination. Sometimes it came to her in those moments before sleep; sometimes it came to her in the middle of the day as a lucid dream. Sometimes she would simply call it up whenever she needed a touch of comfort. The imagination was always the same. She was sitting with Harper at LP's Bar. He was as when she first met him, long ago. Tough-looking but handsome, dressed in his cheap tweed sports coat, his beat-up mackintosh on the stool next to him. She sipped at a glass of white wine, he nursed a beer. Their conversation was always the same, too, and it always started in mid-sentence . . .

". . . that the rain rains upon," Harper said. "That's the rest of it. It was a line from a poem. 'Blessed are the dead that the rain rains upon.'"

"Why did you say that?"

"It's all I could think of in the moment."

"Who wrote it?"

"A British soldier of the Great War. His name was Edward Thomas. He was killed in action on Easter Monday, 1917."

"You knew him?"

"You could say that."

"Why did you die, Harper? Why didn't you leave with the rest of the angels that night?"

"I don't know, exactly. Maybe I got used to the feel of the world under my feet. Besides, this way I get to hear you tell me the story of what's happened in the world when my feet were no longer on it."

"After you died, and they carried you away into the shadows."

"That's right."

"How many times have I told you the story?"

"Many times."

"And you never get tired of hearing it?"

"Not at all. Tell me."

And so she did.

After the comet lit up the sky over Jerusalem, the violence across the Middle East calmed and the world entered a time of reflection. From madman to wiseman, no one could escape the feeling that humanity had been shaken by an intervening force from beyond the planet. And when the Israelis lifted the communications blackout, the world discovered that the point of intervention was the Church of the Holy Sepulchre. The news media were full of stories about great flashes of light and explosions from within the church that night. And there was endless speculation about the droning harmonic that was heard throughout the Holy City. Hundreds of Jerusalemites recorded the sound on their cell phones and uploaded it to the Internet; the sound was heard around the world by more than three billion human beings. The Internet buzzed with theories and interpretations about the meaning of the sound. Scientists had no answers. Millions, then billions, of people began to look to the stars for guidance and meaning. The Hubble Telescope website had become something of a new Bible, where instead of words, pictures of the universe became the new Gospels. Many people began to leave the cities and live in places where they could see the stars and planets. Those people began to perform acts of compassion and kindness wherever they went. They said they were seeking the wisdom of the angels: one soul, one life, one universe. Commentators called it the birth of a new religion.

Months passed, then a year.

Many religious leaders, tired of watching their followers leave their churches and temples and mosques to watch the stars, began to deny that the events of that mysterious night in Jerusalem held any true spiritual meaning. They called on their flocks to return to the true faith and abandon the search for "a false god in the stars." Governments, rattled by citizens who pressured them for social and economic justice for all, encouraged their people to get back to their normal lives. Political and military leaders began to speak of dangers and threats that must be put down. Wars began again. Soon, the press referred to the time of reflection as a short-lived cultural phenomenon, much like the hippies and the days of peace and love in the 1960s.

Then, on the night marking the second anniversary of the comet, the Internet was taken by storm with an anonymous post. The source of the post was never identified. It was a photograph of the rooftops of Jerusalem. The picture was grainy, but clear enough to identify the silhouette of a winged angel standing atop the Church of the Holy Sepulchre as the comet blazed through the sky. The angel held a sextant in its hands as if reading the stars. Under the photograph was the sound of the drone that had been heard throughout the Holy City that night. Then the picture of the angel dissolved and was replaced by a mathematical construct using 420 hertz as a baseline for zero; the construct revealed a message hidden within the drone's tonic note. The message then appeared on screen in its original language, Zend. Then the ancient script fell away and English words appeared on the screen. Then came streams of code showing the same message revealed in all the languages of the world; spoken, unspoken, forgotten:

As you are one with the universe, we are one with you;
we await your ascension to the point of knowing.

"Goose, I bet," Harper said. "He's the one who cracked the code."

"Yeah. And he seriously broke the Internet doing it."

"Well done, him."

Katherine turned her glass, watching light reflect in the wine.

"Will we make it, Harper? Will we make it to the point of knowing?"

"I don't know the answer to that one, Madame Taylor. Like I told you in Jerusalem: it's your world now, it's down to you. And sure, there are ripples of evil in paradise, still. Fear and greed were bred deep. It's going to take time. All you can do is keep Max safe until he's ready to guide the creation."

"That's a tall order, Harper."

"It was your destiny from day one, Madame Taylor."

"No choice."

"No choice."

Harper sipped his beer, Katherine watched him.

"I wish you were still here. I miss you so much," she said.

"I know."

"Can't you come back? I mean, if I can see you in my imagination, maybe you're not really dead. Look at Marc Rochat, he's alive and well within Ella. Astruc lives on in Goose's flesh and blood, Krinkle lives on in Karoliina's heart. Look at Max and Corporal Mai."

"You, Max, and the half-kinds were all born with souls. Human souls were meant to dwell in paradise, moving from one body to another and evolving in wisdom and compassion until they find their place amid the stars. That's the way it's supposed to be."

"We're trying, we're trying so hard, Harper."

"I know."

"We still need you. Now more than ever. Please come back to us."

"Sorry. When an angel's light dies, it's gone forever."

"You're here with me, now."

"No, I'm not here. You, me, LP's bar . . . it's nothing but a collection of imagined images flowing through the neural network of your brain."

"You never learned how to properly chat up a girl, did you?"

"I guess not."

"But you'll always be here where I can find you, yeah?"

"Sure, this joint was always my favorite bar in this town. But I'm afraid it will always be the same imagination. It can never change. Rules and regs, you know?"

"Are you sure?"

"I'm sure."

Harper finished his glass, stood, and fumbled through his pockets. He pulled out some francs to pay for the drinks and dropped them on the bar. He picked up his mackintosh, put it on, and stuffed his hands in the pockets.

"I have to go, now, Madame Taylor. Good-bye."

"Harper, find a way to come back to us, please."

"I can't come back, Madame Taylor, not the way I was. That's just the way it is with my kind."

He walked out the door of LP's Bar.

That's where the imagination always ended. And Katherine would either fall asleep, or find herself staring at the midday sky, or reading a book with Max, or doing any of the things she did these days as the mother of a little boy. This time, she was in Lausanne Cathedral, listening to Ella's music as it sounded through the nave and rose to the cloud of light hovering in the high vault. A new imagination was born in the neural network of Katherine's brain. The cloud of light stirred to the cello's voice as if drawing breath. Then tiny sparks broke from the cloud and became tongues of fire. They descended like sacred things onto all souls gathered in Lausanne Cathedral.

I can't come back, not the way I was. That's just the way it is with my kind.

Katherine Taylor smiled.

THANKS

To David Rosenthal and Blue Rider Press for their guidance and support. To Georgina Capel for believing in the dream from the beginning; to my cats and dog for keeping me laughing; to Afnan, whose brilliance through the darker days got me to the end.

ABOUT THE AUTHOR

Jon Steele was born in the American Northwest. He has worked as a keyboard player in a rock band, postman, liquor store clerk, waiter, radio disc jockey, and TV news cameraman. His autobiography, *War Junkie*, published in 2003, is regarded as a cult classic of war reporting. *The Watchers* was his first novel, published in 2012 as part one of The Angelus Trilogy. *Angel City* was published in 2013. Steele currently lives in Switzerland.